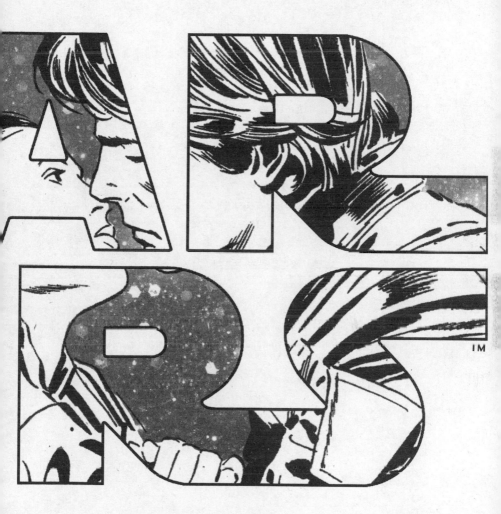

STAR WARS

THE PRINCESS AND THE SCOUNDREL

STAR WARS

THE PRINCESS AND THE SCOUNDREL

BETH REVIS

RANDOM HOUSE

WORLDS
NEW YORK

2023 Random House Worlds Trade Paperback Edition

Copyright © 2022 by Lucasfilm Ltd. & ® or ™
where indicated. All rights reserved.
Excerpt from *Star Wars: Shadow of the Sith*
by Adam Christopher copyright © 2022
by Lucasfilm Ltd. & ® or ™ where indicated.
All rights reserved.

Published in the United States by Random House Worlds,
an imprint of Random House, a division of
Penguin Random House LLC, New York.

RANDOM HOUSE is a registered trademark,
and RANDOM HOUSE WORLDS and colophon are
trademarks of Penguin Random House LLC.

Originally published in hardcover in the United States by Del Rey,
an imprint of Random House, a division of Penguin Random House LLC, in 2022.

ISBN 978-0-593-49936-8
Ebook ISBN 978-0-593-49850-7

Printed in the United States of America on acid-free paper

randomhousebooks.com

1st Printing

Book design by Elizabeth A. D. Eno

To scruffy-looking Corwin
and Jack, the nerf we're herding

THE *STAR WARS* NOVELS TIMELINE

THE HIGH REPUBLIC

Convergence
The Battle of Jedha
Cataclysm

Light of the Jedi
The Rising Storm
Tempest Runner
The Fallen Star

Dooku: Jedi Lost
Master and Apprentice

I — THE PHANTOM MENACE

II — ATTACK OF THE CLONES

Brotherhood
The Thrawn Ascendancy Trilogy
Dark Disciple: A Clone Wars Novel

III — REVENGE OF THE SITH

Inquisitor: Rise of the Red Blade
Catalyst: A Rogue One Novel
Lords of the Sith
Tarkin
Jedi: Battle Scars

SOLO

Thrawn
A New Dawn: A Rebels Novel
Thrawn: Alliances
Thrawn: Treason

ROGUE ONE

IV — A NEW HOPE

Battlefront II: Inferno Squad
Heir to the Jedi
Doctor Aphra
Battlefront: Twilight Company

V — THE EMPIRE STRIKES BACK

VI — RETURN OF THE JEDI

The Princess and the Scoundrel
The Alphabet Squadron Trilogy
The Aftermath Trilogy
Last Shot

Shadow of the Sith
Bloodline
Phasma
Canto Bight

VII — THE FORCE AWAKENS

VIII — THE LAST JEDI

Resistance Reborn
Galaxy's Edge: Black Spire

IX — THE RISE OF SKYWALKER

A long time ago in a galaxy far, far away. . . .

STAR WARS

THE PRINCESS AND THE SCOUNDREL

LEIA

THE FIRES HAD ALL DIED down, smoke trailing in the night sky, dissipating long before it could reach any of the countless glittering stars twinkling through the tree canopy. Leia's hand trailed over the white and black helmets of the stormtroopers and Imperial fighters that the Ewoks had turned into an impromptu drum set. She had laughed and danced along with everyone else when the fires were bright and the drinks had flowed freely.

But now her hand lingered over the scratches and dents on a previously gleaming-white helmet.

A person, a living being, had been under this helmet.

The enemy.

Someone who would have shot to kill—any rebel, of course, but Leia knew that her death would have been the highlight of a stormtrooper's career. Someone shot this person before they could shoot her. And then the dead trooper's helmet had been plucked from their head and banged on like a drum.

She wondered who the trooper had been. Someone indoctrinated as a child, perhaps? That happened often enough. Someone from an occupied world, pressed into service? Had this stormtrooper chosen the path that led to their death and derision on a forest moon, or had they simply been unlucky?

Her fingers slid over the scuffed surface of the helmet, but her hand froze before she touched the next one.

Black.

It wasn't *his* helmet, she knew. The night made the gray-green of the AT-ST operator's helmet appear darker than it was, and the shape was similar but still distinctly different.

A hand fell on Leia's left shoulder, fingers firm, pulling her back. Leia sucked in a harsh breath—the touch was too familiar. The hand pulled her back with the same pressure as before, the same spacing of fingers, one painfully on her clavicle, and when she shuddered at the touch, the same soft, almost gentle rub of a thumb against her shoulder blade.

"It's just me," Luke's voice said, concern etched on his face when she jerked away and turned toward him.

Just Luke. Her brother.

Darth Vader's son.

"You smell like . . ."

"Smoke?" Luke guessed. "We all do." He attempted a smile, but Leia didn't return it. Because the scent that clung to Luke's black tunic was not the same as the smoke that still lingered throughout the Ewok village of Bright Tree. The stench of it made her sick to her stomach—that, and the idea that while she'd danced, he had gone to give Darth Vader a funeral pyre.

Still, when she looked in his eyes, she saw only Luke. And he was sad.

"The whole galaxy celebrated while you mourned," Leia said softly.

Luke shook his head. "I wasn't the only one mourning."

Leia glanced at the stormtrooper's helmet. "No, I suppose not."

"How are you?" Luke's voice was sincere, but Leia wasn't sure how to answer him. This was supposed to be a triumph, but all she really felt was confused. Not just about what Luke had told her about her lineage—their connection was something she'd felt for some time, and it had been easy to accept Luke as her brother. She would not think about what that meant of her biological father. No—it wasn't just that.

"It's the Force, isn't it?" Luke asked.

Leia nodded. She had told Luke that she didn't—couldn't—understand the power he had, but he seemed eerily calm and confident that she *could* actually wield the Force as he did. Leia might not have any real experience with the Force, but there was no denying the power Luke had . . . the power she felt, too, like a fluttering of flitterfly wings just on the edge of her consciousness. Waiting for her to seize it.

"He told me to tell you—" Luke started, but Leia's head whipped up, eyes fierce as she glared at him.

"Don't," she warned.

"They were his last words. He wanted me to tell you—"

"I don't care."

"He *was* good," Luke insisted. "There was still good in him, after all . . ."

My father was good, Leia thought, but in her mind she pictured Bail Organa, not Darth Vader. Thinking of Bail made her think of Breha, her mother. Of her home. Of everything she had lost.

When she had spoken to Luke earlier this night, Leia had told him that she remembered the mother they shared, their birth mother. It had been vague images, feelings, really, nothing more. But she *did* have a memory—of love, of closeness, of things she could not describe. It was impossible to put her feelings into words, but there was no denying their truth. It felt like . . . a connection, a bond made of light.

Yet Luke, who was a Jedi Knight, strong in the Force, had no memory of the woman who had birthed them both.

Did he have memories of their father? Was that why he was so capable of forgiving the monster that was Darth Vader? They had been separated at birth, not just from each other but from their biological parents. Maybe Leia had a connection with their mother, and Luke had a connection with their father.

Leia bit back a bitter laugh. Perhaps it wasn't as deep as that. Perhaps it was merely that Luke had never been tortured by their biological father the way she had.

"What happens next?" Luke asked.

Leia looked at him. Since becoming a Jedi Knight, he had always seemed so calm, so sure of his direction.

He wasn't sure now. His eyes searched hers. *He's waiting for me to decide my fate before he chooses his own,* she realized. Their blood connection may be new knowledge, but he was also her friend. The threads of fate that had pulled them in separate directions could be rewoven.

Beyond Luke, in the shadows, Leia saw the outline of someone else. Han was backlit by a lingering torch, but she recognized his shoulders, his stance. Cocky, even when no one was looking. When his eyes settled on her, he strode directly toward her, his feet loud on the rickety boards of the walkway between the treetop dwellings.

Leia had no idea what would happen tomorrow or the next day or the next. But as she left Luke in the shadows and met Han on the bridge, she knew exactly what would happen tonight.

CHAPTER 1

HAN

Two Days Later

"IT'S NOT OVER YET."

That's what Han had told the rebel Pathfinders after he'd left the Imperial base they'd uncovered on the other side of Endor. While the Death Star had been constructed in orbit around the forest moon, a separate communications base had been built on the surface, undamaged in the aftermath of the Death Star's destruction—until Han and his troops had arrived. Signal intelligence had decrypted some of the messages the base had been sending out, transmitting throughout the galaxy. Blowing up the Death Star may have been fun, but it wasn't enough. Imperials occupied countless worlds, and they weren't just rolling over. The Pathfinders had gone in blasters blazing, but they hadn't been quick enough to stop the signal.

Data, comms, plans. All that info scattered across the galaxy. And it all came down to Emperor Palpatine still giving orders despite being nothing but ash and space debris now. He had calculated for his legacy to live on even if he exploded in space, and that was exactly what they'd been too late to prevent.

One night. They'd all had one night to celebrate and pretend that the war was over. But . . .

It wasn't over yet.

Han cursed. The debriefing with the generals—the other generals, because he now held that rank, too—had been quick and dirty, just a relay of information followed by the others scattering in various directions to make new plans. Time for the brains to work. No one had invited Han to stay and concoct a strategy to round up the Imperials that still remained and hadn't gotten the message that they'd lost. That was fine. They just needed to tell him where to fly and what to shoot. He was good at that part. The best. Sure, he'd had some decent ideas in the past. But now that the blasting was over, it made sense for the others . . .

Beside him, Chewbacca roared.

"Yeah, I get you," Han muttered. It never seemed to end. But then he paused, turning to look up at his old friend. "I haven't forgotten, though, you know that, right? We're heading back to Kashyyyk as soon as possible, kicking the Imperials off your world. You've got a family to take care of."

Chewie started to grumble, but Han cut him off. "No. We stick to *our* plan, and it was always for you to go home as soon as we had a break."

Han grabbed the rung of one of the ladders leading up into the tree village. While the leaders of the Rebellion had set up a base on the ground in order to be closer to the ships in the clearing and the immediate action they anticipated, it was little more than a large tent with a few smaller ones nearby to handle the overflow of quartering pilots and ground troops. The Ewok huts were far more comfortable living quarters. Beneath him, the ladder swung as Chewie followed Han up, his added weight throwing Han off balance for a moment before he could adjust.

Leia hadn't been at the debriefing.

Han knew she'd been elsewhere, recording messages for allies, and he knew that the others would catch her up to speed. But . . .

He wanted to see her.

Han's track record with love wasn't necessarily the best. But this thing with Leia—it felt like more than . . . He couldn't quantify it. It just felt *more*. He'd tried to walk away, more than once. Maybe, if he'd been able to leave Hoth when he'd planned . . .

Han had meant it when he'd told Leia he'd exit her life if she wanted. Of course, that was before he knew Luke and Leia were siblings, before he knew a lot of things. But he'd meant his words. He would have left, not for his own benefit, but for hers. Every other time in Han's life, when he walked away, he did it for himself. But not that time.

Instead of letting him leave, though, she'd come to him.

And Han didn't know if he could let her go again.

Especially not after how much time he'd already lost. He'd been frozen on Bespin and by the time he'd woken up again—blind and disoriented with hibernation sickness—so much time had passed. Leia had loved him for nearly a whole year, and Vader had stolen that year from him. Han wasn't going to let more time slip through his fingers.

Distantly, he became aware that Chewie had been talking to him. Han hooked his leg over the top of the ladder and landed with a thud of his boots on the wooden walkway of the village. "Yeah, buddy?" he asked.

Chewie swung himself up, big arms balancing before he landed fully. He roared, half in amusement, half in discontent at being ignored.

"Sorry!" Han said, throwing up his hands. "I've got things on my mind."

"Oh, am I just a thing?" Leia's voice sliced through Han's brain.

"Hey, now, you don't occupy my *every* thought, Princess," Han snapped back, but the warm smile in his eyes belied the statement.

"You sure about that?" she asked, smirking, her rosy lower lip just begging to be kissed, and Han blanked for several moments, incapable of doing anything more than blink at her.

Chewie chuckled.

"Yeah, yeah," Han grumbled, reorienting himself.

"I was just looking for you," Leia said. Her tone slid from playful to business. "Mon told me about the plans discovered on the Imperial base, and I wanted to check in with the general who made the discovery."

Right. That was him.

Leia kept speaking, unaware that Han wasn't focused on her words. "The timing of that base's communication—even if we haven't been able to decrypt most of the encoded contents yet—indicates that there's far more at play than we originally thought."

Grumbling, Chewie left the two of them alone, heading deeper into the village. Han was far too focused on Leia to really register his friend walking off, though. His mind raced with the impossibility of his thoughts—him, and a *princess*? It couldn't possibly work in the long term.

"We've been monitoring a lot of traffic in the Anoat system in particular, and I wanted to see if any of the transmissions you intercepted indicated that," Leia continued. "Or perhaps you saw something in the base—not everything needs to be online, physical transportation of sector codes could indicate—"

Since when did Han care about the long term, though?

"Han?" Leia asked, her head tilted up at him.

"I want you," he stated flatly.

"Me?" She looked around—although the base below had been bustling with activity, this part of the village was remarkably quiet. "For what?"

"Forever," Han said.

Leia's confusion shifted to something else, something he couldn't quite read. He never could tell everything going on in her mind, and he loved that about her.

He loved her.

She was a princess, the face of the Rebellion, the new government's greatest hope, a symbol more than a person. But she was also just Leia. And she was his. Han needed her the same way he needed the *Falcon*—sure, he could fly without her, but what was the point?

"Marry me," Han said.

Leia, usually so calm and collected, with the ability to face down Vader himself, could not hide her shock in that moment. Her eyes widened, her lips parted, and the rest of her body stilled, frozen in surprise. Han felt the corner of his lips twisting up, watching as Leia didn't try to hide her shock. She didn't hide her desire, either. He was hers, too.

But she had a grander destiny than he could comprehend. Elbows-deep in politics and someone who would always be doing, doing, doing.

Even now, even though neither of them had physically moved, Han could see Leia spinning away from him, out of his grasp.

So he reached out to her. He took her hand. Rubbed the place on her finger where a ring could go.

Han was sure the same questions flying through his mind were in hers as well. How many people were already discussing marriages and settling down with folk they'd only known in combat? It was a common enough thing—emotions ran high after battle, people felt the need to grasp at life when faced with the death of war. The flip side of fighting was loving, and there was a hell of a lot of energy that needed to be redirected somewhere.

This was the part where Han was supposed to tip his chin, laugh, say it was all a joke.

But he didn't.

He didn't flinch as he watched doubt cloud Leia's face. He stood there, and he waited for her to realize the same truth he knew.

They were better together.

And marriage? Well, it was a formality. But it was also a promise.

One he intended to keep.

"Yes," she said. Just that word, but with a smile that went along with it that lit up the entire galaxy.

Something inside of Han eased, invisible bands loosening around his lungs. The days coming were not going to be easy; the Empire would see to that. He and Leia *would* eventually have to separate—there would be battles she couldn't fight, political machinations he couldn't play a role in, worlds and trials and issues that would divide them.

But . . .

It wasn't over yet.

CHAPTER 2

LEIA

LEIA SHOULD BE QUESTIONING THIS, him, everything. But they'd already stolen one night—why not steal a lifetime more? As chaotic as it was, she knew that she would never regret this decision. She was making her happiness an indelible part of her own history, and that was worth the risk.

As Han whooped before sweeping her into his arms and twirling her around the wooden platform above the trees, Leia could do no more than laugh in joy. So much of her life had always been planned. What to wear, what to say, when to work, how to dress her hair, even the meals she ate. She'd never liked ruica, but by the stars she ate it, just as a good princess of Alderaan should.

For so long, everything in her life had been a part of a greater plan, but love could not be scheduled.

Han set Leia down again, his grin wider than she'd ever seen it before. "Wait till I tell Chewie," he said, laughing ruefully. "He always said I'd settle down one day."

Leia raised an eyebrow. "Why does marriage have to mean settling down?"

"See?" Han said, shaking a finger at her playfully. "That's why I'm marrying you."

I need to tell Luke, Leia thought. He was the only family she had left. Her breath caught, but Han, still elated, didn't notice. Leia put her smile back on, a mask.

Han froze. "What's wrong?" he asked.

A bubble of emotion burst out of her. "Am I that easy to read?" She shook her head, her eyes sliding away from his.

"Second-guessing this scoundrel already?" Han asked gently.

"No, it's just . . ." Her voice trailed off. Han put a finger on her chin, pulling her gaze back to him. "I wish my family could meet you."

"Oh, I don't need their disapproval." It was a joke, and Leia appreciated it, weak as it was. His gaze darkened as his teasing smile shifted to a worried frown. "What aren't you telling me?"

Leia's breath came out shaky. If he was going to marry her, he needed to know the truth. She would not entangle him with lies. "When I say family, I mean my mother Breha and my father Bail."

"I know—"

Leia held her hands up to stop him; if she didn't speak now, she was worried she'd never muster the courage to do it. "They adopted me. They're my parents. I love them. But my blood is . . ."

"Luke," Han said, nodding, clearly still confused.

"Not just Luke," Leia said softly. "He found out about our biological father." Han's brow creased in confusion. "Vader." She whispered the word like a confession.

Han blinked several times, the only reaction that revealed he'd heard her. He swallowed, hard, and Leia watched the bump in his throat rise and sink. "Well," he said finally, shaking his head. "Good thing he's dead."

"You . . ." Leia's heart stuttered. "You don't care?"

"Why would I?"

Leia's eyes rounded in disbelief. Han cut her a sharp look. "You care," he said in a voice so low that Leia wasn't sure it was a statement or a question.

"Of course I do."

Han paused, clearly thinking through what to say next. Finally he settled on, "Are you okay?"

She wasn't. She didn't think she would ever be okay with the knowledge of her bloodline. But she also didn't want to mar this moment any more with the shadow of his memory. "I will be," she said.

When he looked at her, he seemed to know everything she wasn't able to put into words. "Okay then," he said, nodding once, that trademark smirk twitching on his lips. "We're gonna get married."

"Seems so."

"I've gotta go tell Chewie the good news. And you've gotta tell . . ." Han nodded his head at someone behind Leia. She turned and saw Luke approaching, a tentative smile on his face but worry lines between his eyes.

Han smirked. "I can't wait to tell Lando. I'm pretty sure there's an old bet he made with me that I could cash in right now . . ." He headed off, clasping Luke's shoulder as he passed the other man, leaving the explanations to Leia.

"You and Han, huh?" Luke asked her.

Leia felt a twist of nerves in her stomach as she waited for his response. What if he didn't approve, what if this soured their friendship, what if—

"*Finally!*" Luke shouted, elation spread over his face.

"Really?" Relief flooded her senses.

Luke pulled her into a hug. "You should know," he said with a chuckle in his voice, "that Chewie was already threatening to kidnap you two and drop you off on some deserted planet until you could both figure out how right you were for each other."

Leia's shoulders shook with laughter. "Wookiees aren't exactly known for subtlety, I suppose."

"Not at all." Luke stepped back, eyes sparkling. "Seriously, I'm happy for you both."

"I told him," Leia said. "I told him what you told me, and he didn't care."

"Of course he didn't. Han's one of the good ones."

Are we? Leia wanted to ask. How did the knowledge of their parentage not disturb Luke the way it did her? For that matter, how had Han's reaction been so calm? He should have been disgusted; he should have been—

Concern washed over Luke's features, but Leia ignored him, wrapping her arms around herself. A part of her wondered at how quickly Luke had come to this deserted landing. She'd sought out Han earlier, intent on reuniting with him after his mission with the Pathfinders. But Luke had seemed to arrive almost as soon as she'd thought of him. Had she somehow unconsciously reached out to him—or did he control their connection? She wasn't sure how she felt about that. Luke had told her that she could have the same power he did, but . . .

Her brother's eyes searched hers, and she knew he didn't need the Force to see the conflicted emotions coursing through her. "How do you feel?" he asked.

He was so different now from when she'd first met him. Years had passed, of course, but the boy she'd met on the Death Star, proclaiming he'd come to save her, had been boisterously excited, full of optimism and opportunities. This man before her now was the same Luke, but . . . calmer. He moved with purpose rather than crashing around, bursting through doors or bumbling across the galaxy. Leia almost mourned the change. She had seen it before, of course, over the years of the war— bright hopefuls who became jaded when they realized they were no longer shooting at inanimate targets. Luke held a deeper sort of stillness within him, like a tree growing on a moon with no air, no wind to shift the branches.

Leia walked away from him and stepped to the edge of the platform. Railings circled the landing, but they were built for the Ewoks' diminutive stature. More than one pilot drunk on jet juice in the celebrations after the destruction of the Death Star had toppled over the barriers that hit them around knee height. Now Leia let the sturdy rails press against her legs as her toes, covered in leather slippers, curled over the edge of the wooden platform. "I feel like I'm on a precipice," Leia answered Luke as she forced herself to look down, through the tree branches to the distant ground below.

She glanced over her shoulder. "I feel like that for all three of us. You, me, Han. This moment, right now, it feels like . . ." She turned back to the railing, but this time her eyes were on the tree-dappled horizon. "It feels like one step, and we'll all scatter in different directions. Right now, we're together. Right now, we're safe."

And I just want to make this moment last forever, she thought, although she guessed that Luke understood her unspoken sentiment.

Luke didn't move toward her; he stayed in the center, near the place where the fires had burned. "When you think of the future . . ."

"I don't want to think of that," she said, her tone pleading. "I want *this* moment to last. When we've won. When we're all together." And, if she were honest with herself, getting married right now would give the moment permanence. To her, if nothing else. Endor was not just the place where the war ended . . . because, after all, the fighting wasn't over yet. The war wasn't over. It might never be over, not if the Empire continued operating despite the Emperor's death. But getting married now, here, turned the battle-that-wasn't-actually-the-end into the day she forgot about the war and chose love instead.

"I think . . ." Luke's voice trailed off. Leia searched his eyes. His brow crinkled in a smile that belied the gravity of the moment. "I think you're forgetting that the end of the war didn't just buy the galaxy peace. It bought you time."

Leia shook her head, confused. In answer, Luke took her hand, pulling her away from the edge. "You *are* right," he conceded. "The three of us have many different paths we could take. And this moment is a deciding one. The choices we make now will . . . linger." He paused. "But following this path doesn't mean you can't follow others. You have the freedom now to pursue any route you want to explore."

"I don't know if I want . . ." Leia's voice trailed off. She knew what Luke was offering, but as much as she was curious about what the Force could offer her, she also knew that every step closer to it was a step closer to the power that had twisted Darth Vader into a monster.

Pain flashed over Luke's face, and Leia realized she had missed the point Luke was making. He wasn't thinking about power at all. He was thinking about her. She wasn't the only one who'd lost family. Luke had, too. He had told her about his aunt and uncle. Leia's heart lurched—had they been *her* aunt and uncle as well? Luke's home had burned, and with it, everything that had represented his past. Tatooine still existed, but to Luke, it was as gone as Alderaan.

Leia leaned in, tucking a lock of Luke's hair behind his ear. Always scruffy, these boys.

"I can help you learn," Luke said, taking her movement to mean acceptance. "After you've had some time with Han, you and I can start training. I have heard of places where I can find more Jedi lore. Yoda is gone, but I can train you as he trained me. And there's so much I still don't know. Yoda called me a Jedi Knight, but I know in the past, Jedi trained from the time they were younglings. There's more for me to learn, too. We can do it together."

His voice trailed off as Leia shook her head. "I don't care about the Force," she said softly. "I would want to go with you because I would like to be with *you*. I would like to get to know my brother as my brother."

Luke kept telling her that she had time to decide, that it wasn't one or the other. But it *felt* like she had a choice to make. Go with Luke and choose a family of a sibling pair, exploring the unknown elements of the galaxy, discovering the Force and all it meant. Or go with Han and choose a family of her own making, discovering nothing more than herself.

"We could do such great things together," Luke said, his eyes unfocused, as if he could see a different future from the one Leia envisioned.

How lonely it must be, she thought. She was among the last Alderaanians, but he *was* the last Jedi. "You could come with us," she offered.

Luke snorted. "On your honeymoon with Han?"

"No." Leia laughed. "I mean you could help us form the new government. My father told me how the Jedi once served alongside the Senate, how they were a part of politics, too. When the new republic is fully formed, you could work with me at the capital. We could build something together." *You don't have to be alone.* For one shining moment, Leia allowed herself the fantasy of a capital city, gleaming and new, with a glorious Senate Hall. She could advocate and bring peace through politics, and then come home to her husband and—perhaps—a youngling or two. Dinner with her children's uncle. A home for them all to center on.

She didn't need to plan every moment of her life as she had on Alderaan, but that stability had enabled love and families to flourish together. It would be nice.

"There's so much left to learn and discover," Luke said, his words shattering her fantasy. "I don't know where I'll be going, but I do know I'll be gone." It was like when he'd disappeared after Hoth, chasing Yoda on a far-flung planet, unable even to comm and let them know he was safe. He searched her eyes, trying once more: "You could go with me."

"I don't think I can," Leia said gently. Luke might believe she could choose multiple paths, but Leia wasn't so sure. Following him would mean chasing power, and that power could help shape the type of galaxy she'd worked her entire life to build. But if she had to choose between power and happiness, she would choose happiness.

Because that was what the choice really was. Going with Luke, becoming a Jedi—it would be an adventure. It might give her the power he tempted her with.

But she had given her whole life to power.

And she was ready to choose, for the first time, what she wanted for herself.

CHAPTER 3

HAN

THE EWOK VILLAGE WAS A maze of bridges and huts. Although Han had found Chewie and told him the good news, after more than an hour, he still hadn't found Lando. When the rebel leaders called a meeting, however, Han stepped inside the tent and immediately saw his old friend.

"What's this about?" Lando asked as Han squeezed onto the bench beside him. "That data compound the Pathfinders uncovered?"

"Probably," Han said. The quick debriefing after the mission now had to be thoroughly analyzed and rehashed in excruciating detail. "Hey, I've got something to tell you. Later." Han glanced at Lando, whose eyebrow arched in curiosity.

Before either could say more, a ray of light cut through the tent and Mon Mothma, followed by Leia, stepped inside. His eyes cut to Leia. She wore a simple green dress but had rebraided her hair, carefully tucking away each strand that he'd run his fingers through the night before. He shook himself. He had proposed with the full knowledge that the war wasn't over, and it was important to act now, before the Empire could dig into any stronger of a foothold in the galaxy. Somewhere over the years, her war had become his war, too, and he was as determined as she was to see it through.

Leia glanced up, her gaze falling on his. Han smirked, deeply aware that she was deeply aware of his presence. She rolled her eyes, but that just made his lips twist up more. They might be in the middle of an impromptu war room with the top generals of the burgeoning new republic, but he had a pretty good guess that the blush staining her cheeks had nothing to do with Admiral Ackbar.

Mon cleared her throat, calling everyone's attention to her, even, eventually, Han's. "We must discuss our next steps," she said, casting her gaze around the tent. A few others had joined via holo—Han recognized some of them, but not all. All hands on deck for this meeting, then.

"We always knew that dismantling the Empire meant far more than simply taking out the Emperor and his weapons," Leia said.

"The Empire is a drangea," Admiral Ackbar interjected. "You can cut off its head, but it will still live as long as it can feed."

Han had never seen a drangea in person, but the legend was common enough. If you could kill one of the massive squidlike creatures, you could sell its roe as a delicacy among people with credits to burn and make enough to fly easy for a year. But killing one was the problem—it had two brains, one in its crest and one that floated freely around its body. Cutting off the head was difficult enough, as the creature lurked in the deepest, coldest waters of Mon Cala. But even if a hunter was skilled enough to do that, the drangea's long, venomous tentacles could still easily continue the attack while the hunter stabbed at it in sheer blind hope of hitting something that would incapacitate the monster.

There were a lot of dead hunters at the bottom of Mon Cala's oceans, and a lot of headless drangeas that fed on the corpses.

"Exactly," Mon said. "But we have delivered a blow to the Empire that could yet prove to be fatal. Obviously the death of Emperor Palpatine and the destruction of the Death Star were vital to our success, and these alone have swayed most of the galaxy to our side. What remains of the Empire, though, is unwilling to cede power. While the Pathfinders were able to destroy the communications base on the other side of the moon, we were unable to stop the data already delivered. Our people are working to decrypt the information that was sent, and we will use it to further our goal of peace."

An aide passed Mon a datapad. "But there are victories to celebrate," she continued, reading from the screen. "I'm happy to report early communications with some key worlds." A screen behind Mon illuminated, showing a series of planets—those already allied with the new government, and those considering. Han noticed that most were Core or Mid Rim. He shot Lando a glance, and the other man nodded tightly. Whatever government filled the vacuum left behind by the dead Emperor had to be able to contend with the Outer Rim. Ignoring those planets would lead to chaos.

The Outer Rim was going to need more than diplomatic talks. And those worlds on the edge—Han guessed those were exactly the places the Empire would target. His jaw tightened. Mon could plan all she wanted to have nice sit-down dinners with politicians on Coruscant or whatever other planet, but he'd bet all his credits that the real action would be in the Outer Rim. And it would be the soldiers like the Pathfinders he'd led who would be in the thick of it.

"Our plans for the Outer Rim are not yet solidified," General Madine said when Mon nodded for him to take over. "But we're keeping transport ships here, ready for dispatch as soon as we acquire our first target."

A pang hit Han in the chest as he looked over the crowded room at Leia. He saw the same worry in her eyes that he knew was in his. Time. They needed time to be together. But Mon was already talking about missions and where to go. Obviously it was important to leverage their advantage and stop the Empire while it was shaken and wounded, but . . . Han figured after a quick wedding, he'd get a week or two with his new wife before everything went to hell again.

". . . and there are key aspects to independence that are being restored," Mon continued, passing the datapad back to her assistant. "Many institutions and businesses that were forced to operate for the Empire are now liberated."

Several logos illuminated on the screen behind Mon, most of which

Han didn't recognize. Lando leaned over, pointing at one. "That's a star line that used to be a charter company," he told Han in a low voice.

"The one the Hutts took over?"

"The very same." Lando straightened and raised his voice. "No ships are going anywhere without fuel," he said. "What are you doing about Bespin?"

Mon nodded tightly. "We are well aware that the Empire is influencing the Anoat sector."

Lando made a disgruntled noise in the back of his throat. "What's going on over there?" Han asked him as Mon answered a question from a lieutenant in the front of the crowd.

"I tried to get through to some of my people. The governor was always an Imperial sympathizer, but now he's resorted to outright lies, claiming the Emperor isn't dead, things like that."

"It's an easy enough lie to disprove," Han said. "It's not like the governor can trot Palpatine out like an orbak and settle the debate."

"It won't matter," Lando said. "How many people ever saw the Emperor in person? He was one man in the entire galaxy, and he held power for a long time. It's easier to believe he's still alive than to take the word of the rebels that he's dead."

Han opened his mouth to protest, but Lando had already turned his attention back to Mon. "It's not just the Empire you have to worry about," he said, standing up and interrupting her. "The crime lords see any upheaval as an opportunity. While you spend your time proving to Governor Adelhard and the people of my sector that the Emperor's nothing more than ash in the void of space now, the crime organizations are going to see this as their way in."

"We know," Mon said, her voice ringing with such authority that Lando sat back down. "Not only will the crime lords reap the benefits of the shifting changes that must come, but they could also be hiding further Imperial supporters. The Empire has been known to work in partnership with crime organizations before."

Han didn't bother biting back his bitter snort of disgust. Boba Fett had been working with Darth Vader and Jabba the Hutt. Han knew firsthand how easily the two groups united.

Mon glanced behind her, to Leia. Mon didn't say anything, but Han could tell she was thinking the same thing he was. Of all the crime organizations out there, the Hutts in particular had a grudge against Leia, on whom they pinned all their hatred. Han had seen the bounty on her head, placed there by the Hutt heirs as payback for her murder of Jabba.

Han was used to making enemies—hell, Jabba hadn't been exactly on good terms with him when he put Han on display in his hall in a carbonite block. Walking around with a death mark hadn't been easy, and it had caught up with him eventually. But Leia . . . Han wasn't very up-to-date on Alderaanian politics, but surely not everyone on the planet loved the political leaders. And Leia had joined the Galactic Senate at a fairly young age—no politician in the galaxy was universally beloved. She made enemies just by being alive. Han hadn't really thought of what that meant before, but now? Now he saw the bounties hanging over Leia's head as clearly as if they were holoprojections. The Hutts, the Empire, political opponents, discontented survivors, businesses ruined in the wake of the end of the war, dissidents on the opposite side . . .

As he watched, Leia stepped around Mon to begin speaking. "Our first goal is to cement the alliances with the worlds that are sympathetic to our cause, as well as assess how well armed each of those worlds is in preparation of defending any type of new republic we form," she said. There wasn't a quiver in her voice, not a single ounce of fear. Maybe she didn't see the targets on her back, or maybe she was just too used to them.

"I'm trying to tell you, you're not going to get anywhere without fuel," Lando interjected. Leia paused, not even flicking her eyes to Han, who sat beside Lando as he bit off his words, spelling out the danger. "Bespin and the other systems in the Anoat sector provide a significant source of Tibanna gas. The Empire knows the entire galaxy runs on Tibanna gas. If they control the fuel, they control the galaxy. And it doesn't matter how many emperors you blow up—as long as they have the goods, they're not defeated."

"Your concerns are noted," Leia said in a calm voice.

"Are they?" Lando muttered under his breath, too low for anyone but those near him to hear.

"They are," Han growled.

Lando shot him a look but kept his mouth closed.

"Imperial control of resources is absolutely a way to undermine our efforts," Leia continued. "But it will look different from before. Previously, the Empire could and did destroy entire worlds in their efforts to bleed them dry of the resources they wanted. The fertile soil of Pyra is now a desert, Cynda was mined of its thorilide until it was nearly unstable, and of course we have our eyes on the Anoat sector, including someone who's been deep undercover at the Chinook Station for years."

Han shot a look at Lando, who raised his eyebrows. So, his old friend didn't know *everything* that happened on his world.

"The Empire will target fuel and food. We must find ways to ensure those resources are protected so that people don't become desperate," Leia continued.

Mon stepped up. "It's a large net to cast—if we prevent the Empire from getting Tibanna gas, they may turn to another sector and target carnium instead. We do know an Imperial station had been negotiating for months on the moon Madurs within the Lenguin system. Our people say that negotiations got heated, but a contract was never signed—"

"Even if it was," Lando said, "it's not like the Empire cared about following it."

Han supposed Lando had more than enough reason to be bitter. He doubted Lando had wanted the Empire meddling with his affairs no matter what lucrative offers had been dangled in front of him, and he knew without a doubt that Lando never originally agreed to the demands Darth Vader later thrust upon him.

It was more than just business though, Han suspected. Lando cared about the profits of the refinery, true, but he also seemed to genuinely care about his people. He'd tried to evacuate them when the Empire seized full control of his refinery. Han shook his head. With Lando, it could be that he cared about both the profits and the people, and it was impossible to tell which he cared about more on any given day. But his hatred of the Empire was one thing Han didn't doubt at all.

"The battle has shifted," Mon stated ominously. "But make no mistake—we are still at war. It will not be open battles with blasters and firepower. The Empire will work covertly to destabilize us before we can truly establish our new and great republic. They'll attack our systems, starve our people, limit our fuel." She paused, looking at Leia. "Rather than open warfare, they'll hire assassins to eliminate key individuals to lower the galaxy's hope for peace."

"That includes you, too," Leia told her in a low voice, not flinching from Mon's gaze.

Han's heart clenched in his chest, black dots momentarily clouding his vision. He wanted nothing more than to knock Lando aside, shove his way through the crowded area, grab Leia by the waist, and carry her to the *Millennium Falcon,* flying her out to the most remote planet he could find (preferably one with sunny beaches) and living the rest of their lives away from all this.

The only thing stopping him was the knowledge that Leia would never forgive him.

And that she'd probably shoot him before he could drag her away.

"Bryn, Kelan, and Maxx, stay behind for additional briefing," Mon stated, and three people peeled off from the crowd, moving closer to Mon and Leia as the rest of the group dispersed. Han caught sight of Leia passing each of the three operatives additional datapads before he ducked out of the tent. Lando disappeared before he could pull him aside.

Covert missions, spies in hot spots, and imperiled supply chains. Han would never say that he missed the dogfights—he *didn't*—but he wasn't really a fan of this sort of thing, either. Han had never wanted to be a part of any military, much less a general, but if this was the way the fight was shifting, perhaps he'd need to find a way to adapt.

On his way out of the tent, Han caught sight of one of his strike team leaders. "Kes," he said, nodding at the man.

"What do you make of all that?" the sergeant asked.

Han shrugged. "Looks like they've found a way to use that information we recovered for them."

Kes Dameron nodded. "Looks like."

"Don't get all disappointed on me, kid," Han said.

Kes shook his head. "No, sir! But . . . it seems like we'll be stuck in the Outer Rim, doesn't it?"

Han had been so focused on how subterfuge would play into the new commands—about how Leia was under even more of a threat now than when she was in the middle of a firefight—that he'd forgotten about what Mon had informed them of at the start of the debriefing. The Empire would hide in the shadows of the Mid Rim and Core Worlds. But they'd be setting up base in the Outer Rim.

And his Pathfinders were ground troops.

"Looks like," Han said. No sunny beaches in his future, then.

Kes nodded, serious. "And no comms in the field, not for spec ops."

Han cursed inwardly. "Yeah." He noticed the fidgety way Kes twisted his gloves. "We don't have a mission yet. Go to your wife."

"She'll probably volunteer to fly us out to whatever world we get assigned to," Kes said, equal parts proud and worried about the pilot he loved.

"Yes, well, *until then*," Han said, wondering when Kes would catch his meaning.

"Oh. Right! You don't have to tell me twice!" Kes snapped off a mock salute before racing back to his bunk, where Shara Bey was no doubt waiting for him.

Despite the fact that Kes had a wife and child, Han knew well enough that as long as there was a mission, he'd fight it, much like Shara. Even in undisclosed locations with no comms and no timeline.

And no promises.

Han had never been a friend to the Empire. But unlike Kes, he hadn't become a fighter in the Rebellion for anything like a noble cause.

For a long time, the only people Han had been fighting for were his friends—for Leia.

But what was even the point of the battle if it drove them further apart?

CHAPTER 4

LEIA

A FEW PEOPLE LINGERED IN the tent as the main briefing ended. After explaining their missions to the three rebels Leia and Mon had selected to infiltrate the Anoat sector, a tall woman with dark skin and a closely shaved head stepped forward.

"Major," Mon said, nodding at the woman. She turned to Leia. "This is Nioma; she works in intelligence."

Leia held out her hand, and the other woman grasped it warmly. "General Draven spoke of you," she said. "It's my honor to meet you."

"He was a good man," Major Nioma said, ducking her head in respect before flicking her gaze to Mon. It was clear that Major Nioma was the type of woman who preferred to stay focused on the task at hand.

"I asked the major to speak with you about possible threats to your safety," Mon told Leia gently. "A member of intelligence is meeting with each public figure of the Alliance over the next few days."

So Leia wasn't being singled out, but she was likely among the first to have such a meeting. She wondered when Mon had been briefed on the threats against her own life.

"You're the face of the Rebellion," Major Nioma told Leia. "That makes you fiercely loved by some . . ." Her voice trailed off—there was no need for her to point out the ways hate ran deeper than love for the princess in some circles.

"I've survived plenty of assassination attempts," Leia said. "I appreciate the concern, but—"

"Major Nioma has prepared a file for you," Mon said, and the major passed Leia a datapad. "I know you are aware of the most common threats, but it will help to be prepared."

"I can assign a protection detail," Major Nioma started.

"I can take care of myself," Leia said.

"The threat is shifting, Leia," Mon warned. "You were a political prisoner, even in war. There were lines that could not be crossed without the Empire admitting the threat of the Rebellion, something they tacitly tried to avoid. But now the Empire is backed into a corner. A caged animal will lash out. Lethally."

Leia had used the ploy of ambassadorship to avoid capture more than once, and it had worked—until it hadn't. Darth Vader hadn't cared that Leia claimed to be on a diplomatic mission when he'd captured her, and her status as a senator and popular figure among the Core Worlds had done nothing to prevent her torture or stop Tarkin from punishing those she loved.

"I am well aware of the threats I face," Leia said. "I cannot let what others are willing to do stop me from doing what I must."

"It's not just you," Major Nioma said. She leaned over Leia, swiping at the datapad. Dossier files displayed on the screen. Luke, Chewie, Han. "Everyone you know is a target; every connection you make is a pathway to you."

Leia kept her face calm, but inside she felt as if she'd plunged into cold water. She could still feel the way Han held her. How much more of a threat would he be under if—when—they married? Even if the wedding happened far from the Core, it would be impossible to keep their union a secret.

She'd already proven she could withstand torture herself, but she could not bear the thought of those she loved being hurt because of her.

"In particular, I'd like to go over the bounties on your head," Major

Nioma said, sweeping past the dossiers of those close to Leia and on to image captures of various postings. "Not all of the bounties have an obvious source, but it's clear that there are multiple threats."

None of this was news to Leia. The Empire wanted her dead. The Hutts. Various political dissidents. She paused, reading one file in particular. "Who is this?"

Major Nioma peered over the datapad. "Ah. This is the chief operating officer of one of the major manufacturing plants on Coruscant," she said, tapping the woman's image. "You legislated for tighter control of refugee labor rights, and that lost her billions."

"And she wants me dead. Because I supported a law that didn't allow her to exploit refugees?" Leia had never even met this person before, at least not to her memory. She hadn't even written the law in question; she'd merely argued for it on the Senate floor.

"If it makes you feel better, she's included me in the hit," Mon said.

"Good company, I guess," Leia muttered.

"We've added several potential threats from business owners here at the end," Major Nioma continued. "Most of them relied heavily on Imperial contracts to remain in operation."

"And they're going to blame me because there's no more need for Star Destroyers or stormtrooper armor." Leia's voice was flat.

"Exactly," Major Nioma said, clearly pleased that Leia was grasping the gravity of the situation.

"Preposterous," Leia said, tossing down the datapad. She hadn't won the war single-handedly; why should she bear the brunt of blame from the discontents who lost?

"Still, these are the viable threats we've identified," Major Nioma said. "So far."

"Fine," Leia snapped. "Half the galaxy hates me and wants me dead."

"Not just you," Major Nioma added. "Also your loved ones and close associates."

Leia froze, her teeth clenched, biting back all the curses she wanted to scream to the sky. Major Nioma opened her mouth to continue speaking, but Mon put her hand out. "That's enough for now. We'll touch back on this later."

Major Nioma nodded and turned to go. Leia grasped her elbow, holding her back. "Let's keep General Calrissian in the loop with anything happening on Bespin. I can reach out to other worlds with energy-rich resources. Can you send me data on Hofsgut, Madurs, Inusagi, let's see . . ."

"Lechra has a privately owned Tibanna gas refinery, and there have been a lot of *Aurore*-class freighters from the Mining Guild coming out of the Lixal sector," Mon added.

"I've got scouts in Lixal, nothing yet," Major Nioma said.

"Can you get me more on Lechra? Oh, and also Forrn—I seem to recall they had a moon with carnium as well."

Major Nioma agreed to get Leia the information as soon as possible and left. Moments after she was gone, General Madine approached. "Is now a good time to talk about the Outer Rim?" he asked.

Mon's eyes flicked over to Leia, but Leia zeroed in on the general. "Yes," she said firmly. General Madine was right to be concerned that the Outer Rim would harbor Imperial remnants or, worse, potentially already had covert bases of operations.

"Sterdic Four is the obvious choice," Madine said, getting straight to the point, "but I have my eye on several other worlds as well."

Leia's recon had told her as much. Although not technically in the Outer Rim, Sterdic IV was on the edge. With a well-populated capital city and a preexisting Imperial presence in the manufacturing district, the planet would not have easily given up the lucrative credits the Empire brought in. "What would be the best approach?" she asked the general.

"Aerial strikes in Cawa City, I think, at the manufacturing district and away from civilian areas," Madine answered, getting straight to the point.

"The optics are good," Mon added. The words made Leia's stomach twist. She knew what Mon meant—Cawa City was large enough, with enough trade going in and out, that a win there would be an excellent show of strength. It would send a message to those who still supported the Empire and those debating whether to join the new government.

But it didn't escape her notice that a strike like that might need the special forces of Han's unit.

Leia gritted her teeth. She could not allow her feelings to dictate her directives, whether it put Han back into battle or not. But try as she might, she could not find the words to speak. She listened silently as Madine and Mon discussed the potential of sending a fleet to Cawa City, nodding along as they brought in Admiral Ackbar for his opinion on which ships to send.

"As for ground troops," Madine continued, "it'll be harder to pinpoint where to dispatch troops in the scattered worlds on the Outer Rim."

Leia let out a breath.

"How much time do you need?" Mon asked.

Madine's eyes grew distant as he thought. Leia had great respect for his opinion. He had originally led a command unit within the Empire before defecting, so he knew Imperial strategies intimately. He had been among the first to support her when Mon had revealed the information of the plans for the second Death Star and Leia had proposed a daring mission as a distraction so they could prepare the attack at Endor. She still remembered the way he'd carefully considered Operation Yellow Moon before firmly and unequivocally offering his approval.

"Let me talk to Solo," Madine said finally. "But I think—a week maybe? Or two. I'll be confident of our locations by then."

A week or two. All the time she would have left with Han before he was off to some Outer Rim war. And before she was . . .

"Where will I be sent?" Leia asked Mon after the other officers had left. The tent had seemed far too cramped before, but now it was cavernous. Mon sat down in front of the strategy board, green light reflecting over her pale dress.

"You're one of our best diplomats," Mon said, smiling up at her. Leia sat down beside her on the bench. "But the Death Star was just destroyed. I think we can afford a bit of a break."

Leia's laugh was bitter. "I know for a fact you were in the same briefing I was just in."

"It's bad," Mon allowed. "We both knew it wouldn't be simple, but . . ."

Leia nodded silently. Her eyes drifted to the strategy board. "So we have a few weeks at best. Killing the Emperor bought us that much time, at least." Leia cut her gaze to Mon. "Enough time for a wedding, I suppose."

Mon's eyes widened, and a rare smile full of genuine happiness graced her face. "A wedding?" She reached for Leia's hands, pulling them into her lap. "You're going to marry that rogue?"

"Are you going to try to talk me out of it?" Leia's tone was jovial, but her heart raced at the thought. She valued Mon dearly, but she knew the older woman saw her as something of a younger sister, nearly a daughter. Leia would do as she wished; she did not need Mon's approval. But she still wanted it.

"Never," Mon said, and warmth flooded through Leia. Mon rubbed her finger across Leia's knuckles. "My only regret is that Bail and Breha cannot be here with you."

Pain lanced through Leia at the thought. Marriage had been something discussed with her before—her aunts, in particular, had always aimed to see her wedded advantageously, despite the fact that such an arrangement had never truly appealed to Leia. She had known from very early on that much of her life would be given to service, and she had no problem whatsoever with resigning herself to long ceremonies or dedicating her work to aiding others. But—despite sensationalizing journalists or nosy family members—Leia had always considered whatever would happen in the privacy of her bedroom to be hers and hers alone. She could not give up *all* of herself to everyone else, or she would have nothing left to give.

Her mother had spoken to her in-depth about love and duty before Leia's Day of Demand, when she was named heir apparent to the Alderaanian throne. Breha had brought with her the Rhindon Sword and placed it on Leia's bed while they'd talked.

The Day of Demand required Leia to prove her worth to the people of Alderaan through three challenges, one for the body, one for the mind, and one for the heart.

"You know," Breha had told her daughter, "the importance of this sword to our people."

Leia had nodded solemnly.

"You will carry this sword when you make your challenges," Breha continued. "And you will raise it before all the court when you succeed in them. But," she added, her tone softer, "you will also wear this sword whenever you marry."

Leia, who had been entirely focused on the upcoming challenges and the rigors of the Day of Demand, blinked, not expecting to discuss something that would be so far in the future. "The sword is a symbol of the monarchy," Breha continued, "and a reminder that it is not blood that chooses the ruler of Alderaan. It is choice. Your father and I—we chose you. To be our daughter and our future queen. And I want you to know, my love, that even though you are a part of a family that has many obligations and duties that come with our privileges, you *always* have the right to a choice. Whoever you marry, it is your choice. And when you marry, I will strap this sword around your waist before you go to meet your husband or your wife. That is what the Rhindon Sword represents to all of Alderaan, but to the rulers especially: that we have the freedom to choose our own fate, and we have the skill and the weapons needed to defend it."

Leia's hands clenched in Mon's grasp now. She had seen her world destroyed, had known her parents were on the surface when it blew up, but the enormity of that loss was still, after all this time, hard to process. It hit her in sharp stings—she might never be able to fully process the magnitude of her lost planet—but the memory of the Rhindon Sword, which had hung upon the wall in the castle for generations, and the loss of that one relic made bile rise in Leia's throat. She could not truly wrap her mind around the whole planet gone. Her grief came in shards—the sword, Appenza Peak, the scent of flowers in the courtyard, her old toy droid Lola, her nanny droid WA-2V, that chipped stone on her balcony from when she'd gotten carried away as a child with a mock sparring match, the little sweetmallow cakes that were sent to her room as appeasement when she was too young to attend her parents' formal functions—it was the details that tortured her, the little memories that could never be re-created or passed on.

Tarkin had stolen her past, present, and future when he'd ordered the strike on Alderaan. Leia could never go back to what had been, and

Breha would never strap the Rhindon Sword around her, and Bail would never meet Han, and their wedding would be on a far-flung moon and not at the palace, and . . .

Mon squeezed her hand, guessing at least some of Leia's thoughts. "They would be proud of you," she said gently.

Emotion welled in Leia's eyes. "Do you really think so?" she asked, her voice breaking.

Mon nodded. "I know so." She smiled sadly. "Bail often fretted about you, you know. He was always in awe of the way you stepped up. You are so giving, Leia, and he loved that about you. But he did worry that you would sacrifice too much of yourself in helping others. So I know without a single doubt that he would be proud you choose to celebrate joy now, in this moment."

Leia let out her breath. It had been an emotional morning, in more ways than one. "Thank you," she said, hoping Mon could hear all the sincerity behind such a simple phrase. "Han and I can get married here—I'll have Threepio ask Chief Chirpa if there is a ceremonial site or a gathering place we can use, or perhaps we should simply be under the trees . . ."

"There is much to plan, and not much time to do it in," Mon said, smiling indulgently.

"Time!" Leia snorted. "There never is enough. But don't worry," she added. "We're not looking for this to be a huge thing, and there's certainly not going to be a honeymoon or anything like that. A simple ceremony before . . ." Before they had to part ways. It was hitting her now, just how abrupt this would be. Leia didn't want to prolong the wait, but at the same time, it was beyond frustrating that they would be pulled in separate directions so soon.

"What?" Mon frowned at her.

Leia concentrated on the timeline. "Han to the Outer Rim with the ground troops. Me to an ambassador mission." She snorted again, the sound softer, more bitter. "I'll be going to the Core, maybe Mid Rim. Worlds apart. In a couple of weeks. I suppose the Ewoks won't mind us camping out here that long, before we ship out."

"No, wait," Mon said, holding up her hands to stop Leia's calculations. "Surely General Madine can lead a Pathfinder mission in Han's place if the need arises." She gave Leia a sardonic look. "We do tend to have contingency plans for if he has to abandon post again."

"The Hutts had a price on his head when he left Hoth."

"You're defending him now? How quickly love makes you turn a blind eye. I remember when he first gave notice. You were incandescent, if I recall." Mon grinned.

"I'm never incandescent," Leia said loftily, but her words were belied with a laugh.

"Still, there *is* time for a honeymoon," Mon said. "If anyone in the entire galaxy deserves time off to celebrate, it's you."

Leia shook her head. She didn't merit any type of special treatment. Everyone had sacrificed; everyone had worked. In war, there was no measuring stick against which to calculate your worth against another's, nor your grief. It was as much about good aim as it was about luck. Besides, there was simply far too much work to be done. Mon was dear to suggest that she take time to herself, but it was impossible.

CHAPTER 5

HAN

IT WAS LANDO WHO SUGGESTED a party to celebrate the end of Han's scoundrel days as soon as Han told him the good news. While Han protested that he was hardly going respectable, who was he to say no to a party? What had started as a small gathering of friends in one of the more sizable huts at Bright Tree Village had spun out larger and larger as word spread throughout the camp of the impending marriage. Everyone seemed eager for revelry now before they all dispersed and separated in the next phase of the war. It was a feeling Han could more than understand—much like a starving child will take what food they can get when they can get it, the Rebellion had been starving for joy and was gluttonous now that even a morsel of it was being offered.

Lando appointed himself as something of a gatekeeper at the hut, a duty he wore with the same grace he held as host, gently turning away those who wanted jet juice more than camaraderie, an effective method to keep the party as closed as possible.

When the Death Star had been destroyed and the tacit defeat of the Empire accepted, that first night of raucous dancing and drinking had been a chaotic release of the pressures the war had put everyone under—adrenaline surged just as much as liquor as, for the first time in years, they no longer lived in a constant state of fight-or-flight. The hut Han was in now was crowded, but it was nothing like the village-wide boisterous party after the Death Star exploded. Han preferred it that way— the party tonight was too big to be called private, but small enough that he recognized every smiling face.

Lando moved to the door when it swung open and a tall, pink Mikkian woman strode inside with sure steps and a confident gleam in her eyes. "My apologies, darling," Lando said, his words emphasized with a seductive smile, "but this is a private party." He bowed his head slightly.

The woman ignored Lando entirely and grabbed a tsiraki served in a wooden cup, downing it like it was nothing. She wiped away a smear of blue liquid with the back of her hand before pouring herself another.

Lando blinked, caught between appreciation of the brash woman and a desire to keep some control of the guest list.

"Ah, Sakas is great," Han said, throwing an arm over Lando's shoulder and shooting the woman a smile.

Lando stepped away from the door and his duties. "I can't believe you're settling down," he said.

"Just following Chewie's example."

Chewbacca roared, a proud trill to the sound.

"And a lucky woman Malla is," Lando said, tipping his glass of wine to Chewie. The Wookiee nodded in agreement, smug pleasure painted across his furry face.

"Where did you even get a wineglass?" Han asked as Chewie wandered over to the table of various breads, meats, and cheeses Lando had arranged. "I mean, the wine I can see, but you have a crystal goblet that looks like it was made on Inusagi and the rest of us are sipping from wooden tankards carved by fuzzballs."

"Very hospitable fuzzballs." Lando raised his glass in the air, as there were no Ewoks present to toast.

"Do you just cart around a full bar wherever you go?" Han asked. He flicked Lando's cloak. "And a wardrobe?"

"Some of us like variety," Lando said. "Speaking of which, my friend, you must let me lend you some more . . . respectable garments for your wedding. If there was ever a time for a man to trade in his vest for something that's been washed this decade . . ."

Han lifted the edge of his vest and sniffed. "It's clean!"

"Yet it could be cleaner."

"Listen, *friend*," Han started, but Lando immediately threw his hand up and backed away. "What?" Han asked.

"Last time you called me friend, you punched me in the face."

"Last time, you deserved it."

"Fair enough. But still, let's get you a jacket at least," he said. "I have something that would fit you. Made on Alderaan, actually."

That caused Han to pause. Leia would appreciate something like that. "Maybe," he conceded. If it wasn't too flashy. He doubted Lando had anything that wasn't, though.

Lando looked around the room and spotted a group playing cards against the wall. "Sabacc?"

"Absolutely not," Han said, grinning despite his words. "I have everything I want, which means I don't need to gamble."

"Wise before your time!" Lando saluted Han with his empty glass. "In that case, you may merely watch as your old friend fleeces your new ones." He winked, and Han laughed.

Before they reached the circle of players, though, the door banged open. Half a dozen Ewoks ran into the hut, arms raised, voices pitched high with urgency. "What's going on?" Han yelled, but the cacophony drowned out his voice.

"*Yip! Yip!*" yelled the littlest Ewok, grabbing Han's hand and dragging him toward the exit. It was the one Leia liked, Wicket. "*Yub, nub! Yub, yub!*"

"Whoa, buddy," Han said, pulling back. In the distance, he heard a gonging bell, deep and resonant, echoing throughout the forest. "What's going on?" He turned back to Lando. "Get Threepio, would you?"

A flash of gold-colored metal outside caught Han's eye. Rather than pulling away from the Ewok, Han grabbed Wicket's paw and headed to the door, the little guy racing to keep up with Han's longer legs. "Goldenrod!" Han bellowed through the noise.

"Oh, I am so glad to see you, General Solo!" C-3PO said, bustling to him. "The Ewoks have spotted a condor dragon in the distance."

Han frowned, unsure of what such a creature was, but if the Ewoks kept guards looking for them and had a system in place to warn others of their approach, it would be best to investigate. He looked around and spotted Luke emerging from the party, one of the few people entirely sober. "What should we do?" he asked.

Luke nodded toward one of the Ewoks, an older fellow with gray fur, beady eyes, and a brown leather hood adorned with teeth and bones. "Ask Chief Chirpa," he said. "Threepio, can you help us figure out what the situation is?" The gonging had stopped, replaced briefly by a high-pitched clacking sound followed by silence, but the Ewoks had all seemed to congregate inside the hut. Han could hear Lando from where he stood, shouting at them not to eat all the food.

"*Yub yub!*" Wicket said, yanking free of Han's grip and running back into the hut.

C-3PO bustled over to Chief Chirpa. The leader of the Council of Elders banged a staff on the wooden platform, swinging the long stick to point at Han as he spoke to the protocol droid angrily. C-3PO put up placating hands, jabbering in Ewokese. A moment later he came back to Han. Chief Chirpa followed him, his brow furrowed over his little face.

"Well?" Han said. "Do we need to get some troops ready to take care of this condor dragon?"

"Chief Chirpa has informed me that the threat is gone; the condor dragon flew in a different direction."

The Ewok stomped even closer, glaring up at Han. "*Yip-yar, nub bree mah!*" he growled, shaking his staff in Han's face.

"So why's the little guy mad at me?" Han asked C-3PO.

C-3PO cocked his head. Han could almost feel the indignation radiating off the droid. Great. Now the finicky droid *and* the Ewok were both angry at him. "Sir, it appears the Ewoks have discovered that you intend to have a celebration? Without them?"

"Oh, no," Han groaned and turned back to the hut. It was positively swarming with Ewoks now. The doors and windows were all slung open, and more fur was visible inside than anything else.

Ewoks squatted on the table, eating the charcuterie display with both hands; they tossed sabacc cards in the air like confetti, dancing as the colored cards drifted down over them; they pounded on the walls to create a rhythmic beat so other Ewoks could dance. Meanwhile, half the invited guests were joining in, cheering the Ewoks on, while the other half slipped away to find less chaotic revelries. Two Woklings climbed over Chewie, swinging from his outstretched arms. Chewbacca roared, and the Ewoks screamed, and while both sounds were joyful, akin to laughter, they were also deafening.

"Seems like the party's gotten away from you," Luke said placidly, observing the riotous cacophony barely contained within the walls.

"Threepio, tell them to leave," Han demanded.

"It is technically their hut in their village," C-3PO informed him.

"It's a party to celebrate my upcoming wedding," Han said.

"What luck," C-3PO chirped. "The condor dragon watch group is made up of the unmarried male Ewoks, who have informed me they have similar celebratory traditions prior to marriage."

Han pinched the bridge of his nose. "That is not the point."

"And it's considered a personal insult to Chief Chirpa if you do not include him in any celebration."

The Ewok elder thumped his staff on the wooden platform, trilled, and strode inside, heading straight to the table with food.

Before Han could say or do anything, C-3PO tottered back into his line of vision, demanding attention. "And might I add, sir, I have been an integral part of your journeys and alongside you since Tatooine. I was shocked to hear the news of your nuptials secondhand."

"Your engraved invitation is on its way," Han growled.

C-3PO considered him for a moment as R2-D2 rolled over the wooden bridge to approach them, beeping cheerily.

Luke, who understood the astromech better than Han, gestured toward the crowded hut. "Oh, go right in," he said. "Everyone is."

"Hey—" Han started, but R2-D2 chirped excitedly, bouncing on his back legs.

C-3PO only had emotionless eye sensors, but Han could have sworn the droid was glaring at him. "I suppose you intended to invite me to this party as well? I would have expected to be included. As a protocol droid, it is quite within my realm of capabilities to serve as an essential part of any social gathering."

"Essential—?" Han started, but before he could stop him, C-3PO bustled into the room.

"This is going really well," Luke observed.

R2-D2 beeped as he whirred behind C-3PO, spinning in the center of the hut to the wild amusement of the more than a dozen Ewoks pounding their feet on the floor around him. As R2-D2 stopped twirling, the Ewoks turned to C-3PO, cheering his arrival and raising their staffs in the air, chanting "*Yub! Nub!*" One of them, wearing an orange-red hood and brandishing a staff adorned with a vine made of delicate green ivy with white berries, seemed to be at the head of the line, leading the others.

"We've got to get the yub-nub commander out of there," Han grumbled.

Luke snorted. "They're kind of cute."

"Did you not see them attacking the stormtroopers? Those little guys are brutal."

"Still cute."

"Chewie could rip your arms off and beat you with them, but he won't, probably. Ewoks would, but they can't. That's not *cute*."

Luke cast an analytical eye at the raging party inside the hut. "So, what's the plan here? Just chalk it up to a lost cause?"

"Eh," Han drawled, measuring the options. "If you can't beat 'em . . ."

"Join 'em?"

Han nodded and headed back toward the deafening drums inside the hut, Luke laughing behind him. Just before they entered, though, Luke touched Han's elbow, holding him back. "So . . . marriage?"

Han gave him a crooked smile.

"What's . . . uh, what's the plan there?" Luke searched Han's eyes. "I didn't think you were the settling-down type."

It was the same question Luke had just asked in regard to the party, and part of Han wanted to give the same answer—he'd met his match in Leia, and that made her the perfect woman for him. *But Luke is her brother*, Han reminded himself. A flippant answer wouldn't do.

He found himself staring at Luke, trying to find the similarities between him and Leia. They weren't just siblings but twins. He couldn't see Leia in Luke's face though, not until his gaze settled on Luke's eyes. Before, when he had first met Luke at that cantina on Tatooine, he would never have pinned that naïve boy as the twin of the princess of Alderaan. Now, though . . . it was in their eyes. Not the same shade, true, but the same depth, calm and assured.

That was the difference. When Han had first met Luke, the kid hadn't known who he was yet. Not the part about being the long-lost brother to Leia or anything like that. He hadn't known his purpose.

Now he did.

Han wondered: If he looked in a mirror now, would his eyes reflect the same certainty? As if he knew both that he was on the right path and that nothing could ever pull him off it.

Luke seemed to see something in Han's expression that satisfied his original question. He nodded at the other man, and the two ducked inside the hut.

And to think, just a few days ago Han had been jealous of Luke's connection with Leia. Han wasn't big on envy; he took what he wanted, and if he couldn't have it, he didn't want it. But he couldn't remember not wanting Leia, especially after—

"What?" Luke asked over the sound of the beating drums and the thudding feet.

Han shook his head, trying to dismiss the image in his mind.

"What were you thinking about?" Luke insisted. "Your face was odd."

"Just—remember that time? After the wampa attack?"

Han watched as the exact memory settled on Luke—when Leia tried to pretend that she wasn't in love with Han and kissed Luke instead. Except, at the time, none of them had known . . .

"Let's never speak of that again," Luke said.

"*Never*," Han agreed.

R2-D2 whirred by, beeping, knocking past Han as he left. Han turned to watch the astromech droid leave the hut, and when he turned back, C-3PO was in his face. Han took a step back as C-3PO said, "Sir, I do believe that this party has gotten out of hand."

"You think?"

"Indeed. I believe it was a mistake to invite so many Ewoks."

Behind him, shadows flickered as a group of Ewoks lit torches and

began swirling them around, casting sparks through the growing darkness. Another one tottered nearby with a wooden mug filled to the brim
with bright-blue tsiraki. Han grabbed the mug from the little guy, who
promptly started shouting in protest. "This much liquor would make a
grown man sick," he tried to explain, but the Ewok leapt at him, grabbing the mug. Most of the tsiraki spilled out, fortunately, and when the
Ewok slurped at the remains, he made a disgusted face, throwing the
wooden mug on the ground and wiping his tongue with his paws.

"Told you," Han muttered to the ungrateful Ewok. The only thing
Han could think of that would be worse than drunk Ewoks was hung-
over Ewoks. "We've gotta shut this down," Han told Luke. "Can't you do
some—" He waggled his fingers. "—and make them go?"

Luke raised an eyebrow. "You'd like me to use the Force to break up
a party?"

"Yes. Can you?"

"I probably could . . . ?" Luke wasn't able to hide the doubt in his
voice.

"But you won't even try."

Luke grinned. Han turned to C-3PO. "Right, well, they think *you* are
a god, so if I kick you out, maybe your faithful followers will . . . follow,"
he ended somewhat pathetically.

C-3PO gasped, affronted.

"It would be a big help," Luke offered, something more appealing to
the droid. "Although you do realize that there's a chance that the Ewoks
will turn on you and avenge their deity instead, right, Han?"

That had not, in fact, occurred to him. But then one of the Ewoks
twirling the bright torches swung the fire too close to the liquor table,
and a punch bowl full of some sort of foul concoction that absolutely
included homemade hooch and might have a splash of literal jet engine
fluid caught a spark and burst into flame. The nearest Ewoks screamed,
charging to the other side of the hut while some of the remaining party
members rushed forward to douse the flames that roared inside the
wooden punch bowl on top of the wooden table placed at the edge of
the wooden hut that was perched very high in the flammable forest dotted with more dwellings that were basically tinder.

"Just go!" Han roared at C-3PO.

"Well, I never!" C-3PO shot back, but at least when the golden droid headed out of the hut, half the Ewoks followed him.

Chewbacca rushed past Han and came back inside a moment later, a huge rain barrel held aloft in his massive arms. He sloshed the contents over the burning liquor table, and a waterfall of ash, spilled liquor, and rainwater poured over the side, splashing on everyone. Pretty quickly, Han discovered that a wet Ewok smelled worse than a dry one.

Lando sidled up. He was immaculate, as always, his crystal goblet refilled with wine from somewhere unknown. He tipped it toward Han, as if clinking his glass against an imaginary one Han didn't have. "Excellent party, Han, best one since we met up with the Tonnika sisters on that casino ship on the Hydian Way."

"Funny," Han said. "Now that all the liquor's gone is exactly when I need a drink."

Lando sipped his wine. "Always the way of it."

CHAPTER 6

LEIA

"HAVE YOU BEEN HERE THE whole time?" Mon's voice cut across the dark tent.

Leia straightened, her back aching. She gave the other woman a guilty smile.

Mon shook her head. "When I offered to help arrange your wedding with the Ewok Council of Elders, I did it so that you could take some time off to yourself, have a moment of peace before you got married."

"I know," Leia said, almost laughing. It was just that as soon as Mon left, Leia had been cornered by all the people who needed Mon or someone from Alliance High Command to proceed with their next directives. General Forell had pulled her away first, so that she could record a message to the Anoat sector, assuring the people that the Emperor was dead and the new unified republic would rise and come to their aid. As soon as that was done, General Cracken had requested another unit added to his reserves, and Leia's opinion on his next plan. After that, Leia had helped the supporting staff with arranging a more efficient system of distributing meals among the troops still grounded on Endor while also clearing another unit for dispersal and early departure from the forest moon.

She had spent the rest of the time in blissful solitude, composing messages to the five worlds Major Nioma had given her intelligence on. Four of them were worlds she'd visited before and whose political leaders were people she already had a connection with. She was able to speak on a personal level in her holomessages to the president of Hofsgut, the chieftess of Inusagi, the viceroy of Lechra, and Empress Eliaora of Forrn. Each of them had either remained independent or had been forced into at least a financial alliance with the Empire, if not more, and Leia was reasonably confident that she could convince them to side with the new republic that was forming in the vacuum Imperial control had made now that it had been defeated. Leia knew the needs as well as desires of each ruler and each world, offering specific aid or personal favors that could be plied for the worlds' entries into a greater union.

The prime minister of Madurs, however, was a different matter. Leia read over the dossier Major Nioma had given her. Dreand Yens was a long-serving elected official, clearly beloved by his citizens to have remained in power so long. Madurs had seen a boom of popularity prior to the Imperial takeover; Emperor Palpatine himself had visited the moon during a fine-arts exposition that had been hosted there, early on in the Empire's development. While Madurs was primarily known for its artistic displays of ice palaces and crystalline creations, which Emperor Palpatine did seem to appreciate, judging from the holos on record, Leia suspected the Emperor had had ulterior motives in his visit. Soon after, appeals to the prime minister for access to the moon's carnium had begun. The prime minister had never agreed to a contract with the Empire, though, and the official records clearly showed that the moon's carnium lay deep within its ocean floor, difficult to acquire and potentially hazardous to the stability of the moon's core.

Leia crafted her initial letter to Prime Minister Yens carefully, opting to compose an electronic missive that showed her appreciation for both the moon's artistic background and the prime minister's resolve in rebuffing the Empire. She knew that reaching out to Prime Minister Yens would give the appearance of the new republic's greed for the resource, but she hoped that her promise to protect the moon's carnium reserves

would be taken for the truth that it was. She cared more about the unification of worlds than the exploitation of them, and she could only
hope that her reputation would reinforce her ambassadorial resolve in
reaching out to Madurs.

Leia didn't know how much time had passed when Mon Mothma
interrupted her. As Leia stretched, her back cracked.

"Your husband-to-be has been throwing quite a party in the trees,"
Mon said.

Leia laughed. "I heard about that." Rumors had spread quickly, and if
only half of what she'd heard was true, this gathering of Han's was sure
to become the stuff of legends.

Mon shook her head. "Take the rest of the night off, I'm begging you.
Crash the party, if you want."

Leia wanted nothing less, but she did take Mon's advice. She left the
base tent, pulling her hood up as she wove through the camp. Her umber
dress trimmed in brown leather was plain enough that she could almost
blend in, especially with her hair tucked away. Closest to headquarters,
she mostly passed rebel fighters and workers, but there were Ewok huts
here, too, the unmarried males who had not yet, according to C-3PO's
translations, won a spot in a family home in the trees. These smaller
huts, dotting the ground under the trees, seemed mostly empty. The
shadows grew long as twilight turned to night. Leia was grateful to have
the warm cloak made of some animal's fur that the Ewoks had gifted her
for being a "maid of the spear," according to C-3PO's translation.

Leia had been warned not to wander too far away from Bright Tree
Village, so she stayed where she could still see the outline of huts in the
trees, the flickering light of torches. She walked with no purpose other
than the chance to be alone. She didn't like sitting still, but it was nice
to have nothing for company aside from her own thoughts and the
whisper of rustling leaves and the gentle wind through the trees.

It was cold, growing colder by the second, and Leia wrapped her fur-
lined cloak tighter. While it was wide enough to cover her shoulders,
the cloak's short length meant that it stopped before reaching her knees.
Soft ferns brushed against her skirt; mud squelched over her leather
slippers.

When she'd recorded the message for the Anoat sector, one of General Cracken's lieutenants had suggested Leia make another announcement, one of celebration for her upcoming wedding. Leia had refused, despite the young man's insistence that the people would love to hear about her romance. "Think of the image it creates!" the lieutenant had said, framing his hands around Leia's face. "The new republic has just begun, and this marriage is timed in a way to be symbolic. *You*, Princess, are literally embodying unification. The Empire loves fractured things, but this new government will join together—"

"No," Leia had said, a touch too forcefully. The lieutenant's face had fallen. "It's just—too much right now," she continued, putting a gentle hand on his shoulder. "Ask me again later."

It had partially been the truth. Recording the message for the Anoat sector had hammered in the idea that the war was still not over; the threat of the Empire still viable. And yet, despite facing the news of clear Imperial babble over the feeds, encrypted data all pointing to that sector, the near-certainty that trouble was brewing, Leia had forced herself to be calm and authoritative, no question of the new republic's strength for the message.

Not that she did question the newly forming republic's strength.

She was just . . . so tired of being strong.

It had drained her to send more messages, more hope to people who would be forced to face more conflict.

But there was also a part of her that hadn't wanted to record a second message, one about her marriage, to the whole galaxy.

For now, under the canopy of the trees of this moon, her love was hers, not the galaxy's. And she knew it would be impossible to remain private for the rest of their lives. But . . . she would hold on as long as she could. This little piece of her heart was not for public display. Not yet.

Leia stopped. She'd wandered farther than she'd intended, but her feet had moved with grace that was unearned. There was no path here; the underbrush was overgrown, roots and vines grabbing at her ankles, waiting to trip her. She had become so distracted that she hadn't realized she could barely see the flickering lights of Bright Tree Village.

Despite being so far away, though, she could smell smoke.

Leia paused, her senses heightening. It wasn't new smoke, but it smelled . . . odd. Damp petrichor scented the air, the general loamy smell of any fertile forest, but the smoky, ashy stench wove through those familiar scents, tugging at her as if leading her.

There should not be a fire so far from the village.

Cold sweat made bumps prickle her arms. There was a push-and-pull to the moment, as a part of her wanted to flee, and a part of her wanted to uncover the source of the smell more than anything else. Leia had felt this way only once before, when she had sensed Luke on Bespin. Her body had wanted to escape the city in the clouds, to pull from orbit and disappear into hyperspace, far away from the threat of Vader. But her soul had called her back, summoning her to the place where she knew Luke was, even though she could not possibly have known Luke would be there.

"Luke," she said aloud, her voice pitched high. She didn't sense him now, not exactly, but—the pull reminded her of the way he had called for her. He had nearly died. Maybe that was what was happening now—he needed her! Leia ignored the fear that made her heart race, irrational as it was, and crashed through the forest, sure that she was going in the direction she needed to go. She would save Luke; she would find her brother, discover whatever it was that had led him into the dark woods on the outskirts of the village. She patted her waist and hip, checking her weapons even as she ran haphazardly through the forest. She didn't care about moving silently; she had to be quick. No time to get help. He needed her—*now*—

Leia skidded to a stop.

There was the source of the smoky smell that still lingered in a sickening haze around the area.

A funeral pyre.

Luke had not summoned her. Whether real or imagined, it had not been Luke who had pulled her forward to uncover what was hidden in the dark shadows of the towering trees.

Gray ash and black soot stained the green-and-brown forest floor. Bile rose in Leia's throat. This had not been a simple wood fire. She knew even without seeing any charred bones. She knew.

Emotion clenched her throat, and for a moment she could not breathe. Her eyes welled with unshed tears, but she turned her face, forcing them down.

She would not cry for *him*.

Leia glanced down. She had stopped right on the edge of the line of ash. Very purposefully, Leia raised her foot and crossed from green moss to gray soot. Soft powder stirred as she strode through the remains of the funeral pyre. She could still see the faint, charred black timbers of the broken base, but the fire had reduced nearly everything to dust.

Good, Leia thought. Her *real* father, Bail, was dust, too. But he had died on Alderaan, which had exploded among the stars. It was not a comfort, not at all, but it made her glad that Bail was stardust, and Vader was nothing but sooty mud. Her father would drift in the heavens forever, and her torturer was scum on the bottom of her shoe.

There's good in him, Luke had said.

But he had not felt Vader's hand on her shoulder as her homeworld was destroyed.

Her toe connected with something heavy and solid. Not a timber. Leia glared down at the ash.

Darth Vader's helmet was twisted and mangled, melted and misshapen but still absolutely recognizable. There was a sort of horror-filled fascination to the way Leia bent at the waist, reaching for the gray-covered helmet. Would there be remnants of his flesh inside? Bone? Would his skull tip out?

But it was empty.

Leia let out a huff of breath, oddly disappointed by the hollowness of the helmet. She wondered what Luke had seen. He'd told her late that first night that Vader had taken off his faceplate and helmet, wanting to die with his real eyes on his son. Luke kept calling him Anakin, not Vader. He had said that Vader died with hope. With pride. For his son.

Leia hadn't seen that.

"Pride." She spat out the word bitterly, looking at the empty, melted eye on the helmet's front. *Pride.*

When Darth Vader had been assigned to find the location of the rebel base, he had enlisted the aid of a mind-probe. Despite that torture, Leia had not cracked. The IT-O interrogation droid had injected Leia forcibly with a truth serum worse than any physical torture. It had made her body feel disconnected, but it had also brought forth hallucinations. Friends begged her to reveal the location of the base. Her emotions were manipulated. People she loved died in front of her when she refused to talk; her worst nightmares came alive.

And when it was over—her heart exhausted from racing, her eyes red and dry, her lungs ravaged from screaming—both her mind and her body were broken, but her secrets were still kept . . .

Darth Vader had walked out of her detention cell, and he spoke of the way she'd resisted the probe with pride.

He had been impressed that she had survived the torture he had given her.

That was what Vader's pride meant to her.

That was what Luke did not understand.

"I'm glad you are dead," Leia whispered to the mask. There was no anger in her voice, only quiet truth. "I will never forgive you."

Something twisted inside her, rising like flame, burning and choking her throat. "I *hate* you!" Leia snarled, and she hurled the helmet into the ash. Her eyes burned, and her nostrils flared, and for a moment she felt *nothing* but the rage sweeping over her. It was feral, and it was *powerful*.

She tasted ash on the back of her tongue, and blood. "You are *not* my father!" Leia screamed. The word echoed around the otherwise silent forest.

And it was in the silence that Leia accepted the truth of the words she spoke. Her mind cleared; her hate faded. No matter what Luke said, no matter what her own blood proved, Vader was not her father.

A family was chosen, not born.

Bail and Breha had chosen her.

She chose Mon and Luke and Chewie and all her friends.

And she chose Han.

CHAPTER 7

HAN

"NERVOUS?" LANDO ASKED, STRAIGHTENING HAN'S collar.

"Of course not."

"It's not every day you marry a princess."

"Are you trying to make me nervous?"

Lando laughed. "Just keeping my friend humble."

"It's just a title," Han said, knocking Lando's hands away. "Titles don't mean much. Especially now."

"Fair enough." Lando raked his eyes over Han's appearance. "Give me half an hour, and I could make you almost presentable."

"This is fine." Han adjusted the jacket Lando had loaned him. It was likely the least flashy thing Lando owned. Lightweight and dark tan in color, the jacket had a thin silver thread running around the hem, the only embellishment visible. It was tight in the arms and Han had to wear it open, but he had to admit it wasn't bad. And if the style reminded Leia of her home, Han was willing to wear it.

"I suppose this will do," Lando said.

"It'd better."

"What do you think, Chewie?" Lando asked.

The Wookiee stood nearby looking through the window at the crowd gathering. He glanced behind him, trilling a high note of approval that turned into a laugh at Lando's preening, self-satisfied smile.

The temple was the largest building Han had seen yet in the Ewok village. C-3PO had informed him that it was not dedicated to any one god—the Ewoks seemed to worship a variety of spirits and deities to varying degrees, some seasonal or based on heroes either in legend or witnessed by the village. While most of the huts built in the trees were round and worked with the flow of the forest, connected by walkways, platforms, and bridges, the temple stood alone. To get to it, one had to descend from the treetop huts, cross on ground to the northern edge of the village, and walk along the small river that provided the Ewoks with their fresh water.

The tree the temple was built into what was called the Great Tree, according to C-3PO's translation, and it was something of a god itself to the Ewoks. "The Great Tree is a part of their origin mythology," C-3PO had explained when Han and Chewie had arrived there that morning. "It gives life and connects them to their land. They say the roots of all the trees in the forest intertwine with the Great Tree's roots. Each tree on the entire moon is both a unique individual and a part of the Great Tree." C-3PO had seemed to consider his translation for a moment. "It is rather confusing," he allowed.

But it made for a great spot to get married, Han had to admit. Separated from the main village, the Great Tree had an air of solemnity to it that didn't really exist anywhere else on the forest moon. And the Ewoks had outdone themselves in decorations. Flower garlands wove around the entire outer perimeter of the temple built high into the Great Tree. C-3PO had tried to explain what each flower symbolized, but Han hadn't even known how to distinguish the different varieties, much less that the yellow bloom wrapped around the pink one was supposed to be a blessing of the forest for many children. Or much food. One of those. C-3PO wasn't exactly clear on the distinctions.

But the furballs really had gone above and beyond, tucking tight little buds of flowers between each rung of the ladder Han had climbed to get to the temple. And it was even better inside.

Not only was the temple the biggest building in the entire village, it incorporated the Great Tree into its design. Standing in the center of the open space, the Great Tree's branches spread wide. Below the temple, stretching to the ground, there was one solid trunk, but behind the walls, the trunk split off into three different directions. Han wasn't sure if the tree had grown like that naturally or if some patient Ewok had bent the branches to form the interlacing design. The three different splits curved around, intertwining and creating a hollow space in the middle of the trunk before they shot off in three different directions, forming the main beams that supported the temple's roof.

"People are starting to arrive," Lando said, looking through the hollow opening in the Great Tree's trunk. Benches had been lined up on that side. Where Han, Chewie, and Lando waited, on the other side of the circular building, there was a platform for the Council of Elders to meet, holy relics, and other items Han could not identify. He only knew he'd been told to wait there until it was time.

Something sour rose in his stomach, but Han swallowed it down. He shook out his arms and legs, dispelling the nervous energy building inside him.

Lando shot Chewie a look.

"What is that?" Han asked, looking not through the hollow space in the tree, but at the thing that rested in the middle. It was large, easily the size of an Ewok's head, and golden in color, but almost transparent.

"A type of amber, I suppose," Lando said.

It sparkled with golden flecks reflecting the torches along the walls, but the giant amber orb seemed to glow from within as well. Han couldn't see how it had been placed inside the hollow cage made of the twisting tree branches, but it also seemed too perfectly shaped to have been naturally made. "Maybe this is why they thought Threepio was a god," he mused. "Same color."

Lando shrugged. "Looks like everyone in camp is crowding in," he said, pointing past the amber toward the just-visible crowd gathering in the temple beyond.

Han tugged at his collar. This many people in one oversized hut made the air stuffy. "Think this place is safe?" he asked. "I mean, that's a lot of people. And the Ewoks aren't used to having everyone crowd up their buildings. It would not be ideal if the floor broke . . ."

Lando laughed. "It's not that many people."

"It's a lot!" Han protested.

"It's fine." Lando stepped to the side, where a curtain had been drawn to hide the place where they stood, giving them a little privacy. He peeked past the roughly woven cloth. "Almost time," he said.

"We should probably stop any more people from coming in, don't you think?" Han asked Chewie. The Wookiee growled, shrugging his shoulders to dismiss the idea.

"Last chance," Lando said, turning to Han.

"For what?" Han asked, louder than he'd intended. "I don't have cold feet, if that's what you're asking."

Lando chuckled. "Last chance to change into something less scruffy-looking."

"I'm wearing the jacket, what more could you want?" Han huffed.

"Pressed slacks?" Lando suggested. "Shined shoes?" He sniffed. "A clean shirt?"

"I'm not changing clothes!"

Lando readjusted the short, dark-blue cape on his own shoulders, rubbing his thumb over the golden clasp, making it shine. "Suit your self." He gave Han a mock salute. "See you on the other side," he said before ducking under the curtain and claiming a seat on one of the benches near the front.

"It's really hot in here, isn't it, buddy?" Han mumbled to Chewie. Why did there have to be so many torches? There was still daylight, although that was fading fast. Too fast. They should have gotten married in the morning. Somewhere off in the woods, where no one else could find them. Luke could officiate and then they could just move on. They didn't need all this. It was ridiculous to gather everyone together in one spot this way; there was no reason to do it like this. As a matter of fact—

Chewie roared in Han's face, finally yanking his attention from his own troubled thoughts. "What?" Han demanded.

Chewie roared again.

"Already?" Han felt the color draining from his face. How could it already be time? But through the spiral hole in the Great Tree, past the huge chunk of amber, Han could just see the crowds of people sitting, their eyes forward. No one talked among themselves. They were waiting. On him. To go. It was time.

He just had to walk past that curtain and take his spot in front of the tree trunk.

That's all.

One foot in front of the other. Everyone was waiting. He just had to walk out there. He just had to *go*.

Han didn't move.

Chewie prodded him, speaking as softly as he could to ask what was wrong.

"Nothing's wrong," Han said too quickly. "Nothing at all."

Chewie poked him again. Han stumbled forward a step, but then his feet felt too heavy to move. He adjusted the lightweight jacket, yanking on its open front. "It's *really* hot in here, isn't it?"

Chewie growled, grabbed Han's arm, and jerked him forward. "Hey!" Han said, running to keep up with the Wookiee's long legs. "You don't have to drag me!"

"*Arr-gryu*," Chewie grumbled back.

"I'm going, I'm going, you don't have to threaten to carry me," Han said, jerking his arm free from Chewie's grasp just as the Wookiee swung the curtain aside.

Every single eye in the entire temple turned to him and his somewhat less-than-graceful entrance. Han tried to grin, but he kept his lips closed, just in case his breakfast decided to join the party. Chewie jabbed him in the back, and Han stumbled forward, moving toward the front of the crowd and taking his spot to the side of the twisted tree trunk. He could feel the rough bark at his back; if he reached through the twisting branches, he could touch the amber orb that rested in the center.

Why was everyone looking at him? The faces blurred together— Ewok, human, droid, various other species—they were all turned toward him. Of course, Han was alone at the front of the temple, so it stood to reason that they would look at him, but still . . .

And then the door in the back opened.

There was one second—just a heartbeat—when everyone was looking toward Han, but Han was looking at the door. And in that heartbeat, Leia stepped inside.

There was no one in the entire galaxy but Leia and Han.

Her eyes met his, and her smile was brighter than any star.

And it was just for him.

Han was rooted to the floor, but it was different from when Chewie had prodded him to take his spot in the temple. Before, what he'd really wanted to do was go somewhere private. But Han couldn't move now if he wanted to—and he never wanted to. Not with her walking between the benches toward him.

Leia wore a gown made of soft meadow green, embroidered with flowers similar to the ones bedecking the outside of the temple. It hung loose over her body, yet it wasn't shapeless. The sides were open, giving her space to move her legs and expose the laces of her white fur boots that went all the way up to her knees. She held a bouquet of wildflowers tied with the same bit of lacing woven in her hair, and Han suspected that Leia had picked the flowers just before she'd climbed the ladder to the temple.

Leia's long hair hung in loose waves down her back, with two small braids framing her face to keep locks out of her way. She wore flowers but no jewels. She looked more nymph than princess.

Han could barely breathe as she approached him, joy in her eyes. Leia had never looked more like herself than in this moment. She wasn't stately or noble. She wasn't the epitome of grace or the face of the Rebellion.

In this moment, Leia was no longer the people's princess. She was all the more beautiful because she was only herself. Just Leia.

CHAPTER 8

LEIA

HAN HELD BOTH HER HANDS with his, rubbing her knuckles with his callused thumbs as he stared into her eyes. "Hey, we're really doing this," he whispered.

"I know."

His eyes crinkled as he smiled. He kept his focus on her, but Leia was aware of some bustling nearby. In her brief stay on Endor so far, Leia had learned a little of the Ewok hierarchy. She was therefore unsurprised when Chief Chirpa strode forward, thunking his staff on the wooden floor with each step, the reverberating sound eliciting full attention. He strode past Han and Leia, going right to the heart of the Great Tree and turning so that one paw reached inside, resting a hand on the amber orb, while his other arm swung out, raising the staff high. An iguana clung to his fur, tail wrapped around his wrist as it stared up at the staff with lazy eyes.

When Chief Chirpa chanted in Ewokese, Leia turned—without releasing her hands from Han's—to find C-3PO. He sat near Mon, who held her bouquet of wildflowers for her. The protocol droid straightened in his seat at being the object of her attention, and he bustled up when she jerked her head. "A translation?" she asked. "For everyone."

"Yes, Your Highness," C-3PO said. He turned to the crowd—a mix of rebels and Ewoks, sitting and standing around the edges of the crowded temple. C-3PO raised his voice. "The chief asks for a blessing from the Great Tree to the union of the happy couple, may they never go hungry in their stomachs or their hearts."

Han chuckled, his fingers tightening around Leia's.

"The chief also asks for bountiful . . ." C-3PO glanced at Leia. "A bountiful bed, and—"

"Okay, that's enough," Han said, and, fortunately, the chief seemed to agree, thumping his staff on the floor three times. Leia noticed it was decorated with the same plants and flowers that adorned the temple outside, the beautiful flora a stark contrast to the long bone the staff was made of. A delicate-looking vine spiraled around the whole length, pale green with a frost of fuzzy white fluff on the outside, with flowers tucked into each loop around the staff. When Chief Chirpa walked, the petals swayed, but the vine held them fast.

Luke stood from his seat in the front bench. Leia had asked him to officiate their marriage, and while he had seemed a little unsure, he'd nodded gravely, rising to the task.

Except, before he could open his mouth or even step forward, another Ewok dashed up. The elder, named Logray, was something of a religious leader to the Ewoks. He had striped fur, alternating between grayish brown and grayish tan, and his face showed more age than most of the other Ewoks. He wore a cap adorned with the skull of a baby condor dragon, its beak forming a point over Logray's eyes. Flowers had been shoved in the empty eyeholes of the skull, giving it a ghoulish yet beautiful look—big yellow blooms with lots of tiny white buds sprinkled between the petals. That same pale-green vine frosted with delicate fuzz had been laced around the condor dragon's beak, and Logray's staff, which was typically topped with feathers and bones, now looked like an enormous bouquet of flowers explosively spilling over the sides and down the wooden length.

"*Yub nub!*" Logray shouted, banging the staff so hard that petals burst around them, fluttering like snowflakes to the temple floor.

Every Ewok in the temple shouted the refrain back: "*Yub nub!*"

"What's going on, Goldenrod?" Han said through a forced smile.

"It's fine," Leia said, trying to comfort him. He wanted perfection for her, and that was dear, but unneeded.

"It seems as if the religious leader has, er, taken over," C-3PO said.

As soon as the droid spoke, Logray stopped his call-and-response chant. He pointed to C-3PO with his flower-bedecked staff, intoning in a deep voice.

"Now what?" Han said. His grip on Leia's knuckles tightened.

"Logray has said that he should not lead the marriage ceremony and will be stepping back—"

"Great!" Han said.

"—so that I may take his place." C-3PO's shoulders quivered in excitement as he straightened to his full height. "Since I am a blessed deity, the temple leader has appointed me as the voice of the Great Tree, and he has stated firmly that I shall be the one to marry you both."

"No," Han said flatly.

"I cannot help what the elder has decreed," C-3PO said. "I am merely the messenger. But I am happy to take over and perform such an important duty."

Luke took a tentative step closer. Logray swung his staff toward him, shouting and waving his arms.

"He says he will defend his god against the usurper," C-3PO said.

"I am not getting married by that droid," Han said through clenched teeth, a mark of panic that this, too, was whirling out of his control.

"Threepio, please tell Logray you do not deign to meddle in human affairs," Leia said.

Luke picked up her meaning. "Tell him that you appoint a human to perform the ceremony. The Great Tree wills it."

"I'll try," C-3PO said, but he sounded reluctant. He turned to Logray to repeat the sentiments in Ewokese. As he spoke, Luke flicked his hand toward the amber orb. It glowed golden, shimmering from within. The Ewoks all gasped, and Logray raised his staff, shouting. C-3PO bowed toward Luke, allowing him to take the spot in front of the amber orb.

Luke looked between Han and Leia at the crowd gathered in the temple, then turned to Leia. "Ready?" he asked softly.

She nodded, and then Han did.

Luke started speaking. His words were soft, but everyone in the temple heard him. It was a simple speech really—about love and unity and trust. But truth lay in simplicity. He spoke sincerely, and Leia felt everything fade away as her brother's words wrapped around her and Han, a comforting promise that they—all of them—were a family, and that this moment would last well beyond this day.

"When I saw Leia for the first time, she spoke of hope," Luke said. "And that is what she has always embodied for me."

Leia almost laughed aloud. That message had been sent to Obi-Wan, a formal, yet desperate, call into the void that she had no idea her long-lost twin brother would find. He labeled her the symbol of hope? No— she did not embody it.

She had been seeking it.

And, somehow, she had been heard.

Leia's hands tightened in Han's, and he met her eyes. *Okay?* he mouthed. She nodded silently, smiling.

Maybe Luke was right. Maybe, to be the embodiment of hope, all she had to do was seek it.

Luke's speech shifted to Obi-Wan. "He told me," Luke said, "that those we love are never truly gone."

Leia's eyes shot to him, but Luke was looking out at the audience. He didn't speak with a placating tone but with a matter-of-fact certainty that told Leia this wasn't a false platitude, but instead his true belief. "None of the people we love are ever truly gone. You will sense them again. Their presence exists in moments of love and joy, of quiet and peace. And so, I ask for a moment of silence," he continued in a soft voice that nevertheless resonated. "Let us remember those who cannot be here, no matter how much they would have wished to share in the celebrations of this day."

Han closed his eyes, and Leia wondered briefly who he was thinking of. There were so many people they'd both known, through the war, who were lost. But there was a whole history of his life before they'd met, and she was sure that life must have seen loss and sorrow. Han's face was open, his emotions easily read despite his closed eyes—sad but accepting.

Leia glanced at Luke—his eyes were closed, too. So Leia copied them. She ducked her head.

Mother, she thought. *Father.*

And she . . . she *felt* something. More than a memory, more than a feeling. She felt a weight around her waist. It tugged at her hips, like something . . . something heavy? It was gentle, yet firm, a definite feeling of—

Leia sucked in a breath through her nose. It felt like someone was strapping a sword around her waist. The Rhindon Sword. She knew its weight well; she knew the feel of it against her body as surely as she knew her hands within Han's.

Leia shifted her weight, and the ghost of the sword was gone. It had never been there. But at the same time, she felt certain that her mother had strapped it to her waist. And, just as she was starting to accept that this—all of it—had been nothing but wishful thinking, she felt a kiss, right on her forehead. She felt the bristles on her father's face scraping against her cheek. It was real—

But it wasn't.

Leia opened her eyes slowly. Her mother did not kneel before her to adorn her with her legacy sword. Her father did not stand beside her, blessing her with his kiss. It hadn't been real.

But it was.

"Those we love are never truly gone," Luke said, and this time, no one heard him but her and Han.

CHAPTER 9

HAN

A RESOUNDING *THUD* ECHOED THROUGHOUT the hall.

"What now?" The words escaped Han's lips before he could bite them back, but only Luke and Leia heard, and they were both smiling in amusement.

The Ewok religious elder—the one C-3PO called Logray—leapt up, beating his staff against the wooden floor in a way that made the yellow petals of the flowers perched in his skullcap tremble. He came forward, his beady eyes almost menacing in his intense movement. "What's going on?" Luke called to C-3PO.

The protocol droid bustled up, speaking quickly. Logray kept his eyes on Han, but he answered the droid.

"It seems as if the Ewoks have a tradition, and the elder is unwilling to relinquish this part of the ceremony," C-3PO explained.

Before he'd even finished talking, Logray reached up with his tan paws and ripped Han's hands away from Leia's. "Hey!" Han said.

Logray growled at him. Han looked past the little Ewok to see the mixture of alarm and curiosity on most of the rebels' faces—and the deep, intense stares of the Ewoks. Whatever the little guy intended to do, it was clearly something important to their hosts. In fact, the chief, Chirpa, bounded up, holding the staff for Logray.

Mumbling under his breath—curses or blessings, Han wasn't sure—Logray gripped Han's left hand in his coarse paw, separating out his middle finger. Han winced, but didn't protest again; those nails were sharp. If this was a marriage tradition, perhaps Logray was used to the tight digits on an Ewok's hand and not accustomed to the way human fingers easily spread apart.

Logray reached with his other hand for his staff, and Chief Chirpa held it closer, the iguana on his arm asleep. Logray pulled out a long tendril of the frosted, pale-green vine. He carefully wrapped the vine three times around Han's finger, chanting with each rotation, his voice creating a rhythmic melody to go with the spiral. Han glanced from Leia, who was watching with bemused wonder, to Luke, who met his confused eyes and gave a little shrug.

With half the vine wound around Han's finger, Logray held his furry paw out to Leia, who stepped closer and placed her fingers in his outstretched hand. Logray brought Leia's palm against Han's and wove the remaining half of the vine around Leia's finger, moving carefully and deftly, but with a gentleness the elder had not shown to Han. When he was done, he stared at his handiwork a moment. One finger on each of Leia's and Han's hands were bound together by the thin vine, tight enough that it would take effort to break free from each other. Logray nodded, satisfied, and then spoke in a solemn voice.

C-3PO chanted. "The Great Tree connects us all, but binds these two directly," he said, repeating the elder's words. Logray held his paw out, and Chief Chirpa handed him back his staff. He plucked the tiniest of the yellow flowers from the top of his staff, no bigger than a dewdrop, and tucked the little bloom at the top of Leia's vine ring. Similar flowers encircled the entire temple, inside and out. Leia smiled at the delicately furled petals.

Logray turned to the crowd and pounded his wooden staff against the floor once, shouting, "*Yoo-ben!*"

Every Ewok in the temple called back in a resounding response: "*Nub-yoo!*"

Han and Leia watched, awestruck and unsure of what to do next.

Logray sighed, passed his staff to Chief Chirpa again, and then placed a paw on Leia's wrist and another on Han's. "*Yoo-ben,*" he said.

"*Nub . . . yoo?*" Leia answered.

Logray looked at Han expectantly. "*Nub-yoo,*" Han said.

Nodding, finally satisfied, Logray jerked Han and Leia's wrists apart. The vine that connected their fingers snapped, and golden nectar oozed from the broken ends. Han held his hand up, marveling at the warmth the vine's sap made against his skin. It glistened and sparkled, and the pale-white fuzz on the green vine soaked up the golden nectar. Han bent his fingers—the vine was now rigid and solid gold-colored. It wasn't as sturdy as metal or even rock, but it felt strong, far more durable than a simple, pliable vine. He tapped a fingernail against the ring, and it didn't scratch; it felt like hardened amber.

Leia held her own hand up—the golden sap had transformed the vine on her finger into a ring as well, although the tiny yellow flower bud was loose and not connected. The amber ring caught the light radiating from the orb in the center of the Great Tree, and Han realized the vine must have come from the same type of plant as this one, and that Logray had meant their union with the tree's blessing to be literal.

Both Logray and Chief Chirpa turned to the crowd. Ceremony over, as far as they were concerned. They raised their arms and shouted, "*Yoo-ben!*"

Every Ewok and most of the rebels in the audience shouted back, "*Nub-yoo!*" The elders repeated it, and soon a call-and-response chant punctuated by Ewoks pounding their wooden staffs or their bare feet on the floor made the entire temple building resound with the chant.

"I guess, kiss the bride?" Luke said, glancing between Han and Leia.

Han didn't have to be told twice. Through the near-deafening chanting and pounding, he grabbed Leia and spun her into his arms. She laughed, joy in her eyes as she gazed up at him, but he was all seriousness. She met his gaze with clear certainty, then she leaned up, claiming the kiss before he could. It deepened, her body melting against his as they sealed the promise of their love at the heart of the temple.

The chanting and thudding stopped, leaving only a ringing silence behind. The abrupt absence of noise made Han and Leia break apart.

"About time," Leia muttered, her half-lidded eyes peering up at him in mirth.

"For what?" Han's voice was low.

"You once promised me a good kiss," Leia said. "I've been waiting."

Han barked out a laugh, but the sound was lost in the flurry of rushing wind. Pulling himself from Leia's gaze, he looked around.

All the yellow flowers that had decorated the temple were not flowers at all—they were a type of flying insect whose wings were what appeared to be delicate petals. The delicate, butter-yellow insects seemed to have been woken from their rest on the vines by the chanting and pounding, and after an initial burst of wings, they now floated lazily in the air, bouncing like bubbles from person to person. Ewok children chased the yellow insects, and even the most stoic-looking generals stood in awe as the impossibly thin wings floated around the temple.

Leia gasped, and Han looked down. The tiny yellow bud that Logray had tucked into Leia's ring before breaking their handclasp unfurled on her finger. Wings twirled out like layered ruffled skirts, billowing as the little insect shook itself free. It pushed its tiny wings out, each one waving in the air as it gently rose from Leia's outstretched finger, drifting along invisible currents. Han caught a glimpse of gossamer strands that reached out—legs, he thought, or perhaps antennae—but they were so translucent he could barely see them.

"Chief Chirpa says that these are a traditional part of an Ewok wedding ceremony," C-3PO supplied helpfully. "They feed on sap from the Great Tree, and they wake with the vibrations of the chant. Their name translates to . . ." He paused, thinking. "Flower-fliers."

"That's very literal," Luke said.

"They're beautiful," Leia said, watching as hundreds of flower-fliers drifted through the room, swirling around. And she was right—there was something magical about the flower-fliers' graceful dance, the way they wove between people and Ewoks, leaving behind laughter and awe at their beauty. Years later, surely, legends would tell about the way the entire Alliance paused to watch hundreds of flower-fliers drift through a room, a brief, beautiful respite between battles.

Every single person watched the magical moment.

Except Han. He only had eyes for Leia.

CHAPTER 10

LEIA

THE FLOWER-FLIERS, ONCE WOKEN FROM their hibernation by the Ewok chanting and the rhythmic stomping, seemed happy to drift among the guests as benches were moved to one side, and the large building transformed from a solemn temple of worship to a place for a more social gathering.

A group of Woklings rushed Leia, pulling her away from Han, who was dragged off by his friends. She crouched down, several of the young Ewoks grabbing her hand and pulling it closer so they could look at her new amber ring, chattering excitedly. Others tucked flowers into her hair, screaming in delight when Leia grinned at them.

"*Totcher!*" An Ewok voice cut through the rabble of children. Knocking the Woklings aside, Wicket, with a cheery flower crown perched on his hood, grabbed Leia's wrist. He pulled her up and, despite her laughing protests to stay with the children, marched with determination toward the rope ladders and slings that descended from the temple's balcony. Wicket pushed Leia into a sling and then perched beside her, waving at another Ewok to lower them to the field below.

"I should have known you cared more about the food than anything else," Leia said, giggling at her little friend as he hopped down and showed her the buffet. "Thank you." She affectionately patted him on the head, and Wicket beamed.

Food had been set up at the bottom of the Great Tree, massive tables laden with bread and berries, some sort of creamy spread that could be fresh cheese despite its green color, and various pitchers of herbed or spiced honey. Three fires burned, each roasting different meats on spits, the sizzling, smoky smell intoxicating.

There were no personal utensils or plates. Leia grabbed a handful of seed bread, spread the cheese on it, and drizzled it with honey; she was nibbling on one end under the tree's shade when Han found her. He procured two skewers of meat for them to share. It was so informal, forcing everyone to laugh and work together to share a meal in the truest sense of the word—Han gave Leia a skewer while she ripped her bread in half to give to him.

"This is nice," Leia said, leaning against his shoulder as Han pulled apart the meat on his skewer.

"It's not exactly fancy," Han said. He spoke with his usual ease, but Leia guessed that he was at least a little self-conscious about what her expectations may have been due to her status.

"This is *perfect*," Leia insisted. "More than I could have wanted." They stood together in a rare moment of silence, partly hidden by the shade of the tree, just the two of them and a few flower-fliers that had drifted down from the temple. The sun was starting to set, and in the dimming twilight, the gossamerlike filaments trailing from the flower-fliers' bodies glowed gently as they wafted by.

The ceremony had been nothing like weddings she'd been to in the past, but it was all the more special because of it. She had held various ceremonial roles in dozens of weddings for relatives and high-ranking officials. Some weddings were days-long affairs with elaborate dresses and specific roles for each individual guest to take. Some were long and solemn, with recitations of passages of holy texts spoken from memory. Leia respected such affairs—there was every chance that, had things been different, she would have married at the cathedral in Aldera, with a customary lace dress, an hour dedicated to the bell service, three different traditional meals with guests of rank, and more.

How could she explain to Han that this wedding was not the wedding of her dreams because she had never really considered allowing herself a wedding at all? As a little girl, she had not been capable of dreaming beyond what she knew, and stuffy ceremony and generations of tradition had not held the fascination for her that it did for some. By the time she had to start seriously considering her future and her role within it, she had put aside notions of marriage. It was an expected thing, to be sure, though not one she particularly looked forward to—but neither had it been an ominous dread. She didn't hate the idea of marriage; it was just that there had been more pressing things to consider. A wedding was, at best, an afterthought to her dreams of the future.

Han had not been a part of her dreams. Endor and Ewoks and a ring made of amber and flower-fliers and eating meat skewers beneath the shade of the Great Tree—none of that had been a part of her dreams.

Leia was beginning to realize her dreams had been far too myopic.

A group of rebels Leia recognized from Han's unit passed by, pausing when they noticed the happy couple. They cheered, and Leia smiled ruefully—their moment of peace was broken. Han kept his arm around Leia, but she saw Mon descending on a sling from the Great Tree, her white dress a bright spot against the dark-brown tree trunk, so Leia untangled herself from Han and made her way over to her friend while Han joined his soldiers for a round.

"Thank you," Leia told Mon sincerely. "I can only imagine how much work you put into this day."

"And it still ended with an Ewok takeover," Mon said, laughing.

"That was one of the best parts. Sincerely, thank you."

"You are very welcome," Mon said. "You deserve this, and more."

Leia shook her head, unsure of how to accept such graciousness. Mon grabbed a wooden mug of sunberry wine to drink but bypassed the food tables. Together, they strolled around the Great Tree, arm in arm. A tiny flower-flier—perhaps the same one that had been on her ring—drifted over Leia's shoulder, its shining filaments briefly making a lock of her hair seem to glow amber before the flier drifted on. Several more floated near the honey pitchers, much to the consternation of some of the Ewoks nearby, who were not too awed by the insects' beauty to smack them away from the food.

"It's nice to have moments like this. To feel like we can afford them," Leia commented.

Mon raised her eyebrow as she looked down at her. "What was the point of fighting the Empire if we do not reap the benefits of peace?"

Leia couldn't help a little sorrow infecting her mood. "True," she allowed. "So, what's on the agenda for tomorrow?"

Mon stopped. She looked at Leia as if she wasn't quite sure what to do with her. "For me? Business as usual. For you? Your honeymoon."

"My what?"

"Honeymoon. It's fairly traditional to take some time with a spouse after getting married. There are several different terms for it, but it's generally agreed that after a wedding a new couple should spend time together rather than working."

"I'm aware of the concept," Leia said, batting at Mon's arm.

"Are you? Because I'm beginning to suspect you've never taken a day off from your duties in your entire life."

"I—well—"

"You're going on a honeymoon."

"There's no time for that!" Leia protested. Mon opened her mouth to object, but Leia stopped her with a look. "I recorded that message to the Anoat sector. I saw your plans for ambassador outreach to Madurs, Naboo, half a dozen others. We both know that Lando's worries are accurate—the Empire is going to target our supply lines, and we need to—"

"You do realize that 'we' involves more than you, right?" Mon asked gently.

Leia's mouth moved for a few more moments, but no sound came out.

"*We* can handle this, especially for a few weeks, without your direct aid," Mon continued. "And besides, if it helps make the concept more palatable, consider the image."

"The image?"

"I spoke to Janray Tessime earlier." Mon took a sip of her wine, watching Leia over the rim of her glass. Janray was an artist who'd survived Alderaan's destruction and had dedicated the past few years to helping to make Rebellion and Alliance propaganda. "She wants to do a wedding portrait of you and Han, start a whole campaign of 'unification stories' with that reporter friend of hers." Mon spread her hands out, envisioning the scope of the campaign. "There's a lot of appeal."

"We can do that without a honeymoon," Leia said, but already her stomach was twisting. Leia wasn't unaware of what her face meant as part of the publicity of peace, but it was one thing to be painted on a poster encouraging others to fight the Empire, and another to exploit her private life to further the cause. Besides, she and Han hadn't really talked about what the boundaries in private and public life would include. She had been raised with the idea that there would be very little she could keep solely to herself, but Han was exactly the opposite.

"The people of the galaxy need to see that the Empire has been defeated and therefore the galaxy is returning to normal," Mon continued, but gentler this time, as if she realized Leia was growing uneasy. "If word gets out that you got married and then went straight back to work, it's going to sound like we're not confident that the Empire is defeated."

"But we're *not* confident the Empire is defeated," Leia protested. "As a matter of fact, we *know* that things are worse than anticipated."

"We know," Mon said, "but the galaxy doesn't have to."

Leia felt her brow furrowing as she took in Mon's words. It made sense, in its own twisted way. The best possible thing to do would be to push the truth of the Empire's defeat, and if the Empire were truly defeated, she *would* celebrate her marriage. It was a publicity stunt, sure, but perhaps Mon was right that it was needed.

"What about a diplomatic mission?" Leia proposed. "We need to confirm unification and the cooperation of several key worlds, particularly any with ties to the supply chain."

"The Anoat sector is too dangerous," Mon said immediately.

Leia thought back to the briefing. "What about the Lenguin system? That moon with carnium?"

"Leia, anyone can go on a goodwill mission to a moon with fuel," Mon said. "You're the only person who got married today and can go on your honeymoon. Unless you'd rather send Han off with Chew-bacca?"

"They're close enough," Leia muttered.

Mon shook her head. "You need it, our new republic needs it, the galaxy needs it."

"The galaxy does *not* need me to go on a honeymoon." Leia shook her head. "Where would we even go? I assume a secluded resort on a tropical planet doesn't suit your idea of a publicity stunt." She wasn't able to keep the bitterness out of her voice.

Mon bit her lip, seemingly aware for the first time how uncomfortable Leia was with the idea. "What about a cruise?" she asked. "A set timeline—you'll be back at work after a week or two. And it would be good publicity for both you and a newly independent star line . . ."

"You mean the Chandrila Star Line," Leia said, recalling the image from Mon's presentation at the debriefing earlier.

Leia had to admit it was a good idea. The independence of the formerly nationalized star line would make it the ideal vacation to draw attention to just how free the galaxy was outside of the Empire's iron grip. She could imagine the story angle the reporter, Corwi Selgrothe, would use—emphasizing the benefits both to the industry and to people on a personal level.

And Chandrila was Mon's homeworld. That added weight to the appeal—it was a statement in favor of Mon and her leadership, a way to bring attention and popularity to the politics at hand.

"I'll think about it," Leia allowed.

Far above them, in the temple built in the Great Tree, music drifted down. Leia tilted her head up, straining to see the temple in the fading light. "What's that?" she asked.

"The next part of the celebration," Mon said with a smile.

CHAPTER 11

HAN

MON HAD DONE HER BEST to put together a classy shindig in the wooden temple on a forest moon on the outskirts of the galaxy, Han had to give her that. She'd pieced together an actual band with real instruments from the various divisions of the troops, and although the dance music was perhaps a little slower than what he was used to, it was still good enough to get the whole crowd moving. That, or the wine. Han was starting to suspect the Ewoks had a higher tolerance for alcohol than he'd originally assumed. Although perhaps they were so chaotic naturally that a little liberation via libations didn't really make a difference.

The flower-fliers still in the temple had merged around the orb in the center of the tree, their wings pulsating with the music but, for the most part, content to rest on the amber. Han twisted his ring around his finger, wondering how long the hardened sap would last. He needed to make sure he got Leia something better when he could, a ring worthy of a princess . . .

"So, where's the honeymoon?" Lando asked. His brow was beaded with sweat; he hadn't stopped dancing since the music started until now. He leaned against the wall, but rather than accept a mug from Han, he pulled a silver flask from a hidden pocket.

"Oh, I dunno," Han said. "I figured we'd just take the *Falcon* somewhere sunny. Nothing fancy."

"Leia's a princess," Lando reminded him. "Maybe she wants fancy."

"It's a honeymoon," Han reminded him. "We don't need anything but a bed, and even that's optional."

Lando laughed. "So, somewhere sunny, clothes negotiable."

"All I've ever wanted in life," Han said, leaning against the wall.

His eyes roved around the temple-turned-reception-hall. He noticed Leia immediately. Like Lando, she had barely stopped dancing since the music started and the party had drifted from the forest floor back up to the temple. If nothing else, this world made one well practiced at ladders.

But Leia didn't show any weariness at all. There wasn't a speck of sweat on her, much less a strain in her eye or a hitch in her step. She smiled with grace and ease at every person who held their hand out to her. Currently she was dancing with a young rebel fighter—Kyrell, Han thought his name was. He wore a black Jelucan armband of mourning, and as the song ended, Leia swept into a curtsy before him then touched the cloth, whispering some words of comfort that made emotion well on the young man's face.

The band started another song, one a little more upbeat. "Back into the fray I go," Lando said as a pair of women—a Twi'lek engineer and a human pilot—both motioned to him. Lando held his arms out wide, accepting a woman on each side and sweeping them into some boisterous dance that had half the floor pausing to watch in admiration.

Not Leia, though. She had moved on to another partner, an Arthurian woman with white gloves and tightly bound hair. Han was too far away to hear them talking, but he could tell that Leia was listening raptly as the woman relayed something highly emotional. Han had seen this before—the way Leia allowed others to unburden themselves to her.

And he realized: She was using their wedding reception to help others process their grief.

Grief was a natural response to war. Han had long ago witnessed how desperation—and what was war if not the last violent acts of desperation—caused people to make choices they otherwise wouldn't, allow sacrifices of people and things they otherwise would cherish, create ties that should be severed or break ones that should be strengthened. And with the end in sight if not actively here, it made sense for people to start to process what they had lost over the course of so many battles.

But it didn't make sense for Leia to assume the mantle of responsibility for easing the burden of sorrow from everyone she met.

"Even here and now," Mon said, softly, her eyes on Leia as well.

Han glanced over at her. He hadn't realized the rebel leader was still at the party, much less that she'd taken Lando's spot beside him.

"Tell me you plan to take her away on an excellent honeymoon where she can forget her responsibilities for a week or two," Mon said.

"Definitely," Han said with full confidence.

Mon smiled. "Where?"

"No idea," he said immediately.

Mon laughed. "May I make a suggestion?"

Han shrugged.

"I'd like to give you two a honeymoon on the Chandrila Star Line," Mon said. "My gift to the happy couple."

"That's . . . kind of you."

Mon waved her hand. "It's nothing. And I want to support my homeworld, too."

Han didn't share that sentiment particularly; he had no desire to support Corellia in anything he did. Then again, Chandrila had treated Mon better than his world had treated him.

"I've been in contact with the Anzellan family that reclaimed possession of the star line," Mon continued. "They'd begun retrofitting their flagship from a wartime requisition to its former glory almost as soon as they were able to, er, remove the Imperial influence."

"Industrious little fellows," Han said.

"They were highly motivated to uphold their family legacy, and they are deeply anti-Imperial. They're on board for a chance to showcase the *Halcyon* in a prominent display of freedom."

Ah, there it was. Mon wanted Leia—and a bunch of reporters and cam droids—to grace the launch of the remodeled ship.

Mon noticed Han's jaded look. "It's the only way we can talk her into taking any time off at all," she said gently.

Han's lips twisted. "Where are we gonna wind up at the end of this cruise, on some committee floor?"

Mon held out her hand, and an assistant appeared at her left with a datapad already keyed onto a page of information. Han blinked at the young Delphidian woman, slender and short for her species; he hadn't seen her before.

"The *Halcyon* has a final destination on Synjax, ma'am," the Delphidian said.

Well. That was better. Synjax was renowned for its pristine beaches, with floating resort houses located directly over the lavender-colored waters, bright-yellow blossoming paradine trees decorating the soft-as-down sandy beaches, lapped by gentle waves. "Yeah," Han said, recalling a poster advertising the planet that had showcased private lagoons with flower-strewn waterfalls. "I think that would be . . ." His mind supplied an image of Leia in the lagoon. "Great."

"Excellent!" Mon clapped her hands together, the decision made. "For what it's worth, I do think this is important. If we don't fill the holonet with images of the Rebellion's success, it'll be filled with speculation about the Empire making a resurgence."

Han nodded, reluctantly agreeing with her. He didn't like the idea of his honeymoon being anything more than time spent with Leia, but if it helped the burgeoning new republic, he was certain it would make his bride happy. And him, too. There was appeal to the idea that winding up on a beach resort would also be a way to spit on the grave of the Empire.

Mon passed the datapad back to her aide. "I'll arrange everything. People across the galaxy are eager to celebrate, but the *Halcyon* will delay launching for your arrival."

"When do we need to get there?"

The Delphidian tapped on the screen and passed it back to Mon. "They're ready when you are."

Han's gaze drifted back to Leia, who was hugging the Arthurian woman. From what Han knew of that species, they rarely showed any emotion or wanted to be touched in any way; it was a mark of Leia's patience and grace and open nature that this woman trusted her enough for a comforting hug.

"Leaving tonight is great," Han said. The only thing better than a free vacation was an excuse to push the *Millennium Falcon* in a race across the galaxy to get there. "Don't worry," Han said, a grin spreading across his face at the prospect. "We won't keep that fancy starship waiting."

Mon left to make arrangements, and Han peeled himself from the wall to seek out Chewie. "Change of plans," he told the Wookiee. "Me and Leia are heading out on our honeymoon, but the good news is the *Falcon* is all yours once you drop us off."

Chewie grumbled in confusion, and Han explained Mon's offer. He nodded, roaring this time in approval of the gift.

"Look, I want you to use this time to go home; you deserve it and your family needs you," Han said. "But if you get a chance, maybe we could add some, I don't know, upgrades to the *Falcon*?"

Chewie made a confused sound.

"Something for Leia," Han said. "I don't know! It's just been us on the ship for so long—she'd like something of hers, you know? Maybe we could get a proper kitchen, change the bunk room . . ."

Chewie chortled, the sound mocking. "I *don't know,* okay? I just want her to feel at home."

With another laugh, Chewie clapped Han on the back, the movement hard enough to make Han stumble forward. "Hey!" Han protested, but Chewie waved him off, already striding away to prep the *Millennium Falcon* for flight.

Now to tell Leia.

There were at least two dozen people between himself and Leia, but Han cut straight across the heart of the room. Someone else was already approaching her, but Han didn't say a word, didn't try to be polite—he just slipped his hands into Leia's and swirled her away.

"I promised him!" Leia said, waving at the man she'd abandoned, even though the Togruta was smiling good-naturedly. No one would begrudge Han claiming his bride tonight.

"Groom's prerogative," Han said. "You don't mind." It was partly a question, but mostly a statement, because he could see the answer on Leia's face—relief.

"I suppose they'll forgive me."

"Who wouldn't?" Han asked.

Leia sank into his arms as they twirled around the room, not realizing that Han was leading her along the outer edge of the dance floor. They swept past the flower-fliers, fluttering on the amber orb. They laughed at Lando, who now had three partners and an entire section of the floor to himself. Leia waved at Luke, who was talking to C-3PO. They caught the tail end of the conversation.

"I was telling Artoo that I was right all along; it *is* pretty here," the droid said as R2-D2 beeped, bouncing. Luke grinned, clearly only half listening. He nodded at Han as if he understood and approved of the other man's intent.

"What do you say we get out of here?" Han whispered in Leia's ear. Before she could answer, he did a quick sidestep toward the door, spinning her around until they were on the landing outside the temple.

The cool night air hit them, and Leia started to pull away, then gratefully closed the distance and allowed Han's arms to wrap around her, warming her. "We can't just leave."

"It's our wedding," Han said, "we can do what we want."

"What if I want to go back inside and dance another round with everyone?"

There was a playful glint in Leia's eyes, but Han could tell she wanted nothing less. "What if you save your energy for tonight?" he asked, his voice deep.

Leia smacked him playfully, but he knew he'd said the right thing. "Come on," he said, pulling her toward the ladder. They still had to cross through the village, get to the *Falcon*, and take off before someone else tried to claim their time. "This is our night," he told her.

Leia's eyes reflected starlight. This high up, they could see past the treetops, into forever. He couldn't help himself; he reached out, brushing his thumb over a loose strand of Leia's brown hair that clung to her cheek. She leaned into his touch, closing her eyes, the movement sweet and full of trust and love. Han let out a shaky breath.

"Hey," Leia said, her eyelids fluttering open. "Don't get all mushy on me."

Whatever quip that usually fell so easily off his tongue died. Han didn't have words for the depth of emotion he felt for Leia in this moment, with music spilling out of the temple, the magic of the moon wafting around them, and her big eyes full of love staring up at him. Han *always* had something to shoot back. But not now.

So he kissed her. And he hoped it was enough for her to know everything he wanted to say but couldn't.

CHAPTER 12

LEIA

"WAIT, WHERE ARE WE GOING?" Leia asked as Han led her around the edge of the village, toward where the ships were docked in a clearing.

"Mon—" Han started.

Leia groaned. She had said she would *think* about a honeymoon. Not that she wanted to leave on one tonight.

Han paused. Behind him, Leia could see Chewie carrying crates to load into the *Millennium Falcon*—one of which was her travel trunk.

"Do you not want to go on a cruise?" Han asked. "Because say the word, and we can take the *Falcon* anywhere we want to go. I was kind of iffy on the whole fancy shindig in the first place."

"It's not that, it's just—"

Han cocked his head. "Or is it that you don't want to go on a honeymoon?"

Leia flinched.

"Work can wait," Han said flatly.

"Can it?" Leia asked, hating the pleading tone in her voice. "The Empire doesn't care that we got married; they'll strike as soon as they can."

"You're not fighting this war by yourself," Han growled.

"I know!"

"You sure about that?"

Leia closed her eyes. She knew she had to be able to take moments to pause, to celebrate, to trust others to pick up the load when it became too heavy to carry. When had that become so difficult?

"Were you thinking you'd just—what?" Han said, caught between frustration and confusion. "Get married and then go back to normal? Like nothing happened?"

Leia shot him a rueful look.

Han reached for her hand, the movement so sudden that Leia didn't have time to react. He wove his fingers through hers then twisted their twined wrists so that their amber rings shone in the pale light from the *Falcon*'s open hatch. "*This* changes things," he said. "I don't know what you expected, but if you want *this* to mean something, it *has* to change things."

Emotion swelled in Leia's throat. "Of course," she said. "Of course. It changes everything." It had all happened so fast—the proposal, the acceptance, the wedding. She had not truly stopped to *think* about . . . anything. About what happened next. Everything had felt like an ending, like borrowed time, ever since the Death Star exploded. The symbolic fall of the Empire, the death of the Emperor that had been the end goal for so long that when it had happened, it felt like *the* end. Like everything else was a happily ever after.

She may be a princess, but not one from a story. Because when a princess from a story reached her happily ever after, that was when the story ended.

But Leia realized this story, *her* story—it wasn't ending. It was beginning.

If only she had the courage to write it.

"I can't believe we haven't even been married for five full hours, and we're already having our first fight," Han grumbled, raking his fingers through his hair.

Leia laughed. "Oh, I can believe that. But we're not having a fight."

"Great. Now we're gonna fight about whether or not we're having a fight."

"I don't know about you," Leia said, flashing him a smile, "but I'm going on my honeymoon. If you want to stay here and bicker, that's fine. I can take Chewie instead."

Han sputtered then recovered quickly, racing to keep up with her. "Wait a minute, your worship!" he called, catching up.

"Your worship?" Leia shot him a look. "Your *wife*."

Han's frustration evaporated. "Wife," he said, agreeing. The smile that spread across his face was infectious.

Together, they bounded up the boarding ramp, then headed to the cockpit. Chewie was already there, and from the low chuckle in his voice when he answered Han about being ready to go, Leia could guess that he knew they'd already been verbally sparring.

"All right, all right," Han grumbled. "Let's get off this moon. I've had about all I can handle of climbing rope ladders." He twisted in his seat to meet Leia's eyes. "Smooth sailing, from here on out."

Chewie roared, punching the flight gear. The *Millennium Falcon* hummed with life, the initial thrusters booting on. Leia's heart surged— they were doing it. She was running off in the dead of night with her new husband to go on a whirlwind trip and extend this liminal moment of joy for as long as possible. Her breath caught.

. . . and then the engine died. The ship sputtered, and the power core flashed.

"What now?" Han groaned. Chewie threw off his safety harness and stood, squeezing past Leia and heading to the control panels in the corridor leading to the cockpit.

"Smooth sailing," Leia said, unable to stop herself.

"Give her a break," Han said in a warning tone. "She took some damage in the fight. I know the rectenna snapped off. Lando wasn't careful enough . . ."

Leia raised an eyebrow.

"We don't need it to fly," Han insisted.

Something loud and heavy clunked behind them, just out of sight in the cockpit access tunnel, the metallic sound almost lost in Chewie's groan of frustration. The hydraulic system, Leia guessed.

"It's fine," Han said through clenched teeth.

"Maybe Mon's cruise ship can just pick us up here," Leia mused. "I doubt this little moon is too much out of the way of a luxury cruise line's course."

"It's *fine*."

Chewie shouted something from the corridor, and Han nodded, slamming his fist against one of the controls. The *Falcon* jolted, and Chewie almost crashed down on Leia as he made his way back up to the copilot's seat. The Wookiee threw himself down, muttering to Han.

"Okay, well, get that fixed, too," Han said, keeping his voice low. "We've got the funds, we can get some upgrades, along with . . . the other stuff. We could probably get another catalyzer from that scrap merchant, you know, the one on Xandros. That's on your way, isn't it?"

Chewie nodded.

"And maybe we can get some civilian parts if we need to. A sensor dish would be cheaper than replacing the rectenna . . ."

Leia looked past the two of them, toward the viewport beyond as the *Millennium Falcon* pointed up and soared over Endor. The curving horizon slipped away, the dark, jagged outlines of trees against the stars shifting to show the glow of the horizon, then the cold black of space.

"Careful," Han muttered, helping Chewie with the controls as the *Millennium Falcon* entered orbital space. Chunks of debris, the remnants of the last battle, floated nearby.

The remnants of the battle in the sky. The twisted metal was too broken to identify if it was shrapnel from the Death Star or broken pieces of Alliance ships, but either way, it represented death.

Silence hung among them all.

That first night, the sky had been filled with shooting stars. Leia had known then—they all had—that it wasn't meteorites falling, but space debris pulled from orbit, burning through Endor's atmosphere. A pretty light display that cost far too much. Even with the fireworks that night, it had still been possible to catch a view of the streaking lights, to wonder if it was friend or foe returning to ash and stardust.

Beyond the orbiting wreckage, Leia could see the outlines of the larger Alliance ships that couldn't dock on the moon. One of them signaled Han, who answered using Mon's clearance. As soon as they could,

Chewie steered the *Falcon* away from the detritus, ensuring there was a clear path before punching the ship into hyperspace, heading to Chandrila.

Leia wished that she had closed her eyes as the *Millennium Falcon* ascended. She wished she hadn't seen that remembrance of the battle. She'd been on the ground when the Death Star had exploded; she'd seen the lights, but it was distant. Removed. She wished the first stage of their honeymoon had not required them to pass through a graveyard.

But as the blue-white streaks of hyperspace blurred her vision, she recanted the thought about closing her eyes.

Not looking had never changed the truth.

"Hey." Han stood in front of her, his back to the seat he'd been previously occupying. "Chewie's got the controls. It won't take long to get to Chandrila."

She stood and followed him out of the cockpit. She knew the *Falcon* well. There was the dejarik table where Chewie played against C-3PO. There was the corridor that led to the escape pod, something she'd sought out after her first trip aboard the ship, just to make sure it was operable. And present.

The *Falcon* was large, but there was relatively little private space. Luke had slept on the seat curving around the dejarik table more often than not, and Leia had sought out the gun well for solitude when she needed it. She had spent as little time as possible in the bunk room, since it reminded her too much of Han.

Han led her there now.

The bunk room was pie-shaped, the outer edge curving along the line of the ship's round end. They were close to the engines and the hyperdrive—it was just on the other side of the wall, and when Leia touched the smooth metal, she could almost feel the hum of the *Falcon*'s life. No wonder Han had claimed this space as his own. One bench stood bolted against the wall to Leia's left, cluttered with a pile of dirty clothes. To the right were a table and some storage cabinets. Leia caught sight of pre-packaged meal kits and boxes of spare parts, all jumbled together; a canister of hydraulic fluid stood next to an un-

sealed bottle of drinking water, which was beside a box with grease
stains in the corners that could have come from a leaking meal kit or
from a recycled part to be repurposed for the ship. Or it might just be
literal trash. Leia wasn't sure; she only knew she wasn't about to open
the box and check.

What drew her attention, however, was the bed.

Leia wrapped her arms around herself. It was one thing to steal a
night together, illicit and exhilarated off the win against the Empire. To
throw inhibitions to the wind and pretend that the forest moon of
Endor was a liminal space where nothing they did together would impact their future. It was an entirely different feeling to look at this
room, this man, and realize she was making this an indelible part of
her life.

But even as she stared at the bunk, Han moved behind her. His body
was warm, his arms strong as they wrapped around her. "I know," he
said. "It's weird."

Relief made Leia's body sag against him. At least they understood
each other. She turned and faced him, looking into his eyes. She found
no answer in his gaze. But she did see love.

In some ways, it felt like she had known Han all her life. She was absolutely certain what he would do or say in almost any situation. But
there was still much of him that was a mystery. He held secrets and a
past she was not involved in. And as familiar as they were, there was still
that slight way he held back, the tentative touch that wasn't yet sure.
They did not share a past; it was impossible to know if they would share
a full future. They only had the now.

He reached out with one hand, brushing her loose hair over her
shoulder. His touch was gentle, almost hesitant. His hand stayed on her
shoulder, his fingers warm. Leia cut her eyes at him, reveling in the way
his grip on her skin tensed at her hooded gaze.

There would come a day, she knew, when there would be no more
questions between them. She would fall and know without a doubt that
he would catch her, would feel his arms cradling her safely even as the
wind whistled past her. She would know his thoughts before he did; she
would know his body as well as she knew her own.

There would come a day when there would be no more questions at all.

And until that time, she would find every answer within him herself.

Han's hand trailed from her shoulder to the nape of her neck, fisting in her hair and pulling her closer to him. She slid her body against his.

Tonight, at least, there would be no need for words at all.

CHAPTER 13

HAN

HAN WAS ALMOST SAD TO see Leia braiding her hair in the morning. She had worn it down for most of her time on Endor, and he liked the way it fell across her shoulders, the little shiver that went down her spine when he ran his fingers through it. But they were nearly at Chandrila now, and she was braiding her hair.

The cruise was a bad idea. He should have just followed his instinct. He didn't need a luxury liner or a resort on a sunny, lavender-washed beach. He could have parked the *Millennium Falcon* out in the middle of nowhere space and done everything he wanted to do on his honeymoon without even leaving the ship.

They would have had to have dropped Chewie off first, though. And they were practically at Chandrila. He supposed they may as well check out the star cruiser.

Han left Leia in the sleeping quarters to finish getting ready while he made his way to the cockpit. Chewie was still at the controls, and as soon as he sat down, the Wookiee huffed at him.

"I'm here now, sorry." Han could see why Chewbacca was on edge. Chandrila was almost as crowded as Coruscant usually was—even as he watched, more ships dropped out of hyperspace and lined up for clearance codes to dock. Still, traffic was nothing Chewie couldn't handle.

Han reached over and checked the comm panel. Mon had set them up with her own personal clearance codes, giving them priority, and Chewie was already angling the *Millennium Falcon* out of orbit. It was nice to know the senator from Chandrila.

"I guess everyone wants to celebrate," Han muttered. A darker side of him wondered who was here for the angle; the Empire nationalized services and goods, and that left a hole in the market.

Han and Chewie worked silently, in perfect tandem, a steadied, practiced routine as they veered the ship toward Chandrila. The blue-and-green world came into focus gently, rolling hills and curving shorelines. As they neared the capital, Hanna City, the skyline of the buildings rising from the ground reflected the soft edges of the world—skytowers didn't shoot up like the pointed trees of Endor, but instead had bowl-shaped tops, smooth semicircular extensions jutting from the side, and spires that sloped rather than jutted up. The *Millennium Falcon* swooped over the Silver Sea, sparkling waters glimmering below, before veering toward the docks.

Han was going to miss this—flying with Chewie. Even after the cruise, it wouldn't be exactly the same, would it? Adding a third person to their small crew would be a change, and even when change was good, it made things . . . different. Han shook his head sardonically as he shifted the *Falcon* toward the city's docking-assist tractor beam. Eloquent as always.

A series of communications pinged as they flew past the landing platform on the edge of the sea and toward a fancier and much larger docking bay Mon had arranged for them to use, a bit farther from the city.

"What?" Han growled, looking at the screen. "We're late? How are we late?"

Mon had told them the ship was waiting for them, and they'd made damn good time. He assumed. He hadn't exactly been piloting the ship all night and checking the clock. Han scanned the comms—a notice to please check in with the cruise director as soon as possible, a second notice that assured him they would wait for such important guests of Mon Mothma to arrive, and a third notice that said the ship's logistics droid would be waiting for them at the dock with a shuttle to take them directly to the star cruiser.

While Chewie handled the landing gear as the *Millennium Falcon* settled into the assigned docking bay, Han sent off a comm to the *Halcyon* that they'd arrived. He threw off his harness and shouted down the corridor, "Come on, sweetheart, we've gotta go!"

Leia met him in front of the boarding ramp. She wore her hair looped in ropy braids, and her simple tan dress was accentuated by a long puffy vest trimmed in a red ribbon that reminded Han of the jackets the officers wore on Echo Base.

"Are we in a hurry?" she asked him.

"Apparently we're late."

The boarding ramp opened, and they started down, Chewie carrying their trunks for them. Leia had barely set foot on the dock when a droid rushed up to them. With a white-and-bronzed body, the slender logistic droid zeroed in on Han and Leia, striding with determined steps and the unwavering focus only a droid had.

"Princess Leia Organa and General Han Solo?" the droid said, looking them both up and down with her yellow eye sensors, spaced apart on her gleaming domed head.

"Yes," Leia said.

"I am Deethree-Ohnine," the droid stated. "I am the logistics droid for the *Halcyon*. Captain Oswin Dicto has asked me to personally escort you to the *Halcyon*."

"Thank you," Leia said graciously.

"I am here to ensure an efficient transfer from your private vessel to the *Halcyon*," D3-O9 said in clipped tones. "We are so very pleased you've elected to join us on this cruise; I am certain you will love the *Halcyon*."

D3-O9 motioned for some nearby service droids to step forward. They quickly relieved Chewie of Han and Leia's trunks and rolled away.

Leia turned to Chewie, giving the Wookiee a big hug that he returned with such enthusiasm that Leia was lifted off her feet. Leia whispered something to Chewie that had him rumbling with laughter, and all of Han's previous tensions eased.

"You know," he heard Leia tell Chewie with a low chuckle, "I wouldn't have been opposed to that, if it came down to it."

Chewie lowered Leia back to the ground. She had tears in her eyes. "You were there for me when I didn't know what to do, when I had no one else to turn to," she told the Wookiee in such a quiet tone that Han almost couldn't hear her. "I'll never forget that. Thank you, friend."

Han's mind spun—when had Chewie been with Leia without him? When had he gone from walking carpet to confidant?

Oh. Right. That damn missing year bumped up against the blank spots of his memory. Jabba would be thrilled to know—were he not dead—how much it haunted Han that he had lost so much time while frozen in carbonite. He hadn't just lost the past, he also didn't have the groundwork for the future that the others did. It unmoored him in ways he didn't like to think about.

"I must say," D3-O9 said to Han, drawing his attention away in a much-wanted distraction from his dark thoughts, "I'm particularly happy to see that you have arrived safely after seeing the circumstances of your travel." The droid's voice was so cheery that it took Han a moment to realize that the droid was slighting his ship.

"There's nothing wrong with the *Millennium Falcon,*" he protested.

"Of course I could not possibly do more than analyze the outward appearances of this YT-1300 light freighter, but I am certain you will feel joy at the comfort and speed—indeed, the luxury—you will find on our beloved *Halcyon.*"

Maybe this star cruiser had the *Falcon* beat on luxury, Han would allow the droid that. But speed? "Appearances can be deceiving," he said. "The *Falcon* can outrun the *Halcyon* any day of the week."

"Factually, it's statistically impossible for your vessel to outperform the brilliance of the *Halcyon,*" D3-O9 stated simply.

Han felt his lip snarling at the droid's words.

"The *Halcyon* is equipped with a unique configuration of thirteen engines, now known commonly as the Drabor Configuration. It's a

Purgill-class ship, the first of its kind, and custom-designed by the greatest ship developer on Corellia or any other world."

"Yeah, well the *Falcon* once—" Han stopped as Leia put her hand over his and pulled his arm down.

"We can compare engine sizes later," Leia said gently. "Let's go on our honeymoon."

Han's hand unclenched, but he still glared at the droid. "It's not about engine size," he grumbled. "It's about *speed*."

"The *Falcon* is very fast," Leia said.

Han turned his glare on her. "You're coddling me."

"Yes, and it's working."

Despite himself, Han felt his lips twitching. "Okay, *fine,* let's go."

Behind him, D3-O9 stood with her hands on her hip joints and her head cocked, not exactly impatient, but clearly waiting for them to finish before she spoke. "Chandrila Star Line boasts its own launch pods, specially designed to carry passengers to the luxury star cruiser of their choice." The droid gestured toward a different platform across the docking bay. Chandrila was a beautiful planet, and the capital city seemed intent on showcasing that beauty, even for people who were merely transferring from one ship to another. As a freighter, the *Millennium Falcon* had been automatically assigned a slip attached to the cargo docks, but D3-O9 pointed to a smaller dock, one across a grassy lawn and showcasing fancier personal transportation shuttles. Han scanned the ships he could see across the way—a shiny *Rola*-class corvette, at least two Drellian yachts, and a K-type Nubian starship that curved in sleek lines.

One end of the shuttle slips held a sparkling sign at least two meters tall and twinkling with embedded crystal lights in the form of a circle bisected by two lines cut off at angles, with a dot in the upper right-hand corner above it. As Han watched, the crystal lights shifted, the logo stretching out into the words CHANDRILA STAR LINE.

Leia followed D3-O9 as the droid headed toward the paved path that cut between the two docking areas. The elegantly curving trail was lined with glowstones in a repeating chevron pattern and had flowers along each side. Fruit trees dotted the manicured lawn; there was even music piped in, a cheery tune with a lot of electronic janglers. The space between the two docking bays was nicer than the entirety of half the worlds Han had been on.

Before catching up with Leia, Han turned to say goodbye to Chewie. "Well, buddy, the *Falcon*'s all yours. Take care of her."

Chewie nodded, roaring his promise to not only care for the *Falcon*, but add in more repairs and the alterations Han had mentioned. Han moved in for a hug, and the Wookiee clapped him on the back, a solid thump that made him choke out a cough as he caught his breath again.

Chewie bounded up the boarding ramp, but turned, trilling a few last words.

"Hey, now!" Han said. "A gentleman never tells."

Chewie laughed, waved, and disappeared into the *Falcon*.

Shaking his head, Han rushed to chase after Leia and the droid from the *Halcyon*. "We are proud here on Chandrila to be the homeworld of Mon Mothma," D3-O9 was telling Leia, "as well as several other ace pilots and decorated soldiers who defended the hope of the new republic."

Han noticed that interstellar orange pennants waved throughout the grassy courtyard, woven around the tree trunks and pillars and strung along the outer edges of the docking bays. It was the same color as the rebel starfighter pilot suits—an appropriate gesture to honor those who'd fought in the war, not just with the color, but also with the location here, among the ships made free by their sacrifices.

The park was crowded, but D3-O9 cut a formidable path through the people gathered, efficiently guiding them past a group heading toward the public transport system that led into the heart of the city, winding them around a large circle of friends eating a picnic on the lawn, and turning down a smaller path that would take them to Chandrila's private docking space. Leia and the logistics droid were close to the same height, and Leia kept pace gracefully, even though the droid marched at such a quick clip that she would soon be running to keep up.

A little boy burst between two bushes close to the curve in the path, knocking into Han. A second later, a bright-yellow kit-flier drifted over the leaves. Without glancing at Han, the boy grabbed the kit-flier and tossed it back over the bushes before crashing through them again, shouting at his older brother to have better aim next time.

Beyond the two boys, a woman looked up, waving apologetically at Han. The boys' mother, he assumed. She had brown hair and a quick smile, but before Han could call over that he was all right, the boys—who both had eyes for the kit-flier—slammed into each other, bouncing onto the ground with audible thuds. The mother rushed over, but the boys jumped up, too eager to play to be bothered with bumped heads. The kids were drunk on joy in a way only kids could be, their excited screeches reaching a deafening pitch as the kit-flier whirled between them, the simple toy providing more entertainment than Han would have thought possible.

Even children could feel it, he supposed. That pressure of the Empire hanging over every world in the galaxy, now gone. Joy burst out of everyone.

Han touched the amber ring on his finger. Past the family playing in the park, over the docking bays, the skyline of Hanna City with its gentle curves and soft lines played in the horizon's puffy clouds. Everything here was so . . . *nice*. He'd gotten used to life on the *Falcon*, he'd even gotten used to the war, but could he get used to a home like this? Or, if not on Chandrila, some other nice world, somewhere . . . somewhere decent.

An earsplitting screech emitted from the youngest child, and it took Han a second to realize it was a noise of happiness and not a response to torture. He blinked, then realized that, despite the cacophony the boys made, he was smiling.

Because for the first time in his life, not only was he considering what it would be like to have a home on a nice world, but he was considering *who* would be in that home with him. Leia, yes, but maybe also . . .

"Do you and Princess Leia intend to have younglings?" the droid inquired politely as she sidled up to Han.

"Younglings? I—what? Why?" This was something he should have talked with Leia about, and certainly not a conversation he wanted to have with D3-O9.

"Sentimentality would perhaps explain why you decided to stop in the middle of the path to stare aimlessly about," D3-O9 explained in a kind voice, as if she were simply trying to figure out Han's logic. "I am merely curious about your lack of urgency to arrive at your destination. The *Halcyon* awaits."

"My lack of—I'm not, argh!" Han growled. He shoved past the droid and headed to the platform where Leia stood just outside of earshot.

"What's the holdup?" she asked him quietly as he stormed past.

"Nothing, let's go," Han grumbled.

"This way, please," D3-O9 said, leading them to a sleek chrome shuttle with the *Halcyon* logo emblazoned on the side, the same curious circle with lines and a dot. "This is Captain Dicto's private shuttle," the logistics droid continued, a clear tone in her modulated voice to indicate that they should be impressed.

And truth be told, Han was. There was an efficient cofferdam locking system built into one end of the shuttle that would attach automatically to the *Halcyon,* and the ion thrusters promised a smooth ride, even for such a small vessel. As he and Leia stepped inside, Leia ran her hands along the plush brown walls, curved in the cylindrical shape of the shuttle. There were only a few seats, angled so passengers could more easily speak to one another. Small circular viewports were spaced beside each seat, the transparisteel rimmed in shining chrome.

D3-O9 tapped on the shuttle's controls. "Preparing for departure," the droid said. "Our journey to the *Halcyon* will take no more than ten minutes. In the event of any emergency requiring evacuation, you will find long vests with thermal heat disks and breathing apparatuses behind this panel." She gestured toward the wall, then took a step closer, clearly thinking she was intimating a private thought to Han. "I would like to assure you that it is *highly* unlikely that such emergency procedures will be needed. You two are under the care of the *Halcyon* now, and you can trust us to provide not just safe travel, but state-of-the-art comfort. You are in good hands with us."

Han ground his teeth, but kept his mouth closed when Leia put a hand on his elbow. The worst of it was that the damn droid seemed to be relaying this information out of *concern,* not to get a rise out of him, which, of course, made him want to toss *her* out of the emergency evacuation hatch. The *Falcon* was perfectly safe and comfortable, damn it all.

The shuttle propelled out of the slip and up, shooting away from Chandrila, the horizon slipping past until they were, once again, among the stars.

"As you can see," D3-O9 stated as the shuttle approached the *Halcyon*, "the star cruiser is an elegant combination of power and grace." The droid cut her eye sensors at Han, as if daring him to challenge her. Han didn't bother. The droid could be allowed her prejudices, he supposed. She was likely programmed to feel that way.

While he would still bet his every credit that the *Millennium Falcon* could outrace the beast, the *Halcyon* was a work of art. Han silently counted the exhaust corridors from the back of the ship. Sure enough, thirteen. It was rare to see such a large ship designed only for leisure. Most of the behemoths were warships.

The shuttle slowed and tilted, giving them a look at the full ship, hanging suspended in space, Chandrila in the background. The *Halcyon* was well away from the crowded traffic, beyond orbital range, and that made it seem all the larger, like the other ships were buzzing pollinators in comparison. The *Halcyon* was long and sleek, with glittering viewports lining up along the hull. The cockpit extended out perpendicularly from the main body, but the long lines on the aft and the fins extending past the cabins gave it balance.

Even as D3-O9 rattled off various details about the ship, a note of pride ringing in her voice, Leia leaned in closer to Han. "What do you think?" she asked.

"I suppose it'll be okay."

Leia's lips curved into a smile. "Thanks for the great sacrifice you're making here."

"I mean, it's not the *Falcon*, but—"

Whatever else he was going to say was drowned out by her laughter.

CHAPTER 14

LEIA

"GOOD JOURNEY," D3-O9 SAID AS they left the launch pod and headed to the Atrium. "If you need anything, I would be happy to personally assist you. I can be reached via the console of your cabin."

"Thank you," Leia said, but the logistics droid had already turned away, heading toward a different corridor.

"That one's swell," Han grumbled.

Leia swatted him. "Be nice."

Han shot her a look.

Despite the droid's urgency to get them aboard the *Halcyon* as quickly as possible, the mood in the Atrium was relaxed as Leia and Han stepped inside the grand lobby area. Sparkling emerald wine fizzed in guests' glasses as people clustered around the expansive room, chatting. Plush cobalt blue seating dotted the area, and Leia nodded to a man whose elaborately embroidered silk robe occupied an entire corner bench that would normally have space for three or four people. He raised his glass to her before draining it.

"Drink?" a server asked, holding out a tray of flutes toward Leia and Han. "Captain Dicto has ordered the finest vintage from his homeworld of Tristall to celebrate the first voyage of the *Halcyon* free of the Empire's yoke."

"Cheers to that," Han said, grabbing a glass.

Leia took one herself, but she didn't raise it to her lips. Tristall wine was sweeter than Alderaanian wine, though they were both made from emerald grapes. The bubbles and fizz would give it a different taste, too, from the flat wine she used to drink at home. Still, the last time she shared a bottle of green wine had been with her family, a private celebration of a little win against the Empire—they had all been little wins, then, but they had been all the more celebrated for it.

It didn't matter how sweet Tristall wine was; Leia knew it would be bitter on her tongue.

Han's glass was empty. "Here," Leia said, swapping with him.

Han looked as if he was going to question her, but then he just shrugged and took it. Leia deposited the empty glass on a tray nearby and then slipped her arm into his, gently steering Han toward the center of the Atrium.

A tall human man strode out onto the mezzanine, looking down at the crowd gathered before him. He wore a captain's uniform, but more than that, his very presence demanded respect. His general appearance—average height, portly build, gray hair, and pale eyes—would have made him seem grandfatherly at best, but he carried himself with such authority that none would dare be so informally presumptuous as to treat him as such. The man both looked as if he had a kind smile and as if he rarely used it. He did not have the same stern, cold authoritarianism as someone from the Empire, though. Rather, this man appeared to love nothing more than to do his job and erred on the side of staunch nobility rather than casual friendliness.

"Greetings, beloved guests," he said, keeping his arms down but tilting his chin up. "I am your captain for this journey, Captain Oswin Dicto. It is my greatest honor to serve you as the *Halcyon* glides through the stars."

He bowed his head, clearly gathering his thoughts. Han shifted beside her, and Leia realized she'd been gripping his arm, hard. Captain Dicto had captured her attention. In fact, everyone in the Atrium had quieted to listen to him speak, and even without voice amplifiers, Leia believed the captain's words could be heard by all.

"Let us pause a moment," Captain Dicto said, "and consider all that has been sacrificed and all that has been won now that peace spreads throughout the galaxy."

The silence that fell over the crowd in the Atrium was different from the type of silence she was used to. Leia realized that while she had lived and breathed the war for so long that she couldn't imagine it *not* being a part of her life, most of the people in the Atrium were the opposite. She settled on her heels and looked around at the crowd. Affluent aristocrats, wealthy merchants, influential celebrities . . . while she had been fighting the Empire, many of these people had been living in it. They had been pretending that nothing was wrong. And now that the Empire had fallen, they intended to keep pretending that nothing was wrong. They had not felt the boot heel of the Empire on their necks, and so they didn't mind if it fell on others. The Galactic Civil War had been merely a shift in power that didn't affect them.

They were here on the *Halcyon* now to joyously mark peace, but these people would just as likely have gone to a party to celebrate the Empire's victory had that been the result. Leia had agreed to join this cruise mostly because Mon had insisted and had leveraged the idea of publicity influencing the populace's view of the rebels' victory. There were others here that Leia recognized—rebel sympathizers like Drelax Lossa, whose deep pockets and endless credits had helped Leia buy ships, and Rothy Trah, who had passed on Imperial secrets to rebel spies—but as Leia's gaze moved from solemn face to solemn face during the captain's suggested moment of silence, she wondered just how many actually cared about the outcome of the war. How many had seized upon the *Halcyon*'s voyage as a carefree vacation after rebels lived and died fighting for freedom.

"You okay?" Han whispered in her ear.

She looked up at him, seeing the concern etched on his face. Leia had let the mask slip, had let her true emotions show. Fortunately, no one but Han had seen. She squeezed his elbow in reply and turned her attention back to the captain.

"The *Halcyon* was the flagship of the former Chandrila Charter Company, and now that we are free from the Empire, the new Chandrila Star Line is determined to honor your journey." The captain's voice grew gruff, and Leia wondered what he was carefully choosing not to say. That was what being a princess had taught her—that the real truth lay behind the unspoken words. Captain Dicto was clearly no fan of the Empire; had he been forced to serve it? Or had he faced hardships for refusing to aid their tyranny?

Still, he must also know that at least some in the crowd today were either apathetic or in support of the Empire. There was a risk to what he said as much as there was a risk to what he did not say.

"This is the first time in a long time that the *Halcyon* has been free to fly for its intended purpose," Captain Dicto continued. "I would like to take this moment to pause and remember that purpose. The Chandrila Charter Company was founded by Shug Drabor with one underlying principle in mind: shared journeys. Our stories have all met at this point, here, now. We are all a part of one another's shared journey, tied together in this moment."

Leia's breath caught. The captain's words reminded her sharply of her own thoughts when she'd accepted Han's marriage proposal.

Han shifted Leia's grip on his elbow, pulling her hand down so he could weave his fingers through hers. She felt the amber ring on his finger, warm. A moment caught in time.

CHAPTER 15

HAN

THE WINE WAS GOOD, BUT Han wanted something more than fruit juice. He swirled the fading bubbles in his glass and wondered where the real stuff was.

It seemed like there was a spotlight on his bride. As soon as all eyes left the captain, they shifted to the center of the Atrium. Seemingly everyone in the lobby area knew Leia, or knew a friend of hers, or "just had to say hello." As soon as she politely greeted one person, another stepped up. Everyone was smiling, and it turned his stomach. They were all fake smiles, all of them except Leia's. They homed in on her because of her title, her fame, her prestige. They wanted to bask in her glow, but they didn't know her. Why were they even bothering?

Han grabbed another glass of wine.

A young Pantoran woman with reddish-brown hair that stood in contrast with her blue skin approached. Her crisply pressed Chandrila Star Line uniform was immaculate, barely creasing despite the fast pace she cut through the crowd. Han touched Leia's arm to get her attention.

"Greetings, Your Highness," she said, bowing her head. "And you must be the new husband." She turned to Han.

"Solo," he said, unaccustomed to being recognized first and foremost by his relationship with Leia. Then again, when people recognized him for his own merit, they tended not to look that pleased to see him.

To her credit, the woman spoke to both of them, not just Leia. "I am Riyola Keevan, the ship's quartermaster."

"Is something wrong?" Han asked, his brow furrowing.

The Pantoran's eyes widened slightly. "No, of course not!" She shook her head. "Apologies; I did not mean—I've been assigned as your personal attaché for the journey."

Han raised his eyebrows at Leia and mouthed the words, *personal attaché*. He was starting to think that the only time things would be normal for them would be aboard the *Falcon*.

"My job is to ensure that this trip is truly a once-in-a-lifetime experience for you," Riyola continued. "Is there anything I can provide for you?"

"Everything is so lovely," Leia started.

"Where's our cabin?" Han interjected.

Riyola pulled up their access details on a datapad. "You have been assigned one of our best suites on the ship," she said. "I am certain you will find your accommodations to your liking, but of course do not hesitate to tell me if there's anything else I can do."

A suite, huh? Han liked the sound of that. He glanced around the Atrium, looking for the lifts that would take them to their cabin while Leia exchanged small talk with Riyola.

"Let's get out of here," Han told Leia in a low voice after Riyola left them.

"Princess Leia, a moment?" a slender man with bulbous eyes said tentatively.

"Yes?" She turned to him, and then her gaze fell on the little girl who clutched the man's hand. Dressed in blue with a puff of curly brown hair on top of her head, the little girl stared up at Leia with clear adoration. Despite himself, Han melted a little at the sight. Here, at least, was a fan of Leia's who was sincere.

"Would you mind?" the man asked. He held up a slender cam with one hand.

"Go on without me," Leia whispered to Han before she bent down to be on the girl's level. Her father clicked a button on the cam, capturing the moment, and Leia turned to talk to the child.

"My mommy was at Yavin," she whispered, her voice barely audible. Han's heart wrenched, noting the use of past tense, the lack of a woman alongside the man. Leia shifted her weight, fully kneeling in front of the girl, ignoring the way the other guests looked at her on the floor, her attention solely focused on the child.

Han nodded at the girl's father, hoping to convey some sentiment. The man didn't notice; his eyes were on his daughter.

Time to make an exit. No one wanted to hear him talk—and he didn't blame them, this wasn't his crowd, neither the elites nor the condolence-seekers. He slipped through the groups of people unnoticed by anyone and found a turbolift.

As he waited for it to arrive, though, Han's gaze drifted to the left. The Sublight Lounge was connected to the Atrium, and music and laughter spilled out of the room. Even though the captain's reception had just ended, people were slipping into the lounge to find something with a little more kick than green juice and a little more action than fake smiles.

Not a bad idea. Leia would shake every hand in front of her, and who knew how long that would take. Better to wait for her in the lounge, surely. The turbolifts made a soft chime as the doors slid open, but Han turned on his heel, getting behind a couple dressed in matching char-treuse robes trimmed in gold. One of the women stopped abruptly, and Han almost crashed into her.

"Sorry!" the woman giggled. "But it's a tradition!"

Han watched curiously as the woman reached to the side of the door, where a bottle of some sort of wine had been added for decoration.

"It's lucky," the other woman said as her partner rubbed the glass bottle.

"If you say so," Han replied.

The women slipped into the lounge, heading straight to a table in the center where a holo display illuminated a sabacc deck. Han turned to the bar.

Blue lights streamed over the bar, and an impressive display of liquors from around the galaxy were stocked on the shelves. A bartender with braids done in the Ming Po style sidled up to him. "What can I get you?" they said.

"Your choice."

The bartender grabbed a nearby bottle and started mixing a concoction into a shaker. Han tried to keep up, but they were quick, adding pours, tossing in ice, muddling herbs, and sprinkling in a handful of some sort of pepper seeds before snapping the shaker's lid, tossing it about, and straining the sparkling purplish liquid into a glass. They slid the cocktail over without a word.

Doubtful that liquor that glittered would suit him, Han tried a sip. Flavor burst on his tongue, citrusy but with a bite of heat. It was nothing like what Han had expected, but it was good. The bartender smirked knowingly at his appreciative smile.

"Cheers," Han said, raising the glass before heading deeper into the lounge. There were no viewports here, but it was still bright throughout the room.

"Join us!" one of the women he'd followed inside the lounge called from the center table. Glass in one hand, Han stepped over.

"It's holo-sabacc," the woman said. "Do you play?"

"I know how to play cards," Han confirmed. He watched as the woman's fingers danced over the cards made of light, the computer shuffling and dealing. "Is there a real game somewhere?"

"This is a real game."

"What's on the table?" Han asked. At the woman's blank stare, he added. "The stakes. How much are you betting?"

She laughed. "Oh, we're not playing for credits! It's just fun."

Han took a sip from his glass.

The other woman leaned over. "It is, actually. Fun," she clarified.

"I'll just watch, if you don't mind," Han said.

The women didn't, and soon enough their table was crowded with both players and other observers. Han could see the appeal in holo-sabacc. Without the need to shuffle—or watch who was counting cards or spot the shifty deal—the focus was on the game itself. Cards flashed quickly as they were selected, tossed, sorted into winning hands. It was clear these women and the other players were excellent at the game.

But that was the problem—it was a game. Han wanted something with a little more bite. He polished off his drink and twirled the empty glass in his hand. Maybe the problem was him. He was used to flying his own ship, not being carted around like a tourist. He was used to having to gamble for something other than fun. He was too rough around the edges to be in a place like this. He didn't fit.

And he wasn't sure he wanted to.

CHAPTER 16

LEIA

LEIA SCANNED THE ATRIUM, NOTING each cluster of people still lingering with their wine. There was strategy in war, but there was strategy in
this, too, the politics of social life, the nuance of interactions, the subtle
alliances made within banter and chatter. Were it not for the life-or-
death stakes, Leia would prefer an actual battle to the social mores.
More straightforward, at least.

The Atrium was slowly emptying as guests made their way to their
cabins or sought other entertainments aboard the ship. Leia was keenly
aware that while this trip was her honeymoon, it was also still a bit of a
publicity stunt. There had been a handful of X-0X units scattered
throughout the crowd during the captain's reception. The discreet recording droids were used by reporters to get a more candid look at
major events. They were there now mostly to celebrate the Chandrila
Star Line's flagship launch after Imperial control, but Leia was savvy
enough to know that at least a few of them had zoomed in on her.

Her eyes caught a familiar face, and Leia crossed over to a group of
people, a ready smile on her face. "Zohma," she said, holding her hand
out to one woman in particular. Zohma had briefly had an affair with

one of the girls in the Elder Houses, and there had been a few months when she had appeared at the same social events Leia had. Quickly, Leia recalled Zohma's details—wealthy, the sole inheritor of a veri ash refinery. Veri plants created a fine, powdery ash that could be added to a variety of adhesives, giving them a bonding power stronger than a steel weld. The rarity of the plant and the precise method with which it must be burned to create the ash made for a lucrative business.

Leia could tell that coming over had been the right thing to do—from the way Zohma's companions turned, Leia was certain the other woman had been speaking of her, of their connection. Acknowledging Zohma first gave her social credit.

"How are you, darling?" Zohma asked, kissing Leia on both cheeks. "I was just telling my dear friends how brave you were to be so personally involved in the war."

"It was . . ." Leia trailed off. If she said it had been the right thing to do, that would imply all the people gathered around her now—a collection of wealthy offspring from wealthy families—had not done the right thing. Then again, Leia knew they hadn't. The veri ash farms had been subsidized by the Empire—it was just small enough of a business that the Empire hadn't seized it, but important enough that it had become a primary customer. Zohma had profited well from the war, and she stood to lose nothing at all now that it was over—the contracts would shift from the Empire to the new republic that formed because there was nowhere else to get veri ash. The war had likely barely even registered as an inconvenience to Zohma, whose easy compliance with whoever was in power had helped secure her family's company's protection.

Fortunately, none of the others expected Leia to finish her sentence. One of them, a young man Leia didn't know, leaned forward. "Is it true," he said, "that the Emperor is *actually* dead? We all saw the feeds of the Death Star, but my uncle knows the Emperor was on Coruscant at the time."

The others tittered; this was gossip to them, an amusement.

"He's dead," Leia stated flatly.

The man gave her a knowing smile and even winked at her. He *winked* at her. Leia felt her flat smile growing rigid. "Of course you have to say that, and no doubt this 'new' republic will . . ." He waved his hand, not saying whatever he meant.

Leia narrowed her eyes. "What are you suggesting?" she demanded. There was an edge to her tone that she knew she should modulate, but she simply could not.

Zohma jumped in. "Oh, he's being silly, darling." She shot her friend a look, but he ignored her.

"I'm being serious," he continued, getting far too close to Leia for comfort. She refused to take a step back, despite the man's lack of concern for her personal space. "The Emperor rarely went out in public. My uncle said—"

Your uncle's full of— Leia cut the thought off in her mind before she accidentally spoke it aloud. "He's wrong," Leia said, the words a little too loud. She didn't care, though, not even if the X-0X droids caught her. "There were witnesses. He's dead."

The *peedunkey* wouldn't back down, though. "Rebel witnesses," he said, looking over his shoulder at his friends, his tone clearly indicating how little he thought of the veracity of their accounts. He spoke loudly, obviously expecting a laugh.

"We're not rebels anymore." Leia's voice was soft, but they were all listening. "Haven't you heard? We won." She didn't blink or break eye contact with the man as she spoke, but she did smirk when he took an unconscious step back.

"Right, darling, see?" Zohma said, pulling her friend even farther back. "I do think he might have had too much wine." She crinkled her nose at Leia. "A delight to catch up, Princess, as always."

Zohma and her friends left, creating a vacuum around Leia in the middle of the Atrium. A gleaming flash of chrome caught her eye; there was the X-0X droid, its lens whirring as it zoomed in on her. A fantastic publicity event. Leia silently cursed herself, but she knew that the feeds from the X-0X units would be edited later. Her smile did not drop. It could not drop. She *must* be the positive, shining beacon for the people, even when what she wanted to do was knock that smug, half-drunk smirk right off Zohma's friend's face. She took a steadying breath, her mask carefully in place, as she crossed the Atrium. She could feel eyes on her, both from people and from droids. But there were no X-0X units lingering near a display case against the wall.

Leia leaned down, focusing on it so that she had something to do, a reason not to face anyone else. As she hovered close to the glass, she knew no one could see the tired ache in her eyes. She let her mask slip, and she allowed her mind to be occupied with nothing more than the beautiful object inside the case.

An ancient hyperspace compass, clearly no longer in use and displayed now as a work of art. The astromeridian etch lines behind the lens showed precision craftsmanship. The entire compass required manual adjustment, not the fully computer-automated navisystems used on most ships, but the simplicity and straightforwardness of the compass was part of the appeal. It could tell the ship which direction to go. It couldn't provide details about the obstacles along the way, the hardships, or the distance, but if one knew where one wanted to go, the compass told the way. Leia could appreciate that, as well as the irony of the compass behind the display case, where it stood as art instead of a useful tool.

The real gem of the compass, quite literally, was the supraluminite lodestone set above the inscribed base. It glowed from within, a shimmering blue that was made more magnificent through the adjustable lens over the top of it.

"Can you believe her?"

The voice from behind Leia was whispered, but the acoustics in the Atrium were particularly sharp where she was standing. Leia didn't move, but her eyes shifted focus from the compass to the glass surrounding it—to the reflection of two people, both human, an older woman and her companion, a middle-aged man. The man was dressed in a fine suit, navy blue and embroidered with silver stars, while the woman wore red silk and a matching turban pierced with an enormous pin set with some sort of glittering red stone.

It had been the man who'd spoken, but the woman replied, cutting her eyes at Leia, unaware that Leia could see her in the reflection and hear her snide, not-quiet-enough words. "How dare she just act as if nothing has happened," she said. The woman swiped a gloved hand at her face. "My son was moving up the ranks on the Death Star. He was poised for a promotion! *So many* died. Just days ago! And she's just tra-la-la, off on a vacation."

"How are you?" the man asked the woman, his voice sincere.

The woman shook her head. "I was better until she showed up. My Bierto, he snatched up reservations for the cruise as soon as he could, to help me get over my grief. And then to find out *she's* here."

They weren't bothering to lower their voices anymore. Leia slowly straightened, hoping the movement was natural, but she didn't turn around. She didn't want to face them.

Leia knew she wasn't universally loved—far from it, she was deeply aware that she had made many, *many* enemies. But she had somehow never thought to add a grieving mother to the list of people who despised her.

She swallowed down the bitterness rising in her throat. She understood why the Emperor was the way he was—a grasping man trying to control everything, greedy for power, a dictator and a tyrant. That was an easy person to hate, to fight.

But she also understood why this woman dressed in red silk was the way she was. And the death of a son? That was a motivation that Leia could understand.

That was a blame she accepted. At least in part.

Her eyes blurred as the pair walked away, the bright-red reflection of the woman's dress growing smaller and smaller. Leia wondered if the woman had wanted Leia to turn around, defend herself. Maybe she had wanted a scene, and that was why she'd spoken so loudly. There were still X-0X droids around. As much as Mon had wanted the publicity stunt of Leia honeymooning aboard this ship, it would have generated far more talk had Leia gotten embroiled in a grieving mother's rage. Not the kind of talk Leia wanted, though.

Leia focused on the compass. Even though it wasn't being used, it was a reminder to stay the intended course, to find a path through the black.

CHAPTER 17

HAN

HAN DROPPED HIS EMPTY GLASS on the bar, along with a few credits as a tip in appreciation of the drink. The bartender sidled over, grabbing the glass and passing it to a server heading to the back. "This not your speed?" they asked.

"Not exactly," Han said. "I prefer cards I can touch."

They gave him the once-over. "You know Lyx?"

Han leaned over. "No. Should I?"

The bartender shrugged as if nothing they were saying was important. "Lyx works on the bridge, but sometimes you can find her in the Engineering Room," they said.

"Thanks, I'll check it out." Han headed to the door, weaving around the stream of people coming into the lounge from the Atrium. He felt a little guilty not rescuing Leia, but then again, she was probably enjoying herself. Just because Han hated small talk didn't mean she did. He caught a glimpse of her chatting with the captain, and he tried to catch her eye, but she was preoccupied.

The Engineering Room was two decks below the Atrium level, and Han took the stairs two at a time, heading portside when he came to the concourse. The large dining room called the most attention. "Crown of Corellia," Han said, reading the sign aloud.

Corellia. Ironic, that. He should have considered the possibility, though—Corellia was known for its shipyards, so even though this was the flagship of the Chandrila Star Line, it had been designed and built on Corellia. Crown, though? Han scoffed. What a grand label attached to the name of a planet that had given him nothing but trouble.

And Qi'ra, a small voice in the back of his head reminded him.

Which just proved his point. Trouble.

Han turned his back on the dining room and spotted another access corridor to the side. He took a chance and, sure enough, found the Engineering Room. A sign by the door said: SPECIAL CREDENTIALS REQUIRED. Credentials Han didn't have. Fortunately, the door was propped open with a tiny screwdriver at the base, enough to leave a millimeters-wide crack. Han stepped inside, noting and ignoring the danger symbols plastered to the interior of the corridor.

The bartender had told him true—there was a game in progress. Not that there was all that much space for it. Han scanned the room, a little surprised he was able to access it so easily. The power core central control dominated the floor space, with coolant regulators taking up an entire corner. Han stepped around the fuel manifold and spotted a makeshift table set up between the mechanical systems and the systems patch bay.

The group here was small. A Cerean woman sat in the best seat, her back to the wall, her chair pushed out so no one could get behind her. Leaned up against the systems patch bay was a Lasat man, too big for the tight space for comfort, his yellow eyes sharp. The human man across from him was about Han's age, with dark hair and light ochre skin, a little short, a little twitchy.

"How did you get here?" the woman asked sharply, looking up from her cards as Han's boots announced him. Her long, pointed skull was offset by the curls at the back of her head, a juxtaposition between harsh lines and soft curves. Her skin was smooth, but her hair was white, so Han was left uncertain of the woman's age.

"Door was open," Han said.

"The door—?"

"Oh, that was me!" The human at the table beamed with pride. "In case anyone wants to join us."

"I'll take care of it," the Lasat said in an aggrieved voice. He stomped over to the door, kicking aside the tiny screwdriver that had kept it open.

"Who are you?" the Cerean demanded of Han.

"Han. I'm just looking for a game," Han said. "You Lyx?"

The woman rolled her eyes. "Kimb send you?"

"The bartender—"

"Mm-hm." Lyx vocalized without moving her lips, and Han suspected the bartender was going to be in trouble later. "Got credits?"

The Lasat returned and claimed his seat. "Mezza," he said, introducing himself.

Han grabbed an empty chair that had been near the engineering computer and slung it over to the table. He didn't like sitting on the end, but at least from this vantage point he could see if any additional people showed up. Han reached into his pocket, pulling out a few credit chips. Not all he had, but enough to get in the game.

"So what brings you to the *Halcyon*?" the human man asked Han.

Han shrugged and looked at the cards the Lasat had passed him.

"Yeah, they don't talk much, either," the man said. "My name is Kelad."

Han glanced at the other players. Mezza, the Lasat, was clearly unhappy with his hand, but it was too early for Han to guess at whether that was a ploy or not—some people made sabacc more about the mind game than the card game. Lyx was a blank slate, completely unreadable, but she seemed the sharpest of them all. The bartender had said Lyx worked on the *Halcyon*'s bridge, and Han wondered if the Lasat did as well. Neither wore a uniform now, but they both carried themselves with a relaxed ease that implied they'd shared games before.

Han had a decent hand, but not a perfect one. He tapped his cred chip on the side of the table, thinking. Mezza paused to watch him. Lyx probably took into account Han's implied tell as well, but the man,

Kelad, blabbered away, only adding more credits to the pile when the woman prompted him.

"I junk," Han said, tossing the hand. Lyx's lips twitched just a fraction.

The other three played out the rest of the game, and Han watched them, trying to learn their habits, pick up how they played. But also, he felt his muscles unwind, his body relax. It wouldn't matter if this game turned into a high-stakes round of chance, this was where Han thrived. The game wasn't fun if it was just a game. He didn't want to play among friends; he wanted to treat strangers like enemies, at least for a few hands.

Next round, Han had fantastic cards, enough to likely win. He made a point not to raise the bet, and he eventually tossed those cards, too. By the fourth round, he was ready to play for real.

"Want some?"

Han looked up from his hand to see Lyx holding a flask out to him. It was made of brown clay and marked with an orange sigil he recognized all too well.

"Where did you get that?" Han asked hollowly.

The woman arched her eyebrow, and Han knew she realized she'd struck an actual nerve by presenting the flask. He didn't care; it wasn't part of the game. "That's Huttese," he said. To the woman's left was a pitcher marked with the same sigil, the long, narrow neck designed to pour boga noga.

"It's strong stuff," she admitted.

Han snorted. "It's not good for anything more than getting the rust off an exhaust or flushing out an engine system—and only if you didn't care too much about the engine in question."

The Lasat laughed. "Can't be that bad." He took the flask the woman had offered to Han and tossed the liquid into his throat. A moment later, Mezza wheezed, yellow eyes bulging, both hands slammed on the table as he hunched over.

Kelad laughed nervously, eyes darting. He seemed like the sort of fellow who wasn't sure when something was a joke or not, but laughed just in case, fearful of missing out more than of appearing foolish.

"Where'd you get that?" Han asked Lyx. Boga noga usually came bottled up, but this flask and pitcher set were just like the kinds Han had seen Jabba use at his palace on Tatooine. These were serving vessels.

The Cerean shrugged. "Found 'em in storage," she said, not clarifying further. She held the pitcher out, inspecting it. "Huttese, you say? The Hutts owned this ship for a while. Can't get caught up in gambling laws when you gamble in space, I suppose."

Ah, that old scam. The crime lords were known to buy cruise ships and turn them into traveling casinos, only letting the betting happen in hyperspace to avoid paying any fees or taxes to a planet. Now that he thought of it, Lando had mentioned this.

Mezza coughed and sputtered, then pounded himself in the chest, one solid, echoing thump. "We don't need that stuff," he growled, his voice more gravelly than it had been before. "Let's just play."

"Right, right, the purity of the game, the integrity of the cards," Kelad said too quickly.

"You eager to lose more?" the Lasat said. He laughed, but from someone his size it sounded almost threatening. Kelad squirmed in his seat.

Han had noticed that Kelad was working with a smaller stack of credit chips than the other two. He'd thought perhaps the man had come to the game with less, but it was evident now that he'd been steadily losing.

"I'm not very good," Kelad confided in Han when he noticed him staring. "I just get distracted!"

Han didn't think this was a bluff. The man truly was that bad of a sabacc player.

"But look at where we are!" Kelad continued as Lyx shuffled the cards for a new game. "This Engineering Room—on *this* ship!"

"Don't start again," Mezza groaned.

Lyx cut the cards, then started to shuffle. Han caught her eye, and she winked. Mezza was a decent player but had had luck on his side. Lyx was an excellent player but hadn't been particularly lucky so far that night. By extending the chitchat between hands, she was hoping to break the Lasat's concentration as well as his lucky streak.

Han could play that game. He turned to Kelad. "What's so special about this ship?" he asked.

Mezza groaned as Kelad threw his hands in the air. "The *Halcyon* is legendary!" he said. "To be on this ship . . ." He sighed blissfully, then leaned over the table toward Han. "And to be in *this* room. I was hoping to get a sneak peek here. That's how I found Mezza and Lyx!"

Lyx began dealing the cards, sliding them over the rough worktable.

"I tried to go belowdecks," Kelad continued. "I really wanted to get closer to the engines, check out the Drabor Configuration firsthand, but I couldn't get by the staff. Maybe you can—" he started, turning to Lyx.

"No," she said flatly, not even looking up.

"You just . . . like engines?" Han asked. He was interested in the way ships ran as much as anyone else, but more for the practical knowledge. Not like a sightseeing tourist.

Kelad shook his head. "Oh, no, not the engines. Not *just* the engines. I like inventions. First things. I like to see the way people do things differently, you know? Solutions that aren't common. Change!"

Lyx tapped the table, where Kelad's cards were still facedown. The man blinked at them, as if surprised they were there, and gathered his hand hastily, fumbling the cards so the whole table saw he had banthas wild—not the best hand, but decently in the middle.

"Nothing," Mezza growled, tossing his hand on the table. "Not even worth trying."

Han tapped his credit chips, glancing at Lyx. She glanced at his faked tell and nodded slightly—this was Han's round.

"I don't have anything good," he said. "But I guess . . ." He tossed a few chips into the game pot. Lyx played along, slowly driving up the pot while Kelad occasionally glanced at his cards, clearly debating the worth of playing it through. But the strong start enticed him enough to keep at it, until Lyx folded and Han called with a fleet, winning easily.

"I'm never lucky!" Kelad cried, but he laughed at himself in a good-natured way. Mezza took over shuffling and dealing. "Same with this war," Kelad muttered.

"What was that?" Han asked, perhaps too sharply.

"Just unlucky," Kelad muttered. When he realized that he had, for once, the undivided and focused attention of someone, he blinked owlishly. "I had a contract working with the Empire, you know. Well, the company I worked for did. I was going places!"

"What'd you do?" This was from Mezza, the deck of cards stacked in his palm. Lasats, like Wookiees, were no friends to the Empire, and if Kelad had a lick of sense, he'd tread carefully.

He did not. "Worked on ship tech, mostly," he babbled, practically beaming with the attention. "Innovative stuff! My division was in gravity manipulation. The new BCL-500 tractor beams? I worked on those! See, someone in the Empire put in a complaint that a rebel ship escaped a tractor beam by messing with the targeting when they redirected toward a planet—the tractor beam couldn't figure out where to focus, on the ship or the planet. I *invented* the new targeting system! That was me!"

Under the table, Han's hands clenched in fists. This wonk was proud of his invention, but Han had been one of those who'd used the gravity of a planet to throw off the targeting of an Imperial tractor beam. And it had saved his life, his and Chewie's, and that maneuver had saved the *Millennium Falcon,* too. And this big-eyed ingénue was bragging about giving the Empire better means to kill him and his friends and his ship?

Mezza, too, was visibly upset, and Han wondered just how close to the war the Lasat was. Lyx didn't seem to care, but she'd proven already that she was good at hiding her emotions.

"'Course, never got credit for it," Kelad muttered. "The Empire doesn't give credit for inventions, they just take them. I *should* have gotten an Ashgad Prize for my targeting system, but *no*, that went to Erso instead."

Han had been so focused on Kelad's muttering that he hadn't noticed someone else coming inside the Engineering Room. "What are you doing in here?" the short Ugnaught sputtered in anger. "You all need to get out of here, pronto-ronto! This is not a place for passengers!"

"Eh, stuff it," Mezza growled. Han glanced at the Ugnaught's uniform and noted he was a junior engineer. "We ain't hurting nothing."

"Not supposed to be here," the Ugnaught said, coming closer, his tone rising. His eyes fell on Lyx. "You don't get to be here, either! Don't care where you usually work. This is engineering!"

Mezza stood up, his chair scraping loudly on the floor. The Lasat towered over the Ugnaught. He glared at him with his yellow eyes, lip snarling over a fanglike tooth.

The Ugnaught looked like he was seriously considering his odds in this fight for the honor of his Engineering Room. His hands curled in fists, swallowing the absolutely tiny little wrench he clutched. It was almost comical.

"It's not worth it," Han said in a low voice. The Ugnaught flicked his eyes at him, but then stormed off, leaving them alone. Between Mezza's threat and Lyx's position on the bridge, he must have realized he couldn't win.

"We playing?" Lyx asked, reaching over the table and taking the deck of cards from Mezza.

Han glanced at Kelad. That man was no card player. He might be some sort of mechanical genius, but he wasn't the brightest. There was more here to learn.

"I'm in."

CHAPTER 18

LEIA

LEIA WAS MORE THAN READY to escape the Atrium when the Pantoran woman assigned as her attaché approached. "May I escort you to your cabin, Princess?" she asked.

"Yes," Leia said. "And no need for the formalities. Just Leia is fine."

The other woman smiled. "Let me be just Riyola, then."

The crowd in the Atrium had thinned enough that Leia and Riyola had the turbolift to themselves. "I've uploaded a schedule of various shipboard activities for you to select from," Riyola said, her own data-pad in the crook of her arm. "If there is any programming you'd like to participate in, I can personally arrange for that."

"Actually," Leia said, "I wanted to go over the ship's flight path."

"Of course." Riyola swiped at her screen, producing a map of the ship's course. After several days of scenic cruising, the *Halcyon* would end up on Synjax.

"Are you looking forward to visiting the resorts?" Riyola asked. She wore a bright smile and seemed genuinely curious about Leia's opinion.

"Mm," Leia said, her eyes still on the display. She realized she hadn't really considered *where* the ship was going; she'd been so focused on just getting to the ship and thinking about how the feeds would show-case her while on board. Although she knew of Synjax's reputation for pristine beaches and private cabanas, she had little intention of soaking in the lavender ocean when there was work to do.

Seeing the ship's route now, though . . .

"A fundamental principle of flying on the *Halcyon* is the idea that the journey is more important, often, than the destination," Riyola said. "I think you'll find the views—"

"What are these pauses in hyperspace?" Leia asked.

"We cruise slowly in some parts of space in order to showcase the galaxy's natural beauty." Riyola's tone spoke proudly of the ship's phi-losophy. Leia could appreciate the sentiment—it was good to slow sometimes, to do nothing but exist among the stars.

"I was just speaking with the captain," Riyola continued. "Do you think you'd be available tomorrow morning for a brief interview? I was going over the feeds, and it's a very positive image, having you aboard the ship on our inaugural flight after Imperial control."

"Sure," Leia said, her eyes still on the map. The turbolift doors opened, and the two women stepped out into the corridor.

"We'll be cruising at regular speed for much of tomorrow morning; it would make for a striking image to have you standing on the bridge with the captain. But of course, I do not want to impose upon your time with your new husband!"

"I don't mind," Leia said. The ship's projected path curved through one sector before winding up to Synjax. The current route had the path heading toward the bottom of the chart displayed on Riyola's screen, but if the route shifted, curving in the other direction . . .

Riyola tilted the datapad to see what had captured Leia's attention. "The meteor storms near the Esseveya system," she said, smiling. "It's a wonder."

"Will we be leaving the ship?" Leia asked, her eyes still on the top of the display, calculating.

"No, but the display from the viewports will be astounding. The me-teor storms go through a magnetic field that produces a brilliant array of colors."

"I haven't heard of it before," Leia said, "but I have heard—"

Too excited by the flight path and upcoming event, Riyola interrupted. "Chandrila Star Line boasts ships suitable for a variety of species, including one specifically targeting underwater species. That ship almost always goes through the Esseveya meteor storms on its itineraries—while the light waves are amazing to us, some species, such as the Mon Calamari, have additional photoreceptors in their eyes that make the display even more breathtaking, with the ability to see a depth of colors that many other beings cannot."

Leia blinked. "Oh, that is fascinating," she said, despite her focus on the display. Although Leia had spent much of her life contemplating how others viewed the galaxy differently based upon their sociological and economic standpoints, she did not always consider how biology might change perception.

A tiny red dot blinked near the point on the display where the path crossed with the meteor storm. "What's that?" Leia asked, pointing at Riyola's screen. Behind them, another set of turbolift doors opened, people streaming out, chatting excitedly as they made their way to their cabins. Riyola pulled Leia to the side so they'd be out of the way.

"It's just a standard warning," she said in a low voice. "The meteor storm has been particularly active lately, but the *Halcyon*'s shields are more than up to the job. Don't worry, Leia; we would never take the ship somewhere dangerous. It's just standard protocol to note the potential hazards."

Leia pointed to the top of the display. "What about this area?" she asked. "Any chance the ship will go there? Perhaps after Synjax . . . ?" Her voice trailed off when Riyola shook her head.

"The Lenguin system is lovely, but there are no excursions planned for it, nor are we getting close enough to see the surface of any of their worlds. You should go there one day, though—there's an ice moon that is quite renowned for its sculptural architecture."

"Yes, I've heard," Leia muttered, swallowing her disappointment. As soon as she'd seen the Lenguin system on the display, she'd hoped that there would be a chance to visit the Madurs moon—one of the locations Mon Mothma had spoken of in the briefing as a possible source for fuel.

A world with which to create an alliance, to break ties with the Empire before the remnants of the Empire formed them. Madurs had been targeted before, but the small moon had protected its carnium and rejected Imperial offers. If Leia could get there now, negotiate a deal with the local government to ensure that, at the very least, no future contracts would be made with the fractured Empire . . .

But it seemed impossible. The *Halcyon* would go in the opposite direction, looping through a meteor storm and ending up on a world that was rich in coastlines and of no interest in the supply chain to fuel the galaxy.

"Ah!" Riyola said, looking at her screen. "I see you do know all about Madurs. I've been alerted that you have received a holo from the prime minister there, Princess. Shall I send it to your suite?"

"A message?" Leia repeated, heart thumping. "Yes, please. This way?" Riyola nodded, pointing out the cabin for Leia and then tapping on her screen.

Leia's heart thudded as she headed to her cabin. This was the first response to the missives she'd sent to the leaders of the various worlds she'd contacted, and surely that was significant? If the prime minister of Madurs wanted nothing to do with her or the foundling republic forming in the wake of the Empire, he would have ignored her message, not responded so quickly. Did he need help? Her message to him had been more of a way to open the lines of communication, but if he was already eager to join the Alliance—perhaps due to the celebrations at the defeat of the Death Star—she would certainly welcome that.

Part of her wanted nothing more than to steal a shuttle and zip over to Madurs, but another part of her felt guilty. She was supposed to be on her honeymoon, not an ambassador mission.

But . . . what if she could do both?

CHAPTER 19

HAN

HAN CONSIDERED HIS ODDS. MEZZA was nearly out of the game, and from the Lasat's frustrated growls at every hand, he knew it. Lyx was a contender, but it was clear that she was growing impatient. She was steadily driving both Mezza and Kelad out, skillfully weaving the bets so that one or the other had hope before she tossed the cards down and collected the chips. Han half suspected that she had a few cards pilfered away, but her top was sleeveless and she kept her arms on the table, hands in sight. She was good at sabacc, but if she was a cheat, she was better than anyone Han had ever seen.

He'd already gambled more than he really wanted to on his first night. He had no real way of knowing the time, but Han suspected that too much had passed. He junked another hand early, letting the others play the rounds while he stretched his legs. He should go—this was his honeymoon, and he had a princess waiting in the biggest suite of the most luxurious cruise starliner in the galaxy. There was no reason to be in the dregs with this lot, crammed in the corner of a stifling Engineering Room.

Han leaned against a wall that put him out of sight of the players thanks to a large pipe. Hands in his pockets, he jostled some of the credits he'd kept in reserve and felt the sharp edge of the trim pry bar he kept there. Shorter than his finger, the little tool was handy in a pinch, capable of popping a rivet or wedging between sticky panels. He should have left it on the *Falcon,* he supposed, although Chewie had his own way of dealing with stubborn panels.

On impulse, Han took out the trim pry bar and scraped the sharp edge against the pipe in front of him, quickly carving out first his initials and then Leia's. He had no doubt that, if she knew he was vandalizing the *Halcyon,* she'd be furious with him, but that made it all the better to leave his mark on the ship. The *Halcyon* should be so honored; it wasn't every day a cruiser carried a princess on her honeymoon, and even rarer that he appreciated any vessel other than the *Falcon.*

Han smirked at his handiwork. He should go to Leia right this moment, but he also wanted to make sure she was safe. As if on cue, Kelad's voice drifted over to him. Han strode over, grabbing his chair and entering the game once more. Time to get this over with. He had a princess to get back to.

"It takes innovation to come up with solutions to problems that don't exist yet," Kelad said, barely glancing at his cards. He looked to Han the way a drowning man clung to a float.

People gambled for different reasons. Money, desperation, the high of it. But Kelad had apparently come to this makeshift table merely hoping for companionship. There was something sad about that, a different sort of desperation, one that made Han uncomfortable.

"That's what the Empire paid me for," Kelad added. He looked down at his little pile of chips, rapidly dwindling with each hand. "Or, they used to."

"Imperial sympathizer?" Han asked, hoping his voice was neutral. He couldn't focus on the cards, even though his hand could be decent with a little luck. He needed to concentrate on what really mattered.

"I don't care so much about the politics," Kelad said blithely.

"Not all of us are given a choice on whether or not to care," Mezza growled.

Kelad didn't seem to notice the Lasat's discontent. "I made the inventions, I got paid for the inventions. With the Empire fallen . . ." He shrugged as if it didn't matter, but he ran his hand along the short stacks of credits in front of him.

"What are you going to do now?" Han asked.

"Make your bets." Lyx's voice was sharp.

Han tossed a credit in, as did the others, and new cards were slung across the table.

"Oh, I don't know," Kelad said, sighing dramatically. "I was working on something big. *Huge.* It was going to make all the difference, really shake things up . . ." He looked at his cards and threw them on the table, junking already.

Han copied him, and Lyx and Mezza faced off. Han leaned over the table. "Something huge, you say?"

Kelad shrugged again. "Doesn't matter, unless I can find a buyer." He shook his head. "That's the problem. War is good business for tech. No one needs a high-level gravity manipulator if there's not a war on."

"How tragic," Mezza said flatly. He threw his hand on the pot in the middle of the table, sending chips scattering. Lyx raised an eyebrow but silently accepted his defeat, collecting the credits for herself. "I'm done. Next time," he said, nodding to Lyx. "Pleasure," he added to Han. The Lasat looked at Kelad and made a noise of disgust in the back of his throat.

Mezza left the room, his feet loud on the metal grating that served as a floor.

"I should call it a night, too," Kelad said, miserably. "I can't afford to lose more." But when Han started dealing, he accepted his hand. "I may have an investor, though. Meeting on Synjax."

There it was. Kelad was just enough of a rube to tell him who this investor was, Han was sure of it. It could be a shell for the Empire. Han wasn't much for nobility, despite being a general, but if he could empty a sympathizer's pockets of credits and get a bead on a potential corporate ally of the Empire by doing nothing more than playing cards, that was exactly the sort of mission he was perfect for.

"This investor going to pay well?" Lyx asked.

Karkarodon in the water.

"If I can entice him!" Kelad laughed, drawing a card and tossing a credit into the game pot.

"This investor . . ." Han said, distracting Kelad while Lyx made her bet. "Rich, I assume?"

"I assume. Unlike me." He laughed in a self-deprecating way and junked. He was getting more careful with his credits. "Not entirely sure where the funding is coming from," Kelad continued. "Could be Imperial, now that I think of it. They may have lost the war, may not. But who else would be interested in gravity manipulation?" He shrugged, but then frowned. "Hey, I heard that Princess Leia was on this ship. When she gets off at Synjax, that may scare away my investor."

Lyx's eyes widened, just a fraction, but in that moment, Han knew: She knew who he was, why he was here, his connection to Leia. Han tapped his credits, tossing an extra handful in. Lyx's lips twitched up, her eyes flicking to the rest of his chips. Han threw in a few more.

When the betting ended, Lyx revealed her hand. She had high numbers, nothing that would normally win the game pot. Han bit the inside of his cheek. He'd had full sabacc, but he tossed his cards facedown on the table. Lyx smirked, pulling the pot closer to her. Her silence had been bought.

"I'm surprised someone like Princess Leia would make such a public appearance," Kelad mused. It was his turn to deal, but he'd proven inept at shuffling, so Lyx took the cards. Kelad picked up the Huttese flask—he didn't drink from it, but he looked at it. "Heard there were bounties on her head," he mused. "Heard someone like her would fetch quite a price. Maybe I don't even need an investor. You know, when I was looking around, I saw the escape pods. How easy would it be to just grab her, throw her in a pod, and shoot off to the closest planet? Some bounty hunter would pay a lot for me to hand her over."

Lyx tapped the sabacc cards on the table. "Turns out I'm done playing," she said.

So am I, Han thought, staring at the oblivious Kelad.

Lyx gathered her winnings and tucked them into a pouch clipped to her belt. She purposefully met neither man's eyes as she slipped silently away, absolving herself of whatever happened.

Leaving Han to take care of the man who'd threatened his wife.

Kelad glanced at Han but didn't seem to notice the rage simmering under the surface of his placid face. "I should pack it up while I'm ahead," Kelad said sadly. "I really shouldn't have gambled at all, not with my luck. But hey! You look like the sort of person who knows bounty hunters, how to arrange all that."

"As a matter of fact, I do know some bounty hunters," Han allowed.

"You think this holds water?" Kelad asked, leaning across the table toward Han. Although they were the only two in the room, he spoke in lowered tones conspiratorially. "I could split the profits with you."

"You think it'd be that easy?" Han asked.

"Oh sure," Kelad said confidently. "I could knock her out or something. She seemed pretty little on the holos. Or you could," he offered. The idea of hitting Leia sickened Han, but the idea of knocking out this incompetent fool had some appeal.

"And then just go to the escape pods?"

Kelad nodded as Han stood up. "This could actually work," the other man asserted, as if he was convincing himself more than anyone else.

And that was the part that burned Han up inside. A detailed, organized plot to kidnap Leia? They would be on the lookout for that. Han could sense a setup a mile away, and Leia was smart enough to see the warning signs. But the sheer chaotic randomness of some unknown, unaffiliated opportunist? That . . . that could work. Possibilities rolled through Han's mind. Kelad had a dopey look about him, not the kind of man to be a reasonable threat. Leia would follow him out of pity if nothing else, and if he turned on her with the element of surprise—

Han could plan for the Empire. He could plan for the Hutts and Leia's other enemies. He had seen some of the detailed dossiers Mon Mothma kept on known threats.

But he couldn't plan for someone desperate who knew just enough to be willing to take a chance on hurting the woman he loved. The *impulsiveness* of it—that was what got to him. Kelad was clearly strapped for cash, and he went from gambling at sabacc to kidnapping for bounties in a flash. How could Han protect Leia from someone like this, someone they couldn't see coming since the man himself didn't know what he was doing?

"I don't need much, just enough to cover my expenses. If I could fund the research, this could be—" Kelad spread his hands wide to indicate how big his invention could go, if he could find the funds to finish it. "There's a tractor beam belowdecks," he added. "I got a glimpse of it before the engineering crew caught me and kicked me out. You want to see? It has such a cool feature—since the original designer was Anzellan, the fittings for the control panel are so close together, and—"

"But first," Han said, "why don't you show me those escape pods you found?"

CHAPTER 20

LEIA

LEIA ENTERED HER CABIN FOR the first time, barely registering the fresh flowers blooming on the table by the door.

"Han?" she called softly.

The cabin was empty. Leia's heart sank a little. He must have found something interesting on board; from the options on Riyola's datapad, it was clear that there was plenty to distract them.

Rather than dwell on where he may be, though, Leia turned to the Droid Link Panel. D3-O9 popped up on her screen immediately. "I was told I had a message from the prime minister of Madurs?" she said before the droid could speak.

The droid nodded. "Yes, Princess Leia," she said, with an inflection of respect in her voice. "I'll transfer it to the screen now."

Leia took a deep breath. Although she knew that neither D3-O9 nor the prime minister could see her, she squared her shoulders and straightened her spine, just as she used to do before presenting arguments on the Imperial Senate floor.

The Droid Link Panel darkened, and a thin blue light illuminated the holographic message from the prime minister of Madurs. The prime minister stood tall, his chin tilted up, but his gaze was off center. It was hard to tell in the flickering image of the low-res holo, but it almost seemed as if the man was reading something, not merely speaking his thoughts. He wore a dark suit with a capelet over his shoulders, an array of badges and honors decorating the sash that crossed his body.

"Princess Leia Organa," Prime Minister Dreand Yens started, his voice surprisingly deep. "Thank you for reaching out to our moon. I am happy to see you are someone who values art, although, as you know, art cannot truly be appreciated unless it is experienced. I invite you to come to our world at your convenience and see how our architecture and other art has evolved since the last Imperial Art Exposition was hosted here."

The message stopped abruptly. Leia stared at the screen. "That's it?" she said aloud. "Deethree, was there anything else? Did the message get interrupted?"

The droid's face popped back on the screen. "I'm happy to inform you, Princess, that the message has been provided for you in its entirety. We received it directly from the prime minister's office."

"Play it again, please," Leia said.

She watched the holo carefully. She was sure now that the prime minister was reading a prepared speech; his eyes shifted, and his body language was stiff. On the other hand, it wasn't that unusual for a politician to carefully select his words before he spoke to another politician, and Leia knew several senators or leaders who wrote statements before reading them, even in private correspondence.

No, it was the content of the prime minister's message that concerned her. He spoke of art—as she had in her own message—but he utterly ignored any mention of the nascent republic or the more salient points Leia had brought up. Her introduction to the prime minister hadn't been long, but it had certainly been more than three sentences of blithe commentary.

"Would you like me to play it a third time?" D3-O9 offered.

"No, thank you," Leia said. She would mull over the prime minister's words on her own.

"Please enjoy your evening. Best journey!" D3 said, and the Droid Link Panel went blank.

Leia stared at it a moment, then turned around. Her breath caught in her throat, and for a moment, she forgot the frustrating message from the prime minister.

The suite was stunning. The service droids had already stowed away her and Han's luggage, and a basket of fresh fruit—tropical citrella, a long green malama, and several crisp omlels—gleamed at her from the side table. The cabin was among the most luxurious she'd ever seen on a starship, grand and opulent.

Leia's mind flashed to the previous night, aboard the *Millennium Falcon*. Han's bunk had been cramped and cluttered, but it had been his— theirs. Leia was certainly impressed by the sheer decadence of such a spacious, elegant place to rest, but the contrast between the *Halcyon* and the *Falcon* had never been sharper.

If only Han were here now.

With a sigh, Leia stepped over to the viewport. Riyola had been right—it was good to have long moments without being in hyperspace, to just gaze at the infinite beauty and wonders of the universe. Any minute, Han would walk through the door. A part of her longed to be back on the *Millennium Falcon,* flying at lightspeed, unreachable and alone with him, no expectations or pressures.

That's what this entire trip is supposed to be, she reminded herself bitterly. But no—as soon as she boarded the ship, she had put on the public relations mask, had sought out the X-0X units to smile, had carefully shown everyone attention *except* her new husband. And when she'd rushed into the honeymoon suite on this luxury liner, she had been most eager to view a message from a government official, not see her groom and make up for lost time.

No wonder Han had wandered off. *He understands, though, surely,* Leia tried to tell herself. Han knew who he was marrying, what the situation was.

Anxiety twisted inside her. He knew who she had been, but neither of them had really talked about who they wanted to become, how they wanted to grow and shift as a unified front rather than individually. She had started her fight to improve the galaxy on the Senate floor, and that battle had shifted to the war. With the Rebellion over, did Han assume she would quit fighting?

Leia huffed a little laugh. No. Han was too smart to think that of her. He knew that the battle wasn't over; it had only changed. She might put aside her blaster and resume her speeches, but she would never stop fighting.

But did *she* expect *him* to change? No—*no*, she loved him for who he was, the scoundrel side as well as the nobility that always won out in the end. She loved that he questioned her, that he pushed her. She loved who she was with him, who he was with her, and who they were together.

They would sort the rest out.

Leia wasn't entirely sure if she was being willfully blind or if she was simply taking a leap of faith. Perhaps there wasn't a difference.

Leia crossed the cabin, past the bed—tightly done up and draped in a blanket bearing the Chandrila Star Line logo—to the small lounge, complete with another viewport and a built-in seating space that was decorated with a terrarium filled with subtropical plants that, Leia suspected, hailed from their final destination, Synjax. Leia collapsed on the couch, relishing the luxurious feel of the cushions. All she knew was that she would take every second of happiness that she could.

A display in the wall promised the latest feeds from the HoloNet. Idly, Leia turned it on for some background noise as she reached for her datapad.

She sent a missive off first to General Madine, to check on the status of the recon for Sterdic IV and Cawa City and to determine if that would be the best place to send the Pathfinders next and root out Imperial influences. The information that had escaped the base on Endor bothered Leia—it was far too clear that Palpatine had created contingency plans even for his own death, like a Chandrilan black-horned net spider weaving multiple intricate traps.

Although Leia doubted that Mon would reply to her, instead insisting that Leia not work during her honeymoon, she brought up a message to be sent to Mon, asking for updates on the Anoat sector.

She tapped her finger on the screen, thinking. She needed to reply to the Madurs prime minister, but what could she say? While Leia was, in fact, a lover of art, that had been the small talk before the business at hand. She wanted to get directly to the point, but the prime minister was being frustratingly obtuse.

Leia leaned back on the couch cushions, glancing up at the display built into the wall across from her. And saw her own face smiling through the screen.

Leia's eyes widened. During the war, the Empire had heavily censored and controlled the feeds. While she had been in the Senate, she had been the darling of the media's eye. Alderaan's destruction had turned her into a martyrlike figure. But for every positive image, an Imperial-run feed had demonized her, questioning her motives, slandering her name.

Leia had long ago gotten used to simply not looking at the feeds. There was the truth, and there was media, and they rarely, if ever, overlapped.

Now, though, she watched as the feed showed an external shot of the *Halcyon* followed by internal glimpses of the Atrium at the Captain's Reception. The reporter's voice narrated the event.

"After a heartfelt speech by Captain Oswin Dicto, the shining stars of the galaxy celebrated newfound freedom from the Empire aboard the recently liberated *Halcyon* star cruiser." A series of flashes showed the elites who had been in the room—Leia, of course, and Zohma. The antagonistic young man she'd been with was identified as Filbert Carta, a rising celebrity who specialized in romantic thriller entertainment feeds. Leia hoped it bothered him that she had absolutely zero idea who he was or what he'd starred in. No bane like obscurity.

The feed highlighted several of the people on the ship, and those whom Leia didn't personally know, she was at least able to draw connections to them, list in her mind which industries they were linked to, which social circles, what ties bound them to other people or other worlds.

"Stop it," she muttered to herself. She didn't *have* to work on her honeymoon; she should be finding ways to spend time with her husband, not exploiting networking links. And at the very least, if she was going to work, it should be an answer to the prime minister.

Leia changed the display to a different feed, this one an economic projection report. A bleak one. War was profitable, and not just for manufacturers of weapons and armor and warships—whole planets worked to provide food packages for troops, for example, and businesses geared toward propaganda would have to pivot. The reporter started analyzing different approaches to revitalizing the galactic economy, emphasizing a return to more local shopping within individual sectors and diversifying shipments.

The reporter's voice was dull enough that Leia could refocus her attention on her datapad. Rather than reply to Prime Minister Yens immediately, she sifted through the dossier Major Nioma had given her, seeking information that could potentially aid her, cross-referencing the data with her own information on carnium, the fuel source on the moon, as well as Imperial presence.

There was surprisingly little relevant information on the moon. Several art journals had done in-depth holographic essays on the well-known ice palaces the frosty moon was renowned for, but even those had dropped off over the past few years. A handful of dates and dry lists of names of prime ministers. The moon was included in a thesis by a student at the University of Bar'leth, but nothing more than a note that carnium was recorded as present but "difficult to access and possibly damaging to the ecosystem." The Empire wouldn't care about damaging any moon's environment, Leia knew that for certain, but beyond a small speculative article that was several years old, Leia could find nothing else relevant.

She frowned at the datapad. It was . . . *curious* that there was so little information available. The Lenguin system bordered the Mid Rim and the Outer Rim Territories, but despite its location there should simply be *more*.

"With confirmation of the Empire's fall coming from multiple reliable sources, tonight we project the impact on the galactic economy," the reporter on the feed said, drawing Leia's attention. A banner flashed along the bottom of the screen, labeling the man Kriz Tray, an economist from Coruscant currently promoting a new series at the Panos Lecture Hall. "While I am focusing on the Core Worlds tonight, it should be noted that upheaval on this scale will certainly trickle down to the Mid Rim and territories beyond. Whether the so-called New Republic will be able to maintain a stabilized credit system is the key issue at hand; swift focus on preventing an inflation and seeing the fulfillment of previous Imperial contracts will help keep the galactic economy on course."

"Well, that's not going to happen," Leia muttered. The Empire's previous contracts were with armament factories and the development of Star Destroyers. It would not be a matter of fulfilling orders for more weapons; the economy would honor the shift to more productive means of goods that could benefit peace.

But that did make Leia wonder—was the relative silence from Madurs a result of an Imperial presence already on the moon? The Empire had heavily controlled lines of communication, and it wasn't unheard of for lies to be printed or information to be scrubbed. While Leia had worked hard to create alternative data points for rebels to access the truth, it was impossible to keep tabs on every world in the galaxy. A tiny independent moon that had little to its name but a nearly inaccessible source of fuel could slip through the cracks. Perhaps the Empire had already targeted Madurs—perhaps Leia was too late.

"Of note, consider these key manufacturing worlds." Tray's words floated over the images of three planets—Corellia, Hindle, and Bleuf. "While Corellia will be able to alter course—the Imperial contracts for additional warships can be restructured to support civilian vehicles— the economies of Hindle and Bleuf may collapse." A series of charts and projections cluttered the display, all of them foretelling doom.

"We could support them while we shift their manufacturing . . ." Leia wondered aloud, but already Tray was reporting just how long it would take to reorganize the economy on those worlds, tossing around enormous sums of credits that would have to subsidize the industry.

"Fortunes were found at the start of the Galactic Civil War," Tray continued. An image of Hindle prior to the Empire's manufacturing impositions showed on the display, with a time-lapse of the Empire's influence—a world that had previously been farmed had reached an ecological disaster through drought, and the Empire developed several factories, provided new housing, and gave support for the locals. Working conditions were not ideal, but compared with what had previously existed there . . .

The Empire had existed for as long as it did because it *wasn't* horrific to everyone. Some people, like Zohma, had not seen much of a difference between working with the Empire and working with the Republic. Others, like the people on the planets Hindle and Bleuf, had directly benefited from increased support of the government and a stabilized industry.

Leia thought of the woman in the Atrium whose son had been on the Death Star. There were legitimate reasons to mourn the loss of the government.

Did the people of Hindle know that their industries supported atrocious war crimes? Were they aware that the Empire would eventually turn on them, exploiting their labor and destroying the economy they'd helped build as soon as it didn't benefit the Empire?

And more to the point: Would the people of Hindle care?

Ideals like the ones Leia lived her life by—freedom and truth, helping others and building a society that benefited all without bigotry and oppression—those were strong beliefs.

But it was hard to believe in such things when a global economy collapsed and families faced starvation.

Leia pinched the bridge of her nose. None of this weighed on her shoulders alone, and she had known from the start that a revolution would take more than a won war.

"Meanwhile, the tourism trade seems to be doing quite well," Tray continued blithely. Leia blinked as her face was splashed across the display again. "Rebel Alliance leader Leia Organa was spotted as a passenger on the luxury star cruiser *Halcyon*, rubbing elbows with other elites who will not need to worry about the possibility of an economic collapse across the galaxy." Tray's professional tone slipped into a sneer.

Leia turned off the display.

CHAPTER 21

HAN

HAN WAS CONSIDERING TOSSING KELAD out of the air lock just to get some silence. The man had kept up a steady stream of chatter as they left the Engineering Room, turning down the corridor to the stairwell. Once on the lower deck, they pushed through a door that was labeled AUTHORIZED CREW ACCESS ONLY and Kelad headed starboard, in the general direction of the hangar bay.

"These generators are for the defensive cannons," Kelad told Han. "Did you know this ship has twelve twin light defensive cannons? I know the Empire controlled this star cruiser for a while, but that seems excessive, doesn't it?"

Han made a noncommittal noise in the back of his throat. Between Lyx giving them leftover hooch from the Hutts and Kelad reminding him of the Empire, it seemed he could never escape his past, even on his honeymoon.

The escape pods were located under the supply docking rings, but since the *Halcyon* was primarily a passenger ship, the route was well lit and had clear signage giving directions in the event of an emergency deboarding situation. When they reached the escape pods, Han gave the system a quick once-over.

"Go ahead and get inside," he told Kelad. "We should get a feel for it, if you think you're going to go through with kidnapping the princess."

Kelad giggled, the sound high-pitched, almost nervous. "You know, I was half joking," he said, stepping into the first escape pod. "But honestly? It's not such a bad idea. She's got to be worth a million credits in ransom, at least."

"More than that," Han said.

As soon as Kelad stepped inside, Han slammed his hand on the seal. Through the small viewport built into the door, he saw the man jump and turn around. Han flicked on the intercom by the hatch release.

"You know what else isn't such a bad idea?" Han said, leaning close to the speaker. "Sending someone who'd threaten Leia Organa off in an escape pod. You're not worthy of being on the same ship as her."

"Wait!" Kelad's voice cracked in his desperation. "Wait! I didn't know you were a friend of hers!"

"Oh, that changes things?" Han growled. "Listen, buddy, Leia has *lots* of friends. Most of them would say an idiot like you deserves a second chance."

"I do! I'm sorry! I wasn't thinking—it's just . . . I was supposed to get paid big by the Empire for my invention. And instead, boom! The war ended, the contract fell through, and I'm flat broke."

"Maybe you shouldn't profit off the death of innocents at the hand of the Empire," Han said. If Kelad hoped his financial hardships would make Han sympathize with him, he was dead wrong.

A noise down the corridor made Han pause. He lifted his finger from the intercom. Kelad, sensing that something was happening, pounded on the door to the escape pod. Fortunately, the hatch was thick enough that no sound escaped. Unfortunately, there was nowhere for Han to hide in the well-lit corridor as a person rounded the corner, mumbling to himself.

It was the same short Ugnaught who had tried to break up the sabacc game in the Engineering Room. "You!" he shouted, pointing some sort of electronic prod in Han's direction. "What are you doing down here? No passengers in this corridor! You, always showing where you shouldn't be!"

Han raised his hands. "Listen, buddy, I was just—"

"I'm no your buddy!" the Ugnaught shouted. He lifted a comlink to his lips. "You need to come to the escape pod corridor, pronto-ronto. Big trouble!"

"No—hey, no, you don't need to bring anyone else down here—"

"Pronto-ronto!" the Ugnaught shouted into the comlink. He turned toward Han. "What you doing down here?" he said, suspicion making his eyes narrow.

And that was when the Ugnaught saw Kelad pounding on the escape pod door, trying to shout through the soundproof transparisteel of the viewport.

Han cursed as the Ugnaught's eyes widened. "You going to throw someone off the ship?" he shouted. He dropped his electric tool, and it clattered on the floor. The Ugnaught shoved Han out of the way and punched a code into the door panel. Moments later, Kelad stumbled into the corridor.

"Oh, thank you, thank you!" he said, clutching at the Ugnaught. "That man was going to kill me!"

"I was not, you big whiner," Han growled, rolling his eyes.

"He was going to send me off the ship!"

The Ugnaught whirled around to Han. "Don't you go nowhere!" he shouted, even though Han had not moved. "I've got big eyeballs on you!"

"Woz, what is going on?" Another man strode down the corridor, picking up his pace when he saw the commotion.

"Great," Han muttered.

The other man—a tall, slender Nautolan—raced forward. The Ugnaught—named Wozzakk, according to his name badge—turned to him. "Chief, I was doing as you say, off to pulse the static discharge vanes, pronto-ronto, as you say, doing my job. And then I find this man—" Wozzakk pointed to Han. "—he trying to send this man out the escape pod!" The Ugnaught swung his arm to Kelad, knocking his arm against his midriff so hard that he made a faint *oof!* sound and winced.

The Nautolan's big eyes grew even wider as he tried to take the situation in.

"Let me explain," Han said.

Wozzakk spun around, snarling at Han, exposing his tusks. Han threw his hands up and backed against the wall, but his eyes went to the Nautolan. From the other man's uniform, he could tell that the Nautolan was the chief engineer, higher-ranked than the Ugnaught.

"Listen, my name is Han Solo," he said. "I'm here on my honeymoon with my new wife, Princess Leia Organa."

Kelad groaned, a sound of pure anguish, and Han knew in that moment that he would win this fight.

"That man there, he threatened to kidnap and ransom the princess. My wife," Han continued. "I wasn't *actually* going to toss him out the escape pod." As appealing as such an idea was ... "I was merely attempting to restrain him and protect my wife—a very prominent public figure whose attendance at this ship's launch was highly recorded on the feeds."

"We have the brig for restraining dangerous individuals who violate our code of conduct," the Nautolan said.

"I'm not dangerous!" Kelad protested.

"And yet you intended to kidnap my wife. For ransom."

"I mean, I just—"

"This wife," Wozzakk said. "She big lady?"

Han grasped the Ugnaught's meaning. "She's a high-profile figure."

The Nautolan had a datapad out and was tapping on the screen furiously. Han was not used to slinging his name—or, rather, Leia's name—for credit, but it certainly was making this situation better. He watched as the Nautolan swallowed, visibly concerned. "Mr. Solo, sir, I—"

"General Solo," Han said, smirking. He could get used to this.

"General, yes, er, sir. General Solo. I'm so sorry that this has happened. I'm chief engineer of the *Halcyon*, Zalma Trinkris. I am certain we can get this sorted out."

"Excellent." Internally, Han was practically whooping with excitement. This was the same high as having the best hand in sabacc. Was this how Leia walked around all the time, so confident she'd get her way? It was a nice feeling.

"And you," Zalma said, turning to Kelad. "Let me have your full name and cabin number, please."

Kelad blanched further. "I, er . . ."

Several things clicked in Han's mind at once. The way Kelad had insisted he needed to get to Synjax to meet an investor, but how he kept complaining about a lack of funds. There were cheaper passenger flights in the galaxy than the *Halcyon*, that was for sure—but Synjax was a well-known resort world, and didn't let any scrapyard ship dock there. If Kelad needed to impress some investor, arriving aboard the *Halcyon* would certainly do that . . . but if Kelad was as broke as he claimed, he couldn't possibly have afforded passage.

"A stowaway!" the Ugnaught shouted, looking over Zalma's arm to see the information displaying on the datapad. "How dare you violate my ship like this!"

"Right, you're coming with me," Zalma said, grabbing Kelad by the arm. "You're going to the brig for the night. The captain can deal with you in the morning."

"But—!" Kelad sputtered as Zalma dragged him away. Han waggled his fingers at the man in a mock farewell.

"You too!" Wozzakk, the Ugnaught, said, poking Han hard in the side. "You go back to your cabin, where you belong. No need to be down here. This here for engineering crew *only*. Get out! Pronto-ronto!"

"Okay, okay, I'm going," Han said, strolling back down the corridor and heading to the turbolifts.

So far, Han had gone belowdecks in the galaxy's finest luxury star cruiser, found an illicit sabacc game, and threatened a man with an impromptu exit on an escape pod. Not a bad first day of a honeymoon, if he did say so himself.

CHAPTER 22

LEIA

THE NEXT MORNING, LEIA ROLLED over in bed, her hair spilling over the pillow. Han had found her the night before on the little couch, datapad still in hand. She'd confessed that she'd tried to squeeze in a little work on their honeymoon, and he'd laughed about finding a sabacc game. It was easy to slip into old habits, but as she woke up next to him, she found it easier still to develop a few new ones.

A little light flashed on the band that served as both her cabin access and an onboard communicator. Leia had spent a fitful night thinking about the prime minister's abrupt message and how to respond, but that didn't matter now. Worrying didn't do the work.

Han groaned. "It's not time to get up yet," he said, keeping his eyes closed.

Leia nestled against his side, but she opened up the comm on her band. D3-O9's shining face beamed at her in a one-way message that had been recorded while she'd slept.

"Good morning, Princess Leia," D3-O9 stated. "Captain Oswin Dicto would like to offer you a tour of the bridge at your convenience. You are welcome to bring your guest with you."

"I'm just a guest, huh?" Han grumbled, still not opening his eyes.

Leia tossed the communicator aside, where it thunked on their rumpled bed. "I should go," she said, but she didn't move to get up.

Han threw an arm around her waist, holding her against him. "What does he need to show you the bridge for?" he said.

"Perhaps he's going to let me fly the ship."

At this, Han's eyes widened, and he shot up in the bed. "Wait, what? You think he'll let me do that?"

Leia laughed and patted him on the head. "Calm down there, Captain Solo, this is just for an interview. I won't get to touch the ship's controls."

Han collapsed back against the pillows. "In that case, just stay in bed."

But Leia was already slipping out from under the covers.

"No," Han groaned, drawing out the word, reaching for her without getting up himself.

Leia laughed. "We're on a luxury star cruiser," she said. "We're *not* going to spend the entire honeymoon in bed."

Han flopped over. "Isn't that the point of a honeymoon?"

Leia raised an eyebrow at him. "I won't be long. Get something to eat and meet me in the climate simulator after?"

Leia worked her hair quickly, smiling at the way Han watched her with wonder. People without experience with long hair always thought it was such a hassle, so difficult to maintain and style, but the reality was that long hair was often easier to deal with than short. Leia braided her locks quickly, needing only one long ribbon to weave through the ends and tie up the braids close to her head. It took just a few minutes to go from bed-rumpled hair to a smooth, bound braid, but it immediately made her feel ready to take on the day.

Leia crossed the suite to the clothing storage, pulling out a pale-yellow gown laced with umber. "If you stay here, you don't have to get dressed," Han said.

"Noted." Leia laughed as she stepped into her shoes and then dropped a kiss on his head. "Don't spend all day in bed."

"I can if I want to!" he called as Leia left the suite. The door zipped closed behind her, and Leia headed down the corridor to the turbolift that would take her to the bridge, sending a quick message to Riyola that she was on her way.

Her personal assistant was waiting for her just outside the lift. "Thank you so much for doing this," she enthused, beaming at Leia. "I hate to impose on your honeymoon—"

"It's no problem," Leia said, smiling. She followed Riyola across the Atrium, toward the bridge. "I *want* to help showcase this ship; I consider it part of my job." It was the only job Mon had left her to do; if this was her only option, she'd take what she could get.

Riyola shot her a look of gratitude, her golden eyes sincere. "It's more than just for the feeds," she confided. "The whole crew—none of us were Imperial supporters, even the ones forced to work during the occupation. It will do a lot for morale if they see you."

Leia felt heat rising in her cheeks, unsure of how to react. She had long known she was a symbol of the Rebellion, but to literally embody that—it was not a gratitude she deserved, and she didn't know what to do with her emotions. She was so much better reacting on the field—it was easier to fight the Empire with a blaster in her hand rather than a smile on her face. But wars were not won with firepower alone.

"I've been monitoring the public feeds as well," Riyola continued. "It's all very positive; people love to see this return to normalcy."

"You said you're usually in the position of the quartermaster on board?" Leia said. "You're very efficient and capable." The Pantoran seemed determined to fulfill her duties not only as Leia's attaché but also as a representative of the *Halcyon*.

Riyola straightened her gray-blue uniform jacket, a blazer over a silk shirt that was more informal than the rigid coats many of the officers wore. "This ship has more than earned my loyalty," she said. Leia wondered what had happened to make this woman so laser-focused, but she suspected that Riyola Keevan's faith was both hard-won and deeply valuable.

Riyola's voice dropped as she leaned in closer to Leia before entering the bridge. "More than the feeds, there's also a sense that, well—if *you* are taking time off to celebrate, well, then there's something worth celebrating, yes?"

"Of course there's something worth celebrating," Leia said.

Riyola's smile was unrestrained. "That's one of the things I love about working on the *Halcyon*," she said. "There's safety in joy."

Riyola strode onto the bridge, waving at the captain, leaving Leia with her words. Safety in joy. She would have assumed the opposite to be true—there was joy in being safe and secure—but it had never occurred to her to flip that phrase. The idea that a feeling of joy created a sense of safety—that was true in a very profound way. Leia marveled at Riyola, barely able to take in the bridge as the woman led her deeper inside. Joy was one of those emotions, like love, that burst forth unbidden and even unwarranted. It wasn't manufactured or cultivated; it simply was. And if one was in a position to feel joy, that necessarily meant there was at least some safety wrapped around one's soul.

It struck Leia that her acceptance of Han's marriage proposal had been rooted in the same idea Riyola had voiced. She had felt joy in his question, and that joy had happened because, for the first time in as long as she could remember, she had felt safe. When there was no security, hope was the thing to hold on to. But once the ground was firm under one's feet, it was possible for joy to exist.

"Princess Leia," Captain Dicto said, striding forward and holding his hand out to her. "You are very welcome on the bridge."

Leia shifted her focus to the task at hand. "Thank you for having me."

Riyola pointed out the ship-owned X-0X units that hovered nearby on the bridge and explained that they were hoping to capture some images of the tour, candid moments rather than a staged interview in order to provide some behind-the-scenes content to entice others to feel confident enough to join the *Halcyon*. With everything in place, Riyola stepped back, out of the spotlight but close enough to be of service if needed.

Leia trailed after Captain Dicto as he showed her the various important features of the bridge. While the *Millennium Falcon* was primarily a two-person operation—and could be piloted alone if need be—the bridge of the *Halcyon* required far more hands on deck. Although several members of the crew turned at their stations to see what was happening, some of them daring a nod or wave at Leia, it was clear that this was a place of work and focus.

Behind them, a window showed the Atrium, already bustling with activity, groups of families and friends meeting up before exploring other areas of the ship. It was so strange to see the warm, inviting Atrium just beyond the glass, a stark contrast with the bridge. The lights were dimmed, both to enable the glowing displays to be more easily read and also to showcase the shining atmosphere of the planet below the ship, just visible from the deck's vast viewport.

Captain Dicto drew Leia's attention to the large circular display unit built into the floor between the Atrium window and the rest of the bridge. He adjusted the controls to showcase the *Halcyon*'s flight path. "As you can see," he said, gesturing from the display to the viewport, "we're cruising over Yotch now. We'll be spending a few hours over this world, circling it so that it's viewable from both port side and starboard."

The dot on the display did nothing to reveal how lovely the world below was from the viewport. "Go ahead," Captain Dicto said, smiling.

Leia crossed between the navigation and bay loader consoles, leaning forward to get as close to the viewport as she could. Beyond, hanging in impossible beauty, was an orange-red planet with streaks of bright silver clouds swirling over the surface.

A nearby crew person—a petite Cerean woman with curly white hair—glanced up from the console she'd been working on. Leia shot her a smile. "It's a beautiful planet," she said.

"Totally uninhabitable," the Cerean woman responded. "Yotch is covered in rheoscopic fluid, which gives it that colorful effect."

"Like glitter floating over liquid." Leia moved her hands, trying to match the smooth flow of the shining particles on the surface of the planet.

"There's a high concentration of iron—that's the red color—but it's in its gaseous form, and swirling with mercurial alloy," the woman continued.

"The planet is a failed star," Captain Dicto added. He looked down at it fondly. "It is essentially boiling metal and constantly shifting in superhot, superfast storms. We are actually watching this gas giant die," he continued. "The iron has made the fusion processes endothermic, and the world will slowly grow colder and colder until it's a solid lump of ash."

"So give it a few millennia," the Cerean woman added, "and Yotch may become inhabitable."

"Unless it explodes," Captain Dicto pointed out in a matter-of-fact voice. "It's too early to tell, but there's a chance this world will cool too quickly, and the gravitational potential energy will create a . . ." He waved his hand, searching for the right word.

"Big boom?" the Cerean woman provided.

"*Big* boom."

Leia watched the world below them, writhing in silvers and reds, in awe that there was, so close and yet so far away, a planet made of gaseous metal, swirling in beauty toward its own death, which would either provide life or explode violently. How small the *Halcyon* was compared with this failed star, how brief their time sailing next to it given the thousands of years that would pass before its fate was seen to fruition. And while they waited, the world was banded in glittering light that reflected starshine, burning.

For a moment, Leia's eyes unfocused, and she saw the gleaming reflection of the Atrium on the window across from the massive forward viewports. "You know," she told the captain, "this is the best view on the whole ship."

Captain Dicto beamed at her, pride radiating off him.

"You may want to consider letting guests see this," Leia continued. "Not just so they can get a glimpse of the awe of space, but also to see the bridge, to understand just how much the ship relies on your whole team to work together. It's really amazing."

Captain Dicto's brow furrowed. "It's rather untraditional to allow guests on the bridge," he said. "But I'll consider it."

"You should come back tomorrow," the Cerean woman said. "If you think Yotch is beautiful, wait until you see the meteor storms."

Leia remembered what Riyola had told her about the itinerary. Before she could comment on it, the captain continued.

"The iron in Yotch and indeed in particles throughout this sector are what cause the aurora display that you'll see tomorrow," he said. "The Esseveya system is renowned for the pillars of light on display, produced by a combination of magnetic waves reacting to the elements in this particular part of the galaxy. It's a rare phenomenon and quite a treat."

Leia's heart sank at the reminder that they would be going through that part of the sector rather than toward the Lenguin system, which held the moon Madurs and a possible powerful ally that could counteract lingering Imperial undermining.

"Is it dangerous?" Leia asked. "Riyola mentioned something about a warning . . ."

"Oh, nothing to worry about," Captain Dicto said. "The high density of composite particles throughout that area makes lightspeed dangerous, but the *Halcyon* has more than enough shields, to say nothing of our defensive cannons!" He clapped the Cerean woman on the shoulder, and she grinned—after regaining her composure.

"We also have twelve proton torpedo launch tubes, in the event of emergency," she told Leia. "Even if every meteor in the storm decided to fall on us, we could easily blast through."

"It's just . . ." Leia started. "I saw on the flight path that there was an alternative route, one that went through the Lenguin system . . ."

Captain Dicto gave out a big boom of a laugh. "Don't you worry," he told Leia. "Nothing—*nothing*—can take my ship off her intended course."

Leia sighed, although she hoped no one could see her disappointment. It had always been a long shot to get the ship to turn a tourist excursion into an ambassador mission, but . . .

Leia followed the captain as he led her around the bridge, introducing crew members and highlighting their roles. Leia made a point to praise them all, to smile at the X-0X units, to provide some good sound clips for the feeds.

At one station, Captain Dicto shifted from magnanimous host to the leader he was. Leia hung back out of respect, but she still heard his commanding voice as he spoke with the fuel technician. "It's the saracore blend that we're running low on," the human man told the captain. "I've got the engineering team monitoring the rhydonium fuel manifold, but the prices for the saracore blend are already increasing. If we bypass the central sublight compressor we can conserve some energy, but Synjax has already stated they will be unable to provide any additional resources for refueling."

It was as Leia feared—the galaxy revolved around fuel. If a ship like the *Halcyon* was feeling the pinch of low resources so soon after the end of the war, that would trickle down to other ships across the galaxy soon enough. Leia was no expert on fuel blends, but it didn't take a leap in logic to assume that there was already a break in the supply chain. The Anoat sector's Tibanna gas would absolutely affect which ships could enter hyperspace. A luxury liner like the *Halcyon* would find a way to make ends meet, surely, but this would hurt smaller businesses and individuals who needed to cross the galaxy.

While Captain Dicto spoke with the fuel technician, Leia turned her attention to the rest of the crew on the bridge. They were used to her presence now, and while the *Halcyon* cruised around Yotch, there was little to do beyond monitor the systems. Leia caught snippets of conversation happening all around her.

"My sister said the parties on Coruscant were *epic*—"

"Yeah, before the riots broke out."

"I'd like to get home after this round, check in with my folks. They're Mid Rim, you know, and the unrest there is . . ."

"My buddy from flight school is a long-haul freighter captain, and he said that the hyperspace lanes aren't safe now, not unless the new government . . ."

Voices swirled around Leia's mind like the red-and-silver glow of the rheoscopic fluid on Yotch. Already, the galaxy after the Empire was in a state of unknown similar to the planet—either it would settle down and become inhabitable or it would explode, destroying everything in its wake.

Time would tell.

CHAPTER 23

HAN

HAN HAD PREVIOUSLY HAD EVERY intention of spending every minute on the *Halcyon* stretched out on the bed in their suite, but the appeal of such an itinerary was somewhat diminished when Leia left him alone in the cabin.

Hunger won out.

Han threw on his clothes, raked his hand through his hair, and headed to the dining room below the Atrium. Rather than stay and share a table with someone—it was too early for small talk with strangers—Han grabbed a pastry filled with some sort of brown stuff and a bottle of pale-orange liquid that could be sunburst juice. He bit into the pastry as he ducked back out of the dining room. The brown was sweet with a kick of spice, melting in his mouth. He devoured the entire thing before he got to the turbolift, wiping flaky crumbs from his shirt.

While he waited for the lift, Han considered grabbing more of the pastries to store in his cabin for later. Before he had a chance to talk himself into it, though, he realized that he was near the Engineering Room—and the brig.

Maybe he should check in on his friend from last night.

The doors to the turbolift dinged, but Han ignored them, veering toward the brig.

The little jail was small, far less comfortable than the suite Han shared with Leia. On the bench built into the wall, a man sat, his head hanging down.

"Hey, Kelad," Han said. "Nice digs."

"You!" Kelad jumped up and crossed the few steps to the locked door keeping him out of Han's reach. "Can you *please* just tell these people that this was all a misunderstanding? I would never hurt your wife!"

Han popped the top off the bottle of juice and took a swig. Not sunburst juice—it was sour citrella, and it made his lips pucker. Han forced it down without making a face. "You only wouldn't hurt her now that you know I'm her husband," he stated flatly.

"No!" Kelad groaned. "I'm just an idiot."

"A desperate idiot," Han said. "The worst kind."

Kelad seemingly gave up, heading back to the bunk and collapsing on it. His shoulders sagged. The man looked miserable, but Han had no sympathy. He was down on his luck because he'd bet with the Empire. The Empire's loss was Kelad's loss, and he had no one to blame but himself.

"You!" Wozzakk, the Ugnaught engineer, rounded the corner. "You have no business here! Get out, or I put you with him!" He jerked a thumb at the brig.

"Hey, now," Han said, throwing his hands up to show he was harmless. "I was just checking on the situation."

The Ugnaught growled, the sound deep in the back of his throat. Before he could say anything else, the Nautolan, Zalma, came down the corridor.

"It's a regular reunion," Han mumbled, but Zalma heard him and scowled. Although the brig area was fully accessible, unlike the locked room that had held the card game, Han could tell the crew wasn't comfortable with him lingering nearby.

"Is it my fault the brig happens to be right here?" Han asked.

"No, it's the Empire's." Zalma's flat tone caught him off guard, and at

Han's widened eyes, the Nautolan explained. "The *Halcyon* never had need for a brig before. The Empire installed it. We'd planned to repurpose this area for storage, but . . ."

"Turns out you needed it," Han said.

"I was going to comm you," the chief engineer told Han with a tired sigh. "I have to speak to the captain about what to do with someone who didn't pay for passage on the ship—"

"Stowaway!" Wozzakk growled, snarling at Kelad.

"—but I needed to ask if you wanted to press any charges against this man for his threats against Princess Leia."

Kelad looked up. "Press . . . charges?" He looked visibly distressed by the idea. "I didn't mean any harm!"

Han gave him a look. He almost wished he could have scared the fellow a little more, roughed him up some, and been done with it. This data-brainer probably spent his life with his nose stuck in a holo and his skull full of schematics. Han was no fan of any threat against anyone he loved, but was this scrap of a person an actual threat?

"I was in the Republic Futures Program!" Kelad wailed. "I can't be arrested!"

Han cleared his throat, waiting until both Kelad and the engineers were focused on him. "I reckon we don't need to get the authorities involved," he said slowly. He looked through the brig to Kelad. "If he ever proves to be a legitimate problem, I have *zero* doubt I can take care of it myself."

Kelad actually trembled. "I'm not a problem!" he swore. "I just— I need another chance. I have ideas—big ones! I can change the galaxy!" His attention shifted to Zalma. "I had a chance to look at your engines."

"Not allowed!" Wozzakk interjected. "Absolutely no passengers allowed in that area!"

"But listen—you're not operating at full efficiency! If you'd let me get my hands on your hyperdrive flux coil, I think I could reconfigure the element base and make the engines at least fifteen percent more efficient."

"Which engine?" Han muttered. "Aren't there thirteen?"

"You're not going to quick-talk your way out of this," Zalma told Kelad.

But Wozzakk was tapping a finger on one of the fangs protruding past his lower lip. "Yeah, okay, maybe you have big idea," he muttered, clearly considering Kelad's proposition.

Well, that was for them to figure out. Han was happy enough to focus on only one engine at a time. With nothing to add to the conversation, he left, dropping the half-drunk bottle of sour citrella in the receptacle at the end of the corridor.

As much as he intended to get more pastries for the cabin, by the time he went back into the Crown of Corellia dining room, there was nothing but slim pickings left. Giving up, Han headed to the turbolifts to meet Leia. Two men stepped onto a lift with him before the door closed.

"Did you hear?" one of the men told his companion. "Princess Leia Organa is on this ship!"

"Oh, stars, I love her," the second man said.

"Anyabe commed me to tell me she's in the climate simulator right now," the first man said.

Great. Kelad had been opportunistic but ultimately far too inept to pull off a ransom threat. But if Leia was so well known that strangers on a lift could discuss where she was, it wouldn't be hard for someone with more skills than Kelad to do some serious damage.

And Han couldn't be there every time.

She's been a princess for a long time, Han told himself. *She doesn't need constant protection. She can—and has—taken care of herself.*

Still, when the lift doors opened, Han barreled between the other two men, knocking them aside and stepping in front of them before they had a chance to get to the climate simulator before him. "Rude," one of them muttered, but Han didn't care.

She is perfectly capable on her own, Han thought as he strode down the corridor. *But—*

He just wanted to make sure she knew that she didn't have to be.

CHAPTER 24

LEIA

AFTER TOURING THE BRIDGE, LEIA had been gratified that the climate simulator was empty. While Captain Dicto had done everything possible to make the bridge welcoming to her, Leia had been unable to completely remove the X-0X units from her vision. It was never good to be too aware of recording units—Leia knew that playing for the cams made for a stiff, false appearance. Unfortunately, the more aware she was of the recorders, the harder it became to ignore them, creating a vicious cycle.

But there were no recording units in the climate simulator. No people, either.

The *Halcyon* glided through the stars so effortlessly that Leia could not feel the rumble of the engines, the vibrations of power. The ship would continue to cruise around Yotch for a few more hours before entering hyperspace and getting to the Esseveya light show. If Leia could have just convinced the captain to alter the course, go to Madurs instead, visiting the ice crystal palaces of that moon and allowing her a chance to lay the groundwork for entering the system into the new republic she hoped to build . . .

Nothing can take my ship off her intended course.

That was what Captain Dicto had said, with the same conviction Leia had spoken with during the Rebellion. She was frustrated to not be able to truly work right now, but what was really bothering her was the fact that she was no longer in control.

Leia had worked with the generals and high council of the Alliance long enough to know that something as grand as a galaxy-wide upheaval of power took more than one person in charge. Ultimately, Leia suspected that the historians of the future would call the mere fact of the Rebel Alliance's cooperation the reason why they had won and Emperor Palpatine had lost. Imperial leadership had been full of singular voices, each one looking out for themselves individually more than the greater whole. The Alliance had won because it had prized the exact opposite mentality.

And yet—

Leia was used to at least being heard, her opinion considered and weighed. Captain Dicto's insistence that the *Halcyon* would not alter course bothered her because she was entirely excluded from any part of his decision.

No—what truly bothered her was the knowledge that it was fair that she be excluded. She was a passenger. Captain Dicto was not the Emperor. He listened—to his crew. What right did she have to suggest the entire ship alter course merely for . . .

For a chance at strengthening the new republic trying to form after war.

Leia groaned aloud in frustration, the sound swallowed up by the serene manufactured waterfall behind the bench. Perhaps if she approached Captain Dicto from that angle, explaining that going to Madurs was not simply a matter of her whims but a chance to aid the galaxy as a whole . . .

But should she? The war was over. Part of the point of her being on this ship was to prove that she no longer had to sacrifice every joy for the good of the galaxy.

Part of the point of her *marriage* was the same.

Leia's eyes fell on the stones artfully arranged on the garden island in front of her. She had not had much time to question Luke about the Force, either before or after the fall of the Death Star, but when he spoke of it, he described it as if the Force illuminated the right path for him to take, assuring him of not only its possibility but its inevitability. It seemed to her that the Force was a type of assurance that provided confidence.

If her brother was right about her—if she could access even a bit of the Force, enough to know what she should do . . .

Focusing on the stones, Leia tried to empty her mind. Luke had never given her any instruction—there had hardly been any time—but she had watched him meditate often enough before she had known that he was her brother. That she may have a similar power to his.

She tried to push his words out of her mind. It was too overwhelming to consider his offer before she'd gotten married. Leia bit back a bitter laugh at her own expense. She had been so certain of the path to take when she had to choose between Han and Luke. But now that she had Han, she was turning to the Force—it was hard for her not to think of it as *Luke's* Force—for guidance.

It's not Luke's Force, a little voice whispered in her mind. *It's his, too.* Vader's.

Leia's mind slammed shut in a way that felt physical, violent. She would not think about *him*.

About the fact that he was her . . .

Bile rose in Leia's throat. No. She would not think about that. Any of it.

She would think of nothing at all. Wasn't that what meditation was supposed to be? Didn't Luke say the Force was like a presence that could be felt if she would just reach for it and nothing else?

Leia closed her eyes and let out a shaky breath. Darth Vader had watched as her homeworld died. Destroyed her childhood. Slaughtered her parents. Tortured her mentally and physically, leaving her with scars that no one could see but that she still felt.

He had taken so much from her.

He would *not* take the Force as well.

She would not let him.

And in that thought, Leia wanted to become a Jedi more than she had ever been tempted to with Luke's promising words. The idea that it was something she could reclaim from his dead and grasping hands . . .

There was nothing but blackness behind Leia's eyelids. These thoughts flared her mind with rage—they were not calming, peaceful meditations.

Focus.

She needed to focus.

On . . . nothing.

She tried again, releasing a controlled breath and emptying her mind. Or, trying to. Perhaps simply being present in the moment would be good enough. She breathed in the climate simulator's air, designed to replicate the warm but salty sea breeze of their final destination, Synjax.

But sweet-scented balmy atmosphere did not fill her lungs.

Instead, there was a heaviness to the air. It was cool and thick. A shiver ran down her spine, and her skin felt damp, as if she'd been standing in heavy fog, not on a sunny, tropical beach. Even though the *Halcyon* was a perfectly stable ship, Leia's stomach swooped as if she were on an unsteady surface—but there was a rhythm to the feeling, like swinging.

Instinct told Leia that if she opened her eyes, she would see the climate simulator. The cold, damp feeling of heavy fog, the slightly acidic humid air, the swaying in her body—that would all disappear. Her grasp on this environment was so tentative that Leia knew it would be easy to break.

Instead, she focused harder on what this feeling was. She felt displaced, not just in space but also time. She wanted, desperately, to find some meaning in this sensation. Was this a vision that would guide her? Had she triggered it by her own thoughts?

Leia's jaw tightened. The more she questioned the sensation, the more it slipped away. Already the smells of the blossoming bosha filled her nostrils, and the sounds of the manufactured waterfall behind her were breaking through . . . through low voices. She could hear *words*. What language was that? Pak Pak?

As soon as she tried to nail down the specifics, the sensation fled from her mind. Leia's eyes opened slowly, but even as she focused on the rocks on the island garden in front of her, the traces of her vision were fading to nothing.

She had been thinking of other planets, potential connections, worlds that could join the Republic—she had imagined it all.

"Why can't this be easy?" Leia asked the rocks. Why must she fight for everything—not just independence within the galaxy but also an understanding of her own self? Meanwhile, her brother could raise his hand—

Leia raised her hand.

—and Luke could just waggle his fingers—

Leia curled her own fingers inward.

—and *move* things with his *mind*.

The rocks on the island garden shifted forward several centimeters.

Leia dropped her arm and her mouth simultaneously. Had—had *she* done that?

She tried again.

The rocks didn't move.

Leia stared at them a beat longer, but nothing happened. The *Halcyon* must have shifted in flight, enough to make the small rocks slide forward. She hadn't noticed the other rocks or the plants shift because she'd been so focused on those rocks. Leia felt silly—at least there was no one here to witness her trying to move rocks with her brain.

And then she heard a footstep.

Leia jumped up, spinning around, but it was just Han. Han with his easy smile and his hands raised as if Leia were a startled bafle that he'd spooked in the forest. "What were you thinking about?" he asked. "You were so focused."

Leia laughed, hoping that he couldn't detect the bitterness in her voice. "Believe it or not, I was trying—very hard, actually—not to think about anything."

Han gave her one of his cocky smiles, the kind that sometimes exasperated her but today seemed endearing. He held his arms wider, motioning for her to step into his embrace, and she did so, gratefully.

With his arms around her, firm and sure, Leia felt every thought that had clouded her mind evaporate. This was the nothing-bliss she had tried so hard to hold on to before.

This was peace.

CHAPTER 25

HAN

LEIA TUCKED HER HEAD UNDER Han's chin, her arms wrapping around him. The perfect fit. Even something as silly as their heights—he towered above her the same way Chewie towered over him—made it seem as if they weren't compatible at all, but instead they were perfect.

Han dropped a kiss on her head; then she rose up on her toes, claiming a different sort of kiss from her husband. Leia's lips parted, a tiny, satisfied gasp escaping before he deepened their embrace. His arms shifted lower down her back, holding her against his body, lifting her a few centimeters from the floor. He supported her weight easily—hell, he was ready to kick down the door and carry her right back up to their cabin.

Han's lips moved from Leia's mouth, down her chin, to that soft place in the corner of her neck, that delicious little spot that he'd wanted to kiss from just about the first moment he laid eyes on her. She smelled of clean things—rain and soap and flowers—and it drove him wild. From the way Leia's back shivered beneath his hands, he knew she wasn't unaffected by his touch, and that? That made it all the better.

"All right, all right," Leia said, gasping and swatting at his chest. "We're in public."

"No one here but us," Han said, barely raising his lips from her skin to answer.

Leia wriggled against him, and Han loosened his grip. She didn't pull away entirely, but she put a little space between them. Disappointing. "Anyone could come inside," she said by way of excuse.

Han shrugged. "The entire galaxy knows by now that you're on your honeymoon," he pointed out. "What do they expect us to do, hold hands and kiss each other on the cheek, all chaste-like?"

"No, but . . ." Leia floundered.

Han took the opportunity to close the distance between them again. "But what, sweetheart?" he said, his lips curving up.

Except Leia didn't throw herself into his arms. Instead she took several steps back and threw up her arms, frustrated. "Someone's *always* watching. I have to be careful."

Han frowned. "You're right. Someone *is* always watching you. That's the problem. If you'd just stayed in the cabin like I suggested, I wouldn't even have been worried about you."

Leia blinked. "Worried?"

Great. The tooka-cat was out of the bag now. "You're too—" He waved his hands in her general direction.

Leia cocked her hip and put her hands on her waist, eyes flashing. "Too *what?*" she snarled.

"Too visible," Han said. "Everyone on this ship—everyone off this ship, too, everyone in the whole galaxy, seems like—always knows where you are."

Leia opened her mouth to snap at him, but then her eyes turned calculating. "What aren't you telling me?" she demanded.

Han sighed. "Last night, there was a card player. Some bum down on his luck. He figured he'd make some credits with sabacc, but when that didn't pan out, he contemplated kidnapping you for ransom instead. And just now on the lift, people were talking about you."

"People always talk about me."

"But talking about you like they knew where you were. Because they did. They knew you'd be here." Had that pair from the lift followed him to the climate simulator, Han knew Leia wouldn't have kissed him like she just did. It wasn't right that other people got to dictate how she acted just because they kept tabs on where she was.

Leia shook her head, refocusing. "A ransom?" she asked. "Do I need to inform Alliance Intelligence?" She spoke quietly, half to herself, then turned her attention to Han. "Was he working with someone specific? The Hutts? The Empire?"

Han shook his head. "No, he's just an opportunistic idiot who couldn't have kidnapped you if you showed up in his luggage frozen in carbonite." Han ran his fingers through his hair. "But don't worry about him. I took care of it."

Leia, rather than taking his advice, absolutely did look worried about him. "Took care of it how?" she asked, her brow furrowing.

Han laughed, remembering the way Kelad's face had twisted in fear on the other side of the viewport in the escape pod. "I wasn't going to throw him off the ship," he said.

Leia's eyes grew wide. "You were going to throw him off the ship?" she repeated.

"No, I said I *wasn't* going to, not really."

"Han."

"Leia."

"Han, do you have *any idea* how bad that would have been? You can't just toss people off the ship if they disagree with you."

"We didn't 'disagree'! He was going to *kidnap you*."

Leia waved her hand as if none of that mattered. "Yes, but you said he wouldn't really."

"No, I said he couldn't. Not wouldn't. There's a difference."

"That doesn't mean you throw him off the ship!"

"I said I wasn't really going to!" How was that for a double standard? Han was being yelled at for threatening to do a thing he didn't do, while Leia was sticking up for Kelad for threatening to do a thing he didn't do. "Also, he was a stowaway!" he added.

"So?" Leia snapped. "What—exactly—did *you* do?" She raised both her hands, her fingers curled as if she wanted nothing more than to wrap her hands around Han's throat and throttle him. "Do I need to remind you that part of the point of this trip is the good publicity it will bring to the newly forming republic, and that murdering dissenters is not good publicity?"

"I wasn't going to throw him out a hatch," Han said, rolling his eyes as he over-enunciated each word. "I just tricked him into going into an escape pod."

Leia made a noise somewhere between a growl and a scream.

"He threatened you!" Han protested.

"I can take care of myself!" Leia shouted.

"Then why am I here?" Han roared back.

The silence that followed was deafening. Leia glared, working her jaw.

"Why are we here?" Han said, his voice low, like the calm after the storm. "You're going off on bridge tours and greeting guests like you're the host at a fancy party."

"And you're roughing up strangers in escape pods."

Han cracked a smile. "When you put it like that."

Despite herself, Leia laughed.

"You know," Han said, "some people would call what I did brave."

"Others would call it foolish." Leia's eyes slid away from him, but he caught the corners of her lips twisting up before she bit back the smile. "I have to go to the brig, see how bad this is."

"I told you, it's handled."

"By you?"

"By ship security."

Leia shot him a look that told him clearly how much doubt she cast on his role in the situation, then strode past him, out of the climate simulator. Han stood there a second longer. The little room was designed to be a miniature version of Synjax, a paradise planet. It was warm and balmy, with sweet-scented flowers and a fresh waterfall.

What was going on that all they could do was bicker when surrounded by all this?

Shaking himself, Han headed after Leia. She stopped in front of the turbolift. "I don't even know where the brig is," she said in a low voice.

"This way." Han pulled her away from the lift toward the stairs, heading down one flight. He led her to the engineering corridor, veering to the brig.

Captain Dicto was already there, as well as the chief engineer. It was clear they were uncomfortable with the situation—since the brig was visible to any guest who came this way, anyone aboard the *Halcyon* would see they had a prisoner.

"Ah, Princess Leia," Captain Dicto said. "I was just being informed of the situation. I apologize for . . ." He trailed off, seemingly at a loss for how specific his regrets should be.

"It's not your fault," Leia said. "And indeed, I commend everyone on the *Halcyon* for their quick action."

Han felt his face sink into a sardonic look, although his wife didn't notice. The *Halcyon* crew acted quickly? All they'd done was interrupt.

While Leia spoke with the captain, Han's gaze shifted to Kelad. The man looked positively sick, and he couldn't take his eyes off Leia. Not in a threatening way—he gazed at her with a mixture of awe and horror, as if he couldn't believe the actions he'd contemplated.

Without even noticing the way Han watched him, Kelad threw himself at the brig's door. "Your Highness!" he shouted. "Princess, I'm sorry. I wouldn't have—I didn't mean anything by my words!"

Han watched as Leia turned from the captain to Kelad. "You don't seem like a violent man," she said, her face serene. Han was almost jealous—she didn't look at *him* that way. But he could tell that this was a mask. That reminded him of Qi'ra, his old flame. She'd been most dangerous when she was smiling, too. And from that glint in Leia's eyes? She wanted to gut Kelad like a scalefish. Han almost laughed. Kelad was bending over backward to ingratiate himself because he thought Leia fit his idea of a prim, perfect princess when the reality was she was the perfect fighter, too.

Kelad shook his head violently. "Let me explain," he pleaded. Then he stopped, as if expecting an argument rather than everyone—including Han, the captain, and the chief engineer—waiting for him to continue. "It's just," he said, flustered by the eyes on him. "I have skills. I headed the gravity manipulation department at Mitikin Industries." He looked around eagerly, clearly expecting them all to have heard of it.

"On Coruscant," Leia whispered to Han. Kelad heard and nodded, grinning, clearly pleased that someone recognized his workplace.

Captain Dicto frowned. "They had contracts with the Empire."

"It was a paycheck only!" Kelad protested. "I'm not political!" Then he turned back to Leia. "But I could be. I can help with the new government. My tractor beam technology revolutionized the process!"

Han watched as Leia processed this information, no doubt coming to the same conclusion that he had—this man had been behind a desk, but he made Imperial ships better at killing rebel ones. Still . . . it was a paycheck. Han didn't want to think too closely about how many people—himself included—had done things or would have done things for the Empire for a paycheck. Not everyone had the luxury of even knowing the Rebellion was an option. Hell, he himself had it thrust in his lap when he was also just looking for a paycheck in the form of Luke and the old man. He hadn't cared then where the credits had come from; it was just by the luck of the stars that it happened to be at the hands of the good guys.

Han bunched his hands in his pockets. He had done a lot of things he wasn't proud of. He'd worn the wrong uniform before he found the right one. He couldn't say he'd exactly been an asset to the Empire during his brief stint as a soldier, but had he the brains to work on some engineering facility on Coruscant, he probably would have done some of the things Kelad had. For a paycheck.

Han looked away from the prisoner, toward his wife. That was a line he knew he wouldn't have crossed, though. Kidnapping an innocent a war hero—for ransom? No. He may run every scam in the galaxy, but at least he was honest about it.

Captain Dicto turned Leia aside. "Our problem is that while this man didn't see through his plan, it would have been catastrophic had he done so . . ."

Leia nodded. "It would have been a shadow over the *Halcyon*'s first launch after Imperial control . . ."

"Not the point," Han muttered.

"And the feeds would have blown this up—that someone would kidnap the Rebellion's heroine within days of the Empire's defeat. The longer we keep him in the brig, the more chance this has of getting out, turning into a story we cannot control."

"Also not the point." No one noticed Han grumbling. Could these people only think about how bad the media would be if Leia had been kidnapped? What about his wife being *kidnapped*?

"But he didn't *do* anything," Leia said, considering.

"He's a stowaway," Zalma, the chief engineer, interjected.

"There is that," Captain Dicto said. "Typically, though, that's a crime that could be made up for with labor, not time in the brig." That made sense at least—keeping Kelad in the brig would give him the thing he really wanted, free passage to the final destination. Working off the debt paid for the ticket he didn't have.

"He is rather adept at engineering," Zalma offered. "I've spoken with him, and the man knows the trade."

"All I want is work!" Kelad offered, hope in his eyes. "I lost my contracts—"

"Because they were with the Empire," Han said.

Kelad's feeble resolve faltered, but he rallied. "I do the job, and I do it well. And while, yes, I came here mostly to get to Synjax and meet an investor, I also really wanted to see the *Halcyon*'s engines myself. They're famous—I did my thesis on the Drabor Configuration!"

The captain and the chief engineer exchanged looks. Han groaned. He could see exactly where this was going.

"Good thing this would-be kidnapper who was a threat to the highest-ranked guest on the ship has *skills*," Han said, loudly enough this time to draw the others' attention. "Guess we should just let him play with your ship's engines and give him exactly what he wants as punishment."

Captain Dicto opened his mouth to speak, but Leia cut him off. "What if, as a compromise, Kelad spends his nights in the brig. He doesn't have a proper berth after all, and it seems fitting. But during the day, he works with the engineers, using his skills to make up for his crimes."

"That seems fair!" Kelad said quickly.

"Of course it does," Han growled, "to you."

Zalma turned to Han. "I'll keep a close eye on him," he said. His Nautolan eyes were huge and unblinking, which was both unnerving and somewhat reassuring. As Captain Dicto moved to release the prisoner, Zalma said in a low voice only Han could hear, "If he tries anything, I'll put him in an escape pod myself."

CHAPTER 26

LEIA

CAPTAIN DICTO ESCORTED LEIA AND Han from the brig, profusely thanking Leia for her assistance in such a tricky situation. Leia glanced at Han. Technically, they should all be thanking him for rooting out the problem in the first place, but since his solution would have been an even bigger nightmare—honestly, how could he expect to get away with something like that, on a ship as well monitored as this one?—she supposed there was nothing really left to say.

"If there is anything else I can do for you—" the captain started.

"Well," Leia said, slowly. It was between meals, so the corridors were crowded, but everyone seemed busy enough to not pay them too much attention.

"Yes?" Captain Dicto asked.

Leia took a deep breath. She didn't look at Han; if she did, she'd lose her nerve. Instead, she stood squarely in front of the captain and looked him in the eye. "I think you need to reconsider the ship's flight path," she said, full of confidence. "As you pointed out, the *Halcyon* is being closely monitored by the feeds. While I know the ship is up to the task, do we really want to risk anything as dangerous as a meteor storm?"

"I would never take the *Halcyon* anywhere dangerous," the captain said. His chest puffed out a little, and Leia immediately recognized this as a reflection of how some people were besotted with their ship. Her eyes went straight to Han.

His gaze pulled to hers like a tractor beam. He contemplated her, clearly calculating what she was trying to do. With a tiny, almost imperceptible nod, Han said, "Captain Dicto, what's this I hear about a meteor storm?"

The captain waved his hand. "It's nothing, really—precursor to the light show in the Esseveya system."

Han's eyes widened. "The Esseveya system?" His tone was incredulous.

"Yes. The *Halcyon* has gone this route countless times. It's very popular with the guests."

"Sure it is," Han scoffed. "This is going to be a *memorable* trip. Hey, any chance I can be on the bridge? Get a tour like Leia did? I've always wanted a front-row seat to the damage that storm can do."

"It's really not—"

"Of course. Normally. I've been through there plenty of times on my ship. The *Millennium Falcon,* have you heard of it? Fastest runner in the galaxy." At the captain's blank look, some of Han's bravado faded, but he plowed forward. "I've seen the meteor storms of Esseveya. I take it you've sent scouts ahead to ensure the extra burst has settled down by now?"

"Extra burst?"

Han squared his shoulders. "When was the last time you went through Esseveya?" he demanded.

The captain shrugged, an uncharacteristic movement that showed his growing concern. "With the escalation of the war, it's been . . . nearly a year since I've taken this route." He spoke with a tone of dawning realization that so much time had passed.

"Oh."

Leia could not believe her eyes. All Han had to do was say that one word—*Oh*—and the captain's nerves twisted inside him like a spitting viper. And Han *knew* it. Seeing Han play someone was a work of wonder. As long as she wasn't the one being played.

"Oh?" Captain Dicto said when Han pointedly did not continue. "Why?"

"Nothing."

"No, what is it?"

"I'm sure you've had the extra scouting droids check everything."

Captain Dicto watched as a few people strolled from the turbolift toward the dining room, seeking a late breakfast or an early lunch, Leia wasn't sure which. "We of course cleared our path prior to departure," the captain said in a lower voice to Han. "But you're right; it has been quite some time since I personally last traversed through the Esseveya way. I value any insight you have."

Han shrugged. "It's just, *I* wouldn't take my ship full of passengers through a meteor storm that's *particularly* active. You've gotta think, Captain, with this war? There's been a lot of extra debris floating through space. The meteor storms are already filled with rocks, but add some collateral damage . . . makes things unpredictable." Han waited a beat. "But it'll be a pretty light show for the guests as huge chunks of doonium burn up in manelle gas clouds."

"I didn't think manelle reacted that strongly to doonium," Leia piped up.

"Not entirely," Han allowed. "I guess it'd be more accurate to say that *partially* melted hunks of doonium are speeding through the overly active meteor storm that's been experiencing violent bursts rather than saying they're entirely disintegrating."

"Partially," Leia repeated pleasantly.

Captain Dicto, meanwhile, looked sick. "I had not gotten news that the meteor storms held this many unpredictable variables."

"Not always," Han shrugged. "Changes almost by the day. You said it, though—unpredictable variables."

Captain Dicto nodded, mostly to himself, as if convincing himself of something. He glanced down at Leia. "And you've been to Madurs?" he asked. "You can vouch for it being a good alternative stop for the ship?"

Leia had not been to Madurs, but she'd seen enough in her records and in Major Nioma's dossier to know that, since it had avoided Imperial takeover, it would certainly suit the elites aboard. She'd recognized at least a dozen people in the Atrium from the art gallery charities she'd attended as a senator.

"Actually," Leia said, shooting Captain Dicto a brilliant smile, "I've been in communication with Prime Minister Yens recently, and he personally invited me to come to the moon. Since the last Imperial Art Expo was years ago, they're eager to host art enthusiasts and nature lovers again. The ice palaces are galaxy-renowned."

"I'll need to consult my navigator and the cruise director," the captain muttered. His gaze refocused on Han and Leia. "May I mention your name to the prime minister should I request a landed excursion on the moon?"

"Of course," Leia murmured, but inside, she was bounding with joy. Not only would she get to see Madurs, but bringing a literal shipload of tourists to the moon's ice palaces would prove to Prime Minister Yens that she had something valuable to offer. Perhaps they could build in additional tourism or other trade as a part of their negotiation deal when she convinced the prime minister to join the new government.

"Thank you, both of you," Captain Dicto said. "Your insight is invaluable." With a small, respectful nod, the captain bade them farewell.

He had made no promises, but the captain seemed to seriously be considering rerouting the ship to Madurs. Although farther away, they'd actually get there sooner than they would get to Esseveya, thanks to being able to use the hyperdrive rather than cruising slowly through the meteor storm and the colorful aurora-type display. Leia needed to get back to the cabin, send a follow-up message to the prime minister, and learn more about the moon so she could be prepared.

If she played this right, Leia might just be able to give herself a new world's acceptance into the growing new republic as a wedding gift.

CHAPTER 27

HAN

HAN WAITED UNTIL THEY WERE back in the cabin before he said, "So, what's the real reason for this little detour? Obviously you're working some angle for the Reb—" He stopped himself, not yet used to thinking the war was over, but then he floundered, unsure of what to call a government not yet properly formed.

Leia beamed at him, eyes alight with excitement. "Remember the briefing before we left? There's a moon in the Lenguin system that has carnium. It was an Imperial target for mining, and with the way the Empire is covertly trying to undermine resources, it's a prime place to visit and set up some strong alliances."

Han blinked at her. "You just talked a star cruiser with hundreds of passengers into diverting its path so that you can play at being an ambassador?"

Leia's face fell—first to disappointment, but then quickly twisting into anger. "First of all, *you* helped me talk Captain Dicto into this. And second, it's not 'playing' at being an ambassador. I *am* an ambassador. I take that seriously."

"You sure do." Han breezed past her, flopping onto the neatly made bed, sending the perfectly arranged pillows bouncing onto the floor.

"I don't see why you're upset," Leia said. She crossed her arms, staring down at Han's supine body.

"Of course you don't, Ambassador." Han rolled his eyes.

"Then why don't you tell me, General?"

Han didn't like her tone—mostly because she'd never speak that way to any of the other generals. The ones she respected. He propped himself up on the bed with his elbows, the better to glare at her. "Listen, sweetheart, if this trip was a mission, you should have informed my secretary to add it to my schedule. I *thought* we were going on our honeymoon."

"I'll have Chewie adjust your agenda then," Leia snapped.

Han threw himself back onto the bed, staring at the ceiling.

"It's not that big of a deal!" Leia protested. "What do you even care about seeing the meteor storm at the aurora in Esseveya?"

"I *don't*," Han told the ceiling. "I care about the way you keep mixing business with pleasure." He sat up. He wasn't arguing with the ship; he was arguing with Leia. "First, you spend more time with the recording droids than you do with me. Fine, I know you told Mon you'd help out with that when she gave us the cruise. But then you care more about your image than the fact that someone wanted to kidnap you," he said, counting up her misdemeanors on his fingers.

"Kelad is too incompetent to be a threat."

"Not the point!" Han shouted. "And now you've shifted the course of the whole star cruiser just so you can take more time away to butter up some chancellor of a random moon—"

"Madurs has a prime minister."

"—over mining rights on the off chance of snagging an alliance."

"Why did you back me up, then?" Leia said. "If you were so against going to Madurs, why did you help me convince Captain Dicto that we should go there?"

Han shot to the edge of the bed and stood up, throwing his hands into the air. "Because you're my wife!" he shouted. "If you're running a con, I'll *always* back you up!"

That made Leia's mouth snap shut, her teeth audibly clacking together. She let out a shaky breath through her nose as she processed what he'd said. "It wasn't a con," she said finally. "And you knew you were marrying an ambassador and politician when you proposed to me."

"No, I thought I was marrying *you*." Han watched his words hit her like a flechette, each one a piercing blow.

Han glared at her, and she glared right back. Leia wasn't backing down. There was nothing he could say that would get through to her, that much was clear. Why should he expect any different? It was almost as if he cared about her more than she cared about herself. It was the same as on Hoth, before they were together. After the command center was hit, Han had come back for Leia, knowing she wouldn't leave. Of course she wouldn't leave, not while anyone else remained on the base. The first thing he'd asked was if she was all right. And all she'd done was snap back at him to go.

They were always coming and going, back and forth, heading in different directions but somehow, always, inexplicably, pulled back to each other.

"It's who I am," Leia said quietly, without looking away.

That was the problem, though. Leia was thinking only about who she was, what *she* wanted. And she kept prioritizing her wants for a utopic government over anything for herself.

"It's who *we* could be, you know," Han said. He wasn't shouting anymore, and he could tell that the softer his voice was, the more she listened to him and took what he was saying to heart. "Think how different this could've been if you'd bothered to give me a heads-up. Talked about what you wanted. Asked me to help. We'd be celebrating right now if you'd let this be something we did together. Instead . . ." He spread his palms wide, indicating the fight that stood between them, the ringing silence of both their anger lingering in the emptiness.

Han watched Leia swallow, watched the emotion rising in her eyes, watched her hands bunch into fists and then slacken.

Because he was right.

And she knew it.

And there was nothing more to say.

So, she left. Leia turned on her heel and strode out the door, leaving Han with the cold comfort that just because he was right, it didn't make the situation any better at all.

CHAPTER 28

LEIA

THE DOOR SLID CLOSED BEHIND her. For a moment, Leia stood there, alone in the corridor. She leaned her head against the smooth wall and shut her eyes.

Marriage wasn't supposed to be this difficult. Was it?

Leia straightened when she heard footsteps approaching. A family of five came through, two fathers, a teenage daughter, and a pair of twins in matching blue dresses. Leia forced a casual smile on her face.

"That's the princess!" one of the twins said.

"Don't be embarrassing," her teenage sister hissed.

One of the fathers gave Leia a sheepish wave as they passed.

"She's so pretty!" the other twin said in a too-loud whisper.

"This family is the worst," the teen groaned as her fathers laughed.

Leia watched the family get on the turbolift at the end of the corridor, but as soon as they were gone, her smile evaporated, an aching pain in her chest.

She should turn around. Go back inside the cabin. Ask for forgiveness.

It's for the galaxy, she thought. *I didn't want to redirect the ship just for myself. Why can't he see that?*

She hesitated. Even though she knew she was right, she also couldn't help but be impressed that Han had her back, even when he suspected she was wrong. And he hadn't said anything in front of Captain Dicto.

Leia believed she was doing the right thing. The ice palaces of Madurs were renowned throughout the galaxy, and both safer and potentially more beautiful than the meteor storm in Esseveya. Besides, wasn't it better to slightly inconvenience some tourists than to jeopardize adding another world to the unification of the galaxy? Leia couldn't help that she had her eyes on the bigger picture—it was important to keep sight of what mattered most.

. . . But Han's parting shots lingered with her. He was right, loath as she was to admit it. He hadn't married an ambassador. He'd married her. And their marriage meant they should have been a team.

Han backed her up without knowing anything about her motives. He may have thought he was helping her pull off a con, but he didn't question her.

And she hadn't even bothered to clue him in on what she wanted.

Leia almost turned around. The door was right there.

But she just couldn't bring herself to open it.

Instead, she went back to the climate simulator. It was no longer empty—and it was no longer filled with tropical plants and balmy breezes. The climate simulator was designed to showcase the weather conditions on the next planet the *Halcyon* was going to visit. When the ship was merely cruising through Esseveya, without extending any excursion on the surface of a planet or moon, the next destination was intended to be Synjax. Now it was Madurs.

"I'm so excited to see *snow*!" one of the twins Leia had seen earlier screamed as her tiny feet slid over a section of the climate simulator that was iced over. Skim-blades had been set up on a small table by the little frozen pond, available for anyone to strap onto their shoes and take a spin on the ice, but the younglings—the twins and half a dozen more gleefully screaming kids—had taken over the area, sliding on their knees, feet, and butts in a chaotic cacophony of childish enthusiasm as snowballs flew through the air.

Parents stood nearby, fondly amused, but it was clear that many of the other guests were not as happy. "I didn't pack for this," a woman near Leia complained. She rubbed her arms and leaned over to Leia. "Perhaps you should complain, dear. I'm going to. If enough of us do, maybe we'll get to see Esseveya as planned."

"I hear Madurs is lovely," Leia said.

The woman shrugged. "Ice is ice. Seeing the meteor storms and borealis in Esseveya? That's a once-in-a-lifetime sort of trip. Not many ships even go there."

"Because it's so dangerous," Leia pointed out.

The woman stared at her flatly. "I'll never know now."

Shivering, the woman turned to go, along with her companion. Leia moved to the corner of the room, watching as guests peeked inside. Most of them seemed to be simply confirming the change in plans, that the ship would now be going to an ice world instead of following the previous itinerary. Some people were thrilled, some skeptical, some dismayed.

And nearly all of them had someone else with them. Family units, friends, lovers—no one in the climate simulator was alone.

Except Leia.

It made sense, she supposed. Who goes on a cruise by themselves? Still . . .

She wasn't supposed to be alone.

Was she? It was such a dichotomy in her life—she believed in the power of unification and alliances. That power had defeated the Empire, after all. But somewhere over the past four years, Leia had begun isolating herself. When she first started participating in seditious rebellion, she had welcomed the aid of allies.

But then she'd seen allies die.

She'd started trying to do more and more missions on her own. When she was forced to work with others, she compartmentalized her attachments to focus on the job at hand. Leia had pushed herself to become a senator at a young age—a full senator, not merely an aide to her father. Someone independent, both of help and of ties that could be easily traced back to the Rebellion. She had Mon Mothma's support, of course, and worked with the Alliance High Command, but

Leia consistently tried to prove, over and over again, that she didn't need help.

Didn't want help.

The more independent she became, the less likely she was to hurt others. Including herself.

And then a couple of laserbrains and a walking carpet had saved her from the Death Star.

Maybe I shouldn't even try, Leia thought. Thinking of the Death Star made her think of Vader, and that made her recoil in disgust. She could not escape her own heritage.

But . . . Han hadn't seemed to care. The entire galaxy would revile her if the truth was out, but not Han.

And she couldn't even give him the one thing he asked of her: time. The very thing the war had supposedly granted them.

Bitter bile rose in Leia's throat. She didn't want a medal or a prestigious appointment, but she longed for the freedom to accept at least a little joy. She had never really considered before that it wasn't something bestowed by peace at the end of war; it was something waiting for her to claim, if only she could allow herself to do so.

A flurry of ice crystals wafted through the climate simulator. She was getting cold, and when some of the *Halcyon* staff came through with carts full of frothy hot drinks, sweet and thick with something creamy, Leia took a cup eagerly, sipping and relishing the burn.

Wrapping her hands around the cup, Leia knew she had to find a way to lower her walls. A true partnership—not just for a mission or a war, but for life—was somewhat new to her. As open as Leia often was, she compartmentalized so much. She had to find a way to let Han past the walls she'd spent the entire rebellion building.

She just wasn't sure how.

CHAPTER 29

HAN

A HONEYMOON SUITE WAS NO fun alone.

Han tossed pillows at the Droid Link Panel built into the wall until he triggered it. D3-O9's voice chirped through the comm speaker, her round white-and-bronze head bobbing in a greeting on the screen.

"Good morning! As a reminder, I am unable to see into your cabin, although you can, of course, see me."

Han looked down at himself. He hadn't really considered the possibility of the video screen displaying his lack of clothing.

"What is there to *do* on this ship?" Han asked from the bed.

D3-O9 straightened up, squaring her shoulders and leaning forward eagerly. "The *Halcyon* provides a wide range of activities for your enjoyment!" The display changed to a map of the ship, highlighting each section as she spoke about it. "There is, of course, the chance to mingle with guests and play holo-sabacc—"

"I'm not in the mood for company." No one's except Leia's, anyway.

"Ah, in that case, I can suggest a peaceful meditation in the climate simulator or even a round of vigorous exercise in our exercise room. That room was developed with—"

"I'm also not in the mood for clothes."

The display featuring the ship's map disappeared, showing D3-O9's face again. It was fascinating, really, the way logistics and protocol droids could express emotion—particularly shock—despite faces made of metal. Han liked to make a game of it.

"In that case, sir, may I suggest you stay in your spacious suite and enjoy the viewport?" D3-O9's voice was somehow scandalized and chastising at the same time.

Han got up from the bed to look out the viewport. It was probably a good thing that the vidscreen was one-way only.

"Of course," D3-O9 continued, "as we are in hyperspace, the view is somewhat . . ."

"Boring," Han finished.

"Hyperspace routes may look the same, but they do represent a wonder of science and technology," D3-O9 started.

"Yeah, yeah." Han crossed over to the Droid Link Panel and disconnected it. A small part of him was impressed. He hadn't felt the shift to lightspeed at all. Still, being in hyperspace when they were supposed to be slowly cruising through a meteor storm reminded him of his wife's . . . it wasn't fair to call it a betrayal, even if it felt like one.

Han pushed the thought away. Food. Food would be good. Some more of that brown stuff—it was delicious. He dressed quickly and headed out the cabin, to the turbolift, and down to Deck Four, where the Crown of Corellia called its sweet siren song of pastries. Voices made his head turn, and he saw Kelad and Zalma walk out of the engineering corridor, Wozzakk trailing behind them. The chief engineer was talking with the former prisoner, heads bent together. They were so wrapped up in their conversation that they didn't even notice Han staring at them. Wozzakk, however, did, and the Ugnaught engineer paused to speak.

"Don't you worry," he told Han. "I've got big eyes on that one."

"Some punishment," Han said. "Guy looks happier than I've ever seen him. He got exactly what he wanted—a chance to look at and work on the Halcyon's engines."

"Big eyes," Wozzakk said ominously. "Don't trust a passenger in the engine room." He watched mournfully as Kelad and Zalma disappeared behind a door marked for the crew only.

"Yeah, me neither."

"Better follow," Wozzakk said, picking up his pace in an almost comical way with his short legs. Before he got to the door, though, Han heard the Ugnaught mutter, "Don't like the way he looks at my tractor beams. They're not his."

Han shook his head. Most ships this size had tractor beams to aid shuttles and supply loaders in reaching the bay. As ships had increasingly smaller targets upon which to land, tractor beams were a safe and efficient means of docking, either to load smaller vessels onto a larger ship, like this one, or to maneuver a larger ship like the *Millennium Falcon* to a small slip on a planet.

Of course, a piece of tech didn't exist that couldn't be corrupted and used for some other means. He himself had once used the *Falcon*'s in a desperate attempt to slingshot a meteor, and *that* had been epic. But it had taken the Empire to turn a tool into a weapon. Imperial Star Destroyers had corrupted tractor beams from something helpful and useful into a way to trap innocent ships.

Han smirked as he crossed the corridor toward the dining room. Okay, maybe the *Falcon* wasn't entirely "innocent." But it was still true that the Empire corrupted everything it touched.

And Han feared Kelad would do the same.

"General Solo?" a voice called. It was the Pantoran woman who'd been assigned as Leia's attaché. "Have you seen Princess Leia?"

"Need her for another interview?" His tone was harsher than he'd intended, and Han immediately regretted snapping at Riyola; it wasn't her fault that Leia was willing to do everything for everyone except herself.

Riyola cringed. "I'm sorry. No, I just wanted to tell her about the agenda for guests on Madurs." She paused, flushing indigo over her blue cheeks. "I really am sorry. I know it's your honeymoon, and I—"

"Forget it," Han said. He headed into the dining room, but Riyola followed him.

Despite the early hour—was it early? Han wasn't sure. It *felt* early—

the dining room was full. He flagged down one of the wait staff and asked about the pastries with the brown stuff inside.

"Those are banchock hand pies," the server informed him. "A delicacy from Synjax. We like to feature the local dishes you'll encounter at the worlds we visit."

"Yes, those. Give me six of them. In a box."

The server had the grace to not even blink at the extravagant order. As she left, Riyola chuckled. "Well, you know what you like."

"I do."

Riyola shifted uneasily while they both waited for the server to bring Han his order. Han wanted to tell her that she could just leave, but she seemed intent on lingering. "I was not assigned only to serve Princess Leia," she said finally. "I am happy to help make your journey better. You're clearly upset by something, but I would like to—"

"I'm not upset," Han said quickly.

Riyola's yellow eyes widened slightly, but she didn't press the matter.

"I just want pie," Han added.

The dining room bustled with activity. They could see the server who'd taken Han's order darting around, helping others. She glanced up and nodded at them, indicating that they were still a priority.

"It's so busy," Riyola commented. "A part of me wants to jump in and help the servers. But it wouldn't be a help. I would just get in their way. An essential part of teamwork is knowing when to offer aid and when to trust others to handle the task at hand."

"Well, they could ask for help if they needed it," Han muttered. He paused, mulling over his own words, then added, "Might get me my pie quicker."

"It's harder to ask for help sometimes," Riyola mused. "Especially if you're used to doing it yourself."

"Some things shouldn't be done alone."

The server brought Han's pastries, and after thanking her, Han opened the box, grabbed the top one, and stuffed it into his mouth as he turned to leave. Riyola followed.

"You're right—some things should *not* be done alone. The banchock hand pies, for example," the Pantoran said. "Did you know they take a full standard week to make? The filling has to be mashed and sweetened before it is fermented at a precise temperature. The final days are crucial, often requiring adjustments to the mixture hourly. Painstaking labor over so many days requires a full staff of chefs to work together."

Han swallowed drily—one of the six pastries was gone before Riyola had even finished speaking. "They're very good."

Riyola smiled. "Most things are when they are created in harmony with others."

"Uh-huh." Han crossed over to the turbolift. *Leia* needed a lecture about working with others, not him. He'd come for pastries; he had his pastries. "If I see my wife, I'll tell her you're looking for her," he said, stepping into the lift and reaching for another pie as the doors closed in Riyola's face.

By the time he got back to the cabin, there were only two pies left. Leia turned around as he entered, the door sliding closed behind him.

"Hey," she said.

Han put the box on the table by the door. "Your attaché wanted to go over the next day's activities with you."

"She can wait." Leia's voice was quiet, almost meek.

He could see that she was nervous. She hesitated, taking a step toward him, then lingering back.

That would not do.

"You know," Han said. "I've seen you command control centers, shoot stormtroopers point-blank when they had us cornered, and stand in front of Darth Vader without so much as weak knees. But I've only ever once seen you afraid."

Leia shot him a confused look.

Han snorted. "Don't you remember? You were shaking like a leaf."

A flush rose on her cheeks as she recalled the moment Han spoke of—the two of them in the *Millennium Falcon,* just before they'd kissed for the first time.

Leia took a step closer, her jaw set stubbornly. "I was *not* shaking."

"Positively quivering." He stalked across the cabin to her.

"Not with fear!" Leia was in his face now, her chin pointed up at him defiantly.

"Then what made you tremble?" Han brushed her cheek with the back of his knuckles, and Leia crumpled against his touch.

"Leia," he whispered. "I don't ever want you to be afraid, but I especially don't want you to be afraid to talk to me."

He brushed aside a lock of Leia's hair that had escaped her braid. The nerves that had wound her up tight melted with the soft, relieved sigh that escaped her lips. She leaned against him, resting her head on his chest as he wrapped his arms around her.

"You should know by now," he murmured, "no matter how many times you push me away, I just keep coming back."

"Stubborn scoundrel," Leia said without looking up, her breath warm on his neck.

"Stubborn scoundrel who came back with pie," Han pointed out.

CHAPTER 30

LEIA

"OKAY, THIS MIGHT NOT BE too bad," Han admitted the next day, when the *Halcyon* orbited around Madurs. From the viewport in their cabin, they had a prime glimpse of the blue-white frozen planet, sparkling like a diamond against the blackness of the universe. This part of the moon was illuminated not only by the system's sun but also by the gas giant planet the moon orbited, a swirling mix of purple and silver. Riyola had uploaded new itineraries into everyone's datapad, with information on the twinkling architecture of the ice palaces and a special planned excursion to ride in submersible vehicles to view edonts, vast underwater creatures larger than most spaceships.

Han turned toward Leia. "But why does it have to be an ice world?" he groaned. "We got enough of that on Hoth."

"On the bright side," Leia pointed out, "there are no tauntauns."

"Have I mentioned how bad those things smell?"

"Maybe once or twice."

"Because it's *bad*."

"I've heard."

"The inside is worse than the outside."

"Yes, that also has been confirmed."

"It's just—"

Leia thrust the day bag into Han's arms, and he took the hint, lugging it onto his shoulders. Although they were only going to be on the moon for three days, Leia had packed multiple outfits, unsure of how formally she would be greeted. Madurs was sending local shuttles to cart passengers from the *Halcyon* onto the moon's surface, although not all of the guests had opted to spend a night in one of the galaxy-renowned ice palaces. Leia adjusted the long cloak made from gwendle wool, draping it around her shoulders. Despite being relatively thin, the white cloak embroidered with silver thread was as warm as any coat she'd ever donned, and elegant enough—she hoped—to impress the prime minister of Madurs. She left the wide hood down and the material pooled at her back then melted over her shoulders. It was too warm now for the full effect, but Leia knew that white was her color, both a fashion choice and a conscious political commentary to remind others of the Alderaanian royal family and the atrocities the Empire had committed against her homeworld.

As Leia and Han headed down the corridor and toward the turbolift that would take them to the shuttle loading area, Leia went over everything she'd researched about Madurs and its prime minister. Dreand Yens was a few decades older than her, somewhere between her parents' and Mon's age. In some of the images on the HoloNet, he appeared almost fatherly, with a warm smile and kind eyes. More recent images showed his age in a harsher way. He had perpetual bags under his eyes, and streaks of gray at his temple. Leia had seen it before—the stress of political office wore on a person, aging them before their time.

D3-O9 stood at the bottom of the turbolift, helping to guide guests to the shuttle. "Ah, Princess Leia," the droid said. "And Han."

"What happened to 'General Solo'?" Han muttered to Leia as they headed toward the Madurs shuttle.

"I imagine she got to know you a little better."

"What's that supposed to mean?"

Leia stood on her tiptoes and pecked him on the cheek. "Have you, by chance, conversed with Deethree when I wasn't around?"

"A little," Han said. "She answered that comm unit display and told me about the ship."

"Did you insult the ship?"

"Not really."

"Well," Leia said, "she 'didn't really' insult you back, did she?"

Han cast a look over his shoulder, glaring as D3-O9 bustled to the front of the group. "'Thank you all for promptly arriving at your shuttle launch," the droid said, amplifying her voice. "We are now ready to begin the boarding process of the local shuttle to Madurs."

The droid stepped aside, allowing all the passengers to enter the shuttle. It was a large vessel, comfortably seating more than two dozen guests and their hand luggage. D3-O9 stepped on board once everyone was settled inside.

"The Madurs local shuttle is entirely remotely operated, but please be assured that it is a perfectly safe loading vessel, with the remote loaders on *Halcyon* aiding in the operation as an additional precaution."

Leia knew that these small orbit-to-surface shuttles were usually fairly simple, operated by a droid or remotely, but it was a nice touch for the *Halcyon* to add in its loader beams.

"Overkill," Han muttered to her. "Bet Kelad talked them into that. Bet they're letting him help on the bridge with the loader beams."

"Are you jealous?" Leia asked, gazing up at him.

"I have more experience flying than he does. They should give me a shot at the controls."

Leia laughed softly as D3-O9 started talking about safety procedures during the launch. "As this shuttle has not had a chance to be inspected by the *Halcyon* to ensure it is up to Chandrila Star Line's standards, I want to further inform you of additional materials we have added to this vessel for your safety and comfort."

"You don't even know for sure Kelad is on the bridge," Leia told Han, continuing their conversation.

"I know he's not in the brig, and that's reason enough to be angry."

Leia shot him a look, but he ignored it.

"Please also note," D3-O9 continued at the front of the shuttle, her voice cheery. "In the event of emergency, supplies are available for your safety." D3-O9 held up breathing apparatuses and a long vest with thermal heat disks attached that would provide warmth when activated. It wasn't a full spacesuit, but it would be enough to keep someone safe long enough for a rescue crew to reach them. "These are located in these crates, along with explosive evacuation flare shells to help locate survivors."

"Are we going to need those?" an elderly man asked. He turned to his companion. "I told you we shouldn't have come here. I signed up to go to Synjax, not an ice moon. Synjax shuttles don't need emergency equipment."

"All shuttles have emergency supplies," Leia said.

The old man craned his head around to look at her. Leia raised an eyebrow. She clocked the exact moment he recognized who she was— a slight widening of the eyes, a small parting of his lips—and she registered the moment half a second later when he remembered the true rumors that Leia had influenced the shift in the ship's flight path. With a huff, he snapped his head back to D3-O9, but he didn't protest any further.

"As Madurs was not a part of the original itinerary," D3-O9 continued, "we will begin passing out thermal heat disks for personal use. Straffle wraps have also been provided for anyone who would like additional heat support." The droid gestured to a crate at the front of the shuttle, which Leia presumed was full of cloth wraps made of the intensely thermal woven straffle material.

A server droid passed out thin thermal disks to everyone aboard. Despite her cloak, Leia took one—the severe cold on an ice planet required more than simple cloth, no matter how warm it was. The single disk strapped over her clothing, discreet but providing electric radiant heat to her core.

"Don't need those on Synjax, either," the old man muttered, pitching his voice purposefully loud enough that Leia was sure he wanted her to hear.

Han, who likewise wanted a beach more than an ice palace, started to get up, his hands bunching in fists. Leia pulled him down and patted his knee. He couldn't fight every battle for her, and Leia had learned long ago that not every battle was worth fighting anyway.

D3-O9 concluded her introductory speech and moved to the shuttle doorway, sealing it closed and beginning the launch process. All around her, passengers chatted about the excursion. At least most of them seemed happy with the change in agenda. Madurs was fascinating from an artistic perspective, but several people in the shuttle hoped for a more adventurous ice fishing expedition.

Ice fishing . . . Leia should have looked closer at the ecological side of the moon's resources. The Empire wanted Madurs for its carnium. Most of the galaxy knew it for its ice palaces. But fishing must surely be a prime food source for the people, which would absolutely affect the sociopolitical environment.

Leia's hands clenched, her eyes staring at her lap, but she saw nothing. Ice fishing meant ice fishers. Where were they on the hierarchy of the society on this moon? What other food sources were there? There was too much at play here—Leia knew too little about this world, and that meant she wasn't going to be able to come into her work as strong as she wanted. At least she was going to be there in person. True ambassadorship meant really being present, listening to what the people needed—the prime ministers *and* the fishers.

Injustice, inequity, and a lack of needs met for the lowest members of a society echoed like ripples in a disturbed pool of water into issues on a global level. An individual world that experienced troubles likewise spread out further and further into a galactic problem. Helping people was never as simple as just gifting money or supplies, which is what many of the world leaders requested. Leia had learned that the hard way. She'd saved a hundred refugees on Wobani when she was sixteen, but that hadn't been enough. She had helped those few, but the planet itself had continued to deteriorate under the Galactic Empire, eventually only used as a labor and prison camp site. She hadn't created the type of change she'd wanted to.

Leia needed to find a way to seek out the working people of Madurs, listen to the voices of those who weren't commonly heard. But she had so little time—her status had afforded her and Han a spot at a banquet the prime minister of Madurs was hastily arranging to welcome the guests, but how much time could she angle with him to speak about these issues? Riyola had helped her with that, working in tandem with the prime minister's people to ensure that he knew Leia wanted an audience to talk about a possible alliance. But would Prime Minister Yens be open to discussing the needs of his people and how the new government could help, or would he be antagonistic toward Leia? If she knew more—both about the man and the moon—she would better know what to say.

Han reached over, breaking her clasped hands and weaving his fingers through hers, giving her a squeeze.

She looked up and smiled at him. He wore an expression that told her he knew exactly what had been twisting her nerves. Leia felt herself relaxing as the shuttle broke into Madurs's atmosphere. Leia was unprepared to meet with the prime minister not because she wasn't a good diplomat but because she was on her honeymoon.

And being on her honeymoon meant she wasn't facing this problem alone.

CHAPTER 31

HAN

THE SPACEPORT OF MADURS HAD seen better days. Leia had told Han about the Imperial Art Expo several years ago, and Han doubted the docking bays had had much upkeep since then. The shuttles had docked near the front, and there'd been some obvious effort to clean up, but even he could tell that the port was well below most *Halcyon* guests' standards.

When the guests stepped outside, though, all grumbling about the spaceport disappeared in the face of the glittering, frozen moon.

Han knew Madurs was ice-covered. He had been expecting something akin to Hoth—harsh winds that cut through his coat, snow that crusted in his eyelashes, tiny ice crystals that mercilessly cut into any exposed skin.

Instead, he was met with a world that was mostly silent. There was cold, yes, but no wind. As his feet walked across the thick ice, there was barely the crunching sound of snow beneath his boots. Rather than growing louder as more and more people stepped out onto Madurs, the crowd grew quieter, speaking in hushed, nearly reverent whispers.

Han hated it.

It was the brutality of Hoth that had made it bearable. This silent, soft cold was far too similar to the cold of being frozen in carbonite. Han shuddered at the memory. The creeping silence and darkness still haunted him, the claustrophobic feeling of being utterly trapped in his own body. His vision blurred, and he vividly recalled the moment he realized he had become temporarily blind from the process, the terror at being lost under his own skin.

Leia slipped beside him, tucking herself under his arm. She had been the one who had come for him, who had saved him. And for all that she was the one who had dragged him to this blasted cold moon, she was also the one who stood beside him now.

"It's beautiful," Leia said, nodding to the sky.

Cresting the horizon, the big gas giant planet Madurs orbited rose like a pale-lavender sun. Its colors were muted through the wisps of clouds and thready, gray-blue sky, creating a ghostlike image.

Nearby, others were marveling at the ground. Under a dusting of snow, the thick ice was clear as glass. Deep, dark-blue water shone through the ice, and, distantly, there were darker, moving outlines of massive sea creatures beneath their feet.

An earsplitting *crack* echoed through the otherwise silent ice plain. Several guests screamed in startled surprise or ducked, looking for the source of the noise. In the echoing wake of the splintering sound, a low rumble drew everyone's attention. They could see a group approaching quickly—a mix of individuals each riding some sort of machine and groups in sleds pulled by large, four-legged animals. They were far enough away that Han wasn't able to see any individual's face, but the smooth, flat horizon of the ice plain meant that they were visible even from a distance.

In moments, the welcome committee arrived. Ice-zippers sped by first, spraying snow and bits of ice in arcs, an impressive display that made those closest screech in delight, young and old. The little ice-zippers had curving refracting lasers as blades, cutting razor-thin tracks through the thick ice. Each one had a platform that could hold a driver and one passenger, and several of the guests, especially the younglings, clamored to claim one.

Behind the ice-zippers, regal sleds approached next. Each one was pulled by an enormous white pronged beast. The animals—one of the locals called one a proose—had legs that were roughly as long as Han was tall, with relatively slender bodies covered in silky white fur. Their graceful—for they were graceful, despite their disproportionately large size—bodies were strapped to heavy, corded ropes that were woven over their backs and threaded into reins. The prooses' narrow faces ended in slightly pointed muzzles, with long, draping ears beneath elaborately twisting white horns. Everything about them, from their fur to their hooves, was solid white. Except their inky black eyes. It should be eerie, Han thought, but there was a gentle kindness to their gazes. Despite being so large, they tapped the ice softly, scratching their hooves over the snow in a way that could only be described as prancing.

Leia let go of Han's arm, and she approached the closest beast with her eyes full of wonder and not a trace of fear on her face. One of the locals jumped down, offering her little white cubes to feed to the proose. It lapped at her fingers with its split-lip muzzle, leaving a long strand of sticky drool on her palm. Leia laughed, completely charmed, the sound somehow rising above the excited chatter of the other guests. The proose was so tall that it could easily arch its long neck over Leia's head, resting its chin on the small of her back, its breath coming up in pale clouds. Leia reached up, petting the proose.

Han took a moment to appreciate the image. His wife, in a white gown, with a white cloak flowing down her shoulders, the hood barely covering her hair, reaching up to pet the enormous—but gentle—creature.

"The ears are soft!" Leia called to Han. She was so joyful in the moment, almost childlike in her excitement over the beast. All Han could do was smile in return as Leia stroked her fingers over the proose's drooping ears. When she stopped, the animal nudged her with its head—a gentle motion, but its weight was enough to make Leia stumble.

Han caught her before she slipped on the ice. She giggled up at him. "Oh, they're so dear," she said.

Han forgot about the bitter cold of Hoth, the even worse cold of being frozen in carbonite. His anger at the ship's diversion and Leia's ridiculous focus on work evaporated. She was happy in a way that showed him that for a moment she'd forgotten about the war, their problems. She saw only a beautiful animal with soft ears that nuzzled her when she petted it and fed it, and she was content. And so was he.

"Are you ready?" the local guide said. She was a petite human with two long braids of hair sticking out under a woven knit hat. Han looked around and realized that nearly all the other sleds were taken—this guide and her proose were the last one, and some of the others had already departed, cutting a neat line behind the chaotic ice-zippers across the frozen plain.

The girl introduced herself as Nah'hai, and she helped Leia up into the sled first. While Leia snuggled under the heavy blanket, reclining in the back of the sled, Han took the chance to examine the vehicle. It used regular metal blades, dulled to even out the weight, but although the proose was more than capable of pulling it, there was also a propulsor built into the undercarriage so that it could be operated without animal aid.

"The prooses get mad if we don't use them," Nah'hai told Han as she gestured for him to sit beside Leia.

Beyond her, the proose strapped to their sled tossed its head, flappy ears audibly slapping against its neck as it huffed impatiently. All the other prooses and sleds had taken off.

"How fast can they go?" Han asked.

"Oh, you like fast?" Nah'hai said, a gleam in her eye Han recognized.

Before Han was fully sitting, Nah'hai ululated, a deep, resonant sound bursting from her lips. With a snort of excitement, the proose kicked up snow and ice, setting a fast clip over the plain. Han stumbled, partly falling on Leia before she pulled him under the blanket and onto the seat next to her.

Nah'hai set their proose on a path circling wide out, away from the others. "Over there!" she called, pointing to the right.

In the distance, the smooth, flat plain was broken with jagged cliffs that stuck straight up, like a vertical wall of ice. Han hadn't noticed it before; the gray-white-blue of the ice faded into the gray-white-blue of the sky.

"The ice fishers," Leia muttered. Squinting, Han could see the slightly dark spots in the ice—horizontal ledges cut into the wall, leading to round holes that must indicate doorways to dwellings.

"Think we can go there?" Leia shouted through the wind to their driver.

"Why?" Nah'hai said. "It's just cliff dwellers." She made a loud call again, her voice haunting, and the proose diverted, roughly curving back toward the others.

They could see the main ice palaces now. The ice-zippers had already arrived, but a few—those who had been commandeered by some of the older kids, Han suspected—were spiraling in tight loops in a way that made his stomach churn, despite some of the more chaotic moves he'd done on the *Millennium Falcon*. The largest palace, the one where the other proose-pulled sleds were already pulling up, towered above the others. It was easily seven stories high, reflecting light so that it looked silver in a way that reminded Han of one of Leia's necklaces, the one she had worn after the Battle of Yavin.

From this distance, Han could truly appreciate that the ice palaces—there were roughly a dozen, but only three large ones—were truly architectural works of art. They were lavish and almost ostentatious. Unlike the cliff dwellings, there was no attempt to blend into nature. No, these ice palaces demanded to be seen, to be recognized as human marvels, not natural wonders. They rose as if by magic from the ice field, jutting straight up and glistening in the cold air.

"What are those?" Leia asked, pointing past the city. Han hadn't noticed the other ice palaces, the ruins. Giant blocks of ice had cracked and tumbled, smashing into the thick ice plain. They were barely visible, caught in a nether region between the cliffs and the beauty of the other crystalline buildings to the left.

Nah'hai slowed the proose. She didn't otherwise acknowledge that Leia had asked a question, and when Han opened his mouth to repeat Leia's words to the driver, his wife put her hand on his knee under the blanket, shaking her head at him. Nah'hai stared out at the broken ice palaces as if she were . . . sad. It was a look of mourning on her face, but so stoic that Han almost didn't recognize it.

Even the proose was silent as they gazed at the broken ice palaces. Han counted them—thirteen grand buildings, with remnants of the metal underpinnings that kept the ice blocks in place twisting up. They had been larger and more elaborate than the current ice palaces, with some lacy filigree edging still glittering along one broken roof.

Leia strained her eyes, leaning forward in the sled to see better, ignoring the way their cover fell to the floor, letting the cold wash over them. "Nah'hai?" she asked tentatively, so soft that their guide could have easily pretended not to hear. Instead, Nah'hai's shoulders slumped. She looked back at her passengers.

"The old city," she said, her gaze distant. "It's the nature of ice. It's not permanent. Ice melts, it breaks, it cracks. Our art is temporary, and all the more precious because of that."

Leia pulled the cover up and settled back into Han's arms as Nah'hai clucked at the proose and their sled approached the main—new—city. Han dropped a kiss on the top of Leia's head, but he could not help but recall the way Nah'hai's voice was so deeply sad as she spoke about the way the art she so clearly loved simply could not last forever.

CHAPTER 32

LEIA

HAN AND NAH'HAI WERE SILENT as the proose pulled the sled away from the broken ice palaces. Nah'hai turned her head away from them; Han couldn't take his eyes off them. But Leia was looking past them, through the cracked and crumbling ice of the shattered palaces, to the long black tower rising over the horizon.

"Nah'hai!" she called as the wind picked up. "What is that?"

Nah'hai did not stop the sled. In fact, she turned sharply away, slapping the reins against the proose's rump to make it go faster. Leia stood, and Han reached for her—to pull her back down, she thought, and make her sit again, but no—he was offering her a steadying hand on the swift sled. Leia leaned over, using Han for support, and grabbed the back of Nah'hai's fur drape.

Reluctantly, Nah'hai pulled up the proose. The animal stomped its cloven hooves, snorting clouds of white breath. Nah'hai's shoulders slumped, but Leia couldn't quite tell why—was that guilt? Slowly, the girl turned around. "Yes?" she asked. From the tone, it was clear that Nah'hai was trying to make it seem as if she were in a hurry, and perhaps she was as the others had all already arrived at the grandest ice palace in the city, but there was something shifty about the way the driver wouldn't meet her gaze.

"What is that?" Leia said, getting directly to the point. She swung her hand toward the black tower, still visible through the cracked and broken ice palaces.

"I told you, the old city—" Nah'hai started, but Leia shot her such a withering look that the girl's words died on her lips.

For a moment, the two women glared at each other. With her dual braids and round face, Leia had been thinking of Nah'hai as a girl, but the stubborn set of her jaw made it clear that she was not a naïve youngling. Leia respected her attitude, but she also wanted an answer.

Because this stank of the Empire.

She had seen it before. People hated the Empire, but the Empire didn't care. They came to worlds regardless of invitation, forcing their presence on people. Ignoring the Empire was easier than fighting it. And so the Empire's flag decorated the city square, stormtroopers patrolled the streets, Imperial rules superseded traditional practices, and, like a black ink stain spreading over white cloth, the Empire seeped into the world.

And the people looked down. They kept their eyes on their own work, their own lives, trying valiantly not to think too much about how the circle of their previous life was shrinking and shrinking, their gazes narrowing smaller and smaller.

It was easier to pretend the Imperial flags weren't there if you didn't look up at them.

But that never made them go away.

Leia saw now the way Nah'hai purposefully didn't look at that black tower. She turned her back to it. But it didn't matter. It didn't make it go away.

And Leia would not deny what she had already so clearly seen.

"What's over there?" she asked, more gently this time, but still with a tone that said she would not back down.

Nah'hai opened her mouth, and for a moment Leia thought she might be given the truth. But instead, Nah'hai said only, "That area's dangerous."

Despite her words, Nah'hai's eyes searched Leia's, almost pleading with her. Leia nodded once, and hoped Nah'hai understood that the small movement of her head was a promise.

Nah'hai turned back to her proose. She didn't look at the black tower on the horizon. Rather than call out to the proose, she pulled on the ropes and clucked her tongue, the sound almost inaudible. The proose, however, responded, turning toward the new city.

In moments, they pulled up to the main ice palace. Leia looked up at it in wonder. If she unfocused her eyes, she could see the fine silver grid of wires running through the center of the ice. The outward walls were crystal clear, shining under the sun's light and the planetary glow of the nearby gas giant still cresting the horizon. The structure, despite being made of ice, seemed so grand, so *solid* that it was hard for Leia to believe that it could crack and crumble like the ruins they had seen in the distance.

Nah'hai hopped down from the driver's seat of the sled and Han—impatient as always—left before she could offer him a hand up. He slipped on the ice, and Leia caught Nah'hai's knowing, smug look and shared a silent smile with the other girl. She held Nah'hai's hand as she stepped gingerly off the sled and got her footing on the snow-covered ice.

"Nah'hai!" One of the other drivers approached, his voice sharp as a cracking electrical whip. He had on a dark capelet lined in cerulean silk and a smart hat with a square brim. His shoulder was decorated with gleaming bronze and gold badges. He seemed to be something of an authority figure. "Why are you so late?" he demanded of their driver.

"Captain, I—" Nah'hai started, looking flustered.

Leia rushed forward. "I'm so sorry; it's my fault," she said. "I specifically asked Nah'hai to take us a bit farther so we could see the beauty of your moon. She did try to stick to the schedule, but I'm afraid I insisted that she show me—" Nah'hai cut her a sharp look under her knit hat, and Leia paused. She was smart enough to know not to mention the black tower, but was she not supposed to bring up the cliff dwellings, or was she supposed to keep her knowledge of the broken ice palaces a secret? "—more of the ice fields," Leia finished weakly.

Nah'hai's shoulders relaxed, but only for a moment.

"We are on a *strict* schedule, you know that," the captain told Nah'hai, his voice stern but low, glaring at her in a way that spoke of secret knowledge. Why was the timing of their arrival so important? Or, more relevant, what was the thing Leia wasn't supposed to know about?

The captain glanced back at Leia, then visibly registered who she was. "And an honored guest of the prime minister!" He swept into a bow. "Princess Leia Organa, it is my great privilege to escort you into the palace."

Leia hesitated, about to insist that Nah'hai, who was so kind, be the one to escort them. But it was clear the girl wished nothing more than to disappear with her proose. With an apologetic smile, Leia said farewell to their driver.

"I'm here, too," Han said. The captain looked at him curiously, which did nothing to abate Han's sullen attitude. "Han Solo? General of the Rebel Alliance? Captain of the *Millennium Falcon*?" The captain's gaze remained blank. Han sighed. "Leia's husband."

"Oh!" the captain said, offering Han a small bow. "Please, follow me. The prime minister asked to be introduced to you, I mean, you both, as soon as you arrived."

The captain proffered his arm for Leia to take, but Han claimed her first, glaring at the other man until he turned on his heel and led the way into the glorious, crystalline ice palace.

The steps shone like mirrors, but when Leia placed a tentative shoe on them, her footing was stable. She bounded up a few of the stairs, her cloak billowing behind her, then paused for the others.

"We take care to ensure that our art is both beautiful and functional," the captain said, noting Leia's hesitation. "And you will find the accommodations inside to be comfortably warm, despite being made of ice."

"Amazing," Leia murmured. She turned her attention to the giant blocks of ice that made up the palace. She could clearly see the grid of silver, woven in a lacelike pattern that added to the elegance of the ice palace and—yes. There it was. Red twinkling through.

"How are the palaces given energy?" Leia asked innocently. Through the doors, they could see glittering lights, and the guests had all discarded their heat wraps. A blast of warmth enveloped them as they drew closer.

"Ah, we have a networked grid of power built into the ice," the captain said. He paused in the doorway, drawing their attention to the center of the nearest block. "See that?"

Leia nodded.

"It's a mix of doonium laced with copper-infused carnium. Stable, strong metal that naturally generates and holds conductive power."

"Fascinating," Leia breathed as if she didn't already know this information. "I've never heard of carnium before. It must be quite rare."

"Most ships in the galaxy are powered by Tibanna gas, or proprietary fuel blends, such as rhydonium," the captain said. His voice held a note of pride as he added, "But Madurs has a natural strain of carnium running through it. It enables us to safely build our palaces, as well as fuel our shuttles, such as the one you arrived in, and our underwater vessels."

"Underwater ves—" Han started, but Leia nudged him.

"I had no idea that such a rich resource was under Madurs's ice," she said, hoping to draw more details from the captain.

But she had gone a step too far. He squared his shoulders, physically moving away from the ice block. "The prime minister is waiting," he said, gesturing with his arm for Leia and Han to enter the main palace.

Madurs had remained independent, slipping unnoticed through the grasp of larger political entities for the entirety of its colonization. Independence had its benefits, even Leia could see that. But worlds were better when they worked together, ensuring the prosperity of all in good times, the survival of all in bad times.

Stepping into the ice palace now, it was hard for Leia to believe that Madurs had ever experienced bad times. The doors opened up to a grand reception hall, with towering ceilings that dripped glowing icicles twisting in graceful curves. Glimmering lights twinkled within the long strands of clear ice, casting the entire room in a sparkling glow that shifted as people moved about.

Han steered them toward a table with a display of drinks. Stemmed goblets were perched sideways atop glass cylinders that rose from the floor, clustered together in a display. Each goblet held just enough glittering bright-green liquid in the bowl so that it didn't spill over the tilted lip.

"It's hot!" Leia said, picking up a goblet. Steam bubbled up from the cylinder that had served as a stand for the sideways goblet.

"You hold it by the stem," a man said in a deep voice, showing her the way he held his. Han took a goblet, too, sipping the emerald liquid. Leia emulated him.

A burst of heat filled her tongue, followed by a different type of burn down her throat.

"The secret to living on Madurs," the man said, raising his glass. While Leia had sipped her liquor, the man downed the contents in one swallow, put the goblet on the tray of a passing server droid, and picked up another one. A cloud of steam rose up from the vacant cylinder that had held the goblet on its side. "Warm kistrozer."

Warm? It was practically lava. Han had discreetly gotten rid of his goblet, and Leia wanted to do the same but didn't. She took another sip.

"I should introduce myself," the man said, having already finished his second glass. "Yens."

It took Leia a moment to realize that the man meant he was Dreand Yens.

"Oh!" She ducked her head in respect. "It's an honor to meet you, Prime Minister." She hadn't realized he was the same man who'd sent her the holo before, and despite having seen various images of him in the dossier Major Nioma had given her, she simply hadn't recognized him. His voice was relaxed now, not stiff like he was reading from a prompt. The holo had shown him wrapped in official wear—a suit, a capelet, a sash full of honors and medals. But he was more casual here, wearing a dark-brown fur cape no different from a dozen or more similar capes. Prime Minister Yens chatted easily and stood casually; the captain who'd escorted them into the palace seemed more of an authority figure than this man.

"Thank you for replying to my original message," Leia said, aware of using her diplomatic tone of voice, but unable to stop doing so.

"Thank you for bringing a shipload of tourists to my moon!" The prime minister laughed, tipping his glass of kistrozer toward her. Leia caught Han's eye, raising her eyebrow. He stepped closer to her, his elbow brushing hers, a quiet certainty in the way he stood so solidly strong at her side.

"I wanted to discuss—" Leia started, but the prime minister waved her words aside.

"Drink, drink," he insisted, nodding to her glass. "I did not invite you here for a diplomatic mission. You came to see art and experience the natural beauty of the world. Let's not mar that with political talk."

"But—"

"And here, you as well!" the prime minister said, reaching for another glass of kistrozer and pushing it into Han's hand. "This is the time for drinking!"

Leia caught Han's eye. His expression was grim. They could both tell the underlying meaning of the prime minister's unspoken words—this wasn't the time or place where it was safe to speak.

Too much was being left unsaid. The black tower jutting out past the broken ice palaces, the pointed way the prime minister insisted on talking about nothing more in-depth than art . . .

Not a single person in the entire palace wore an Imperial uniform, but that did not mean the Empire wasn't there.

CHAPTER 33

HAN

"THIS IS OUR GRAND PALACE," Yens told them as he led Han and Leia around the room. Han kept his kistrozer in his hands—the hot glass warmed him—but he didn't take another sip. Not even Leia in full-politician mode dared to grace her lips with the noxious stuff. Just the smell of it made Han want to cough. The prime minister must have guts stronger than the fuel intake on the *Millennium Falcon*.

"Art must have function," the prime minister told them conversationally. "It is true of nature as well—stars twinkle prettily, but it is only because they burn to live."

As they strolled around the outer edge of the expansive reception hall, Han became aware of the way everyone in the room seemed to have at least half their attention on them. Even though Han knew they weren't looking at him—it was Leia and Yens who were the focus—it unnerved him. He didn't like looking that closely at his own life, much less letting others do it.

"Each of our palaces is built directly on the ice, but we sink a metal platform base into the building site. It is the source of both the power and the heat inside the building—we pipe in hot water from the sea near the moon's molten core, and we lace the walls with a rare energy-providing metal." The prime minister spoke lightly, but Han didn't trust the razor's edge underlying the words.

"Yes, carnium," Leia said. Her voice dropped. "I was serious about my offer to help you protect your reserves."

"Despite being made of ice, our moon can often have a dehydrating effect on the skin," the prime minister continued blithely as if Leia had not spoken. "The steam helps by giving us both heat and moisture."

In that moment, gentle waves of steam radiated from the walls and ceiling. Like clouds covering the sun, the entire room was blanketed in the soft, airy steam, just warm enough to be refreshing instead of oppressive. Nearby, several of the guests from the *Halcyon* started to unclasp their thermal disks, feeling too warm with them on, despite being encased in a building made of ice.

"We use the same technology for the guesthouses," Prime Minister Yens continued. "You arrived late; did you get a chance to see them?"

"No," Han said.

The prime minister led them to the other side of the reception hall, where an oversized door with a round pinnacle led them to a courtyard framed by a spiky wall that looked as if it were made of stalactites of ice. The courtyard was decorated with delicate, twisting branches that were white and encrusted with snow, giving it the appearance of a forest, even though the branches only reached about knee height on Han.

But what really grabbed his attention was the tall, wide cylinders perched atop the ice, and the huge cubes that sat crookedly atop each cylinder.

"It's more . . . modern," Prime Minister Yens said, as if he were admitting to a foul secret. "I campaigned for a different design, myself, but the artist was very passionate about the guesthouses."

"These are the guesthouses?" Leia asked.

"Each cylinder contains a short turbolift that takes you to the residence," Yens said, pointing to one. Steam obscured the interior of the ice tube, but there was a shadow of the internal working of the lift inside them.

"But the cubes are . . ." Leia framed her hands, then shifted them to show how cockeyed the cubes on the cylinders were. The angles jutted out oddly; without the cylinder to support it, the cube houses would have had to balance on one single sharp corner.

Yens laughed. "Let me assure you, the floors inside are not crooked. The angle of the walls provides more room than you would think, and getting to be inside an object that seems impossible—ah, well, it's not visually my taste, but the concept is strong, and the artist truly is a genius. She'll go far in the galaxy."

Han had stayed in worse places than a piece of modern art made of ice, but he was still dubious about the situation. The cube houses had walls opaque enough that it was impossible to see through them, granting privacy despite the material. They were each a little larger than the cabins on the *Halcyon*, and judging from the number of guests who'd elected to stay on the moon for the excursion, it was a good thing so many of the cube houses were built and ready to be occupied.

Then it hit him.

He silently counted—twenty-five guesthouses lined the courtyard, little cubes perched on cylinders like the kistrozer rested on the heat stacks. They truly seemed to be guest residences, not intended for any of the permanent residences of the city, who all had their own, normal homes to go to.

"How long does it take you to build one of these things?" Han asked.

"One? Oh, probably a month or so from inception to completion, depending on the supplies at hand."

Han caught Leia's eye as the prime minster blathered on about some other aspect of art Han had no care for. His wife's brow furrowed, trying to get his meaning, and Han jerked his head toward the guesthouses. It would have taken months, perhaps a whole year, to complete them all.

Leia's eyes widened as she grasped his unspoken comment. Prime Minister Yens had indicated that the *Halcyon* guests were the first visitors the moon had had for quite some time, at least since the Emperor's visit years ago. These cube houses had been constructed recently, when Yens said he had no expectation of future guests.

So why did he build residences for fifty or more people to stay at the palace? Who—or what—had the prime minister been expecting?

Leia cast one last look at the numerous guesthouses, then reached for Yens's arm. "Prime Minister," she said, "while I do deeply appreciate the art of your moon, you must know that I had hoped to discuss the possibility of Madurs joining the new republic forming in the wake of the oppressive Empire. I would be happy to give you information about—"

"No need," Yens said brusquely. Han narrowed his eyes as the man shook his arm free of Leia's grasp.

"But—" Leia started.

"We need no one and nothing," the prime minister said. "Do you not see how our moon flourishes without being under the boot of a grasping galactic government?"

Han kept his mouth firmly closed—although he could see the prime minister's point, he had no desire to put himself in his wife's line of fire.

"What would any republic or alliance do for us?" Yens continued. "We are a truly independent world."

"When I first reached out, however—" Leia tried again.

"You came for the art, my dear, and the art alone. You'll see. Madurs can play the political game, but we stand alone."

Leia looked as if she wanted to protest some more, but Yens ignored her. Han studied the man. He spoke confidently, with a tone that brooked no argument. And the way he kept speaking over Leia . . . it grated on Han's nerves, but not because he felt like his wife needed defending; she could handle herself. No, it bothered Han because Yens was reminding him of Lando on Bespin. The man wore a smile to hide his fear.

Well. Nothing like confronting an issue head-on. "What about that black tower?" Han said loudly, his voice bouncing off the odd-angled ice walls.

Yens froze. He made a show of checking the time on his wrist chrono. "We should go inside," he said. He started to head to the doors leading back into the reception hall, but Han grabbed the man's elbow, yanking him around.

Leia widened her eyes at Han, clearly wishing for a more politic approach, but niceties had never gotten Han very far. "We saw a strange black spike sticking out of the ice. Beyond the broken palaces. What was that all about?"

"I'm sure I don't know what you mean," Yens started.

Han smiled with all his teeth. "I'm sure you do." Yens opened his mouth, but Han cut him off—the same way the prime minister had kept interrupting his wife. "It was twenty-five, maybe thirty meters tall. Huge metal thing, but black." *Black as the Empire,* Han almost said. "You can't miss it."

A muscle worked in Yens's jaw, but he met Han's gaze unflinchingly. "About a year ago, the Empire came. They wanted our carnium. Gave me a deal, they said, I couldn't refuse."

"And what did you do?" Leia asked quietly.

"I refused them."

Before he could say anything else, the ice beneath their feet shuddered. A splintering crack echoed somewhere nearby, and inside the palace came the sounds of startled screams. Han watched with wide eyes as the ground—made of a solid sheet of ice—shifted. He grabbed for Leia, catching her arm before she lost balance. Yens stood with a wide stance, balancing as the ice moved. "Simply a quake," he called to them. "Nothing to worry about."

It was over in less than a minute, but the ice quake left Han's heart racing, his breath catching. Leia's cheeks were flushed, and she gripped his arm tightly. The ice fields had felt so solidly strong, as firm as any ground Han had ever stood on; the quake had rattled him.

Yens looked down his nose at Han and Leia. "I advise you not to leave the safety of the city without supervision," he said. "After all, anything can happen on the ice."

CHAPTER 34

LEIA

THAT WAS SIMPLY NOT A good enough answer, and an ice quake was not going to stop Leia. "You said the Empire came here," she said, marching over to the prime minister as an aftershock shuddered through the ice. "What *exactly* did they offer?"

"Credits," Yens said. "Not as much as the carnium was worth."

"And the black tower?" Han asked.

"Used to be a station. It was in orbit; they treated it like a base as they scouted the other moons and planets in this system for more carnium."

Leia raised her eyebrow, not even bothering to hide her doubt at his words. Was the prime minister implying that they had shot down an Imperial space station? Han looked grim, and she was reminded that even though he hadn't wanted to come to this world, he still had her back no matter what.

"As you can see," Yens continued, "my people defend what's theirs. We need no alliance with whatever republic emerges from the ashes of what used to be the Empire. A year ago they came; now you're here. It makes no difference. Madurs wants neither of you."

"A year ago," Leia muttered. That would line up with the time when the Empire annexed Cloud City on Bespin—a primary source of

Tibanna gas. While she had not known it at the time, Palpatine must have been deep into the construction of the second Death Star then, but to her knowledge, it did not need carnium—could he have wanted it for another purpose? Leia and the high council had speculated that the grip in the Anoat sector was tightening now as a sort of precautionary plan Palpatine had set up to control the supply chain and cut off the budding new republic at the knees before it could fully stand. But Madurs and its carnium was an alternative source of energy, and if the Empire had come a year ago—at the same time as it seized control of Bespin—perhaps there was something more nefarious at hand than a complication in controlling fuel supplies for the galaxy.

Han scowled darkly at the prime minister, who seemed oblivious to the foul look. But Leia also knew that Han's disconcerting reaction wasn't just to this new knowledge of the Empire seizing control of fuel supply lines.

About a year ago was when he had been frozen in carbonite.

What must it be like for him? Only a few weeks had passed since Leia had been able to steal into Jabba the Hutt's palace in the Northern Dune Sea. Han had gone from Bespin to Tatooine with no memory or even awareness of the time that had passed. To him, Leia had confessed her love, then he'd been frozen, then he woke up in her arms. His recovery hadn't been smooth—Leia was still worried about long-term repercussions of Han being frozen for so long, and his temporary blindness had truly scared her—but he had lost a year of his life.

A year Leia had lived.

So much had happened that year that Han knew nothing about. He was aware that Leia had saved him, true, but he didn't see the endless nights of planning. The frustration at delays.

Han had not yet noticed the new scar on Leia's arm, the one that she refused to let the meds fully erase. She kept a hairbreadth of that scar as a memorial, a gift from a commander with a particular need for vengeance against her specifically, a reminder that sometimes the choices people made resulted in situations where there were no longer choices to be had.

Leia hadn't told Han about the long struggle even to *find* him. When he'd been frozen, Boba Fett had been right there, ready to take him to Jabba. But things had gone sideways, as always. For a while, Leia had thought he'd died. She'd crossed paths with Qi'ra and Crimson Dawn. She'd made deals she hadn't wanted to make. And in the end, Han had still ended up on Jabba's wall, and Leia had still had to fight to save him.

Han knew only the beginning and the end of that story. And she should tell him the middle, she knew that, but so far she couldn't seem to put into words just how much had transpired while he slept.

She had only found the courage to say the words "I love you" moments before he'd been frozen. And she had spent the year that followed with those words as a chain around her heart. There was no closure in silence. Every decision she made, every action she took, was pulled down by those words, still lingering, forming a question she could not find the answer to.

Leia twisted her wedding ring on her finger, but a piece of the crystallized vine seemed to shift at her touch. She forced her hands down; she didn't know how delicate the ring was, and even though it felt like amber, it wasn't truly. It could break. Everything could.

Prime Minister Yens gestured to the big doors leading back inside to the reception hall. The party was starting to wind down, the glittering distraction of the palace and all it had to offer somewhat dimmed by the ice quake. Leia and Han followed him inside.

"Let's smile for the holos." Yens put down his now empty glass on the tray of a server droid, grabbed Leia by the elbow, and steered her to another part of the reception hall, where a series of reporters and X-0X units were mingling. Leia could hear Han's footsteps behind them, but she didn't turn around, even though she didn't like the way the prime minister held her arm so firmly, his fingers digging into the inside of her elbow.

"Here she is!" Prime Minister Yens said loudly. "Sorry to have stolen away our guest of honor!" A few reporters captured her image.

"I wasn't expecting a media conference," Leia told him quietly.

"Then you're not as savvy a politician as I was led to believe," the prime minister replied in a low voice, his lips curved in a politician's smile for the cams.

"This is the first time in years that we've had attention on our little moon *solely* for its merits in the art realm," he said louder, his voice picked up by the recorders. "We greatly value the attention your presence brings to our ice palaces. Perhaps we can convince the *Halcyon* to make Madurs a regular stop on its cruising itinerary, especially now that we have intergalactic peace!"

Leia reminded herself that she *was* there to reassure the public that the galaxy no longer needed to fear the Empire's stranglehold. Being unable to convince the prime minister to join the unified new government left a bitter taste in her mouth, but Leia had been raised a princess and had worked diligently to become a politician.

She knew when to smile.

And so she did, graciously praising the wonders of both Madurs and the ship that had brought her to the moon, leading the reporters down a story path full of art and beauty. Yens kept his hand on her elbow and his own smile fixed firmly in place.

"And what about that ice quake?" one of the reporters asked.

For the first time, Yens's cheery attitude faded. "A mild inconvenience that rarely causes harm. Ice quakes are a fact of life on Madurs, nothing to worry about."

"Was it the ice quakes that led to the ruins we passed on our way in?"

Leia cut her eyes at the inquisitive reporter—while most of the people gathered here were clearly under Madurs's employ, this journalist was one Leia recognized from the *Halcyon*. Riyola had promised to send someone trustworthy who would help ensure that the narrative was presented truthfully. This woman, with short-cropped silver hair that belied her youthful face, had a pin on her collar identifying her as working with *Contempora News,* a holonet show with a reputation for balanced information that was vigorously fact-checked.

The woman noticed Leia's attention and flashed her a smile. "Mira Khun, for *Contempora*," she said. "I'm pitching a story to the network about this jaunt."

Leia wasn't sure if Mira meant her honeymoon, the *Halcyon*'s premier voyage out of the shadow of the Empire, or their impromptu visit to Madurs, but for the first time that night, her smile back at the reporter wasn't false. "The prime minister was just talking to me about his moon's natural resources," she said, turning to Yens. "Of course I care about more than just the economic welfare of any world; Prime Minister Yens has offered to allow us to inspect the ice fields near the ruins so that we can advise him on any conservation efforts that are needed for this moon's stability."

As one, every lens whirred as they focused on the prime minister's face. Leia blinked up at him innocently. Yens had said nothing whatsoever about leading any tour of the ruins—and the black tower beyond—but now that Leia had put him on the spot, denying her access to that area would look even more suspect.

"Of course," Yens said gruffly. "All art is temporary, even this palace." He swept his hands up, clearly trying to divert attention.

But he had forced Leia into the spotlight, and Leia was going to use it to her advantage. "And there is beauty in broken things," she said, cutting him off. "Such a good idea to juxtapose the grandeur of this ice palace with those that have fallen. Shall we visit them today?"

The prime minister sputtered. "If you're concerned about the conservation efforts, I will be happy to explain more during our forthcoming visit to the underwater fishing base so that you can see just how in touch the people of Madurs are with our environment."

"Of course, that sounds delightful!" Leia gushed. "And on the way back, we can stop at the broken ice palaces. What a wonderful idea, Prime Minister." Before he could answer, Leia turned to the journalists, singling out Mira Khun. "Would you like to come with me, for your story?"

Mira grinned rapaciously. "Absolutely."

With plans settled, the little media corner broke up, reporters mingling with the fading crowd, droid cams drifting higher for a different perspective for the feeds. In all reality, Leia hoped that the exposure would work well for Madurs's art world; seeing the ice palaces on the feeds must surely incentivize some to come see them in person.

Feeling it her duty, Leia forced herself to make her way around the reception hall, greeting guests from the *Halcyon* and residents of Madurs alike. Even the most reluctant of the tourists from the *Halcyon* were eager to don the thermal disks and venture out to explore this harsh but beautiful moon, and Leia was gratified to see that this part of her plan, at least, had paid off. Clearly the prime minister had been pushing the art angle of Madurs; perhaps invoking the promise of more star cruiser stops on this moon would be the economic leverage needed.

The server droids had switched out the warm kistrozer with something bubbly and light, and Leia happily claimed a glass for herself. The party was starting to break up as guests from the *Halcyon* made their way to the cube houses in the square behind the main palace. Eager to change clothes for the excursion, Leia downed her drink quickly and looked around for a place to put the empty glass.

A server—a human, not a droid—stepped forward with a tray. "Thank you," Leia said.

The server nodded, but he looked as if he wanted to say something. Leia waited, and, sure enough, the young man spoke after furtively looking around. "Is it true what they're saying?" he asked in a low voice. "We—" At this, he glanced behind him, and Leia noticed a cluster of servers lingering near the wall, watching them raptly. "We all wanted to ask. Is it true that the war is over?"

Whatever Leia had been expecting, it hadn't been this. "Of course," she said.

"But . . ." The server sat his tray down on a table, giving Leia his full attention. "But *really* over? The Empire fell?"

"The Emperor is dead," Leia said in as clear a voice as she could. She enunciated each word carefully, strongly. It was disheartening that even here, the Empire's propaganda and power were leveraged against the truth. "The Empire is gone. The galaxy is free."

"But—" he started, but then the young man's eyes widened, and he turned on his heel, grabbing the tray he'd set down. Glasses clinking together, he bustled off.

Leia turned to see what the server had seen. Prime Minister Yens raised his glass to her from across the room in a mock salute.

CHAPTER 35

HAN

DESPITE BEING MADE OF ICE, the guest residence Han and Leia were given was luxuriously appointed, warm, and private. From the ground, the cube house looked as if it was perched cockeyed on a tube, much like the precariously warmed kistrozer glasses, but inside, the floor was flat and made of some sort of metal panel that radiated heat. The walls all angled oddly, but the sharp corners allowed prisms of rainbows to glow across the white furnishings. The city resided at the northern pole of Madurs; it would never get fully dark while they were visiting, and the gentle, hazy light cast everything in cool-toned softness.

"It's not bad," Han said, shrugging as he sat down on the bed. He leaned back, his boots on the white coverlet until Leia knocked them down.

"What do you think of Yens?" she asked, sitting down in the spot where his feet had been.

Han didn't bother opening his eyes. "He's lying."

"Obviously." Leia paused, watching a beam of light that cut through the room. "But about what?"

Han raised his hand in the air from his position on the bed, counting down with his fingers. "The black tower. The ruined palaces. The real reason he invited you here. Take your pick."

Leia frowned, shoving his legs again. "The Empire got here first."

Han snorted. Not everything had to lead back to the Empire. He didn't bother arguing with Leia now; he knew she would never see it from his point of view. But little worlds like this, ones that could not only self-sustain but thrive enough to develop their own art and culture—they didn't want to join any larger government, Imperial or Republic. They just wanted to be left alone.

Han could respect that.

Leia stood up from the bed and headed to the clothing stand in the corner, where two straffle cloaks were draped, waiting for them. They'd been informed that, after a brief respite, the first tour to view the ice fishing and underwater base would begin. Leia tossed one of the cloaks to Han, who let out a breath of air in an audible *oof!* as the heavy material hit him in the stomach.

"You do realize we don't have to go, right?" he said, shoving the cloak to the floor.

"Come on, this is our chance to check out that black tower."

"There's no way he's gonna actually take us to see that," Han said with a snort. "Bet you he'll take us in the other direction and then give some excuse about how we can't go there."

Leia frowned. "Either way, we're not going to just stay here."

Han finally sat up. His eyes searched hers. "Do you really think the Empire has some hold here? Sure, that black tower is pretty damning, but Yens made it sound like the Empire came, and they fought them off."

"A little moon like this can't just fight off the whole Empire alone."

Han shrugged. "Could have been more trouble than it was worth. And the Empire was losing its grip."

"Not a year ago. Not while you—" Leia stopped herself.

But Han knew what she'd been about to say. *Not while you were gone.* He'd lost a whole year, and within a week of him waking up, both Jabba the Hutt and the Empire were dead. Everything had happened so *fast*— but not for Leia. Not for anyone who hadn't been trapped in carbonite.

"It doesn't *have* to be the Empire," Han said sullenly. "Sounds like Yens just doesn't like *any* overarching government."

Leia cut her eyes at him, twisting her ring on her finger. "The new republic we make will be different."

Han couldn't hide his doubtful expression, but before he could comment, a beeping sound emitted from Leia's bag. She bent to root around in its depths, withdrawing a holocomm. She sat down on the bed beside Han as she flicked it on.

Riyola Keevan's form illuminated on the holo. "Leia, Han," she said by way of greeting, her words clipped.

"What's wrong?" Leia asked, concern etched on her face at the Pantoran woman's dark tone and serious expression.

"The prime minister has rescinded his invitation for the media," Riyola said.

Leia shot Han a look. She may have more experience with publicity, but it didn't take a genius to know that a government that wanted to hide from the media had something big to hide.

"Khun contacted me," Riyola continued. "I'd arranged for her to cover this event in the first place, and when I spoke with the prime minister, he was on board for all media to stay the duration of the excursion. She planned for an entire special documentary covering not just your visit, but more of the moon's history."

"But not anymore?" Leia asked.

"The prime minister's chief of staff escorted her off the moon personally."

Han let out a low whistle. Yens wasn't being subtle here. And he'd acted quickly—the press conference had been only about an hour ago. The reporter had been packed up into a shuttle while he and Leia were polishing off their drinks.

"I guess that reporter's not coming with you to examine Madurs's conservation efforts after all," Han said softly.

Riyola's mouth stretched in a grim line. "I don't like it. Do you want me to come to the surface myself?"

"No, that's okay," Leia said. "I like knowing I have support from the *Halcyon* if I need it."

Han doubted Riyola knew much of Leia's plans. The attaché's primary focus was the ship; if Leia revealed that she was mixing business with pleasure, he doubted the *Halcyon* would have allowed the excursion to the ice moon to happen. But Riyola was also smart; she had to at least suspect something was wrong when the media was blacklisted.

"I'm standing by, then," the Pantoran said. "Keep in touch."

Leia nodded and turned off the comm. She looked to Han, her eyebrows raised in a challenge.

"Fine." Han groaned, falling back on the pillows. "Looks like there's either the Empire or something else bad happening on this moon." They just couldn't catch a break. He sat up on his elbows, though. "But . . ."

"But what?" There was already a fight in Leia's voice, as if she could guess what Han wasn't saying.

Han didn't finish the sentence. There was no point in saying he wished things were different, easier. They weren't, and both he and Leia wouldn't turn a blind eye or sit idly waiting for backup.

However, there was some emotion warring behind her eyes that worried Han. He had seen her slip into a mask before when presented with someone she needed to be polite to, or a cam droid, or up on a stage.

He didn't like that she was wearing a mask now, when it was just the two of them.

He straightened on the bed, pulling her closer. She felt so delicate in his arms, almost fragile, like a bird newly hatched, unsure of whether or not to plunge from its nest and take the first flight.

"I can't stop now," Leia murmured. Han didn't answer, just rubbed a rhythmic circle against her back. After several small moments, Leia added, "I have to do as much as I can while I can."

That made him stop. "*While* you can?" The wording made it sound ominous, and Leia's defeated shoulders and low head only added to that.

She twisted around in the bed to meet his eyes. "Not everyone in the galaxy is like you," she said.

Han smirked, reclining on the pillows so that Leia could get a better view of all he had to offer. "Why, thank you."

That actually got a laugh out of her, but a grave shadow passed quickly back over her countenance. "I *meant* that not everyone will take the news of my, er, parentage as well as you did."

Han blinked a few times. He had to remind himself of what Leia meant. When she'd first told him that Vader was her father, it had been so preposterous, news given to him so suddenly and after the rush of her acceptance of his proposal that he'd mostly put it out of his mind. Leia, linked to Vader? That was impossible. It didn't make logical sense. So his brain had shifted it away, sidelining the truth so completely that he'd been able to ignore it.

That had been a mistake.

Not only had Han not seen just how heavily this information continued to weigh on his wife, he'd also not allowed himself time to accept the truth.

Nothing like repression to rear its ugly head at the worst moment. Han forced the thoughts back down. Again. As much as he could.

"It's not going to—" he started.

"It matters," she stated flatly. "Once the galaxy knows my secret, people will see me differently. It will limit what I'll be able to do to help others; they'll question, at the very least, my motives." Leia had a distant look in her unfocused eyes. It reminded Han sharply of the way she'd spoken about Luke, just after the second Death Star had been destroyed, the certainty with which she'd known he had survived.

That look put Han on edge. It spoke of unknowable things, of that strange way Luke had turned from a kid to a Jedi, and Han didn't like it one bit. It made him feel as if the entire galaxy was passing him by, like he was stagnant while everyone else went into hyperdrive.

But when Leia's gaze centered on him, he saw only fear inside her. And somehow, that was worse.

A part of Han wanted to kiss her worry away, to make her forget about whatever was causing her such trouble. And he knew instinctually that she would let him. Ice fishing and tours be damned; if Han scooped Leia up and tossed her down on the bed, he was certain she would let him distract her from the dark thoughts troubling her now.

But he couldn't do that. Not to her.

Leia closed her eyes. "I have to do as much as I can, while I can," she repeated. Leia let out a defeated breath. "A secret like this, it cannot be hidden forever. So if there's something I can do, I have to do it. *Now.* I can't stop doing my job," she continued, speaking quickly, as if her words were a confession. "I can't stop helping others. I can't just quit being myself. And part of it is because this is the way I believe I should live my life. This is the work I love. And part of it is because I have to keep the guilt at bay. I commanded the battles. I knew people would die—good people—and they did."

It was a war, Han wanted to say, but he was too afraid that his words would silence hers.

"But also, I know I will no longer be trusted if . . . once people know. If I have a position in the new government, it will be recalled. Any work I've done will be criticized, possibly dismantled. I'll lose everything."

"Except me." The words slipped past Han's lips before he could even process the thought, but he saw the way Leia looked at him, the hope rekindled in her eyes. "Face it, sweetheart, you're stuck with me."

She laughed again, the sound sweet and true.

"But," Han added, "it seems to me like you're wasting all your precious time worrying about the future. Maybe the galaxy finds out. Maybe it doesn't. Right now, we have a prime minister to work around so we can find out what that damn black tower is. One thing at a time."

He didn't want to dismiss Leia's thoughts too much; it was clear this truly worried her. But Han wasn't bothered. Leia, he had no doubt, would rise above any challenge. And he knew better than most that it was possible to reinvent yourself beyond your past.

She leaned over the bed, cradling the side of his face before drawing him in for a kiss. When they parted, she whispered against his lips, "How are you so remarkable?"

Han grinned, satisfied. "Just naturally perfect."

Leia laughed, and with that, the last of her reservations seemed to break away. "Right. Focus on the now. Which means we need to get ready to go on a tour of an ice fishing base."

Han groaned, the sound half a laugh, as Leia bent to gather the cloak Han had tossed to the floor earlier. Han could convince his wife that her lineage didn't matter, but nothing could convince her to stay in bed all day.

CHAPTER 36

LEIA

LEIA TWISTED HER RING AROUND and around her finger. She cast a fur-tive look at Han as they descended in the guesthouse turbolift. He seemed utterly unconcerned, but would that extend to her following Luke's guidance and learning about the Force? She still felt that such a path was not her fate, and she wasn't sure it ever would be. But then again, she had never really expected to marry a rogue on a forest moon in the Outer Rim before, and that had happened.

One part of Leia was curious about the Force. Luke's words about how they could work together to bring a stronger peace was tempting. And even though she knew that he was going on his own quests for more knowledge and she would be involved in the formation of the new republic, that didn't mean the door was closed forever. The chance to learn about the Force would arise again.

And she might take it.

Would Han be as comfortable with the idea of his wife learning about the Force considering the damage her father had done while wield-ing it?

Worry about the now, Leia reminded herself.

The turbolift doors opened, and a blast of cold met them. Han stepped out first, looking around at the small crowd gathering in the courtyard. Leia lingered beside him, unwilling to let social niceties drive her thoughts away.

It would be so much easier to convince Prime Minister Yens to ally Madurs with the new galactic government if she had the gravitas of being not only a senator but also a Jedi Knight. Leia had watched Luke meditate before; the serenity on his face had been real, and something that seemed impossible for her to share.

No—the Force was a temptation. While it brought Luke peace, it had brought her father war.

Vader brought himself war, Leia thought.

"This way, please," the captain Leia had met earlier called from the reception hall, waving the gathering crowd over. He led the group through the palace and toward the grand entrance, where sleds strapped to prooses awaited them. Leia looked for Nah'hai, the woman who'd driven them from the spaceport, but she and her proose were not among the entourage.

Prime Minister Yens himself offered a hand for Leia to step into a sled. "Will we be stopping by the ruined palaces before or after our visit to the fishing area?" she asked.

"After," the prime minister replied with a confident smile.

"He's not going to let us see a damn thing," Han muttered in Leia's ear as they snuggled closely together on the sled.

Once everyone was in their own sled, the captain let out a whistle, and the drivers all called to their prooses to start the journey. Sure enough, the sleds took them in the opposite direction of the broken ice palaces and the mysterious black tower.

They moved too fast for easy conversation, so Leia didn't bother trying to answer Han's I-told-you-so smirk. She leaned into his arm, unconsciously fiddling with her wedding ring again.

If this honeymoon was partially a public relations trip to assure the populace of the safety of the galaxy, it only proved that the citizens of the galaxy loved a love story and wanted a glimmer of happiness. And yet Leia knew from experience that the only thing people loved to see more than a hero was a fallen hero. The more they celebrated her, the more people would seek her flaws, exploit them, and use them to topple her image.

It reminded her sharply of her mother, Breha Organa, and her experience with the Day of Demand. Breha had climbed Appenza Peak confidently. But every step closer to the summit led to an even greater fall when she lost her footing and nearly died after tumbling down the side of the mountain, her injuries so severe that her body was permanently damaged and some organs had to be replaced with cybernetics.

Every moment of joy Leia felt now was only raising her higher so that, when she inevitably fell, the crash would be that much harder.

Leia felt a snap against her finger, and she jerked her hands apart. Her nervous fidgeting had damaged her ring made of vine. Inwardly, she cursed herself. Although it had felt like amber, the ring had been made of nothing more than a bit of delicate plant, and she had been too rough with it. She lifted her hand, squinting through the cold air that rushed by, looking at the damage.

A hairline fracture splintered over the surface. Her ring had not broken, but it would—and soon.

She stared so intently at the cracks that Leia was startled when Han grabbed her hand, weaving his fingers through hers and wrapping her cold palm with his warmth. He couldn't have seen the barely visible splinters in the amber—he merely saw Leia's hand and claimed it as his.

Han was right. The future wasn't worth worrying about. Her ring would eventually break, but that didn't matter if he was still holding her hand.

Leia had never seen a more efficient means of ice fishing. Prime Minister Yens turned everyone's attention to Anyel, a marine biologist who worked at the base they were gathered around, floating in the center of an enormous hole cut directly into the ice. From their vantage point, the guests could see that the ice was five or six meters thick, although they were warned that some areas of the ice field were nowhere near that thick and could even be dangerous enough to fall through.

"As you can see, although the surface of our moon is barren, our people find plentiful resources under the ice. We do not merely survive on Madurs; we flourish." Anyel grinned at the guests as Prime Minister Yens swept his arm toward the elaborate fishing center.

The hole carved in the ice was about a hundred meters in diameter, and while there was a ring of empty space in the outer perimeter, showing the cool gray-green waters of the sea that covered the moon, the majority of that space was filled with a large, bubble-like transparisteel building that connected to the rim with four bridges. Anyel led the group across the nearest bridge, waving merrily at the anglers who cast long lines into the sea from the outer edge.

"The anglers primarily get salna, a large fish that often swims close to the surface," Anyel told the group. "You'll be getting a taste of it for lunch. But the real action is inside."

Leia worked her way to the front of the group. "What about the ice quakes?" she asked. "Do they affect the wildlife?"

Worry passed over Anyel's face, and her eyes flicked to the back of the group, where Prime Minister Yens lingered. "The ice quakes are of deep concern," she said in a low voice. "We're doing all we can to offset them."

Leia opened her mouth to ask more, but a bustle of excitement erupted to the left, and everyone peered over the railing of the bridge to watch as one of the anglers pulled up a massive fish. The woman had a pole fitted to a harness strapped to her torso, but the taut line dragged her half a meter closer to the edge of the hole. Leia gasped, but the angler was clearly in her element, sliding her feet into grips and using her entire body to pull the fish up. This was no high-tech operation; the anglers at the edge used the same tried-and-true methods of catching fish that people had no doubt implemented for millennia. Leia—as well as the entire group of tourists from the *Halcyon*, watching from the bridge—cheered as the angler was able to swing up a huge, silver-blue fish with a spiky dorsal fin. That one fish could easily feed a large family, and the entire group of anglers around the edge of the hole worked together to bring more in. As soon as the woman had landed her salna, more people rushed forward to process the fish or cast more lines in the hot spot.

"This way," Anyel said, motioning the group toward a pair of open doors at the end of the bridge, leading into the transparisteel building floating in the water.

Han held Leia's arm as they stepped through, not as a form of endearment, she knew, but because Leia's eyes were wide, looking all around except at her feet. "Watch it," he said in a low voice, pulling her back from a railing on the edge of the platform.

Leia couldn't help herself. This building was a marvel. Not only was it artistically designed—she expected nothing less from the people of Madurs—but it was also highly functional. The transparisteel walls curved to give it a natural flotation in the water, but Leia noted the carnium web embedded in the transparisteel, providing efficient energy to the various resources, including the turbine wheels that kept the building steady both in the water and where hooked up to energy reserves. The platform they stood on overlooked the main hall below, but it also gave them a view of the center tube that Leia hadn't been able to see thanks to the ultraviolet protection on the transparisteel from the outside. The tube flared at the top but sank well out of sight, into the darkened parts of the floating bubble that were underwater. And it was filled with every type of plant, from flowering sakoola to edible root vines. Herbs, peppers, edible seed pods, various fruits and vegetables—Madurs had it all growing right in the center of their main harvesting building.

"Some of these plants are tropical," Leia muttered to Han, pointing at a citrella that she recognized from the climate simulation room on the *Halcyon,* a fruit that was native to Synjax.

"Thanks to a mixture of carnium, hydroponics, and individualized regulators, we have a variety of plants that would otherwise be impossible to grow on our icy moon," Prime Minister Yens said, noting the fruit Leia had indicated.

Anyel and the Prime Minister escorted them to an efficient series of turbolifts built into the outer transparisteel. The group was deposited on the main working floor, where a series of portals cut into the walls would lead directly out into the cold water. Leia watched with wonder as underwater fishers departed from the dock through magnetic-shield-protected bays that led to bubble-domed submersible vessels. While the anglers on the surface caught the prized salna one by one, these under-water net fishers brought in whole schools of fish. Another group of underwater fishers wearing skintight radiant heat suits and breathing apparatuses lined up and down a corridor that led to a hatch—these were elite harpooners with jet propulsions strapped to their backs who hunted the most prized prey.

A squelching noise nearby made Leia jump, and Han laughed at how easily she'd been startled. She'd been wrong, though—the underwater net fishers didn't just target schools of fish. Bright red kelp slopped on the floor as one fisher returned from his haul.

The people of Madurs had learned to gather the bounty of the sea right below their feet. Nothing grew and little lived on the surface of their cold world, so they went below. And they ate better than many worlds Leia had visited.

Anyel took them one more level down, to an underwater viewing platform. Looking up at the swirl of green from the growing tube and the glittering light from the surface of the water made Leia dizzy, but when she looked down, down, down into the depths of the deep dark water, a sense of cold peace settled over her. Everyone was breathless and silent as they watched flashes of bioluminescent creatures glowing in the dark, providing glimmering lines of light that hinted at schools of fish. One of the underwater speeders zipped by, its net fisher waving to them. The speeder swooped down, and a floodlight cast a warm glow through the murky depths. The bioluminescent creatures scattered, dis-appearing instantly. But far off, shadows of larger creatures were barely visible, gliding through the water.

"Is this where we are going to see the edonts?" a young boy with yel-low hair said, his hand stuck up in the air.

Anyel deferred to the prime minister; she was only there to speak to them about today's tour. Yens smiled at the boy. "No, you'll all be riding a submersible tomorrow. Edonts live in the coldest waters; they don't get this close to—" He paused and redirected his thoughts. "You'll see them tomorrow. And you won't believe how big they are!"

"It's amazing how much you can harvest from the sea," the child's mother said. "Do the harpooners we saw hunt for edonts?"

"Oh, no." Anyel laughed, taking over again. "Edonts are not food; in fact, their flesh is poisonous. Unlike krackles, there's no part of their body that can really be used."

"They just . . . are," Yens said, a soft smile on his face. "Their only purpose is to exist. Which is, I suppose, why we love them so much. They are big and beautiful and they simply *are*. Much like art. Keep in mind that even things that are functional can reflect an aesthetic viewpoint. You'll see this better when we go to the artists' commune later, but for now . . ."

While Yens continued, Leia moved closer to the marine biologist, drawing her to the side. This platform circled the entire underwater base, with floor-to-ceiling transparisteel windows and enough lights pointing into the dark to give the illusion that they were truly in the ocean. Leia spoke in a low voice, partly due to the reverence this place inspired, but also so she wouldn't be overheard.

"You mentioned that the ice quakes were concerning," Leia said. "I wanted to let you know that I can connect you with some universities I know—the University of Jenrand on Mon Cala may be the most helpful in this situation, with the best underwater sciences. And, of course, when the new government is fully operational, I could—"

"No." Anyel's face shuttered, her tone no longer friendly. She pushed past Leia, sweeping her arms out to get the group's attention. "If I can direct your attention this way, please," she said loudly.

Prime Minister Yens had clearly arranged for the underwater net fishers to put on something of a show for the guests. Soon, the first diver was joined by half a dozen more, each of them equipped with floodlights that cast diffusing beams of illumination through the water. The platform the guests were on completely encircled the bottom of the transparisteel building, and Leia was able to follow the lights of the underwater divers and the decorated bubble-domed submersible ships.

Although troubled by Anyel's abrupt change in demeanor when she was only trying to help, Leia's eyes strained into the darkness, eager to see something new, something unique. A tiny crustacean, bright blue with glowing fronds, skittered over the outside wall before sliding down into darkness. She got a better view of the massively large creatures that were nothing more than shadows in the water—her perspective was off, but she guessed they were at least twice the size of the ice sled, with wide bodies and protruding flippers—two on each side in the front, and three at the tail. Leia longed to grab one of the underwater speeders and race out into the depths, really get a good look at the creatures.

Leia was barely conscious of the way she moved. Most of the others had lingered near the divers, who played with the school of bioluminescent creatures, their long, featherlike bodies wafting in the water, each ripple a different glowing color.

It was eerie and beautiful simultaneously. She turned immediately to Han, who, like her, was staring into the depths of the underwater world.

"You like it," she said, only a hint of a question in her voice.

Han nodded. "Being underwater isn't that much different from being in space."

"The danger," Leia said, nodding. All that separated them from suffocation and death were the transparisteel walls, and that was true of both the underwater base here on Madurs and the cockpit on the *Millennium Falcon.*

"No," Han said in a bemused tone. "Not just the danger. The unexpected."

Leia smiled. Han loved space the way she loved him. The thought rose within her like a tide, and she felt it viscerally, like drowning. Swallowing down her emotion, Leia turned, moving around the circular base, away from him, from everyone. Her hand glided over the cool metal railing, her feet practically running as she chased one of the underwater fishers around the perimeter of the building. The beams of the floodlight bounced off shadows of creatures—

Until it didn't.

Leia paused, and Han, who had started chasing after her, bumped into her. "Look," she breathed.

"There's nothing there." Han leaned over the railing, his face centimeters from the cool transparisteel wall, but he was right.

While the rest of the sea was alive with creatures and plants, bustling with activity, that area—northwest of the main ice palace, Leia guessed—was empty.

Except for the faint outline of one long, black tower driving deep into the water.

There were no underwater creatures there, not even a lone curious crustacean. The underwater fisher seemed to realize that they'd highlighted a forbidden area, and the speeder zipped by, racing in the opposite direction.

Leia and Han stood at the railing, both squinting into the dark. That area, where nothing lived, was where the black tower was embedded in the ice.

"It's time to go." Leia looked up as Anyel approached. Behind the marine biologist, the tour group was leaving.

Mostly alone, Leia tried once more. "I'm not sure what the prime minister has told you," Leia said. "But my offer before was truly meant to help this planet. I know of some grant applications that might—"

"I said no." Anyel's voice was softer now but just as firm.

"Wow," Han said, catching up with the conversation. "Yens sure has a hold on you."

Confusion flickered over the marine biologist's face, and in that moment Leia realized that Anyel's hesitation to accept help might not be coming from coercion on the part of the prime minister. As she followed Anyel toward the door, Leia saw Prime Minister Yens watching them from the corridor. His face was as dark as the water, and as unknowable.

Her eyes drifted to the blinking red light embedded in the ceiling directly above the prime minister's head. She reached for Han, pressing her fingers into his arm and flicking her eyes to the blinking light. It was obvious what it was, more so as they drew closer.

A security feed.

Prime Minister Yens wasn't the only one watching them.

CHAPTER 37

HAN

AS HAN HAD PREDICTED, PRIME Minister Yens had found an excuse to bypass the broken ice palaces and the ominous black tower, re-diverting the group from the ice fishing to the proose stables, neatly winding up back at the palace for a tour of the ice sculpture gallery. While Madurs was most famous for its livable art, from the grand palaces to the cube house residences, there was a thriving trade in ice sculptures, both grown and made. The traditional methods were still used, but the docent leading the tour had been particularly proud of the modern sculptors who started with a base—usually metal, but some artists used proose horns or bone—then dipped it in water from various parts of the moon with slightly different shades, freezing to the frames and forming organic, twisting designs that were sometimes enhanced with the judicious application of a laser blade. These nomadic sculptors traveled the surface of Madurs seeking just the right temperatures, ice floes, and glaciers to include with their art.

Leia fell in love with a painting made of deep indigo ice. It stood in the center of the room on a silver stand so that guests could walk all around it. The artist had etched white lines in the front to create an abstract image of expanding circles that reminded Han of a star map. He leaned forward to read the placard with information on the piece. *The Broken Galaxy*, it was called, made to represent the entire galaxy, from the Core Worlds to Wild Space.

"Art is not static," the docent, a young man named Nondi, said. Everyone from the *Halcyon* gathered around as Nondi showed how the artist included a pendulum made of twisting black metal. The docent held the pendulum to the side and then let go, allowing the metal to skid across the back of the ice painting.

At first, Han couldn't tell that anything had happened. But then he realized the back of the ice painting was deceptive; the ice was clear enough that he hadn't noticed the careful ridges built onto that side. As the metal pendulum swung against the bumps, splinters formed over the back of the painting. The crowd gathered around the work of art had only a moment to see the damage the pendulum cracked along the back of the painting before a small floor heater kicked on, melting the cracks away.

Han watched the water drip to the floor, evaporating in the heat.

"But the painting is weaker now," Leia protested. The metal broke the ice, and while the heat melded it back together, it was thinner. How many times could the brittle, thinning ice be scratched before it shattered?

Nondi smiled sadly. "That is the point of this work of art," he said.

Leia shook her head even as the docent walked away. "It's so beautiful, though," she told Han. "It doesn't have to be broken. All you have to do is not smash the pendulum into it." She reached her hand out as if to touch the painting, but held back. Even the warmth of her fingers would hurt it. "I want to find out more about this," she told Han as she hailed the docent. Han could only shake his head. Leave it to Leia to argue about art.

After trekking through the cold climate back to the main palace, everyone in the party looked forward to an evening inside. Even, admittedly, Han and Leia, who had both noted the distractions that had pulled them away from the ominous black tower embedded beyond the broken palaces.

Leia dressed for the banquet that night, choosing a slinky, drop-waisted gown of deep indigo that was the same color as the ice painting she'd admired earlier. When she moved, the material shifted in color, flashing dark purple and shifting to gold highlights. Ribbons of prismatic crystals hung on gold chain formed the sleeves, leaving the rest of her arms exposed. She paired the dress with a long, ropy strand of versilk pearls harvested from the oceanic world Wrea, and she loosened her hair into similar loopy braids that went halfway down her back before being tucked back into a gold band around her head. Han liked the effect; it made her look good. But it also made him think about how amazing it would be at the end of the day, when he helped her take those braids down.

Han didn't change clothes.

He was quiet throughout the banquet that followed, but only Leia noticed. They were seated at the prime minister's table, and Han was more than happy to let Leia do the talking. This dinner—false smiles, forced civility—it reminded him of that last time he'd been on Bespin. He had known something was wrong then, despite Lando's assurances that all was well, and he knew something was wrong here . . . although Prime Minister Yens didn't seem to be trying that hard to hide the truth. It had been as if he'd stood under the surveillance droid on purpose, so that they would notice it. He had taken them to see art where black metal broke native ice. Earlier that day, he'd set the route for the prooses when they'd first landed. Yens was not a subtle man. He could have had the shuttle land to the east on an open field away from the spaceport; he could have told the drivers to swoop south. But instead they'd gone just close enough to that strange black tower that it *could* have been an accident that they'd seen it.

Han was beginning to think it wasn't.

These "accidents" of seeing things the prime minister seemingly didn't want them to see no longer felt like accidents. And even if Yens kept insisting that they shouldn't look or question too much, it no longer seemed as if he truly wanted to avert their gazes.

Lando had been that way, too. Saying just enough—and not saying even more—that Han had known something wasn't quite right. Leia had, too. And once again, they were stuck in a position where they had to wait for—

Han dropped his fork with a clatter against his plate, a morsel of salna splattering on the table. Leia looked up at him curiously, but he gave her such an easy smile that she turned back to her conversation with the prime minister.

The last time Han had walked into a formal dining room had been on Bespin. And Darth Vader had been at the head of the table.

Darth Vader.

Leia's father.

Han's stomach soured at the thought. He didn't bother picking his fork back up.

He didn't care that Leia shared a bloodline with that monster. He did not care.

Leia reached under the table, touching his knee. Even though she hadn't stopped talking with the prime minister, she found his hand, wove her fingers through his. She squeezed his palm.

She could tell something was wrong.

She didn't even have to look at him to know.

Is that the Force? Han wondered. Vader had been able to anticipate blows or block shots before a blaster had even been fired. Was this the power Leia had inherited?

Her thumb stroked his knuckles under the table.

When Han looked up, Leia was watching him. Her brows creased, and he knew immediately what she was thinking—not because of some sort of strange power, but because her concern was painted vividly across her face. And so was her love.

Han gave her a watery smile, unable to push every dark thought away. "Just tired," he muttered.

Leia raised her eyebrow. She didn't believe him.

She was getting better at reading him.

Before Vader, before Lando's betrayal had been made clear, before it all, Leia had told Han that she knew he'd be as good as gone once the *Falcon* had been repaired. Han thought of that moment often.

It was one of the few times Leia had been dead wrong.

How had she not seen it before? Even if he had actually gone—he did have to face Jabba still—he would have come back.

He would always come back for her.

Han was so lost in thought that he didn't realize Leia had been making an excuse for their early departure from dinner until she stood up, and so did all the political leaders of Madurs. "Please, stay sitting," she said, smiling graciously as she tugged on Han's hand. Han pushed his chair back and stood. "Thank you for a lovely evening." Leia inclined her head at the prime minister.

"You don't have to leave early on my account," Han said, following Leia as they wound through the tables that had been set up for the banquet in the reception hall.

"It's fine," Leia said, not breaking her smile as she nodded at various people from Madurs or the *Halcyon*. Soon enough, they reached the doors that led to the courtyard. An icy blast of cold met them, and Han clicked his thermal disk back on, even though it was just a short walk to the cube house.

The air was frigid as they raced through the gently falling snow across the courtyard to their guest residence. Leia laughed, great clouds of her breath twinkling under the delicate lights that had been strung overhead. The turbolift to their rooms opened, and Leia stepped inside, pulling Han behind her.

Leia leaned against the wall as the lift rose. Han marveled at her. Moments ago, she was the epitome of a graceful diplomat, making polite excuses to leave the table early after having a conversation with the leaders of this moon. And now she was giggling, snow caught on her eyelashes.

It was like she was two different people.

But, Han understood now, she wasn't. She was not just his wife, nor was she just the people's princess. She was Leia, and Han had to love all of her or none of her.

Even her blood.

Han wasn't sure he would ever be able to let go of the rage and terror Vader instilled in him, even if the monster was dead now. Han had lived with those emotions trapped inside of him for nearly a year while he was frozen in carbonite. They had left scars, deep ones no one could see.

But he could separate those emotions from Leia.

And he could see all the sides of her. Leia fractured herself for everyone—the strong warrior for the Rebellion, the savvy politician for the Senate, the gracious leader for the people. But she was whole in front of him, multifaceted and, sometimes, cracked, but whole.

He had to love the whole of her, or nothing at all. That was the way of it with Leia—all or nothing.

He chose all.

Leia, who could not possibly guess at the dark and ultimately revelatory turn of his thoughts, grinned up at him as the turbolift doors opened and she yanked the headband from her hair, letting her braids tumble loose. "I'm so glad you talked me into leaving that banquet early."

Han laughed, following her into the room. "Talked you into it? Sweetheart, I didn't say a word."

"Oh, you were quite insistent," Leia confirmed. "And I couldn't agree more." Her smile turned feral. "Now let's go to bed."

CHAPTER 38

LEIA

LEIA WOKE UP WITH A start. Not only had Prime Minister Yens deftly delayed their viewing of the black tower—not unexpected—but Leia was keenly aware that there would be little opportunity for her to continue any talks on Madurs joining the new republic. The *Halcyon* had only stopped on the moon as an alternative to cruising through the meteor showers, something that was scheduled to only take a few standard days before arrival at Synjax. Short of abandoning her own honeymoon, Leia would have to go when the shuttles left tomorrow.

Han rolled over and looked at the time. "Skim-blading," he groaned.

Skim-blading was a charming excursion, but Leia shared Han's sentiments. It was even worse when they arrived at the area set up for the guests, partway between the spaceport and the ice palace, where Leia and Han could almost see the point of the black tower in the distance. It was as if Yens were taunting them.

While the other guests from the *Halcyon* strapped on skim-blades, Leia had her eye on the proose-driven sleds that had brought them to the area. The younglings on the trip squealed with joy as they wobbled on the thin blades of pulsating light that cut razor-sharp lines in the thick, snow-dusted ice.

Han looked on, amused, but Leia interrupted his thoughts. "Do you think we can just take a sled for a bit?"

Han cast an evaluating eye at the nearest sled and the enormous proose strapped to it. "Absolutely," he said confidently.

"Really?"

"Sure," Han replied. "We could take one right now. But taking one without being seen?" Han made an exaggerated show of looking around the barren ice field, flat on all sides with clear vision right up to the ice cliffs where the anglers lived. "That's not happening."

Leia nudged him. He knew what she'd meant. Fine. They'd have to use a different tactic. She marched over to Prime Minister Yens, who was yelling at the children.

"Don't go over in that area!" he called, pointing to a spot that had been marked off with red powder. "That ice is too thin to be safe."

"Prime Minister," Leia said, smiling at him warmly. "Thank you so much for arranging this." Before Yens could respond, Leia continued. "Unfortunately, I'm no good at skim-blading."

"Practice makes perfect," Yens said.

"And it's my honeymoon, as you know. I was hoping to take a sled out, a little romantic moment with my husband . . ."

Prime Minister Yens looked at her so intently that Leia's words died on her lips. "Yes," he said, "A good idea. Out in the open air."

"Exactly," Leia said cautiously.

"I'll drive you myself."

Leia hid her surprise, but she couldn't very well deny the prime minister's offer. So, while the younglings slid and bladed across the ice, she and Han bundled into the back of a sled as Prime Minister Yens himself took the reins.

Yens drove them straight out onto the ice. Once they were far enough out that they could no longer hear the children screeching in joy on the ice, Yens pulled the proose to a stop. The pronged beast stomped on the ice, the sound echoing.

When Yens spoke, his voice was soft, but in the cold, clear air, Leia and Han could easily hear him. "Do you know why we had to build the docks for shuttles so far away from the palaces?"

Leia glanced at Han, who shrugged. "To create a dramatic entrance?"

she asked, thinking of the ice-zippers and the sleds and the awe she'd held when she first saw them.

"The environment is delicate on a water world," Yens said as if Leia hadn't spoken. "Despite being frozen, this world is made of water, make no mistake. Beneath the ice, pollution spreads quickly. Debris falls on the ice, we can pick it up and take care of it. But waste that seeps into the water becomes diluted, poisoning everything a fraction at a time."

Leia frowned. It was hard to imagine this pristine world polluted. But she dared not speak and break the prime minister's thoughts.

"We are a small moon," Yens continued. "Our only fame is in our art. And when the Empire first reached out to me, I thought, *What does the Empire want with art?*"

He was silent then for a long while. Han eventually lost patience. "Well?" he demanded. "What did the Empire want with your art?"

Yens turned around and faced them for the first time since they boarded the sled. "Not a damn thing," he growled. Then he jerked the reins, setting the proose directly toward the black tower.

The Empire had only wanted Madurs's carnium, Leia knew that. And Yens knew it now as well, too. They sped along the ice, drawing closer to the broken palaces. Leia thought about Nah'hai, and the way she emphasized how all art is temporary, a belief backed up by the ice painting they'd seen yesterday. But this town had sharp cracks, ridges that cut into the sky. The broken edges were not dulled by time or weather; the intricate, lacelike details of the awnings still seemed new.

Yens pulled the sled up before they left the confines of the last building. It was not just shattered castles; there were smaller buildings here, built of more solid materials. "It's not safe beyond this point," Yens said flatly. "I'm telling you this not because it's some ploy to keep you from the area, but because it is a fact. The ice quakes hit stronger in this area, and the ice is thinner. We evacuated the city for a reason."

Leia leaned forward. "Is the area unstable because of the black tower?" she asked. It loomed on the horizon, closer than she and Han had gotten before.

"Obviously." Yens turned around in his seat, his back to the tower, but his eyes past Han and Leia, toward the broken, glittering walls of the destruction around them. Even here, there was beauty. Sorrow, too. "A sculptor may use any material," he said softly, although Leia wasn't sure the prime minister was talking to them or himself. "We choose to use ice because it is a part of the art. It melts. Everything passes. Nothing lasts forever."

Han opened his mouth, but Leia pressed her hand down on his leg, silencing him. Prime Minister Yens's gaze slid to Leia.

"You say the Empire is fallen." The prime minister's tone held a question, one Leia was coming to hate.

"It's as fallen as that space station," Leia said, pointing to the tower. She still had no idea how the tiny moon had been able to make an Imperial station crash into their surface, although it was clear now that they had sacrificed a city to do it, and the presence of the station was harming their environment. The prime minister hadn't been subtle in the link between the tower and the thinning ice.

This fallen station was significantly smaller than Calderos, an Imperial-controlled waystation in space near Wobani in the Bryx sector. The Rebellion—before Leia had officially joined it—had destroyed that station, and Leia had witnessed its remains after returning from a diplomatic mission. Perhaps she was wrong to be surprised at this station's destruction. The entire moon seemed to support Prime Minister Yens's vision of independence, and with a concentrated effort, it was not impossible to destroy something of the Empire's. She knew this to be true. And she should appreciate Madurs's effort, not question it.

But her words did not seem to comfort the prime minister. Rather than believe her assertion that the Empire was truly fallen, he raised his eyebrow, smirking in a defeated way. He glanced at his wrist chrono, then turned back to the proose's reins. "We have to go," he said.

"Punctual," Han muttered as if that were the worst possible insult he could toss at someone.

They had barely begun their sled ride, and Yens was already attempting to make them leave. But before they'd reached the skim-blading arena, the proose let out a keening bellow. A moment later, the air echoed with the violent cracking sound of ice, a sharp pinging noise echoed by a dull snap.

Leia had time for just one thought—*The ice quakes are happening on a schedule—they're not natural, that's why Yens checked his chrono*—and then the proose, panicked, leapt up, jerking the sled so violently that Leia crashed into Han's side, and they both tumbled toward the edge of the open sled. Han wrapped his arms protectively around Leia, but his legs swung out of the tilting sled, his boots skimming the ice. If they crashed now, there was every chance they'd both be crushed under the weight of the sled.

The ice cracked again, violently shoving one side up by almost a meter. Fortunately, it bumped Han back into the sled as it teetered toward the other side. Prime Minister Yens was shouting at the proose— sounds that Leia couldn't identify as words, perhaps just calls the proose recognized—but whatever it was, it didn't make a difference to the animal, who careened forward.

They were nearing the skim-blading area—heading straight for it, right at the children zipping along in their skim-blades. Leia's heart seized in fear—the enormous animal would surely plow down anyone in their path, youngling or not—but then flashes of red cut through the sky. Leia and Han clutched each other, and when the sled came to an abrupt stop, they both crashed to the floor.

Shakily, Leia stood and saw that several of the local proose drivers on the ground had cast disruptor rays at the sled, causing the proose to fall to its knees. As soon as it was down, they rushed the animal, throwing lines over its bent neck and back, securing it to the ice, while a pair of other drivers ran close to its head, gently soothing it with calming words, wiping away the froth at the animal's mouth.

"Is it okay?" Leia asked, standing up and peering over the edge of the sled toward the proose. Its chest heaved, and foam glistened on its fur, but its large floppy ears were drooping, and its head was lying on the ice, as if it were almost asleep now.

"I was going to ask the same of you," Prime Minister Yens said. His cheeks were flushed, eyes wide. The rampaging animal had scared him, Leia could tell, and although it was clear that the locals had known how to deal with a panicked proose, it was just as evident that this had been a dangerous situation for everyone.

"We're fine," Leia said, checking on Han, who nodded sharply.

Prime Minister Yens's shoulders sank in relief. "It's always dangerous to get close to the Empire," he said, just loud enough for them to hear.

CHAPTER 39

HAN

IF THEY WANTED TO KNOW what was going on, they were simply going to have to figure it out on their own.

Han shot Leia a look as the children started to reluctantly take off their skim-blades to head back to the palace. Leia nodded, understanding what he meant without words. But then she shrugged, as if to say: *But how are we going to get away from the group?*

That was the problem, of course. Put Leia on a battlefield, and she shot her blaster without question. Put her in a diplomatic situation, though, and she deferred to politics and politeness.

The setting didn't matter to Han. Everywhere was a battlefield, even if it was dressed up differently.

Not that he could shoot Yens to get his way. No, he'd considered that option and knew it would be more trouble than it was worth.

"Hey," he said when Yens walked past him, carrying a pair of skim-blades for a tiny youngling. When the prime minister paused, Han continued. "My wife and I are going back to the shuttle." He jerked his thumb toward it.

The other man's brow furrowed. "Why?"

No reason to lie. "Gotta get something from inside."

"What?" Yens asked.

"Does it matter?" Han shot back, trying to inject some authority into his voice. If Yens refused this request, then they were prisoners, not tourists, on this world. Leia might consider Han's approach rude, but rudeness was just a weapon on this battlefield.

"I don't suppose so," the prime minister said, but he may as well have said: *I don't suppose I can stop you.*

Good. They were finally getting somewhere.

"But I cannot give you a sled," Yens said. "The proose we used before is in no condition to carry passengers now."

Handlers had gotten that proose up again and attached leads to its harness. They had begun walking back to the ice palace, the handlers practically running to keep up with the proose's long-legged ambulatory stride. With that sled down, Prime Minister Yens had probably expected to double up a few sleds to get everyone back to the palace for lunch.

"We can walk," Han said. It wasn't that far. They had thermal disks for warmth, and unlike Hoth, this planet had clear skies and no real risk of a blizzard to cause them harm. Even if foul weather did arrive, the ice fields were flat, with easy targets to get to—the ice palace was huge and plainly visible. "Unless," Han added, "you think another ice quake will arrive sometime soon." He made a show of looking at the prime minister's wrist chrono. "But I don't think one is due for several more hours, do you?"

He was tipping his hand here, showing that he knew the ice quakes happened on a schedule rather than randomly, but Prime Minister Yens's face remained blank. "No, I don't suppose so," he said. Without another word, the prime minister turned and headed to the cart carrying the skim-blades.

Well, that was pretty much permission, wasn't it? Not that Han needed permission, but at least this meant they shouldn't be hassled as they walked away. Leia smirked at him as he held his arm out pretentiously for her to hold, as if they were stepping into a ballroom.

"Where are you going?" one of the guests from the *Halcyon* demanded as they strolled by.

"Romantic afternoon stroll," Han said in a superior tone.

"On the *ice*?" the woman asked incredulously.

"Where else?" Han said, and he led Leia out onto the barren ice field.

Getting inside the spaceport was easy enough; there was no security. But the shuttle itself was locked. Han had vaguely hoped that since the shuttle belonged to Madurs and since there was so little travel on the remote moon, it would be easily accessible, but no such luck. Han tugged a second time on the release bar, just in case, but the hatch didn't budge.

"Don't tell me a locked door is going to stop you," Leia said.

"How much of a thief do you think I am?" Han said, fiddling with the scanner lock frame under the release bar. "You expect me to know how to break into any ship I come across? I happened to run respectable jobs before Luke got me all tangled up with *your* Rebellion."

"I just meant—" Leia said, her eyes widening a little in surprise at his response.

"I may be a scoundrel, but I'm not some common criminal." Han's voice was wounded as he turned away from Leia, facing the shuttle.

"I'm sorry," Leia said, gentling her voice. "I only meant that—"

"There." Han pocketed the code breaker he carried on his belt as the locking mechanism in the hatch popped open and the door swung open. Leia gaped at him, and Han gave her his most roguish grin.

"You!" Leia snarled at him, but she was laughing.

Inwardly, Han breathed a sigh of relief that the ploy had worked. The code breaker wouldn't break anything with higher security, but Madurs had put only a basic lock on the hatch, probably to keep out curious passersby. Not that there were many people meandering around the ice fields. Still, the locking code had been simple enough, thankfully.

Once inside, Han went straight to the crates by the door, Leia at his heels. It was the observation deck in the fishing station that had given him the idea. Being underwater truly wasn't that different from being in space; Mon Cala even had a shipyard where they constructed ships underwater, pumping the liquid out only when the ship was ready for flight, and Mon Calamari ships were among the best.

Inside the first crate were emergency evacuation flare shells, but the second contained spare breathers and vests with thermal disks attached, emergency supplies needed in the event of an untimely departure from the shuttle while in space. Unlike the thermal disks they wore for comfort on the icy moon, these heavy-duty units were designed for use in space and could withstand changes in pressure. And were, hopefully, waterproof.

"Here," Han said.

Leia plucked a breather from the top. Combined with the vest, it would allow an oxygen-breathing being to survive in the void of space, providing heat, air, and minor protection. "This is the big plan?" Leia asked tentatively.

"The water is cold on this world, but not colder than space," Han said, taking off his trademark vest and swapping it for the one dotted with thermal disks before fitting a breather over his nose. "All we need is warmth and air, and this has us covered."

Han felt his lip curling into a salacious smirk.

"What?" Leia demanded.

"It's just . . . if we're going underwater to inspect the remains of that Imperial station . . ."

"We can't just walk up to the front door and knock," Leia said, exasperated. "We have to inspect it, obviously. Something's causing the quakes. It's got to be some form of blasting ray, or . . ." She caught Han's look again. "*What?*"

"Oh, no, it's just, I absolutely agree we should go underwater to investigate," he said. "But . . ." He gestured to all of her. "Those clothes may get in the way." Leia had worn a fur-lined suit for the day's activities, dressed up with her white gwendle cloak.

Leia stared at him flatly. "Are you expecting me to skinny-dip?"

"The thermal disks would keep you warm, and—" He stopped talking when Leia threw her white gwendle cloak at his face. She didn't strip down entirely, but the bodysuit that remained would both enable her to easily swim and also . . . Well. Han didn't mind it one bit.

"And you?" Leia asked, hand on her hip.

"Not all of us bring multiple outfit changes with us."

"I suppose if they get wet, your clothes are halfway to being washed for once," Leia grumbled.

"My clothes are clean!" Han protested.

"At least you wore something nice for our wedding," Leia muttered.

Han preened. "Noticed that, did you?"

Leia shot him a confused look. "Noticed what?"

"The jacket."

"Yes, it was nice."

"And Alderaanian."

Leia blinked. "No, it wasn't."

Han's eyes widened, and his jaw shifted ruefully. Lando had played him. That shiny jacket was just something from his closet, not anything special. Han couldn't believe he'd been so easily tricked.

Leia laughed, guessing at what had happened. "Remind me to thank Lando next time I see him."

She peered out the shuttle's window, where the edges of the black tower of the half-submerged Imperial station were visible over the low wall of the docking bay. "Good thing that last quake broke the ice," she said.

Han, remembering the terrifying way the cart had swerved and nearly crashed, simply said, "Yeah, good thing."

But she was right. It didn't take them long to reach the first areas of cracked ice when they went north. They traversed the broken sheets carefully—the quake had caused the ice to splinter, and it did indeed seem thinner in those areas, but some of the breaks were no larger than a handbreadth, and the sides of the rift too heavy for them to push apart farther.

Thinking of the surveillance droid, Han kept his eye out for spies, mechanical or otherwise. The Imperial space station may have fallen into the icy crust of the moon, but that didn't mean it was inoperable.

Leia seemed to be thinking along the same lines. "Those ice quakes happen so regularly that I suspect some residual operations are still happening." She paused, looking from the black tower protruding from the ice up to the cloudy sky and back again. "No one likely survived the crash, but that doesn't mean there's not still danger."

She stopped in front of a wide gap between two broken ice sheets. The splintering crack stretched all the way toward the remains of the Imperial station, but it was separated enough here for them both to slip through into the water below. Without looking back, Leia took a deep breath to steady herself, then leapt into the abyss, the water splashing as she disappeared under the surface.

Han loved that about her. Just like on Endor, when she leapt on a speeder to take out the stormtroopers that had invaded the forest, leaving him behind—she didn't hesitate. She just dived headlong toward the task she knew needed to be done, without question, confident in both Han and herself.

She knew he would follow.

And he did.

CHAPTER 40

LEIA

THERE WAS ONE BRIEF SHOCK of cold, then the thermal disks ramped up, adjusting for the abrupt change in temperature. Heat didn't quite reach her fingers and toes, but her core was protected, and the radiant warmth would be enough, at least for an hour or so, if she kept moving. Leia gulped at air, and a thin stream of icy water trickled down her throat. Focusing, she forced herself to regulate her breathing, to allow the breather machine to filter the air to her.

A thin beam of reedy light cut through the water from the crack in the ice above; all else was shadowed. She had plunged into the water feetfirst, and she had gone deep enough to feel the pull of the currents. Han dived in as well, his brown hair floating around his head, his eyes wide and panicked as he got his bearings.

Panicked? That wasn't like Han.

The cold, the dark, the shock of it all. Leia knew it the same way Han did.

Carbonite freezing.

It was supposed to be painless. Quick. A flash, and then nothing until thaw.

Supposed to be.

But it wasn't.

One needed only to see the look of sheer and utter pain on Han's gray, frozen face to know that it was neither quick nor painless. Leia would never forget the way his eyes had been scrunched in pain, the way his whole body bucked against freezing. It had been primal, a bone-deep response to pain that could not be hidden.

Han had spent close to a year in carbonite, long enough to get hibernation sickness, for his eyes to regress, for the chance for long-term damage to rear up years from now.

Long enough for the trace effects to rise within him when he was submerged in system-shocking cold water.

Leia swam over to him, blowing bubbles out of her nose with the aid of the breather. She grabbed both his hands, searching his eyes until he focused on her. He nodded tightly. He was with her again.

Swimming down, Leia checked the readout on her vest. The thermal disks adjusted temperatures based on external sensors, and, as she suspected, the closer they got to the crashed Imperial station, the warmer the water was. That would account for some of the extensive damage from the ice quakes—warm water weakened the ice. But the quakes were timed, which implied something was going off in the station, maybe the laser array that had been intended to attack the moon's core to reach its precious carnium. If they could get closer, find a way in, and then disable the array, perhaps that would be enough to entice the prime minister into believing that the new government truly did mean to help, not exploit them.

Although she knew the water was frigid, the thermal disks enveloped her in warmth. Leia relished the freedom to swim, the silence of it, the pure simplicity in movement. A school of fish with flashing silver scales darted by, veering as one away from the warm water Leia swam through. Long-nosed spike eels flitted through the water. Leia paused to watch them. When their quivering bodies shot too close to current drifting from the sunken Imperial space station, they diverted their paths, wiggling away.

Even the fish don't like the Imperial presence, Leia thought. Then she remembered what the prime minister had said about edonts preferring the cold. It was warmer here. The station was changing the climate under the ice.

The cracks in the ice grew wider the closer they got to the sunken space station. It caused beams of light to cut through the pale-green water, highlighting the few aquatic animals that ventured this close to the black metal. Far in the distance, Leia could see the shadow of some huge creature—perhaps an edont, or the many-toothed sawkill she'd read about.

Han shot forward, grabbing Leia's arm and jerking her back. Startled, she adjusted her focus to the submerged space station.

Red lights blinked along the perimeter. Security monitors.

Why monitor a broken, defunct space station? Leia thought.

Because it wasn't broken. She could see it now. People in the viewports, dressed in crisp Imperial uniforms. A few troopers patrolling inside. The round viewports were scattered in a pattern throughout the spiraling, conical shape of the base of the station, and through many of them, Leia could see lights, profiles of people working, droids, and more. This was very much a station in use.

But Yens had said . . .

He'd said that the Empire was as dead as this station.

And while he'd also said that the space station had crashed into the ice after being destroyed by Madurs, the evidence to the contrary was right before her eyes. Leia would have laughed sardonically if she wasn't underwater. She had known all along, hadn't she, that Madurs simply did not have the firepower to destroy an Imperial space station.

Han had said before, "Being underwater isn't that much different from being in space." And while other mining blasters could fire from orbit, this station was designed to be . . .

Her eyes squinted through the water that grew increasingly dark the farther down she peered. This station narrowed to a point, like a child's top. Like a drill.

This station had always been designed to drive into the core of this moon. Not to orbit and blast it from afar, but to sink deep into the ice, shoot directly at the core. This station had not even remotely been destroyed.

It was fully operational.

And—

Leia watched with horror as the base started to glow red. With the quake earlier, she had been sure they would have more time before another strike.

But they'd miscalculated. It was going to fire *now*.

CHAPTER 41

HAN

HAN GRABBED LEIA BY THE elbow, pulling her closer to the station. He'd already been concerned about being spotted—they were two humans floating in the water right at eye level with some of those ports, and it was only by luck and chance that none of the Imperial officers or storm-troopers had glanced out one of the viewports at them, and that the ports they were closest to were empty. With the core blaster charging up, they could either try to make a run for it—a swim for it, rather—or hide closer to the station. Not knowing just what the core blaster would do, Han figured it was safest to cling to the side of the sunken station like a mynock.

The station vibrated with power as the core blaster charged. Han and Leia found stabilizer bars to hold on to, floating in the water just above a large viewport. They had warmth and air thanks to the thermal vest and breathers, but neither of them had comlinks now. Instead, Han and Leia both watched in horror as the clear, pale-green water glowed eerily beneath their feet, first with a bright-white light, then with a focused, red beam blasting straight down into the core. The burst of power was so strong that the station shifted in the ice, bouncing back into position with repulsorlifts, half a dozen of them spaced above the core blaster.

Leia tapped Han's chest, drawing his attention from the vivid glowing water to his vest. The temperature monitor was changing sporadically, trying to adjust for the increased heat in the water.

Oh, karabast, Han thought. The water near the station had been warmer than in the frigid, icy depths farther away, but the core blaster was making the whole area as hot as the beaches of Synjax. The thermal disks couldn't keep up with the quick change in temperature—it was designed to keep a being warm if they were thrown into the cold void of space; it had no way to do the reverse and keep a body cooler if things got hot. The disks fritzed out, turning themselves off and exposing Han to the water's current temperatures.

Which were rising by the minute.

Hotter than any bath Han had taken, the core blaster had turned the ice-cold moon into a sauna. He cast his eyes up, squinting at the ice above them.

For several meters around the perimeter of the station, there was no ice. Han hadn't realized that—they hadn't gotten close enough to the station from aboveground for him to see, and the shadow of the enormous base had prevented much light from leaking through. But while the ice around the fishing base had been several meters thick, a more solid ground than most terrestrial worlds, the station was like an enormous rod of hot metal, burning away this world's crust.

And its core.

Han looked down—the core blaster was still firing a red laser beam straight down. The water was getting hotter now. Not boiling, but not comfortable. Han glanced at Leia. Her eyes were calculating—should they flee, or should they stick it out?

The station churned and shifted like a ship with a bad catalyzer, jarringly abrupt and chugging nastily. Through the metal, Han could feel the station grinding out a different sort of vibration. If he had to guess, it was a type of tractor beam. No ice was directly holding the station upright; far too heavy to stay afloat otherwise, the station must be using gravity manipulation against the same core it was blasting, aided by the visible repulsorlifts.

Which would mean—

Han's eyes widened, and he swooped around Leia, pushing her body against the side of the station and gripping a stabilizer bar with each hand. His feet sought desperately for a foothold, one boot tip finding a gap near a viewport and the other jammed into a third stabilizer bar. He used his full body weight to cover Leia, pressing her hard against the unforgiving metal just moments before the ice quake erupted.

The reverberating force was enough to make Han feel as if his arms and legs were being pulled out of their sockets. As much as he'd joked about Chewie ripping a person's arms out before, this pain made him rethink the quip. His teeth ground as he clenched his muscles. While Leia had been initially shocked by his sudden movement, she curled against him, accepting his protection in a way that made him all the more determined to not let go, even as the water seemed to be trying to rip him away.

This was an ice quake. And they were in the center of it.

The station alternated between blasting the core of this moon and then shifting to a tractor beam, creating a push-and-pull sequence that disrupted the entire environment. It wasn't just the water movement from the blast, although that contributed—it was the use of the gravity manipulation to restabilize the station after every blast that really disrupted everything.

Straining against the pull, Han was able to blearily confirm his theory by looking up. The solid field of ice that extended from all sides past the station rippled underneath the surface as if the meters of thick sheets were nothing more than one of the gwendle drapes of Leia's cloak. It was disorientating and plain *weird* to see something that was supposed to be unyielding instead bend and break. The more the ice field wavered under the force of the water and the gravity shifting, the more it strained and splintered, cracking apart.

Almost as abruptly as it started, the quake ended. The station was stable. Han relinquished his hold on the bars and yanked his foot free, shaking his stiff ankle in the water. Leia stayed close, still holding him by the arm.

The water remained too warm for his thermal disks to kick back on, but it was definitely getting cooler by the minute. Han shifted his gaze from the ice, which was resettling after the quake, to the depths below.

There was no longer any bright laser beam to make the water glow, but something shimmered in the dark water, growing closer.

A giant bubble escaped Leia's lips, and she let go of Han's arm to cover her mouth in horror. Silver-speckled fish—thousands of them—floated up from the seabed. Whether it had been the disrupting blast or the surge in temperature that had killed them, Han didn't know. They had long fins with silky-thin membranes that wafted through the water like flower petals, a graveyard of gentle beauty. Rock and bits of coral were scattered between the fish corpses, gritty sand drifting in waves, swirling around it all.

Han reached out and grabbed a thin red tendril lazily twirling through the water.

Carnium.

Bubbles alerted them to an open hatch nearby, and Han and Leia pressed against the wall of the station again. Submersion droids jetted through the water, sucking up the tiny red threads of precious metal, darting around dead fish and useless rock. They were small enough that they worked on sensors, not by visuals, so Han was fairly certain the droids wouldn't detect them.

Still, it was time to go.

CHAPTER 42

LEIA

LEIA BURST THROUGH THE ICE a moment before Han did. She grasped for leverage as the water tried to drag her back under, her fingers clawing at the snow-dusted ice. She slipped once, but then clambered up before turning to give Han her arm.

For a moment, they both sat there, shivering before the electronics in the vest kicked back on. The thermal disks struggled, the mechanics whirring. Perhaps something designed for space wasn't perfectly functional underwater.

Han glanced at Leia, no quip at the ready. There seemed little left to be said.

Leia had known the Empire was trying to grapple back the power that had been destroyed with the second Death Star. She had seen evidence of the growing blockade in the Anoat sector, and she had listened as Lando and Mon had both confirmed that the Empire sought to seize power by controlling the energy sources. The carnium at the heart of Madurs was too valuable for the Empire to let one art-loving people protest their presence, and the little moon never stood a chance against an Imperial station.

And Leia knew firsthand how easily the Empire would destroy a world to get what it wanted.

Her head sank, hair dripping into her lap, faint steam wrapping around her thanks to the thermal disks. Madurs was breaking apart at her feet. The ice quakes happened according to the Empire's mining schedule, and the violent shaking of the moon's core combined with the rising temperature of the blaster drill were scarring the moon's environment.

"The core of this moon can't withstand constant blasts," Han muttered, his eyes on the crack in the ice they'd escaped from.

"No," Leia agreed hollowly. But that wouldn't matter. The Empire would take as much as it could and then leave the shell behind, nothing more than debris.

It wasn't supposed to be like this.

They'd defeated the Empire.

It was supposed to be *over*.

Leia stared down at her hands in her lap. She was so *tired*. So deeply tired of it all—every victory was met with more loss, more fight. Every attempt she made to do more, be more, was undermined by a callous universe that seemed to revel in watching her struggle. And she tried, so hard, to hold on to hope. Not just for herself, but for the whole galaxy. And what did she have to show for it?

Leia sucked in a hard breath.

Her ring, which had slowly been unraveling, was gone. The amber ring made of vine and blessed by the Ewok elders, the ring that symbolized her marriage—

Gone.

It must have broken apart in the water, the remnants slipping from her finger unnoticed. The loss of it sent a sharp pain through her. Leia knew that saving Madurs, defeating the Empire—that was all far more important than a ring made of organic material that was always doomed to break apart.

But it still hurt, the way sacrifice hunted her.

Her fingers curled into a fist, hiding the place where her ring should be.

CHAPTER 43

HAN

IT HAD BEEN TOO EASY to leave.

That was the thought that chased Han over the ice fields. The Imperials knew that Madurs couldn't oust the station from the ice, but the Empire always expected insurgency, even from worlds that had already bent to them.

Probe droids, surveillance cams, stormtroopers on watch . . .

How had they been able to swim right up to the very viewports in the station, see everything, and just leave?

No. It had been too easy.

As Han and Leia raced across the ice back toward the docking bay where the shuttle waited for them, it felt as if the hot breath of the Empire was on the back of his neck. He knew he was going at a dangerous pace. He wasn't like Yens; he didn't know where the thin spots and cracks in the ice were. But even when they were back inside the shuttle, Han's heart didn't still.

"We need help," Leia said, a little breathless from the run. Han nodded, already moving to the shuttle's communicator.

His hands paused on the controls, hovering over the hail button that would call the *Halcyon*. Huh. His chin tilted as he bit back the self-deprecating smirk budding on his lips. All it took was a few years and the Skywalker twins to make him realize that he *could* ask for help. No strings, no favors, no paybacks. It was possible to just ask and get the aid needed. Who could have seen that as an option for Han Solo?

"What's wrong?" Leia asked at his shoulder.

"Nothing." Han hailed the *Halcyon*, hovering in orbit around Madurs, waiting on the guests to return the next day.

D3-O9 picked up immediately. "*Halcyon* to shuttle, how may I assist?"

Leia pushed Han aside. Han threw up his hands, but he knew this was a force he wasn't going to win against. "Deethree, this is Leia Organa. I need to speak with Captain Dicto immediately."

"Of course," D3-O9 said. Han rolled his eyes. He had a feeling if the request had come from him, the droid would have disconnected the communication.

A moment later, another voice came through the shuttle's speaker. "Captain Dicto here. What's wrong, Princess?"

Leia glanced at Han, doubt in her eyes. They were not on an official ambassador assignment, nor was the *Halcyon* a warship capable of going on the offensive against a fully operational Imperial station equipped with a core blaster and, presumably, a full arsenal and a battalion or two of stormtroopers.

"Ask for someone from engineering," Han suggested. He could tell Leia understood his meaning. While she and Han might be able to sabotage the station and buy some time before *real* help could arrive, an engineer from the ship might also be able to figure out how the star cruiser could give immediate aid and convince the captain of that course of action.

Leia shook her head, disagreeing with Han.

"Princess Organa?" Captain Dicto asked in the silence.

Leia turned back to the communicator. "Captain, we've seen evidence that there's an Imperial stronghold on Madurs," she said. "I'd like to request aid, and—"

"Evidence?" Captain Dicto asked, cutting Leia off. "What sort of evidence?" Before she could answer, he continued, "If the Empire has infiltrated this moon, we need to evacuate the tourists immediately, including you and Han. The safety of the *Halcyon*'s passengers is of utmost importance."

Leia paled and looked up at Han with panicked eyes. Fleeing the moon would leave the people of Madurs in grave danger. Their world was literally cracking apart at their feet.

Han leaned over the communicator. "Captain, you'll have to excuse my wife. She's been in the Rebellion so long she sees everything through a soldier's eyes."

"A *general's*," Leia hissed.

"There's no evidence of the Empire, and no evidence of danger to anyone. Don't cause a panic among the crew or the passengers," Han continued.

There was a moment of silence, and Han could almost picture the captain scowling. "Why did you hail the *Halcyon* then?"

Han cleared his throat. "I happened to notice that the shuttle that will take us back up to the *Halcyon* seems damaged. Not from sabotage," he added, "despite my wife's concerns. But I think you should send an engineer down to inspect it. Make sure it's safe for flight."

Another long moment passed, and Han raised his eyebrows at Leia in triumph. But then Captain Dicto's voice filled the cockpit. "We just ran a diagnostic report on our end. All shuttles linked to the *Halcyon* are rigorously inspected, and we get constant updates remotely. We see nothing wrong with the shuttle," he said.

That was less than helpful.

Leia stepped away from the communicator, waving her hand to indicate that Han should keep talking. Shrugging, Han leaned over the mic. "Captain, I really think you should send someone to investigate. I have a lot of experience as a pilot, and these small vessels—"

Out of the corner of his eye, Han saw Leia lift something huge over her head. He slammed his hand over the mic. "*No*," he murmured at Leia.

"Why not?"

"That's a flare shell!" Han waved his free hand at her. "It. Will. *Explode*."

Leia looked like she was still considering it. Han shook his head forcefully. Shrugging reluctantly, Leia placed the flare shell back in its crate and grabbed a particle-suppressant foam fire extinguisher, about the size of a milliaw ball, painted bright orange. Han gaped as Leia deftly smashed the spherical metal unit on top of the shuttle's navigational console, cracking the glass and denting the base.

An alarm beeped on the other side of the communicator, a tinny sound coming from the *Halcyon* monitors.

"Er," the captain said, no doubt relooking at his diagnostic report.

Calmly, Leia shoved the hose of the fire extinguisher into the crack on the monitor and depressed the mechanism, filling the entire unit with a thick gray foam.

"My apologies!" Captain Dicto shouted over the comm unit. "Our prior scans must have been in error; we're reading a major malfunction in the shuttle's nav unit. I'll send our lead engineer to the moon immediately!"

"Thanks," Han said, grinning at Leia. He disconnected the comm and turned to his wife. Her grin at him was rapacious. "Where'd you learn a trick like that?" he asked, knowing the answer.

"From the best," Leia said, dropping the empty canister and pulling him in for a kiss.

CHAPTER 44

LEIA

THE THERMAL VESTS HAD DRIED their clothes as they raced across the ice field, but Leia was more than happy to dump the breather in the shuttle's recharger. It was better than some of the less manageable helmets or face shields she'd used before, but it was still uncomfortable. She happily zipped herself back into her fur-lined suit, cinching the silver belt at her waist.

"It's going to be at least an hour before the engineer gets here," Leia said. "We've got time."

"Time for what?" Han stretched his arms over his head; the swim before hadn't been exactly easy, nor had the climb back onto the ice.

"We need to get Prime Minister Yens on board."

Han rolled his eyes. "He *knows* the Empire is here. I don't think he's thrilled, but he hasn't been exactly helpful."

"He didn't think he could be," Leia said. "He's been warning us away from the start, not because he thought he had a chance at getting help, but because he feared we would be hurt."

"Or he didn't want the Imperial officer in control to think he sympathized with the enemy."

"Regardless, we know now. And I'm certain that Yens isn't pleased with the damage to Madurs from the station. We need to let him know that we intend to help and, more important, see what he can do to help."

"He could have been helping his moon all along," Han pointed out.

Leia crossed the shuttle to Han, reaching for his hand and weaving her fingers through his. "It's hard to believe you can do anything when you think you're alone," she said softly.

"Not everything is an analogy, Leia."

Leia's fingers gripped harder, and she yanked Han's arm to make him follow her. "Come on," she ordered.

"Back and forth, across the ice," Han groaned as they stepped out of the spaceport and their vests' thermal disks kicked back on.

Leia rolled her eyes but did not dignify that statement with a remark. She knew—thanks to Riyola's meticulous planning of the schedule— that the *Halcyon* group was set to return to the fishing docks after lunch, this time for an underwater tour in one of the larger submersion vessels.

Her stomach was aching from all the running around without a meal, so she pushed the thought of the lunch everyone else was having from her mind. The enormous fishing hole with the underwater dock was at least a shorter walk from the shuttle than if they'd had to go all the way back to the ice palace. She and Han made quick time. They waved at some of the anglers fishing from the edge of the ice as she and Han hurried across the bridge to the floating transparisteel building.

The captain from the first night's reception met them at the door. "You are late for the tour," he said. "The last submersion vessel has already departed from the underwater dock, I believe."

"That's fine," Leia said. "We just want to speak to Prime Minister Yens."

The captain seemed surprised. "You didn't want to see an edont? We have some smaller vessels designed for two to three net fishers. They're not as fine as the edont-viewing vessels, but—"

"No," Leia said, too abruptly. "Thank you. But no. We need to find the prime minister."

"Is everything okay?"

Han sighed, clearly losing patience. "He's still at the underwater docks?"

"Yes, but—"

Han grabbed Leia's elbow and steered her past the captain, heading to the turbolift. In moments, they stepped out on the dock.

Prime Minister Yens stood near a series of hatches. The larger ones were sealed, and through the clear transparisteel windows, Leia could see that the vessels that had been docked there had already launched. As the captain had indicated, there were a handful of smaller hatches that were open, revealing submersible vessels that were clearly used by the fishers, littered with nets and scythes, perfect for either capturing large schools of fish or harvesting the long stalks of ila kelp that grew in spots close to the surface.

"They're here," Prime Minister Yens said into a comlink, then he looked up at Leia and Han. The captain must have alerted him that they were coming. "How can I help you?" Yens asked politely.

With so many of the vessels launched, the dock seemed smaller than when they'd passed it on the tour the day before. The lights were dimmer, too, with strange patterns cast along the walls and floor from the underwater signals used to guide vessels to the proper bays. Leia took a step closer to Han.

"Prime Minister Yens," she said, "we know that the station you said was destroyed is not, in fact, even damaged. We know what it's doing to your moon. And we want to help."

Yens showed no emotion on his face, and that, more than the darkness and the shadows, unnerved Leia. This straightforward confrontation with the truth should have made him angry or relieved, sad to be caught or joyous to have help. But the blank emptiness was . . . eerie.

"The Empire was never supposed to come here," the prime minister stated in a flat voice. "They sent an ambassador, and at first, I was told to prepare as if for another art expo." He laughed bitterly. "That's why we built the guesthouses in the courtyard. The ambassador told us that Madurs would be integral to the galaxy. She encouraged us to spend our time building up the little city in preparation. But that was just a distraction so we wouldn't notice the groundwork laid for the mining processes. When it came time to advance the negotiations, it turned out the only thing the Empire wanted was carnium. I turned her down."

Yens stared blankly, his eyes unfocused, as he continued. "The ambassador left that meeting on her shuttle, and then the station attacked before that night. That whole hulking station we thought was just in orbit had spent all that time scouting where to strike. We never thought something that big would actually *land* on the surface. To be fair, I don't suppose it did. It slammed into the ice. Apparently, the best mining spot was right next to the old city. That first blow destroyed it all."

His words were soft but Han and Leia heard the heartbreak in his tone. They had both seen the broken buildings, the rubble. The ice quakes they had felt since then were nothing compared with the initial impact.

No one on Madurs had expected it, least of all the prime minister, who'd thought the negotiation process would mean he had a voice for his people. "They wrapped us in chains while I was making polite conversation," he said.

Leia shook her head. If one is put in chains, one should turn them into a weapon and squeeze the life from one's oppressor. She felt the rage boiling inside her, a dark thing that swept through her. And for a moment, she allowed it to seep into her bones, tighten her muscles, remind her of the time she had looked in Jabba's eyes after the light had left them.

She had hated every single moment on Tatooine except for that one.

She had never felt more powerful than in that instant.

I understand why he did what he did, Luke had told her on Endor. *I don't agree with it, of course, but I understand it. Don't you?*

Leia closed her eyes.

Don't you?

She opened her eyes. She focused on the prime minister. She felt rage, but he exuded grief. She could see that, if she looked.

"How many died?" Leia asked gently.

Prime Minister Yens's eyes were hollowed out and haunted. "Two thousand, two hundred and forty-eight."

Leia could picture it all too well. If she was heartless, she could even see the logic of it. The aftermath would be so catastrophic, there would be no way to fight back. The grief that followed the entire society—the guilt, the tragedy—sometimes that was the emotion that sparked a rebellion. But those flames could turn inward and burn a heart to ash.

"And they won't go?" There was a lilt to Han's voice, as if he were asking a question, but everyone in the room knew the answer. "Despite the Empire falling, I mean." Because no one thought the Imperial station cared about the destruction of the moon.

The prime minister's laugh was bitter. "They say it's all operations as usual." His eyes cut to Leia. "Politics don't change the 'deal.'" He spat out the last word, but then his eyes shifted, focusing away from Leia, as if he didn't want to face her with his next words. "But they promise to leave soon," he said. "They'll pay the invoices, the reparations. And they'll go."

"Sure, when this moon cracks apart or is too polluted to be habitable," Han said.

"They've received orders to wrap it all up soon. The lead officer assures me—"

"Orders from whom?" Leia demanded. Not the Emperor. Not Tarkin or Vader. They'd cut the head off the Empire; why wouldn't it die?

"From me," a woman said, striding forward. She had been on the far side of the underwater dock, hidden in the shadows. As she came closer, something red flashed near her temple—a cybernetic eye, whirring as it scanned over Leia and Han. The woman's blond hair was slicked back in so tight a bun that she nearly seemed bald. She wore the crisp white uniform of an officer in the intelligence division of the Empire, and she walked with the certain confidence of someone with deadly experience.

"May I introduce Ambassador and Senior Commander Alecia Beck," the prime minister said. His head hung low, a sign of both respect and defeat.

Beck strode past him as if he were nothing. She ignored Leia as well, her red eye targeted on Han, who tensed beside her. Leia's gaze flicked between the Imperial officer and her husband and back again. "You two have a history?" Leia guessed.

"Solo," Beck snarled. "You cost me a promotion. I've been waiting a long time to kill you."

CHAPTER 45

HAN

"YEAH, SHE'S, UH, SHE'S NO fan of mine," Han said. "She thought it would be best to torture information out of a rebel prisoner, and we disagreed on that point. Guess she held a grudge." Although he kept his tone light, Han was careful to keep Beck in his vision. She snapped her neck to the side, letting an audible crack release. The senior commander smirked at the way Leia cringed at the sound.

Han shifted his arm, touching Leia's hand. A warning. He knew Beck. He knew her aim.

Leia, however, seemed to misinterpret his signal. "Why are you still here?" she demanded, clearly hoping to antagonize the senior commander. "The Empire has fallen."

Beck laughed. "I don't believe rebel propaganda."

"We're not rebels anymore," Leia said viciously. "We're the victors."

Han saw Beck's hand move a second before Leia noticed it, and he used that second to slam against her with his whole body, knocking them both to the ground before the blaster shot through the space where they had been standing. Emotionless, Beck shifted her stance and her aim.

"Run, run, run," Han said urgently, dragging Leia up. He lingered just long enough to know that Leia was steady on her feet and already racing in one direction before he darted off in the other, hoping to draw Beck's fire away from his wife.

It worked—for a second. Beck seemed unsure who to shoot first. Leia was the bigger enemy to the Empire, but Beck had a personal vendetta against Han.

Han cast a look behind him just in time to see Beck leveling her weapon at Leia, who had the sense to zig rather than go in a straight line as she ran toward the relative protection of a stack of crates near the turbolift. Carbon scoring marred the floor and wall as Beck chased Leia with blasts, her gun steady and her eye focused. It was mere luck that had kept Leia from being hit so far.

Beck's loyalty to the dead Emperor was stronger than her personal need to see Han dead.

Barely.

Han charged at Beck, intending to knock into her, but in one deft motion she stepped to the side. Without the impact he'd been bracing for, Han stumbled, and Beck slammed the butt of her blaster into the back of his skull, causing black dots to dance before his eyes.

"How considerate," Beck said, grinning at him as he took a few more staggering steps. "Giving me a reason to kill you first."

A harpoon sliced through the air, cutting Beck's biceps. A red line of blood blossomed over her white jacket—perfectly straight and neat, so clean it looked as if it were a band of honor on her immaculate uniform and not an injury. With a snarl, Beck adjusted her grip on her blaster to steady her now injured arm. Leia ducked back behind the crates, a flash of white as she scrambled for both a better position and another weapon. Han used Beck's distraction to dart away, taking cover near the protruding ridge of a magnetic shield housing that protected the docking bay from the water on the other side.

"Stop!" Yens shouted, his voice breaking. "This doesn't have to end in violence."

Beck snarled, but it was Han who snapped, "Of course it does; this is the Empire!" He could almost account for the tragedy of the situation leading to Madurs being trapped, but surely this man wasn't so much a fool he didn't see how this would inevitably conclude.

Beck swung around, aiming her blaster at Han, the easier target with less cover. The plasma blast hit the magnetic shield, dark carbon scoring streaking the metal housing centimeters from his face. The shield rippled like water, but held.

"Don't flood the dock!" Yens shouted.

Beck cursed at him, a moment too late to hit Han as he darted to a different bay. This one was connected to a ship and therefore had no shield up, but Han was not foolish enough to step inside, trapping himself in a submersible vehicle locked into the bay. He could probably figure out how to free it, but the entire time he'd be an easy target for Beck's dead-eye shot.

From his new vantage point, he could see behind the crates. Leia was frantically rifling through the ones she could reach without exposing herself, looking for a weapon. But while the harpoon had been effective, most of the contents were nets. That'd worked on Endor, but Beck was smarter than the average stormtrooper.

Leia's gaze met Han's for a split second.

This isn't the end, he wanted to say, even as glowing red blasts burned through the air between them.

Leia's brow raised, her meaning clear: *I know, laserbrain, but you got any ideas?*

That woman sure knew how to talk with her eyes. Stars, he never loved her more than when they were in the middle of a battle.

"This isn't right!" Yens shouted. It seemed as if the man was confirming what he'd known all along—the Empire was never going to uphold their "bargain" with his moon, they would continue to take and take until there was nothing left. That, or cold-blooded murder right in front of him was a bridge too far for him to tolerate.

Beck ignored him utterly. Han and Leia were cornered, close enough together that she could advance without losing sight of either. The only reason her steps were slow and methodical, Han knew, was because she didn't know what else Leia may have found behind the crates.

Han curled against the protruding metal of the magnetic shield housing. He knew what Beck didn't—there were no weapons left.

He caught Leia's eyes, subtly moving his head to the submersible. It was a long shot to even get it unlocked from the bay, much less operating, before Beck killed them both.

Good thing Han was used to long shots.

Leia nodded once, but rather than run over to him, she bunched her hands in fistfuls of netting, twirling the thin material around her wrists.

Beck took another step closer.

Leia leapt up, throwing the nets to the left, the material streaming out in gossamer threads at the same time that she hurtled herself to the right, toward Han. She kept her grip on the nets, letting them wave behind her.

By the time she crashed into Han, sending both of them tumbling into the submersible, there was nothing but burnt ends of strings dangling from her fingers; the rest of the nets had been burned away.

Beck no longer trod lightly. She thundered toward them, not pausing as she fired, not caring what else she hit. Her arms—even the injured one—didn't falter. There was no cover inside the submersible, not even seats. It was little more than a hatch, a control panel, and a glass bubble dome, used for work and efficiency, not comfort.

The entire submersible shuddered, nearly sending Leia to the floor. What was that? Not a quake—not a result of the blasterfire.

The magnetic shield lowered.

Han's eyes flew through the glass to Prime Minister Yens, who had his hand on the control panel in the docking bay. His jaw was set as he prepared the launch of the submersible into the icy water.

Beck cursed, but rather than lose herself to rage, she skidded to a stop just in front of the faint blue-glowing light of the shield. Legs splayed in a firm stance, Beck raised her weapon, not flinching as she fired blast after blast not at the shield but at the metal housing that covered the mechanics that operated it. She had already caused enough damage to make the metal glow red and sizzle through one layer.

"It can't hold!" Leia screamed. If Beck blasted directly into the circuitry that operated the shield, it would fail.

"I *know*," Han growled, frantically slamming his hands on the controls. Slow to wake up, the old submersible was barely churning water, chugging resolutely but painstakingly slow.

Through the shield, Han saw Yens rush at Beck, but she easily knocked him aside and continued calmly firing, carefully aiming at the same spot, over and over again.

And then the shield broke.

Water flooded into the docking bay, the force hard enough to knock both Beck and Yens down before the metal fail-safe sealed the bay closed.

But not before Beck shot one perfectly aimed blast through the water and against the glass dome of the submersible.

Through the growing, splintering crack in the glass between them and the frigid waters, Han and Leia saw Beck stand, straighten, and smirk.

She hadn't been able to kill them directly, but as soon as the dome shattered, the sea would do it for her.

CHAPTER 46

LEIA

DRIP.

Leia watched as a tiny droplet of pale-turquoise water dribbled from the crack and plopped between them. She raised her eyes to Han.

Even in those brief seconds, the crack in the glass splintered more.

"It won't hold," she said softly.

Han shook his head.

Their best bet was the open area around the dock, where the anglers tossed their lines down, but even as Leia thought that, she saw glimmers of red plasma snaking through the water. Stormtroopers—perhaps aided by Beck herself—were shooting through that open area directly into the water, hoping to hit them and further damage the ship. There was no escape that way.

Leia closed her eyes. She allowed herself one moment of fear. To visualize what would inevitably happen. The glass dome was breaking. It would split apart under the pressure of the water soon. They still had their thermal vests, so they wouldn't freeze. But they had tossed the breathing apparatuses aside. They would drown. Even if they could reach the surface in time, it was frozen, meters-thick ice that they could not break through with nothing but their bare hands.

I am not *going to die underwater on some moon.*

She opened her eyes.

I am not *going to die today.*

She tried to believe it.

"We have to get as close to the surface and as close to the station as possible," she said, her eyes on the growing crack. The ice was thinner there, the water warmer; it was the only chance. There could be Imperials there, too, but . . .

It was their only chance.

The submersible launched forward as Han leaned into the controls, little more than a joystick and a pedal. Leia reached forward, hands on the cold glass, looking up. If she could see a beam of light, a place where the ice was thinner . . .

In the shadows, Leia spotted dim outlines of sea creatures. In another life, she would never have even noticed that there was something wrong with Madurs. She would have piled into the luxurious underwater shuttle and gone edont sighting with the tourists. She would have had a normal honeymoon, without a worry in her head. Another life.

One where she'd probably live longer.

Bubbles roiled behind them as the tiny vessel puttered along. It was never designed to rush people to the surface and air; it was designed to plug along through the water, slow enough not to startle big schools of fish and steady enough to pluck kelp. It was no more designed to be the *Millennium Falcon* than Leia was designed for a life of peace.

The crack splintered more, cold dribbles of water leaking over her fingers.

Leia glanced at Han. His jaw was set, his eyes focused, his whole body straining to push the little submersible farther, faster, farther.

Leia felt so useless, just standing there.

Could . . .

Could the Force help?

Luke had reached out to her for aid on Bespin. And she had heard that call. Her twin was too far to help her even if she could reach him, but . . . could *someone* hear her? Could someone help?

She let her eyes unfocus, past the crack, through the water, into the murky blend of colors. She tried to listen—not to Han's muttering, or the grinding of gears, or the splintering glass—but to something deeper, something mystical.

If—when—*I survive this, I must reach out to Luke for proper training,* she thought even as she strained her will to hear, feel . . . something.

Nothing.

With a growl of frustration, Leia spun away from the window. She didn't have time for whispers of power she couldn't control.

"When it breaks," she said aloud, her voice hollow but authoritative, "kick up. Hard. Take as big a breath as you can before the water floods us."

A plop of icy water landed on Han's forehead.

"Swim to the light," she continued resolutely, clinging to the only hope that remained. "Look for weak spots."

She turned her eyes upward again, to the dark uniformity of the solid ice above them.

CHAPTER 47

HAN

PURE PANIC FLOODED HAN'S SENSES as the crack in the dome above them widened. He didn't want to die, but more than that he didn't want to die *cold*.

Not again.

"You're not going to die, Han," Leia said, her voice as calm as the underwater sea.

Han snorted. "How do you know that?" They were near the surface now, but it didn't matter. The ice remained impenetrable.

"Because I am not going to die," Leia said with certainty.

That? That he could believe.

But then Leia said in a small voice, "And I need you."

Those four words shot through him with the shock of an electrical pulse. This wasn't her roping the *Falcon* into one more mission for the Rebellion. This wasn't some higher purpose or noble cause.

It was her. *She* needed him.

She could love him all she wanted. Plenty of women had loved Han in his life. But need? That was different.

His hands slipped off the feeble joystick of the submersible as he looked right into her eyes.

Need was real.

An ear-piercing crack of breaking glass shattered the silence.

The glass dome above them finally gave out, the crack breaking apart under the pressure of the cold water, flooding the submersible before Han could do more than suck in one mighty, last breath of air.

His senses rioted—water stoppered his ears from sound, the salt of the ocean blurred and blinded him, the cold washed over him before the thermal disks in his vest kicked on.

The water rushed in, knocking both Leia and Han down with the force of a plasma blast. The ship itself swirled toward the bottom of the sea, the explosive flood of water driving it down, down, and Han and Leia with it.

Han clawed through the water, kicking frantically, trying not to be dragged into the depths. Once he was able to pull away from the current, his body hung, temporarily limp in the water, as he strained to see through the rapidly fading depths.

Trying to see Leia.

Instinct drove him up, toward the reedy, barely visible relative lightness of the ice-blanketed surface. A desperate bubble of air escaped him when he saw a flash of white against the unyielding ceiling of ice.

Leia.

Han shot to her, and together they beat against the ice above them. The dim, pale glow above only served to highlight just how thick the ice was.

Sure could use an ice quake about now, Han thought, half expecting one to rattle the ice and break them free.

But no. As usual, his luck ran out right when it counted the most.

Leia was still beating against the ice, both fists pounding loudly enough that the sound reverberated through the water, but not nearly loud enough for anyone to hear them, even if they were standing right above them.

No one knew where they were.

No one was coming to save them.

Han's lungs ached, but he fought the instinct to breathe in, knowing that would mean nearly instant death.

Han grabbed for Leia's hand. She struggled, shooting him a desperate look, fighting to the end. But Han cupped her cheek with his other hand, his fingers slipping through her loosely flowing hair. He pulled her to him, drawing her into one last longing kiss.

When their lips met, there was no cold water, no lack of air. Just the two of them, floating in the sea. Together.

Leia's body sagged in the water, defeated. No. Not his wife. She was never defeated. Han wrapped his arms around her, pulling her against his body, so tight that their thermal disks clinked together. She clung to him, their two bodies the only heat in water as cold as the void of space.

Black spots danced in front of Han's eyes, so he closed them. Nothing would mar this moment, not even a lack of oxygen.

She'd said she needed him. Well, he needed her. More than air.

But some air would be nice about now.

Cold washed over him. The thermal disks couldn't function well underwater.

This was it.

Then the ice above them exploded.

Han and Leia were ripped apart, their bodies swirling in the aftermath of the blast. Cold water filled Han's nose, mouth, lungs. He gagged, choking on the salt.

Something—*someone*—slammed into him. Had he any air left, it would have been knocked from his chest. Vaguely, Han was aware of something swimming, hard, propelling him through the water and then somehow tossing him bodily out a new hole that had been blasted in the ice. The force of the landing on the hard ice rattled something loose, and Han found himself vomiting salt water onto the jagged edges of a cracked ice sheet.

"That's it, get it out."

Han almost recognized the male voice, but his mind was a chaotic mess of flooded senses. "Leia," he croaked through a raspy voice. He turned at the sound of gagging and saw Leia's body hunched over nearby. He crawled to her, pulling her into his lap. Her whole body shook as she curled into him. Han closed his eyes, his head sinking against her wet hair.

"We've got to get you both something dry," the voice said again. Han forced his head up to look at their rescuer.

A Nautolan. Well, that explained how well the man had been able to swim and save them. His eyes drifted to the black scorch marks at the edge of the hole in the ice. Three empty flare shells had been lodged into the ice, their explosive force just enough to blow a hole through it.

"How?" Han croaked.

"Those flares are serious business," the Nautolan said. Zalma. Han was able to piece the memory of him together. Zalma Trinkris, the head engineer of the *Halcyon.* "I don't know why they were out on the shuttle, but—"

"No," Han said, tightening his grip around his wife. "How'd you find us?" His teeth were starting to chatter, but not hard enough for his words to be incomprehensible.

"Oh!" Zalma beamed. "The trackers."

"Trackers?" Leia asked without releasing Han.

Zalma nodded as he reached over and tapped a now malfunctioning thermal disk on Han's vest. "This is from the *Halcyon,* and it has trackers. If you had to evacuate a shuttle, you'd be glad we could find you in the vast emptiness of space before your oxygen ran out."

"Glad you found us in the vast emptiness of the sea," Han said.

Zalma laughed, the sound dissonant given the situation. *Leftover hysteria from the close call,* Han thought, noting the manic edge. Zalma sobered, looking down at Han and Leia huddled for warmth together. "We need to get you back to the shuttle. Or somewhere safe."

Han accepted the Nautolan's hand to help him stand, pulling Leia up with him. Zalma was wet, too, and exposed to the cold air of Madurs, but he had his own thermal vest on. He caught Han's eye, starting to unbuckle his vest and give it to Leia.

"No," Leia said, forcing herself to walk forward. Han shook his head. He knew his wife. She would freeze before she made her savior cold.

"When I got to the shuttle, I knew something serious was up," he said. "And that it wasn't just a malfunction in the navisystem. Nice use of the fire extinguisher, by the way."

Leia gave him a little bow as they plodded across the ice. Her feet slipped, and Han gripped her elbow to steady her. They were both weak, and this exposure wasn't good—it was cold enough on the surface of Madurs, let alone when they were wet.

Zalma seemed to realize this, too; he walked faster, leading the way, and he talked faster, as if he hoped his words would distract them from the cold.

"Anyway, I saw the missing thermal vests. I figured it would be easiest to just find you and ask what happened."

"With evac flares?" Leia asked.

"Look, I can read between the lines," Zalma said. "I know about you two. I know your reputations. I didn't think I'd *need* the flares, but—" He shrugged. Han could respect that sort of resourcefulness. Although he did kind of wish the Nautolan had thought to pack some blankets, too.

"I was halfway to the ice dock when your signals headed in the other direction," Zalma said. "And it was pretty obvious you weren't walking on the ice like me. So I changed direction. And then your signals stopped."

And he'd blown a hole in the ice and saved them.

Han's fingers wove through Leia's, and he squeezed her hand. He'd been wrong. His luck hadn't run out just yet.

CHAPTER 48

LEIA

LEIA WAS SO COLD THAT it was hard to think of anything beyond putting one foot in front of another. She did not even have the energy or concentration to consider the ice quake that rattled the ground.

Zalma, however, cursed quite a bit, big eyes growing bigger as the aftershocks rumbled. "Has this been happening often?" he asked, gaping at them.

"Like clockwork," Han muttered.

"Every time the Imperial station blasts the core," Leia added through chattering teeth.

Zalma frowned, shaking his head, his long green tentacles sweeping his back. "I've seen this kind of thing happen before, although not on this scale. On an aquatic world like this one, once you start feeling the quakes, the damage is done. It's too late to just withdraw."

Leia plodded forward, each step like the pound of an impact drill into her skull, but somehow his words still penetrated her mind. She stopped. "Wait," she said, still sifting through her foggy thoughts. "Are you saying that even if we destroy the station somehow, this moon is doomed?"

Zalma frowned. "I could be wrong. I'm an engineer, not a geologist. But . . . the core is unstable. What's true of a ship is true of a world, when it comes to cores."

The ice quakes wouldn't stop, even if the Empire did.

What hope remained for this world? She had only just visited it, but the beautiful art was shaking apart. The people, the prooses, the edonts she had only seen shadows of. This was their home, and there was *nothing* she could do to save it.

They had arrived too late.

It was worse, somehow, to have had the hope that they could potentially save Madurs. To believe that there was a chance, no matter how slim, that just a handful of rebels could, once again, go against a station far larger than they were. But to think that they had nearly died facing Beck, that they had spent so much effort to uncover this mystery—and this world would still be left as nothing but broken ice . . .

"Evacuations," she muttered. "We'll have to evacuate everyone." Senior Commander Beck wouldn't like that. She was operating under the assumption that the Empire still reigned; and that meant no witnesses. Leia frowned, trying to think. It was so *cold,* but there was so much to do—

"Hey." Han stood directly in front of her. Beyond his shoulder, Leia saw that Zalma had gone on a little, giving the two of them privacy. "Look at me." Han's voice was the warmest thing on this ice moon.

Leia shifted her focus to him. He put both hands on her shoulders, grounding her. "How you doing?" he asked, searching her face.

Leia didn't bother biting back the bitter laugh that erupted past her chapped lips. "Not bad, you?"

The corner of Han's mouth twitched up. "Same. Bit cold."

"Bit."

"So." He didn't let go of her; he didn't break his eye contact. "How are you doing?" His tone had changed. It wasn't a question. It was an offer. To ease the burden on her mind, to help carry the load that weighed her down.

Leia tried to shift her gaze, but Han ducked down, holding her focus, not letting her escape her own truth. "Luke could have broken it," she finally said. Han's brow furrowed, confused. "The ice," she added. "Luke could have broken it. He wouldn't have just . . ." Her fingers curled into a fist, relishing the pain of the budding bruises and cuts the ice had made in her skin when she'd been underwater, pounding on the underside of the seemingly impenetrable sheet.

"Look, the kid's some sort of wizard; you can't expect—"

"It's in my blood," Leia spat out. "*He* could have done it. *He* could have broken that ice and saved us both."

They both knew she wasn't talking about Luke now.

"What is the point of power if it cannot save the people I love?" Leia asked, her voice breaking.

"We're okay, though." He tucked her hair behind her ear, and they both noticed the crackling sound; ice crystals were forming in it. They needed shelter and warmth, and they needed it fast.

But Leia couldn't summon the will to move. "I can't be Luke," she said finally. "If I had even a fraction of his power, I could do something with it, but I don't. I just cannot be him." Luke spent every second he could honing his Jedi power, but Leia had her own missions. She couldn't walk away from those responsibilities. She didn't need to find herself on a Jedi quest; she knew who she was already. She was a rebel.

But even after the short time Luke had spent on Dagobah, he had come back so different from when she'd first met him. Peace ran through him like an unyielding axis of strength. He still had doubts; she knew him well enough to see the way they haunted him. But like a light in the dark, he could see past them all, see straight into the heart of certainty.

See the Force.

And she couldn't. Not even when her and Han's lives depended on it. She *couldn't* tap into the power Luke had.

"Here's the thing," Han said slowly, as if he were still thinking through his words. "You say it's in your blood, and maybe you're right. But Luke's not Vader."

"Of course he's not," Leia said immediately.

"So that means you don't have to be Luke."

Leia blinked at him, the truth of his words falling like snow on her skin.

Han dropped a cold kiss on her forehead. "Luke had to dump his X-wing in a swamp to find the Force. You just need to find your swamp."

Leia laughed—without a trace of bitterness this time. "I don't think I'm going to find a swamp on this moon."

"So?" Han shrugged. "All I'm saying is, you need to be yourself. Find *your* way to the Force—if you even want to."

"I don't understand you," Leia said, slipping her hand into his and pulling him forward, to where Zalma was waiting for them. "You're so good at saying exactly the wrong thing so often that I come to expect it, and then the perfect words just fall from your lips."

"I just like to keep you on your toes," he said airily, but he squeezed her hand.

When they reached Zalma, they realized he wasn't just waiting for them to catch up; he was also waiting for a mounted figure to approach. Leia squinted as the enormous proose came closer.

"Nah'hai!" she exclaimed.

Nah'hai jumped off the back of the proose. "I'm so glad I found you!"

"I'm glad you did, too!" Leia said, teeth chattering.

Nah'hai grabbed a satchel strapped to the proose's back, pulling out warming cloaks, which she passed to Han and Leia. "Sorry, I don't have more," she told Zalma, who showed her his own thermal disk vest. Steam rose from Han and Leia's bodies as the warming cloaks activated, heat seeping through their wet clothes and to their skin.

"How did you find us?" Han asked.

"You mean other than following the giant blast in the ice?" Nah'hai laughed. "The prime minister alerted us."

"Beck will know where we are," Han said immediately. "If Yens contacted you with a comlink, you can bet it's been monitored."

Nah'hai shook her head. "We know. He used the anglers."

"The—?" Leia asked.

"The anglers. When the stormtroopers crossed into the dock, Yens passed word on to the anglers, who dropped one-way signals into the water instead of bait. The underwater fishers saw the flashing lights and went to the dock built under the palace. They told the captain, the captain sent the proose drivers out. No communication to be sliced. If troopers even saw the flashing lights, they certainly wouldn't know the signals mean anything."

Han leaned back, looking impressed. "Why didn't Yens tell us about this elaborate system of communication going on?"

Leia shook her head. "It's not just communication. You've got a whole resistance happening." She frowned. "Why didn't you tell us?"

Nah'hai hesitated. "There was some debate over whether to bring you in," she said.

"Of course we would help!" Leia said.

Nah'hai shook her head mournfully. "No, it was . . . if you succeeded, great. But if you failed, the retaliation of the Empire against us . . ." Her gaze flicked from Leia to Han.

Leia could understand, especially now that she knew the depths of destruction the Empire had leveraged against this moon. She and Han were only two people, and Leia had reached out as an ambassador to talk politics, not to offer military aid. Even the prime minister's original holo to her had been carefully scripted so that if Beck saw, she would see nothing more than chatter about art, not politics or carnium. Openly working with Leia would mean that Beck would have amped up her attacks on the moon's core. Worse, she could have shifted her abuse of the planet to a battle against the people.

That was why Yens had held back. He had wanted them to discover the truth, but he couldn't be open about it, not with Beck monitoring him, not with the risk to Madurs and his people.

"The prime minister was going to gift you some art at the end of your tour tomorrow morning," Nah'hai continued. "It was going to have a message attached so you could send troops or some other help. We all voted that it would be safest. You two were just impatient."

"Who voted?" Leia asked. "Do you have a council, or a—"

"The survivors," Nah'hai said. "We all voted." She looked around the barren ice field. "Come on, we should move out."

Nah'hai didn't have a mounting block, but she cupped her hands, indicating that Leia should use them to help mount the proose. When Leia stuck her foot in the girl's palms, Nah'hai all but flung her in the air. Leia scrabbled to hold on to the patient animal's fur, then turned to help Han mount behind her.

"I'll walk, thanks," Zalma said, staring up at the proose.

"That commander has troopers looking everywhere."

"They're not looking for me," Zalma said, taking a step back.

"Mount up, Trinkris," Han growled. Reluctantly, Zalma clambered astride the big animal. Nah'hai tapped the proose's foreleg, and it bent a knee, giving her leverage to swing herself up. Everyone scooted closer together, and while cramped, the proose's wide back had no issue at all accommodating so many riders.

"Where are we going?" Leia asked Nah'hai. Going to the palace put countless people at risk. And Beck would have the spaceport monitored by now.

"I've got a place," Nah'hai said, clucking at the proose. Soon they were trotting across the ice.

Han wrapped his arms around Leia, and she was glad to lean into his warmth.

"Commander Beck won't believe we're dead until she sees our bodies herself," Han said in her ear. "She's a hunter."

Leia had no doubt of that. The resistance network the people of Mad urs had already built had bought them time, but no doubt Commander Beck had sent droids through the water and to scan the icy surface.

"How many people are aboard the Imperial station?" Leia called to Nah'hai.

She shifted around to see Leia. "They started leaving almost as soon as the station was established in the ice. It's a skeleton crew now, mostly just those needed for the collection and shipment of carnium."

Leia frowned, exchanging a worried look with her husband. That wasn't how the Empire worked—stormtroopers were disposable to them, and they wouldn't mind whole contingencies on the surface of a conquered moon that provided a valuable resource, no matter how peaceful and conquered they seemed. From what she'd gleaned from Yens, the station had been there for a year or less, so the removal of forces would line up with . . .

With Luke training to become a Jedi Knight, Leia thought. Something Vader must have known. Had that been enough for the Emperor to start shifting his focus, changing the locations of his heaviest military presence, or did something else spur that movement? Leia shook her head, trying to clear it. This was a strategy she would need to analyze in the future, determine how it played out. The Emperor had been strategizing for a much longer game of holo-chess than she had realized, setting up pieces to be in play even after he fell, a year in advance.

The proose moved swiftly, and in the distance Leia could see more of the enormous animals scattered over the ice—a distraction to any probe droids or troopers that were looking for them. Soon, Nah'hai's destination became obvious.

"The cliffs," Leia said.

While Leia hoped that Commander Beck wouldn't think to inspect the cliffside dwellings where the anglers and net fishers who worked below the ice lived, a part of her was more relieved to go there than to the luxury of the guesthouses. Leia may have grown up in a palace, but she knew better than anyone that the strongest rebels were usually not the ones who lived in luxury. Yens cared for his people, and he mourned for their losses, but the workers of this world? They didn't just mourn. They *burned*. Hot enough, Leia hoped, to excise the Imperial station from this frigid moon.

CHAPTER 49

HAN

THE CLIFF DWELLERS GREETED LEIA and Han as if they'd known they were coming, which, judging from the underground resistance network, it seemed likely they did. It still worried him. If the cliff dwellers had known they were coming, Beck would figure it out, too. He could only hope that she hadn't bothered to learn about the cliff dwellers, but he doubted such a thorough and astute officer would have skipped that.

Leia guessed his thoughts at his dark look. "Maybe she will think we drowned," she whispered, unable to keep the doubt from her low voice.

"She'll find the hole Zalma blasted," Han muttered.

There were no footprints on the ice, though, and with dozens of prooses on the plains, there was a good chance Nah'hai's proose had escaped notice. At least for now.

The cliff dwellings were far different than the ice palaces and the cubed guesthouses in the courtyard, but there were still some similarities in their construction. Although the ice palace had tried to incorporate the carnium lace used to provide power and heat to the buildings, the cliff dwellings used a networked pattern of pipes and wires to connect each of the many levels without any attempt to hide the utilitarianism of the carnium, which they harvested personally in a safer, gentler way than the Empire's core blaster. The dwellings were made of hand-dug caves cut directly into the ice, but even here, there were some artistic touches that were the trademark of the people of Madurs—fish scale patterns pressed into the floor, carvings of harpoons crisscrossed above the doorframe, rounded windows that resembled the glass domes of the submersibles, made of ice that had been distilled for crystal-clear translucency.

The inhabitants, too, were different from those in the ice palace. While the people in the palace had known the schedule of quakes, they tried to ignore them. But the cliff dwellers cursed them roundly and loudly, in a way that immediately put Han at ease. That, and the copious pours of kistrozer, which still burned when Han drank it, but at least he had been cold enough now to appreciate the liquid fire down his throat.

"Aye, we knew the bastards were here the whole time," one of the anglers told Han after they'd shared a third round of kistrozer. "And we knew the deal was rotten and stayed rotten. We all had people we lost in the original city."

Han nodded sympathetically, but he also had his eye on the plate of sliced fish being passed around, raw but drizzled with a green sauce. When it came by, he grabbed a piece, gobbling it eagerly. He wanted more, but hesitated.

"Here." The angler—his name was Janyn, Han recalled—handed him another glass of kistrozer. Han started to refuse, but Janyn pushed it into his hand. "It helps with the hunger," he said gently.

Han took the glass, but stared into the steaming liquor, frowning. He knew that trick. "You're an angler. I saw the size of those fish you were pulling up. Why do you need liquor for that?"

Janyn snorted. "Half of what we pull up has toxin levels that are too high for human consumption. The prooses like 'em."

"Toxins?"

"You think the Empire's dumping their waste in hazard containers that are processed correctly? A fish can't avoid the chemicals when they're bleeding into their home."

"What about the kelp and other plants?"

"We go farther and farther out, but our submersibles can only go so fast."

"Trust me, I know."

"They don't grow if the water's too warm. They thrive in the cold. And—"

"Yeah," Han said, "I get it." If the world didn't shake apart at its roots from the core blaster, the Imperial station would leave behind nothing but poison and blight. "How can you stand it?" he said, unable to keep the incredulity from his voice. "How have you all just been sitting around, hoping Yens would negotiate some deal to make the Empire leave?"

"Oh, we tried! Didn't we, Balangawa?"

A gruff woman, Balangawa, turned at the sound of her name. "'Course we did," she said.

Leia, who'd been standing by the door, came over. "Please, tell me more," she said, eagerly.

Balangawa and Janyn animatedly started talking with Leia, detailing their previous sabotage attempts on the station. Leia listened raptly, dedicating her full attention to the anglers, not blinking at their hard language or thick accents. Han took a moment to appreciate his wife, the ease with which she switched between speaking with senators and conferring with fishers. She had no trace of contempt for these people—for any people. That was a rarity, Han knew firsthand. Some of the roughest mob bosses sneered at elites for their lack of space smarts; some of the most prestigious people on the right side of the law belittled anyone with a little dirt on their hands. Leia never did that, not with anyone.

Han felt a slight pressure on his arm, and turned to see Zalma nodding toward the door. He followed the Nautolan outside, onto the open ledge that served as a corridor granting access to the front-facing entry of each of the dwellings. There were few people here as the sun crested the rim of the planet Madurs orbited, casting the moon in shadow and adding a chill to the air. Still not over the cold from their dunk, Han had kept his robe around his shoulders, something he was grateful for now.

"Any news from the *Halcyon*?" Han asked Zalma, assuming that was why the engineer had asked him to go outside.

Zalma palmed his comlink. "I encrypted my message to Captain Dicto, just in case the Imperial station was watching."

"Smart. They would be."

Zalma shrugged the compliment off, and Han could tell he was delaying bad news. "Well?"

"Captain Dicto can't help."

Han growled, turning his back to the brilliant view as he leaned against the fence that prevented someone from falling the roughly ten-meter drop to the ground. Made of fishing netting that had been reinforced with carbon threading, it wasn't quite stable enough to casually trust with his weight, Han decided, so he started pacing on the packed-snow walkway. "Why not?" he demanded. "The *Halcyon* is big enough."

"Size has nothing to do with it. It's a luxury star cruiser, not a warship. What do you want the captain to do, blast the station with defensive light cannons from orbit?"

"Can't you juice them up?" Han asked.

Zalma shook his head, tentacles moving over his shoulders. "You know we can't do that. To say nothing of the—"

"Don't you dare mention 'optics' or 'public relations' or what the news feeds will say," Han growled.

"You know the captain has to consider that. We were *just* freed of Imperial control, and Chandrila Star Line has always been envisioned as a peaceful, exploratory line."

Han glared at the Nautolan. "These people need our help."

"I can't manufacture an armada to fight against an Imperial station just because you want one," Zalma said, frustrated. "Can't you contact the Rebellion? Can't they come?"

"Leia is going to get in touch with the leadership." He ran his fingers through his hair. Another quake rumbled. He couldn't be sure, but they seemed to be coming more frequently. "So you think the core of this world is unstable, huh?"

Zalma nodded gravely. "Listen, like I said, I'm no geologist. But I've lived most of my life on different aquatic worlds. They've got a different nature to them. And if the core goes . . ."

"Which would happen after being blasted into multiple times a day for a year," Han said.

Zalma flinched. "The ice may be the only thing that's kept this world together. And you and I both saw how it's thinning and cracking."

Madurs was being destroyed from the inside and the outside.

"Besides, we have to face facts," Zalma continued. "The warmer water has effectively created a climate change that may not be reversible. Add in the pollutants in the water, which directly affect the inhabitants' only food source."

"No need to sugarcoat things," Han grumbled.

"The *Halcyon* can and will aid with evacuations, if there's imminent need," Zalma said. His tone was confident, but Han wondered if Captain Dicto had confirmed this.

That was, at least, something. And the lives of thousands of people was no small matter.

But Han had seen the way Leia grieved. There was a difference between leaving home and having no home to go back to.

CHAPTER 50

LEIA

"WE'VE BEEN MAD AS HELL the entire time," Balangawa said, and all the anglers and net fishers that had circled them cheered. It had very nearly turned into a drinking game, shots of kistrozer downed every time someone cursed the Empire.

"Tell her about the time Ardyn plugged their sewage pipes!" someone called from the group.

Balangawa laughed, detailing how a single teenage boy had sneaked around to the waste disposal vents, stopping them up with rancid edont blubber, a simple but effective action that had stopped drilling for three whole days.

Leia laughed along with the others, and even if there was a desperate pitch to the guffaws, there was real mirth, too. She had not met any of these people before that night, but she admired them already. They had never expected to be saved, but they were always going to fight.

All around her, the others were still regaling one another with the stories of their heroics, some of the star players already reaching legendary status in the epic recounts. "Tell me," Leia said. "Where have you targeted before?"

Balangawa waved her arms, clearing a space where a few people had been sitting on a fur. Whipping it up, she flipped it around. The underside of the white, thick fur revealed smooth suede decorated with thick black lines. Leia's eyes widened as she took in the schematics of the Imperial station, carefully etched with the precise lines she should have expected from a world known for its artistic rendering.

"Ardyn's sewer ploy," Balangawa said, pointing to a circle with an X mark on it. "Comm unit attack here, that was Blinna and her girls." Another circle crossed out. "We've tried to get to the core blaster, but that's impossible. Tried a couple times to net the droids gathering carnium."

"Useless," a voice from the crowd said, and several of the people nearby muttered their agreement.

"What about an attack from the top?" Leia asked. "I understand how it's easier for you, in the submersibles, to attack underwater, but—"

Balangawa was already shaking her head. "The ice surrounding the station is very thin and unstable. Not only would we be out in the open, but it's just too dangerous."

Leia's eyes sparked. "Which means they would never expect it." She jumped up, pointing to the valves along the side of the station. "It's above the ice for a reason. Air valves?"

"As far as we can tell," Balangawa confirmed.

That made sense—oxygen generators were difficult to run, and once the station had breathable air, it could redirect power to the core blaster and simply use the atmosphere of Madurs. "So we attack here. If we're quick—"

Balangawa snorted. "We could never get there." Before Leia could protest, the other woman held up her hand. "There are guards watching, probe droids. They'd see us long before we got there. *If* we were able to navigate the thin ice. And they'd have the advantage, shooting at us from the shielded station. Trust us, Leia. We've thought of this, too. We can't approach from topside."

"Wait a minute." Leia looked up as Zalma and Han walked inside, a dusting of snow on their shoulders rapidly turning to steam in the warm room. The *Halcyon* engineer frowned at the drawing. "That station is at least forty meters aboveground. A core blaster drill like that—" He used his hands to imitate the funnel-like shape of the base of the station. "If it's not embedded in the ice, how could it possibly stay in position?"

Balangawa pointed with her staff to a series of protruding disks encircling the top of the core blaster. "Repulsorlifts," she said.

Zalma squatted down, carefully examining the drawing. "This is accurate?" he asked without looking up.

"As good as we can do from memory."

"Right. I've never seen a design like this, but clearly the Empire knew they'd have to mine an aquatic world differently from a land-based one. They were smart about this."

It was a mark at how intensely they all hung on Zalma's words that no one commented on his compliment to the Empire.

His hand drifted down to the main housing of the core blaster. "That's certain death," Balangawa said before Zalma could speak. She counted off her reasons on her fingers. "Shields. Patrols. Constant monitoring. Plus radiation and boiling heat from the blast itself."

"Right." Zalma's gaze shifted up. "Where're the—"

"All life-support systems are internal, including the power generator," Balangawa said, defeat threading through her voice in a way that broke Leia's heart. "All major functions are heavily protected."

"The station is operating with a stripped-down staff now," Leia said. "Not as many troopers, and . . ." Her voice trailed off at the look of sheer pity Balangawa shot her.

"There are fewer, I suppose," she said. "Still too many to fight."

"No." Leia bit off the word as she stood, drawing nearly every eye to her. She felt the power in the moment. This was her element. A battle planning room. A troop of soldiers. It didn't look like Endor or Yavin or Hoth, but it was still the same. Her father had started as a senator and become a rebel, but Leia had always been a fighter first, even before she'd realized that about herself. War rooms were her home now. She paused, meeting as many eyes as she could before settling on Balangawa. "It is not too many to fight."

It was Zalma who'd given her the idea, but she hoped she wasn't incorrect when she leaned over his shoulder, pointing to the repulsorlifts.

"We attack these," she says. "We make them think we're going for the core blaster, but it's a misdirect. We attack the repulsorlifts."

Zalma started nodding, getting more excited as Leia spoke, seeing her vision. Triumph blossomed inside her chest. *This could work,* she thought.

"When the repulsorlifts fail, the entire station will sink into the water," Leia said. "The ice won't hold, like you said. The air intake valves will flood."

"They might have redirectional jets or some other fail-safe," Zalma said. He rubbed his chin. "But they might not. That's the problem with a station that started in space and ended up being functional on land. If they have redirectional jets, they're probably geared for orbital adjustment, not sea steadiness. Big difference."

"But there will be some shields—" Balangawa started.

"Of course there will be," Leia said. "Can you send someone tonight, a scout? Your best artist, who can give us some details here?"

Balangawa looked at the crowd. "Filli," she said, pointing at a slender boy almost as tall as a Wookiee.

Leia motioned him closer. "Zalma will tell you what to look for."

"I need to know exactly how many repulsorlifts are supporting this thing," the Nautolan said. "And I want you to look for the shield generators. They'll be separate units, protected in a casing that looks like . . ." He drew the boy aside, explaining in more detail.

Leia turned to the others. "Tomorrow," she said. There was no point waiting.

She relished this feeling, the moment when planning tipped to action, when every single person in the room stood on the edge with her and peered past the smoke of the battle yet to come and caught a glimmer of the shining possibilities beyond it.

CHAPTER 51

HAN

LEIA AND HAN ESCAPED TO the top of the cliff for a moment of peace before the attack against the Empire the next day. They were waiting for word from Captain Dicto through Zalma, unable to proceed in their plans without confirmation of the *Halcyon*'s help.

A million stars stretched out above them, a million more twinkling on the clear parts of the ice below. Leia leaned into Han, her back against his chest, his arms around her.

In the dark, Leia said, "I met Qi'ra."

It was such an odd thing for her to say that it took Han a moment to register her meaning. "Qi'ra? My Qi'ra?"

Leia craned her head around, her eyes piercing. "*Your* Qi'ra?"

"You know what I meant."

"It was when you were frozen," Leia said, settling back into his arms and facing the stars. Han started to ask her what had happened—Qi'ra was enmeshed in the Crimson Dawn crime syndicate, and he could think of no good reason for the two to cross paths. But Leia continued, "She told me a story about you."

"Oh, no," Han said.

"It was a good story."

"I highly doubt that."

"She said you got in a fight to help out a boy you didn't even know. That the goons were going to kill you until your crime boss stepped in."

Lady Proxima was as much a slaver as a crime boss, but Han didn't bother trying to correct her.

"Qi'ra made it sound like you were a fool to help," Leia said.

"I was."

Now that Leia had dredged up the memory, Han could remember it—and the conversation he'd had with Qi'ra after, two dumb kids trying to survive. Lady Proxima hadn't cared about any of the children and teens she forced to work except for the labor they could provide. Qi'ra had cared—a bit, at least—for him, but she hadn't lifted a finger when she saw a child being beaten. It wasn't hate that made Corellia so bad. It was the way no one cared. *That* had choked him, clawing at his breath, trying to drown the man he wanted to be.

He'd jumped in that fight just so he knew he could feel something other than apathy.

"You made a difference to that kid you saved," Leia said.

Maybe he did. It was nice to think that, at least.

Leia turned around, shifting her gaze from the stars to his eyes. "You've gotta start somewhere," she whispered, brushing a lock of hair from his face. Han closed his eyes and leaned into her touch, and tried to believe in change the way Leia did.

Footsteps interrupted the moment. Zalma's approach was a disruption to the quiet Han had hoped he could selfishly extend a little longer.

"There you are," Zalma said. Leia shot Han a reluctant look as she stepped out of his embrace and turned to the Nautolan. "We have a lot to discuss."

"We need to talk about evacuations first," Leia told Zalma. Han could see the sorrow in her shoulders. Leia knew—they all knew—that there was a good chance the people of Madurs would become refugees as their moon splintered. The damage the Empire had done was irreversible.

"I've been in contact with Captain Dicto. Encrypted, of course,"

Zalma said. "The *Halcyon* is fully prepared to take as many refugees as possible. It will be uncomfortably tight, but the current population of Madurs is within an acceptable limit for us to evacuate everyone."

Han could imagine that the guests on vacation wouldn't be thrilled about sharing cabins with fishers, but at least the captain understood the gravity of the situation.

"Is there no hope?" Leia asked in a voice that broke Han's heart.

Zalma didn't pretend not to understand. "Destroying the station and making it crash into the seabed will eliminate the threat of the Imperials, and I *do* think it will work," Zalma said. "Especially given the instability of the moon at this stage. Those ice quakes; they worry me. They seem scheduled now, but when the end comes, it'll be fast and violent, the quakes spinning out of control as the world cracks apart. We can't really afford to wait."

No doubt the Empire would start evacuating well before that time came—although, Han realized, perhaps they already had. Nah'hai had told them there was only a skeleton crew left. There was every chance the Empire was already preparing to abandon the world, knowing it was doomed.

"Do we have any idea of when the moon will collapse?" Han asked. If they were successful in taking out the station, they might buy the moon more time, perhaps long enough to figure out a way to save not just the people, but the entire world. It would be a broken, polluted world, forever tarnished by the taint of Imperial destruction. But it might survive, despite that.

Many things broken by the Empire found a way to survive.

"I spoke to the locals. Given the regularity of the blasts, I would think a few weeks. A month or two, max." Zalma sighed heavily. "A year of regular, heavy blasting . . . that kind of damage can't be undone. It's a miracle this moon is as stable as it is."

Leia let out a shuddering breath.

"Taking out the station is our best bet to ensuring everyone has time to evacuate, and it will enable us to save as much as we can," Zalma said. "The design of the station makes me think that the Imperials expected the ice to support it and didn't factor in the heat of the core blaster warming the water as much as it ultimately has. That makes the repulsorlifts an even more vulnerable spot to attack."

It wasn't much consolation. They could take down the Empire, but it wouldn't be enough to save the moon. Once destabilized, the core was doomed. Madurs was a ticking time bomb. The only thing they could hope for was enough time to turn the citizens into refugees.

Leia squared her shoulders. "First, evacuations," she said. "I'll start organizing that."

Han watched his wife descend the steps carved into the snow. He knew it weighed upon her to watch another world die. Even if they were able to save all the people, they wouldn't be able to save the art, the prooses, the edonts. Nothing would exist of Madurs but memories.

Zalma turned to Han. "All right, look, I know you're not going to like this," he said in a rush. "But you know who we really need right now?"

Han turned slowly to the Nautolan. "No," he said flatly.

"He's a *genius*. I've been talking with him, and—"

"He tried to kidnap my wife."

"Unsuccessfully!"

"That does not support your 'genius' argument."

"Just—hear me out," Zalma said. "His specialty is tractor beams, remember? Gravitational manipulation. Like with repulsorlifts. He could help, Han."

Han glared at him, but he didn't see the man. He saw scrawny, sniveling Kelad, the academic-turned-mercenary, but only for a night, when the opportunity arose.

"He worked for the Empire before."

Zalma glared. "So have I. I didn't want to. I also didn't want to die."

Han released a breath through his nose. He didn't want to go down that line of thought again. He didn't want to think about what he had done for the Empire to survive. And he definitely didn't want to consider the men and women aboard the Imperial station right now who might be killed tomorrow, who were only doing a job with no concept of what that job entailed. *They have to know by now,* Han thought. *The Death Star destroyed, the Empire's darkest secrets being exposed. If they still haven't bothered to look at what they're doing . . .*

He shook his head. No. He couldn't think about that. Not when an entire moon full of people and life stood in the balance.

"He kept talking about his theories. It was the only reason he stowed away on the *Halcyon* in the first place," Zalma continued. "Kelad knows gravity manipulators, which includes repulsorlifts, and that's exactly the experience we need right now."

If Han was willing to give him a chance.

"Fine," he said. "Get him down here, too."

CHAPTER 52

LEIA

AS LEIA DESCENDED THE STEPS, she sent a comm to Mon Mothma, re-questing evacuation ships for the people of Madurs and fighters for the Empire. Mon confirmed that aid was coming, but it would take a day or more to reach the moon.

Leia had just turned off the comlink when an explosion lit up the night, a thundering boom echoed by loud thuds and the eerie pinging noise of splintering ice. Chaos immediately erupted as the cliff dwellers burst from their rooms, rushing for the stairs, evacuating the cliffs in case the ice quake reached them.

But Leia recognized those sounds.

That had not been an ice quake.

Rather than push her way down the steps with the flow of the crowd, Leia raced up, back to the top of the cliffs where she'd last seen Han. He and Zalma stood near the edge, watching smoke and steam cloud the starry night sky.

"What was that?" Leia asked, panting.

Han pointed. "The spaceport."

From this high up, the source of the explosion was evident. Someone had blown up the ice that supported the spaceport. Leia had no doubt that the culprit was Senior Commander Beck. The docking bays and all the ships and shuttles they had held were sinking into the cold depths of the sea that covered Madurs.

"Why would the Empire do that?" Zalma asked incredulously. "This entire world is covered in smooth ice thick enough for shuttles to land on. We don't need a spaceport to get the shuttles from *Halcyon* here. We can still evacuate everyone."

Leia met Han's eyes, horror dawning on her. "Wait," she said. Her comlink was still in her hand. Leia opened an encrypted holo to Riyola.

"How can I help?" the Pantoran woman said immediately.

"Do you already have shuttles coming to Madurs?" Leia asked urgently.

Riyola's brow furrowed. "Zalma told us to send down the stowaway. I have him on Captain Dicto's personal shuttle, waiting for departure."

"Get him off," Leia ordered. "Right now. The shuttle doesn't need to be crewed to fly, correct?"

"You want me to send an empty shuttle to Madurs?" Riyola asked, clearly confused.

"Yes. Immediately."

Riyola nodded firmly. "Consider it done."

Han, Leia, and Zalma looked up at the stars. The *Halcyon* was barely a speck in the dark sky, and it was impossible to see Captain Dicto's personal shuttle zoom away from it, empty. But soon enough, Leia spotted the craft, a bright dot swooping closer. It burned through Madurs's atmosphere, close enough for her to see the sleek, curving lines of the vessel.

And then a laser blast fired from the Imperial station, incinerating the shuttle.

Below, Leia could hear the screams of horror from the people gathered at the base of the cliffside as they witnessed another explosive blast, although they didn't know what had been targeted.

Leia's communicator beeped, and she brought up Riyola's holo. The woman looked grave. "The shuttle was destroyed," she said.

"We saw."

Riyola's jaw tightened, and then she said, "Are we to assume that any shuttle that enters or leaves Madurs will also be destroyed?"

"Looks like it," Han answered for Leia.

"The Empire is making sure no one escapes," Leia said.

"Why?" Zalma was clearly rattled by both the initial attack on the spaceport and Kelad's last-minute escape from the shuttle. "The Empire has destroyed this moon, why do they care if people leave? So there are no witnesses?"

Han shook his head sorrowfully. Leia knew what he was thinking.

It was them.

Beck was willing to let the entire world crack apart and trap every single person on it just to be sure that she killed Leia and Han. That was why she hadn't hunted them down. Rather than try to locate Han and Leia, Beck had laid explosives under the spaceport and prepared to target any additional shuttles that came down. Her meaning was clear: They were trapped. All of them, on a dying moon. Beck was ensuring that not a single person on the moon who wasn't Imperial could escape.

"Maybe we can negotiate with her," Leia told Han. "She might let the others go if we . . ."

"She doesn't work like that," Han growled. "I know her. She doesn't mind killing everyone on this moon if it means . . ."

If it meant Han and Leia died.

CHAPTER 53

HAN

THE NEXT MORNING, HAN WATCHED Leia pull up a fur-lined hood over her head, tugging it low around her scarf-covered face. The one good thing about an icy moon was that disguises were a little easier. All the anglers and net fishers wore layers of warm clothes rather than thermal disks. The anglers needed to stay flexible when a salna fish bit their line, and the tight chest harness restricted them too much. The underwater net fishers wore their own suits that had heat generators attached to the back, alongside breathing apparatuses.

Han, Leia, and Zalma stuck tight with the group that would be heading down in the floating dock to the submersibles, intermingling with the regulars in a way that they all hoped would keep them hidden from the droids obviously stationed around the fishing area. Yens had been right—the Imperial station was definitely operating with a thinned-out crew. The fact that there were only half a dozen probe droids circling the perimeter of the bubble dock spoke volumes on how little Beck had to work with.

Han shuddered as he thought of Beck's cold, imperious gaze boring into him from both her biological and her cybernetic eye. He was surprised to have found her here, on such a remote world. But Han had been to worlds poorer and more repressed than Madurs, and they had been plagued with far more troops. Leia might have the right theory: The Empire was willing to mine this world dry, but it had directed its military force elsewhere. And that was a problem they were going to have to solve.

Inside the dock, two stormtroopers stood on either side of the door, scanning faces. Han ducked into a group of fishers, holding a heavy bunch of netting in his arms, obscuring his face. As practiced, the group veered, shifting around to keep Han hidden within the crowd. Simultaneously, one of the younger fishers purposefully tripped on his netting, crashing into the closest trooper. It wasn't much of a disturbance, but it was enough for Han to slip through. Once inside, he dared a look behind him, watching as Leia made it past the checkpoint in a similar way.

Too easy. It made Han sick to his stomach, wondering what was coming. Beck was using the moon's destruction to kill them all just so she could take out Han and Leia, but Han knew she would have more plans in place, not trusting their deaths if she did not personally touch their cold bodies.

Inside the dock, Beck's damage was clear. Carbon scoring streaked the walls, and the hatch she'd damaged was still sealed by a locked metal door. Even the broken crate and the spent harpoon were on the floor where Leia had left them.

While anglers stayed at the top, on the ice, the net fishers worked underwater. Most of them went in the bubble-domed submersibles that Han and Leia had experienced, but the many elite and experienced fishers were upgraded to harpooners, suiting up and diving solo into the water.

These were the men and women chosen to be the strike force against the station, Han, Leia, and Zalma among them. The three stuck close to the harpooners as they veered to the dive corridor and the other fishers made a point of flapping their nets over the surveillance cams in the corners. Once in the narrow hallway that ended in the dive hatch, they all stripped off their layers of outerwear and stepped into the synthprene underwater suits. Designed to stretch and fit a variety of sizes, the full-body suits weren't exactly comfortable, but Han would rather wear one than step inside another bubble-domed submersible.

"Wasn't sure you three were actually going to be on the front lines," Balangawa said as she helped Han shrug into the shoulder harness and plug in the cords that would enable him to breathe and stay warm in the icy depths.

"Then you don't know us," Han said. He staggered under the weight of the unit Balangawa strapped to his back.

"Don't worry; it's lighter in the water," she told him.

Han hoped so. Balangawa showed him how to read the gauges—not just oxygen and heat, but also the power of the underwater jet propulsion unit that would enable him to shoot through the water quickly. She checked his communicator piece as he stepped into the oversized flippers and adjusted his gloves. After her approval, Han got in the dive line between Zalma and Leia.

Harpooners were more underwater hunters than passive fishers. The anglers waited on the ice, dropping hooked lines in the water. The net fishers gathered mindless schools of fish. The harpooners tracked their prey, hid and waited, attacking the biggest sea creatures directly, darting out to face down sawkills and krackles, stab them, and pull the bodies back to the floating dock. Sawkills were used both for food and leather; the krackle was harvested for trade—its oil was used as a natural preservative in an array of industries, and it was second only to Madurs's export of art for the colony's income.

All fifteen harpooners for the day's shift—all of whom were going to attack the station rather than any sawkill or krackle—walked through the first pressurized hatch. With their suits on, it was hard to tell one from another, but Han knew Leia, and not just because she was the shortest harpooner in the hatch. He stepped closer to her as the metal floor shifted and water started rising from the base.

It was a strange sensation, letting the water rise higher and higher in the enclosed hatch. He knew, logically, that this would prevent them from getting pressurization sickness and ease their transition into the cold sea, but he had to fight his body's natural inclination to resist drowning as the water reached his chest, his neck, his chin, over his head. He breathed heavily, and oxygen flowed freely from the filter tank at his back through the tube in his nose.

"You okay?" Leia asked, her voice oddly tinny in his earpiece. He shot her a thumbs-up, but she knew him too well. He hated this. It was different from the carbonite freezing, but the suit didn't insulate him entirely, and that same feeling of being trapped raced down his spine.

There was no time for panic.

The hatch door opened, and the harpooners were swept into the sea. Only Zalma was really distinguishable now, big eyes and tentacles open in the sea as he swam without a breather. They turned on their jet propulsions and shot through a stream of bubbles in different directions in groups of two or three, spreading out but all heading in the same direction. The bubble-domed submersibles tailed the group, straight toward the Imperial station.

Now that they'd made it to the water, there was little point in hiding their goal. Senior Commander Beck would be expecting an attack, and they were going to give her one. The first wave of fishers—the majority of them—were sabotaging the sewer pipes and vents, a repeat of the failed attack that had happened last time, just on a larger scale. They all knew it would fail to take down the ship, but that wasn't the point. The point was to cause distraction and chaos while a dozen harpooners, including Leia and Han, attacked the repulsorlifts.

"It's not an exact science," Zalma had told the strike team the night before, showing them how to operate the hyperbaric welders. There were six repulsorlifts circling the lower half of the station. Teams of two would attack each one—one to cut into the arm holding the repulsorlift, one to serve as backup and cover their partner in case the battle got heavy. "Just cut deep as you can, then stick the damn thing up the unit," Zalma had told them. "That'll fry 'em out."

Simple and efficient. A plan Han could get behind.

The strike team had lingered behind the others, and by the time they arrived, it was clear the goal of chaos had been met. The water was already churning with submersibles actively clogging up every pipe and vent they could while the spare harpooners took down each droid sent out. Just as the strike team arrived, a hatch opened up on the station, and troopers in underwater armor shot into the water, blasters already firing.

"Let's go," Zalma ordered.

The Nautolan hung back—not only would he be an obvious target, given his tentacles, but he was the one with the most experience disabling repulsorlifts, there to guide any of the harpooners who couldn't manage their unit or to help if something went wrong. The rest of the strike team each took one of the six repulsorlifts in the station in pairs. Even through the chaos of droids and troopers blasting at harpooners and submersibles, each of the dozen fighters went straight to their station.

Han and Leia zoomed to their repulsorlift. Han pulled out the hyperbaric welder, angling it at the base, attacking the arm's weak spot as Zalma had suggested.

It would take roughly ten minutes to completely disable the repulsorlift, with the longest time spent breaking through the metal housing that protected the circuitry. Han didn't even glance at Leia as she got into position to cover him, blaster at the ready. He knew he could trust her to protect him.

Ten minutes. That was all they needed.

All around them, the water churned, a frothing sea of blasterfire, bubbles, blood, and broken droids.

Nine and a half minutes.

The station started to rumble, the vibrations throwing Han's aim off balance, the beam of the hyperbaric welder sliding off the line he'd made.

They only had to survive for nine minutes more.

But from the red glow at the tip of the core blaster, it was clear that the station was charging to fire.

CHAPTER 54

LEIA

BLASTS SIZZLED THROUGH THE WATER as one of the bubble-domed submersibles retreated, listing heavily portside. Harpooners jetted about, using their own propulsors to zigzag through the water and avoid the stormtroopers blasting at them. It was utter chaos, but at least their team had clear directives.

"Watch out!" Zalma called over the networked communicators. "You all have been spotted."

"What do we do when the core blaster fires?" Leia said.

There was a crackling pause in her earpiece before Zalma answered. "Hold on."

Han cursed, but he didn't take his eyes from the hyperbaric welder as he cut into the repulsorlift's base. Leia spared a glance to know that hardly enough time had passed for him to cause any real damage.

Leia kept her eyes sharp and her blaster ready. More Imperial harvester droids had been released—the same ones they'd seen gathering the carnium when they saw the first core blast. Those were harmless, but they clogged her sight line, enabling the attack droids to get closer. Leia pulled the trigger on her blaster, an attack droid exploding so close that bits of it slammed against the metal station wall, ricocheting hard enough to make Han curse again.

"Team down!" Zalma shouted. "Can anyone go to the one under Bay Four?"

Leia felt a pang, but she pushed the friendly faces of the pair who'd been assigned that repulsorlift out of her mind. They were down, but perhaps just injured. She could let herself believe that for the next ten minutes.

"Trade with me," Han told Leia, holding out the hyperbolic welder. She passed him her blaster. He'd gotten enough of the metal casing off that he could aim the blaster directly into the sensitive electronics inside. It wouldn't be as efficient, but taking out two repulsorlifts slowly was better than only taking out one.

Now without a weapon, Leia shot off around the edge of the station, aiming for the repulsorlift that had been abandoned. She grabbed a hold bar, her momentum still pushing her through the water as she reached her destination.

No vibrations.

Leia had the hyperbaric welder on and driving into the repulsorlift's arm by the time the thought formed in her mind. Where had the core blaster's vibrations gone? She risked a glance down—the red tip of the plasma beam still glowed, but it hadn't fired.

It didn't vibrate like that before.

When she and Han had seen the core blaster at first, it had rumbled, but not that sharply. The chaos of the fighting had distracted her from this logic, but now—

Light flashed near her face, and Leia jerked instinctively to the side. These blasts were getting closer. *Focus.* She drove the hyperbaric welder into the metal, watching it glow red with heat. *Focus.* More blasterfire. The water was getting hot. Leia's eyes flicked—all she saw was the white of stormtroopers, the black of the droids. Not the yellow submersibles, the bright-green harpooner suits.

"How's it going, Zalma?" It was Han's voice in her earpiece, and Leia let out a breath. He was still okay.

"Three down!"

Just as Zalma shouted the words in triumph, Leia felt a lurch—the station was going into overdrive, trying to maintain balance. She pressed into the hyperbaric welder, burning into the metal a little harder.

"We need someone at Bay Six!" Zalma called.

"On it!" Balangawa, Leia was pretty sure. The other woman's voice was tight.

"Need help?" Leia glanced up as Han reached for the grab bar near her, blaster in hand. "Almost got it," Leia muttered.

"My cover's down!" Balangawa shouted. "I'm wide open!"

"Keep at it," Zalma ordered. "There're just yours and Bay Four left."

"Four's almost done," Leia said. "We're coming for you, Balangawa."

There was a hole just wide enough for Leia to cram the hyperbaric welder into place, the magma-hot tip shooting straight into the inner workings of the repulsorlift. Once she was sure it was lodged, she turned to Han, motioning for him to follow.

Three submersibles shot through the water, barreling through the droids and taking out two stormtroopers, knocking them wildly off course. The unwieldy vehicles sputtered as they tried to turn around, but the stormtroopers who hadn't been struck resumed their rapid-fire assault, plasma blasts slicing through the water. Han and Leia reached Bay Five, pausing to reassess.

There was a long black streak of carbon scoring on the metal, and a cloud of red blood still lingering in the water.

But the repulsorlift was down.

"Anytime!" Balangawa shouted over the communicator. "It's getting hot over here!"

"Almost there," Han shouted. He kicked up his jet propulsion and started out, but Leia shot after him, grabbed his ankle, and swung him around, slamming him back moments before the sonic detonator slammed into the station at the exact same spot he'd almost been in. Not strong enough to damage the metal hull of the station, the sonic detonator would have been more than enough to disrupt all of Han's organs. Even from the distance they were at, the results were enough to make Leia feel as if her brain were clanging like a bell ringer.

Dazed, both Han and Leia struggled for clarity through their muddled minds.

"Balangawa's down," Zalma called.

"No, I can—"

She's not dead, Leia thought with relief as she heard the woman's voice.

"The hell you can. Han, Leia—can you get to Bay Six?"

They could see the last repulsorlift, straining valiantly in an effort to keep the station balanced. The worst activity was here, as all the Imperial forces were gathering at this point, with the fishers hot on them. A harpoon was wedged through a grab bar, a bit of shiny white stormtrooper armor and the arm inside it still attached to the end.

Another sonic detonator flew by, forcing them to retreat even farther. "We can't get to it," Han said.

"Keep trying," Zalma ordered. "They've sent droids out already to fix the damaged ones."

"No." The word escaped Leia's lips, but it drowned under the screams and shouts cluttering the sea. They were *so* close. They had come so far. She tried again, but the stormtroopers had clearly been given orders: *Protect the last repulsorlift.* Leia spun in the water, looking back at the lift near Bay Five. So many black droids swarmed over that one that it was clear it was only a matter of time before the damage the resisters had done would be repaired.

"We have to take out that last one before the others are fixed," Leia said desperately, but there was no point. Saying what needed to be done didn't make it happen. The stormtroopers were casting detonator after detonator in the water, timing them to explode in a protective radius around the last repulsorlift. It did nothing but send shock waves through the water—far too little to harm the station—but more than enough to ensure that Han and Leia couldn't break through, not with their feeble synthprene suits.

An eerie calm washed over Leia in the face of such sure defeat. There was nothing she could do now, nothing but accept the truth of the situation. And accepting the truth meant *seeing* it. Leia was well accustomed to seeing every possible path, thinking three steps ahead, guessing at what the enemy would do so she could lay a trap or stop a battle or win the war.

But there was no path she could see now. She had reached the end.

Through the churning water, through the bright flashes of blasters and the ripples of sonic detonators, through the tangle of bodies that writhed in hand-to-hand underwater combat, through the too-still bodies that floated down and down and down—Leia looked at it all.

Accepted it all.

Her eyes went farther. The dark waters seemed so still, but there was something darker yet in them. The edonts were out there, enormous aquatic beasts, floating through the shadows.

Leia's mind stilled.

She did not try to summon the creatures. She did not order them to help. She made no effort to control or even use the Force.

She simply existed within it.

And in the deep silence, it answered the one word she couldn't let go of:

Help.

CHAPTER 55

HAN

HAN FIRED BLAST AFTER BLAST. They may not be able to get to the repulsorlift, but he'd damn sure take down as many stormtroopers as he could while he could. Trapped with an Imperial station at their backs, sonic detonators to their right, and a fraught battle all around, there was little more Han could do than shoot, so that was what he would do.

"Leia, do you think you could—"

Han's words died on his lips when he saw his wife's face. She was so often *doing* things—doing everything, actually—that to see her so completely still, her eyes unblinking . . . it stopped him.

"Leia?" he whispered.

She didn't answer, but her lips formed a word he recognized: "Help."

Then the screaming started.

Not from her—Leia remained focused on whatever it was she was looking at. But Han's earpiece was filled with such piercing screams that he clawed at his ear to get the communicator out.

In front of them, the battle stopped. Stormtroopers and harpooners fled with equal urgency, clearing the space before them.

Something was coming.

Han didn't need to see what it was to know that he needed to get the hell out of the way, but what he saw was enough to instill terror. Huge and black, hulking through the water with long, thin tendrils snaking out. Grabbing Leia's arm, Han jammed his jet propulsion into overdrive and shot through the water toward Zalma, towing her behind, dodging the tendrils, unsure what they would do.

Han had not fully disconnected his earpiece, and so he was able to hear through the muffled receiver the disbelieving and awed shock from the fishers. An edont—an old and unusually large one from the chatter—had cut through the water.

Han and Leia had only seen edonts from a distance, in the shadows. He had known they were huge, but he could not process his thoughts to comprehend the sheer size of it now, up close. The edont's body was easily twice the size of the *Millennium Falcon,* but its dozens of gossamer, filament-like tendrils extended three or four times that length, and the fluid way its entire body shifted in the water made it seem even larger than it really was.

As Han drew farther away, to a safer distance, Leia tugged at his arm. Han was grateful to see that she was no longer staring vacantly; she must have been stunned by a wave from a sonic detonator or hit by some debris, but she'd been able to shake it off.

The edont moved with a mixture of graceful flowing pulses and a near-comical clunkiness as its body drew even closer. The back of it was solid and curved in an egg shape, but the front half, the part zeroing in on the station, flowed like gwendle wool underwater. It reminded Han of Leia's cloak, the way it had rippled over the steps as she entered the main ice palace. Just as there had been purpose in her strides, there was purpose in the way this edont moved, sucking in water through a gaping, black-beaked maw in the center of its baggy front and ejecting that water through vents in its solid back, propelling it forward.

"Look." Leia pointed. Han had been right to avoid the long, thready tendrils wafting around the edont's body. They seemed directionless, but the moment they connected with droids, the mechanical bodies fizzled and sank. Some of the tendrils wrapped around the remaining stormtroopers who had not yet fled, and even through the sleek white underwater armor, the troopers screamed in pain, thrashing and flailing the moment they connected with the gossamer threads.

"Han! Leia! *Han!*" Even with his earpiece hanging awkwardly below his ear, jammed near his jawline under the synthprene suit's hood, Han could hear Zalma calling for them. Leia led the way, using her jet propulsion to head over to the cluster of remaining harpooners and bubble-domed submersibles.

"Did you disable the last repulsorlift?" Zalma asked urgently.

Han shook his head.

The Nautolan's face fell, but even through his disappointment, he kept half his attention on the edont, unable to look away. Han could understand the inclination. This ragtag group of battle-worn fishers was all that remained of the strike force and distraction troops. Several sported injuries, arms held awkwardly against their body, little clouds of red lingering in the salt water, some people hanging from nets being used as makeshift floating gurneys to carry the ones too hurt to swim on their own. There were far fewer people than before, and Han could only hope that meant one wave had already fully retreated back to the base, not that they had lost that many in the fight.

They were not retreating now. The arrival of the edont had effectively stopped the skirmish in the water. But the massive creature was not merely drifting through. It propelled itself closer to the station. As Han watched, the edont sucked in a huge spout of water, flattening the loose skin and revealing a spiny prehensile horn through its beak.

"How does it know?" he muttered as the edont slammed its horn into the last repulsorlift, the one they had not been able to reach. Balangawa may have weakened it, but the edont decimated its remains, shattering the arm and ripping the entire repulsorlift off.

The station listed down but didn't sink. The edont's flattened front curled, stretched, forming six long tentacles that wrapped around the station. They weren't quite long enough to completely encircle the base, but it was close enough.

The edont *pulled.*

The Imperial station moved slowly—without the repulsorlifts supporting it, it would fall, but it was still massive and somewhat buoyant.

The edont hastened its demise. As the bottom shifted, they could all see the red glow at the base of the station. The core blaster was still charged and primed.

"Why hasn't it fired yet?" Leia asked.

Zalma shrugged, unsure. There was no reason the core blaster didn't fire; despite the battle that had raged in the water, there would still be Imperial officers on board. If anything, they would have hastened to discharge the plasma, hoping it would defray the fighting, even if the blast hurt their own troops.

But they all watched the red eye of the unfired core blaster sink lower and lower, dragged down by the edont. A rush of bubbles rose up—the air vents were being flooded, the oxygen inside the station replaced with water.

It was a hell of a way to die, Han knew.

"They'll have locking seals internally. Any vessel designed for water or space would have safety measures," Zalma said.

"Yens will want to send us to aid survivors," Balangawa, her arm hanging limply at her side, said as they all watched the edont sink the station, its glittering tentacles all that remained visible. Several minutes later, a burst of white sand clouded the water. At least part of the station had touched the seabed.

"Do you have anything that goes that deep?" Leia asked.

"No," Balangawa said softly.

It was so strange, the way the sea was still now. The fighting had been furious, the station looming, the red eye of the core blaster a constant threat.

And now there was nothing but water, the currents washing away any trace remains of the battle.

Far, far beneath them, a burst of red light filtered through the murky depths. The core blaster housing must have cracked, the plasma ray melting down. The red light illuminated the deepest parts of the ocean, burning and bright and beautiful in its destruction, like fire blossoming beneath the water.

Han turned to Leia. Her eyes were focused on the last whispers of the sparkling silver gossamer tendrils from the edont as it drifted away, back into the shadows. Some of her hair had escaped the synthprene suit's hood, and her brown locks gently floated in the pale water. It was the only thing about her that moved as the edont faded from sight.

Han watched her blink as she seemed to come back to the moment. She turned to him with a smile, but he couldn't force his face to mask the emotion rising within him. A question.

And a fear.

CHAPTER 56

LEIA

BY THE TIME THE LAST group of fighters returned to the floating dock and made their way up to the surface, the celebrations had already begun. Yens greeted them personally, passing out hot kistrozer while others waved long sticks shooting off sparks that still burned even when they hit the ice.

Prooses were all around, shying from the sparkling sticks and snorting puffs of steam. They weren't strapped to sleds; instead, they had metal harnesses and saddles on their backs, and the people nearest them carried beautifully smithed spears.

Yens, it turned out, had led a ground attack after the spaceport had been destroyed, a fight that had quickly moved from the palace to the floating dock after their initial success. There had only been probe droids and a handful of stormtroopers at the dock, but more had been in the palace—Commander Beck had clearly thought that Han and Leia were hiding out there and hoped to corner them. The cliffside dwellings hadn't been a secret, just naturally camouflaged and ignored by the city, buying Han and Leia precious time from the Imperial officers who had never bothered to learn where the workers who harvested food lived.

Prime Minister Yens pulled Leia aside as soon as he could. "We've arrested all the troopers who attacked on the ice, and we're seeing what we can do for any survivors of the station." His brow furrowed. "I must confess, I don't know what to do with them."

"Detain them somewhere secure," Leia told him. "I have reached out to the Alliance leadership, and ships are on the way; they can take it from there."

The prime minister's body visibly relaxed. "This experience has made me both more wary of entangling my moon with galactic politics and more open to the concept."

On the one hand, the Empire had only pretended to care about negotiations. Yens could have signed an agreement and gotten token payments, but even when he clearly refused the Empire's presence, they simply ignored the will of the government and the people and did what they wanted to. On the other hand, Leia had approached him with no more ulterior motive than unification, and it was she, as a representative of the budding new republic, who was cleaning up the mess the Empire had made.

"You don't have to decide now," Leia assured him. "We would help even if you didn't join us. But I hope you'll at least listen to what we have to offer."

Behind them, a roar went up from the crowd. The Imperial probe droids had been piled in a heap of broken black metal contrasting with the white ice, and despite not being good fuel, the locals had found that krackle ink made them flammable. A bonfire erupted, smoke billowing up.

"I don't know how safe that is," Leia muttered, watching the putrid, dark-gray smoke drift up, but it was too late to do anything about it now.

Zalma rushed over to Han and Leia, pulling Yens closer. "Word from the captain," he said, holding out his communicator. "I thought there was something wrong about the station when it sank. It was hard to see—"

"Did an edont really attack the station?" Yens interrupted. "I heard the rumors, but . . ."

Leia nodded at him, but turned to Zalma for the message, which was more urgent. Beyond their group, she could see the fishers animatedly discussing the attack. Even Balangawa, with her injured arm, made an attempt to use her hands to show just how vast the edont had been. Leia had to laugh. No matter the world, fishers always pulled up tall tales.

"Oh, the wildlife always knows!" Balangawa said loudly.

"It's true," another added, nodding in agreement. "Didn't the proose always shy away from the thin spots of ice before we knew it was dangerous?"

"And that core blaster was going to go—bet the edont was sick and tired of it." One of the harpooners laughed. "Good thing it decided it'd had enough today and not tomorrow!"

Laughter washed over the crowd. This was the stuff of legends, that was for sure. But Leia's focus drifted, and she remembered the strange silence as she'd stared out into the water, reaching with—something— calling for help.

And not . . . not hearing the answer, but *feeling* it.

Was that the Force?

The bonfire raged, the crowd loudly recanted tales, the prooses stomped around. All of that was enough to make Leia unsure of the rumbling at her feet at first. But one by one the voices died as the trembling grew stronger, horror replacing joy on the faces of everyone around her.

The Imperial station was gone, but the ice quakes continued.

"I thought—" Yens said, looking from Han and Leia to Zalma.

Zalma shook his head. "That was always the fear. The damage has been done."

Yens's face fell as the impact of Zalma's words hit him. "There's nothing we can—"

Zalma put up a hand to make him stop. "There's more. What we didn't know was that part of the Imperial station could be detached as a shuttle. It was in the design—that core blaster drill was made in space, could easily move to space as it was launched and rest in orbit. But once it was lodged on a planet, or moon in this case, with gravity, that core blaster was never coming up again. Should have thought of that. It only makes sense. But—"

Han cut him off. "You're saying part of the station broke apart?"

"And launched." Zalma looked grim.

Leia met Han's eyes, understanding flashing between them. Leia remembered the heavy vibrations of the station when they tackled the first repulsorlift. She had thought it was the core blaster charging, but had felt it was more violent. And the core blaster never fired. Those vibrations had come from the shuttle detaching from the station.

Beck and anyone higher up had left the station and the stormtroopers to their fate. It was a cruel thing, the certainty that those who had died on the Imperial side of the battle had been the ones least deserving of the punishment owed. It accounted for the lack of leadership, the chaos in the water, the ease with which the troopers on the ice had been dispatched.

"Beck would not have abandoned her station, especially not that early in the fight," Han muttered. "I was a little surprised she didn't don underwater armor and dive into the battle personally."

Leia nodded grimly. Beck could not possibly have gotten orders from the Emperor since Han and Leia had arrived on Madurs—Palpatine was dead. No, the fact that she fled on a shuttle meant that she'd gotten orders from *someone* else. Someone with the authority of the Emperor.

Was it a puppet, a shadow figure operating under the rumor of the Emperor's survival? Possible, but if so, who was pulling the strings? Or had the Emperor named an heir, one already assuming command?

Zalma cleared his throat. "Fortunately, the *Halcyon* was on alert, and once that part of the station detached, it engaged."

"Engaged?" Leia gaped. "I thought Captain Dicto wasn't going to fight."

"This is a rogue hostile shuttle—not a fully armed Imperial station," Zalma said.

Han cast his eyes up. In the daylight, it was impossible to tell what was happening in orbit around Madurs, but he damn sure wished he was there instead of here.

"I have a private shuttle," Prime Minister Yens said. "It can only hold a handful of people, but I kept it at the palace, not at the spaceport. It's yours if you need it."

"Get me up there," Han said immediately.

"Hoped you were going to say that." Zalma turned to Leia. "Can you organize the evacuation? We can't risk shuttles in hostile airspace, but as soon as the *Halcyon* takes out the Imperial shuttle, there are launch pods on the *Halcyon* that we could use."

"I'm on it," Leia said, understanding. Time was of the essence as the ice quakes continued even without the Imperial station blasting at the core.

Leia watched as Han and Zalma raced toward the ice palace and the prime minister's personal transport. She dug her palms into her eyes, driving away the stinging sensation. This wasn't Alderaan. She would be able to save the people, if not the world.

That would have to be enough.

CHAPTER 57

HAN

ZALMA GAVE THE TRANSPORT COMMAND over to Han, and he was glad to be in control as soon as they broke orbit. It was more than just a simple shuttle that had detached from the Imperial station—it seemed like roughly half of the station that had been above the ice was designed to reenter spaceflight. And that was the half with all the firepower.

The *Halcyon* had a dozen twin light defensive cannons and a dozen more proton torpedo launch tubes, but the Imperial shuttle was smaller and had speed and maneuverability on its side.

"The Imperials are trying to jump to lightspeed," Zalma said, "but Captain Dicto is blocking them. I don't know how much longer he can draw this out."

Han twirled the prime minister's transport through plasma blasts. Knowing Beck, it wouldn't be much longer. The hangar on the underside of the *Halcyon* was open and waiting for them, and Han came in hot, ignoring the way Zalma gripped his harness with white knuckles. Before the transport had even finished decompressing, Han leapt up and raced to the gangway, Zalma on his heels.

They took the service corridor to a direct lift to the bridge level, by-passing any guests. "I'm glad you're here," Captain Dicto said, pointing at Han. "Can you take on a defensive cannon?"

"Happily."

"Lyx, you're relieved," Captain Dicto barked, and Han took the seat the Cerean vacated, nodding at Lyx. "Go to the engines, help out Woz-zakk Grimkin," he ordered the woman.

Han settled into the seat, reaching for the console's controls. The *Halcyon*'s shields were strong, so while the Imperial shuttle had more firepower, the *Halcyon* could outlast it. The problem was that the shuttle kept dodging.

"Why haven't you got this shuttle locked down with the tractor beam?" Zalma asked.

"You think I haven't tried that?" Captain Dicto barked. "Go with Lyx, see what you can do."

Zalma followed after the Cerean woman, talking quickly. Han was able to gather that the shuttle was too quick, slipping just out of range of the tractor beam that would doom it. It made sense. The tractor beam was not a part of the *Halcyon*'s original design, it was added on when the Empire took over the ship. Beck would know those specs, and she would know how to avoid the trap.

What she didn't know was that Leia had called in aid. All they had to do was run out the clock, then corner the shuttle.

"We want to disable it, not blow it out of the black!" Captain Dicto shouted when one of the gunners sent a proton torpedo at the Imperial shuttle, close enough to damage the hull. Smart man. Han knew Leia and Mon would have some questions for Beck—namely, who was running the show.

"All passengers, secure yourselves," Captain Dicto barked into the in-tercom, his voice echoing throughout the ship. Good thing most of the passengers were on Madurs—although if they couldn't evacuate them in time, perhaps not such a good thing. The captain leaned into the comm system again, flicking over to the crew channel. "Grimkin! Why can't you lock on with the tractor beam?"

But it wasn't the Ugnaught's voice that replied. Han rolled his eyes as

Kelad answered the captain. "We need to redirect the engine's efficiency directly into the gravity-manipulating generator in order to—"

The captain cut him off. "*You* are not altering my ship."

"A little more," Han muttered, hands on the trigger. As soon as the Imperial shuttle danced over his targeting system, Han deployed the defensive cannon, a blast ripping through the black of space, just enough to knock the shuttle around, forcing it to divert its thrusters and stay within range.

"Give us more power!" Captain Dicto bellowed into the comm system.

This time, the Ugnaught engineer answered. "Pronto-ronto," he said, and the *Halcyon* lurched forward, boosters burning through the back engine. "Now, proton torpedoes, starboard, aim below and above the hull. We need to pin her down!"

"It won't work," Han said, leaning over his console. Sure enough, the Imperial shuttle, under Beck's command, dropped *backward*, flying not away from the *Halcyon* but under it. Rather than outrun the star cruiser, Beck was going to shift down, closer to the moon than the *Halcyon* could safely go, and shoot into hyperspace from that angle. It was smart. It was exactly the move Han would have made.

"We need to drop," Han shouted, leaping from his seat.

Captain Dicto paused, hesitating and wasting precious seconds. Han pushed the captain aside, taking the main controls. "This is going to get rocky," he said, flipping to the engineer comm and ordering Grimkin to reverse the thrusters and drop.

"Who is this?" the Ugnaught growled. "Not permitted to take captain's comm!"

Captain Dicto slammed his hand against the comm, realizing Han's intent. "Do it!" he roared.

A moment later, the *Halcyon* dropped like a stone tossed in water.

Defensive cannons and proton torpedoes were one thing, but a physical bump from the *Halcyon* against the Imperial shuttle was more than enough to knock it out of jump readiness. The impact and sudden shift in direction also tossed the *Halcyon* crew who hadn't been ready to the ground, and Han relished the idea of immaculate Beck getting knocked on her ass.

"That trick won't work again," Captain Dicto warned.

"It doesn't have to." Han pointed through the viewport as a dozen A-wing starfighters and a boarding craft popped out of hyperspace.

"Heard you could use some backup!" a female voice hailed.

"Shara, that you?" Han asked. Captain Dicto frowned, but Han knew he'd forgive him for taking over now that help had arrived.

"Green Group, here to save your ass again," Shara called.

"Why're you—" Han cut himself off. He'd been about to ask why Shara was leading the Green Group. At the Battle of Endor, Arvel Crynyd had been Green One. Han had forgotten for a moment the man had died, sacrificing himself and his ship to bring down the Super Star Destroyer. Crynyd had been among the many memorialized that first night as reports had come in, the joy of winning counterbalanced by the reminders of sacrifice.

It was gutting, the way loss could be forgotten, even for a moment.

Fortunately, Shara Bey didn't need to make small talk. The *Halcyon* bridge heard through her open comm her orders to surround and detain the Imperial shuttle. The A-wings were smaller than the Imperial shuttle, but Han could just imagine Beck's rage at being outmaneuvered. With the entire Green unit firing shots, it was only a matter of moments before the engine on the Imperial shuttle was fried.

"We're boarding the hostile now," Shara informed the bridge.

"The *Halcyon* is standing by to aid if necessary," Captain Dicto said.

The tension was thick enough to slice as everyone on the *Halcyon* waited for confirmation of Green Group's success. An eon seemed to pass before Shara got on the comm again.

"Prisoners have been secured, we'll be towing the unclassified vessel back to base with us for inspection."

Everyone on the bridge cheered, and Han leaned over the captain, tapping on the comm. "Tell Beck that I sent you," he said.

"That might have already come up." Han could hear Shara's amusement laced through her voice.

"How'd she take the news?" Han couldn't hide his grin.

"She's a big fan of yours," Shara said with a laugh. "You sure do know how to make friends."

"I'm a friendly guy," Han said.

Captain Dicto glared at him, clearly done sharing his bridge. "Safe flight," Han said before stepping back and letting the captain take over. The bridge watched through the viewport as the A-wings got into formation, towing the Imperial shuttle through a lightspeed jump that would take Beck straight to the temporary headquarters for a tribunal. Maybe now they'd get the answers they needed.

A part of Han wanted nothing more than to race back to the hatch, jump onto the shuttle, and follow the fighters back to base. He may have joined the Rebellion for Leia, but he joined it for this, too—the brilliance of a flight maneuver that worked, the breathless anticipation of a dogfight. Beat shipping cargo, illegal or not, every time.

Han fell back into the seat in front of the defensive cannon. At least he'd gotten to grab the controls of the luxury star cruiser, if only for a moment.

Not a bad way to spend a honeymoon.

"Captain!" Zalma's voice cut through the relieved chatter on the bridge. Han straightened, watching the Nautolan cross over to Captain Dicto, Kelad at his heels. Han stood and headed to the center console. Kelad visibly wilted under Han's glare, but Zalma shook his head at Han.

"Captain," the Nautolan said. "Now that the shuttle's taken care of, we need to talk about Madurs."

"With the hostiles neutralized, I'll order Deethree to deploy launch pods," the captain said.

"That's good, and it's needed. As I told you, that moon's core is not stable. It's a highly dangerous situation."

"We're doing all we can," Captain Dicto said. "We only have so many shuttles."

"It's not that," Kelad interjected. "I think we could stabilize the moon's core."

"What?" Han said, loud enough to draw attention from others.

"The moon's destabilization comes from the disruption to the magma core, which has seen significant damage from mining, enough to make it essentially collapse." Kelad held his fingers spread out in a sphere—

the shape created by gravitational forces—then pushed his palms together and twisted his hands. "Gravity is heaviest at the center of a world, and with the Empire drilling out the dense carnium, it left too hollow of a space, making the world cave in on itself."

"So, we use the tractor beam," Kelad concluded, as if the answer were obvious.

The captain gaped at him. "The tractor beam?"

Kelad nodded eagerly, but it was Zalma who explained. "Tractor beams work through gravity manipulation, just like the repulsorlifts on the Imperial drilling station."

"But tractor beams can push as well as pull," Kelad said. "And we could push the moon's core with the *Halcyon*'s beam. It wouldn't work with a terrestrial world, but Madurs is aquatic, and water flows easier than dirt or stone."

"This is too risky. We need to focus on saving the people," Captain Dicto said.

"This moon may have weeks or months, but we don't know what additional damage the station caused to the core when it crashed into the bottom of the sea," Zalma protested. "It could destabilize in hours. And besides, you said it yourself—we only have so many launch pods. There are no more on the surface. We can only bring up a fraction of the population at a time, and meanwhile if the quakes break the ice surface, we will have nowhere to land . . ."

"The core could collapse at any moment," Han said. Mon had told Leia evacuation ships would arrive to aid, but they were slower than the fighters. And they needed a solution *now*.

"This will work?" Captain Dicto asked Zalma. "You really think you can use a tractor beam to stabilize a moon's core?"

"Oh, absolutely," Kelad said cheerily. "But I'm going to need to dismantle some parts of the *Halcyon* to do it."

CHAPTER 58

LEIA

"WALK ME THROUGH IT AGAIN?" Prime Minister Yens asked, leaning over the holoprojector. Blue light illuminated Kelad as he spoke animatedly from the *Halcyon,* explaining the complex balance of gravity and pressure to the moon's core.

Leia's brow furrowed, trying to keep up through the jargon. Luckily, Han pushed Kelad aside. "He wants to put a gravity lock on the moon's core," he said.

"It's so much more complicated than that!" Kelad protested, resuming his position in the center of the holo. "It's a thermal oscillator. I could craft it and install it directly on the core of the moon. I would need the base parts of the *Halcyon*'s tractor beam, and Zalma tells me that there's enough carnium plates that I could use—"

Yens nodded eagerly. "Carnium we can get you, even if we have to strip down the palace."

That made Kelad's eyes light up. "Excellent," he said, "because we still haven't discussed payment."

Leia's eyes widened at the man's audacity.

"Payment?" Prime Minister Yens said.

Kelad smirked as if he had a winning hand and knew it. "I've done *all* the testing. My thermal oscillator was designed for a major space station, but I could adapt it for a planet or a moon, I'm certain of it. It is *my* design." He paused. "I had a buyer on Synjax."

"We need to stabilize Madurs's core!" Yens said.

"Oh, you definitely do," Kelad nodded, agreeing. "And I need to be paid for all the research I did for the—"

He stopped just in time, but everyone in the conference room of the ice palace and on the bridge of the *Halcyon* surely knew what he was about to say. He'd initially designed his thermal oscillator for the Empire. Who else would want technology like that—who else would need it? And with the collapse of the Empire, he was left without the promised credits. Leia wondered who the buyer on Synjax was; if that was linked to whoever had been giving Beck orders. She made a note to contact Mon, have the interrogators press Beck for information on this.

"Fortunately, the *Halcyon*'s tractor beam is Imperial-made," Kelad said, oblivious to the scowls now being directed at him.

"Fortunately." Leia couldn't see the captain, but she was surprised Kelad didn't notice the seething anger under his voice.

"Imperial tractor beams have phased targeting arrays, and we're going to need that. So, between the tractor beam from the *Halcyon* and the carnium from Madurs, I can rig something up."

" 'Rig something up'?" Yens said, incredulous. "Sir, this is my homeworld we're talking about. I don't want a patch job that can leave us in an even worse situation."

Someone on the *Halcyon* cleared his throat, and then Zalma stepped into view. "Yes, I've been considering that as well. You're going to need help to install such a large item on the seabed." Zalma turned, his blue holoform presumably looking at the captain. "I'd like to stay on Madurs and help with the installation and monitor it after, ensure that everything is on the up-and-up."

"Trinkris, are you positive?" The captain's voice was sad but unsurprised.

"You know I've been considering returning to Glee Anselm for some time," Zalma said. "I miss the water, the one thing even the *Halcyon* can't provide enough of."

"I was preparing a recommendation for you to transfer to one of the aquatic ships," Captain Dicto said. "But if you'd prefer this . . ."

"Excellent!" Kelad said cheerily. "So, I have the parts, I have a crew, now I just need a contract with my payment stipulations." The man threw out a number that made Leia's eyes pop.

Yens shook his head mournfully. He had the method to save his moon, but not the means. The Empire had been bleeding the moon dry, blocking trade and limiting their regular exports. Leia didn't know the details of Madurs's coffers, but she could guess that Kelad's demands were impossible.

"The new republic will pay once it is established," she said, leaning over and taking the prime minister's spot in the holo.

"I cannot sign away my people's freedoms, not again," Yens said in a low, tight voice, clearly torn. How could he choose between paying an impossible debt and saving the world he lived upon?

Leia shook her head. "The new republic will pay," she told him. "Not as a loan. As a gesture of goodwill." She was sure Mon would approve the funds, but if not, she would drain her own accounts. Leia would not let another world die at the hands of the callous Empire, not if she could help it. "In time, I hope you will learn that this is the function of a good government—to give aid when it is needed, to prepare for it when it is not."

Yens nodded, his lips tight, as if he did not trust himself to speak in this moment. "And Captain Dicto?" Leia added, turning back to the holoprojector. "Let us negotiate the cost of the tractor beam when I'm back aboard."

"Take the hateful thing," Captain Dicto said. "It's Imperial. We don't need it—we have bay loaders. It is my goal to scrub every vestige of the Empire from this ship."

"Perhaps, then, we can come to a different agreement, one that suits all. The Imperial battle aside," Leia said, laughing a little, "Madurs has proven to be a hospitable stop on the cruise. Maybe we can develop a different tour, one for citizens of our democracy that can showcase how the Empire damaged worlds, but how we try to repair them."

The captain nodded, thinking. "Perhaps."

"So!" Kelad interrupted. "I should bill the government then?"

Leia glared through the holo. *Opportunist* was too kind a label for the man. "The government will not be dealing with a private . . . individual," she said, unable to keep her disgust from her voice. "I'll draw up a contract with Yens and Zalma as representatives of the business venture." She stated another sum, one far more reasonable.

Kelad opened his mouth to protest the lower amount, but Leia could just hear a grumbling growl that sounded remarkably Wookiee-like. Kelad's eyes widened, and Leia almost regretted not hearing the full extent of her husband's threat to the man. But he turned back to the holo and nodded. "Fine," he said. "Deal. That was more than the buyer on Synjax offered anyway."

Leia could now see exactly why Han had wanted to throw the man out of an air lock.

CHAPTER 59

HAN

THE SPACE ABOVE MADURS WAS crowded.

Mon's promised evacuation ships had arrived to cart the people of Madurs into orbit while the moon's core was being worked on. Several of the underwater fishers, including Balangawa, remained on the surface despite the danger in order to help in the underwater installation of the thermal oscillator.

Leia was among those who stayed, so Han joined the engineers when they went down to Madurs. Captain Dicto assured Han that the *Halcyon* would wait to depart in order to ensure the safety of the people of Madurs. Kelad, meanwhile, assured Captain Dicto that he would have the moon stabilized within the day, although Han was doubtful the quick talker could actually deliver. At best, he expected the initial install would be done in a day, but it would take far longer to truly neutralize the ice quakes.

"Isn't she a beauty?" Kelad asked, running his hands across the *Halcyon*'s dismantled tractor beam.

"No," Han said flatly.

"Behave," Zalma warned.

"You just don't see my vision," Kelad said. The transport shifted as they neared the surface of Madurs. Kelad brought out his datapad, and schematics for his large-scale thermal oscillator illuminated on the screen.

Kelad chatted away, pointing out which parts of the tractor beam he'd already altered, which others would be taken apart, and how he would put it all back together with the plates of carnium from the ice palace. The transport landed on the barren field near the floating dock. The gangway door opened, and Han walked past the man, utterly ignoring him even as he sputtered at the way Han obviously wasn't listening.

Han stomped out of the transport, his eyes skimming the icy surface of Madurs. There she was.

Leia was deep in conversation with someone via holo on her comlink, but Han completely ignored that, wrapping his arms around her and silencing her protests with a kiss. As soon as they broke apart, Leia raised the comlink. "Sorry, Mon, Han is impatient."

The holoprojector showed a somewhat bemused Mon Mothma. The leader wasn't with the evacuation ships, instead remaining at the temporary headquarters. "I'll be in touch later," she said. "Don't forget to have this so-called genius you found get back in contact with me. If he's really this good, I've got some engineers with new ship designs that could use some upgraded tractor beam technology."

Leia's gaze flicked up to Han, hurt in her eyes that he wished he could make disappear. The war was over. But the need for newer, better, stronger warships might never be.

"Leia, Han. Happy honeymoon." The holo disappeared.

Before Han could say anything, Leia's eyes settled on Zalma. "The Nebulon-B frigates Mon sent are equipped with tractor beams that are already engaged in order to help stabilize the core while you work."

"That's a good temporary fix," Zalma said.

"I thought of it!" Kelad interjected.

Leia's cool eyes looked right through the man as if he were not even there. Instead she turned to Han. "The frigates obviously cannot stay in orbit forever. And we're still getting ice quakes. Milder than before, but . . ."

Han cast his eyes up, even though he couldn't see the frigates from where he was. All the inhabitants of Madurs who evacuated were on the ships above, no doubt watching their moon, hoping it wouldn't shatter.

"Well, let's get this thing in the water," Balangawa said, striding forward with her crew.

They loaded the dismantled tractor beam onto carts and headed to the dock. With the fishers all either evacuated or on the crew to help, the floating dock was mostly empty. It was strange, Han thought—they had just been there in the crowd of work crews, voices filling the corridors. Everything was quiet now, but not enough time had passed to remove all traces of the people who'd been there. Even though it felt as if this world had been abandoned, there were personal items left in the lockers, half-eaten snacks on one of the desks. Dust had not had time to settle. Bait buckets along the ring of the fishing hole had not even yet begun to smell bad, or, at least, no worse than they had before.

The entire world was paused, waiting to see if it would be saved.

"So, the initial process is pretty simple," Kelad said. "If this works, it'll be enough stabilization to see us through the bigger build."

Even though Han had dismissed Kelad's schematics before, the ragtag crew gathered around, going over the plan. The initial stage would ensure stability enough to bring the evacuees back to their moon. Kelad's long-term plan, which would take more than a year to see through, would build a housing unit connecting the thermal oscillator all the way to the surface for easy, consistent maintenance and checking.

"Meanwhile," Balangawa said, "the water temperatures are already tracking cooler than before. And we installed this while we waited." Balangawa showed them the radial seismograph display.

While Kelad, Zalma, and Balangawa's crew went into the under-ice ocean with the pieces needed to install the initial stages of the thermal oscillator, Han and Leia stood around the radial seismograph display. Tiny lines jittered in circles on the screen, indicating the mini-quakes that rattled the moon's core.

"Do you think we have a chance?"

Han turned to see Prime Minister Yens. He nodded to the man, an appreciative look in his eyes. Han had initially believed that the prime minister was weak and bending, but he had seen the steel in the man's resolve, the way he worked with his people instead of against them.

"See for yourself," Leia said. A burst of energy trembled on the radial seismograph display, but then the lines dropped harshly. The thermal oscillator worked quickly.

Prime Minister Yens's body sagged in relief.

They stayed on the surface of the moon long enough for the first shuttle of evacuees to return to the surface. If the celebration at the defeat of the Imperial station had been joyous, the reunion of the citizens of Madurs on their icy moon was effervescent. It was the difference, Han thought, between the fires that had burned on Endor, the dancing and the music that had happened in the wake of their victory, compared with the more solemn awe of the Rebels at the flower-fliers that had emerged after his wedding with Leia. One was relief for surviving bursting out chaotically. The other was quieter, a recognition of what was lost, a solemn appreciation of what was not.

Han and Leia returned on the shuttle to the *Halcyon* after saying farewell to Zalma and the people of Madurs. As the ship came into view from the shuttle's small windows, Leia nudged Han.

"So, did you get to fly the fancy ship after all?"

Han grinned. "Fired some cannons at the Empire, that was nice."

Leia laughed. Han had liked being at the helm of the *Halcyon,* even if it'd only been for a moment, but it really just made him miss the *Falcon* even more. That was home. It wasn't just piloting; it was the *Falcon.*

He couldn't wait to get back to *his* ship.

The shuttle connected to the loading bay of the *Halcyon* so smoothly that it was almost undetectable. The door opened, and D3-O9 stood there, ready to welcome the pair back aboard. Leia walked out first, but Han caught her by the wrist and spun her around, claiming her lips in a kiss. He had one sort of home with the *Falcon,* but he was already looking for a different one with Leia. Would life always be that push-and-pull, similar to the gravity working against the tractor beams, as he oscillated between ship and wife, adventure and peace, one home and the other?

He didn't know.

But amid all the uncertainty that the past few days had exposed to him, she stood in the center, the clear vision of the one thing he truly needed. He didn't know how to put any of that into words, and he could only hope his kiss was enough. Leia's head tilted up, her arms going around his neck, her lips claiming his with the same urgency, the same desire, the same love. This wasn't a gentle kiss; it was a mutual vow.

D3-O9 made an impatient noise. "This area is for loading and un-loading purposes only," the droid informed them. She refrained from shooing them, but only just.

Leia laughed, and Han's heart twisted. If he had known his honeymoon would have turned into a rescue mission and a battle against an Imperial holdout, if he'd been told that he would face Beck again and the cold, if he'd foretold the fate of this trip . . . he didn't think he would have taken it.

But if he hadn't taken it, he wouldn't have gotten that one moment of pure joy glowing in Leia's eyes when she was breathless from his kiss.

And that would have been a damn shame.

CHAPTER 60

LEIA

HAN HAD INSISTED ON GOING to the dining room himself to procure a much-needed meal and bring it back to the suite so they could dine in private, and Leia was more than happy to oblige. Almost as soon as the door zipped closed behind him, though, D3 O9 pinged Leia at the Droid Link Panel.

"Riyola Keevan would like to speak to you," the droid said politely. "Should I schedule a meeting?"

"I'm not busy now," Leia said. "Should I meet her somewhere?"

"She says she can come to your room, if that's acceptable."

Leia agreed, and a few minutes later, Riyola arrived. "I'm so sorry to bother you," she said.

"Come in," Leia offered.

Riyola shook her head. "I just—I wanted to tell you personally how much I appreciated all you've done. Not just turning your honeymoon into a chance to help strengthen the galaxy after war, but then all you did on Madurs—"

"I was actually thinking about that," Leia said. "I saw a work of art on Madurs that really stuck with me. The artist no longer lives on the moon; she's studying art on Hosnian Prime now, but I wondered if I could contact her, perhaps I could commission a work of art for the *Halcyon*. Would that be acceptable?"

Riyola flushed. "I'll have to clear it with the captain, but I cannot imagine it would be an issue," she said. The Pantoran paused. "Although . . . it wouldn't be made of ice, would it?"

Leia laughed. "According to the docent, the artist left in order to study media that won't melt." She would have to speak to the artist, but she hoped that as the Empire fell, Madurs was saved, and the new government formed, the artist would be in favor of something more permanent to reflect a unified government. If there was one thing Madurs had taught her, it was the power of art to exist even in the darkest times, to silently stand in opposition to the destroyers.

Art was a form of rebellion.

Leia and Riyola chatted for a bit more, and after another sincere thanks, Riyola left. Han still wasn't back, so Leia sent a comm to Mon to update her on the status of Madurs and secured a promise of more engineers to arrive to aid in the development of the thermal oscillator—and to ensure that Kelad could actually do the job he'd exploited the situation to procure. She closed her holocomm with a heavy sigh. Leia was used to the invisible work of politics, the minute details and the layers of negotiations and compromises, all the labor that wasn't glamorous.

This had been different.

No one—except, she thought, Han—had seen her use the Force. It was already a legend on Madurs, excused as coincidence or ignored as exaggeration, but she knew it had been real, even if it hadn't been seen.

All those other times, she had *tried* to use the Force. She'd called for it in privacy, in the climate simulator. She'd screamed for it underwater, nearly drowning and freezing. But this time? Leia hadn't been trying to use the Force. Or, rather, she hadn't been trying to *control* it.

Leia let out a harsh breath. She should have known better, but perhaps that was her legacy from her biological father—a desire to control. After all, wasn't that how Darth Vader had always used the Force? As a weapon, as a means to—literally—force those around him to bend to his dark will? No wonder the Force hadn't worked for her when she emulated him; she would have learned to hate it as much as she hated him if it had.

Or I would have become him.

Leia demanded that she dwell in the thought, not push it away. She had only brushed against the Force on Madurs, but even now, she felt the power of it seeping into her, making her long for it all the more. It was intoxicating, and—

And she craved more.

"I need to speak to Luke," Leia said aloud, then repeated it. She wasn't sure if this need—this hungering longing for power—meant that she should learn to control it, or if it meant she should deny herself the use of it.

Her hands bunched into fists. Now that she had tasted the power of the Force, she . . . she couldn't deny that she longed for more.

But if claiming the Force meant following in Vader's footsteps . . .

No. Never that.

When she had brushed up against the power of the Force on Madurs, it hadn't been in an attempt to destroy, not like Vader had. She hadn't been commanding the edont to attack; she hadn't even meant to reach the edont.

She had simply wanted help.

Tentatively, Leia reached out again, simply hoping to feel . . . *something*. She closed her eyes, trying to recall the peace, the silence, the stillness of the sea.

No—she hadn't felt the Force in the water. She'd felt it inside herself.

That was also the difference. All those other times, she'd been reaching forward, trying to grab something in the great beyond, but . . . it had been threaded within herself the whole time. The Force as much felt her as she had felt it. And so, when she had asked for help rather than trying to seize control, it had answered.

As if it had been waiting for her to simply ask all along.

The door to the suite opened, and Han came inside carrying a tray that he set on the table in the corner. Leia stood, and Han wove his arms through hers, holding her against him, demanding nothing of her but her presence.

Love was like the Force. She hadn't asked for it. In a lot of ways, she knew, their love was only going to complicate things.

But something inside her had called out to Han, and something inside him had answered.

CHAPTER 61

HAN

HAN KISSED THE TOP OF Leia's head. "Hey, sweetheart," he said softly.

She looked up at him with those big brown eyes of hers, and he shook his head. Unfair of the universe to give her eyes like that.

"What?" she asked, laughing at his look.

"Just wondering if, now that we've fought off the Empire *again*, saved a whole world *again*, and proved ourselves to be the heroes of the new republic, if *now*, finally, we can celebrate our honeymoon." He smirked. "Or did you have some committee you needed to go be on first?"

"Now that you mention it," Leia said, "I do need to send a quick message to the chieftess on Inusagi." She turned on her heel, heading back to the sofa, where she'd left her communicator.

As she started to retreat, Han held on to her wrist, spinning her back to him. "Uh-unh," he said, a wicked smile curling over his lips. "No way."

Leia laughed. "For the rest of this trip, you—no, *we*—come first." Her words were a solemn promise. "If Mon needs me for something, she's going to have to pilot a ship to Synjax herself and pull me off the beach."

"If she tries that," Han said, his words also a promise, "I will blast her."

Han rubbed her fingers in his hand, and she looked down at the way he held her. Turning over his palm, he revealed a ring.

Leia gasped. The dark-gold metal fit her finger perfectly as Han slipped it on. It was a large ring, with gold snaking down to showcase a round, purple-blue stone at the base of her finger and then looping up to display a second stone past her middle knuckle. It was a ring that demanded to be noticed.

Han had bought it on his way to pick up dinner, the whole reason he'd bothered to step foot outside the suite as soon as he got his wife into it.

"Did you think I didn't notice the other ring broke?" Han asked softly.

Leia looked up at him with a watery smile. "Yes."

"Well," Han conceded. "You were right. I didn't notice it was gone." Just as he hadn't been aware of when his own vine ring had broken apart, although he hadn't bothered buying himself a replacement yet. "But I noticed you were sad. And I figured it out."

Emotion welled up in Leia's eyes. Oh, no. He didn't mean to make her *cry*. He'd been trying to set an entirely different mood instead. "This one's not going to break," he said, hoping that would reassure her.

Leia's fingers traced the looping gold ring, lingering over the two stones. There had not been a large selection of jewelry at the shop, and he'd known that ring was large and showy, but he'd liked the two different stones because—

"One for me and one for you," Leia said, echoing his unspoken thoughts.

"And the gold reminded me of the amber vines."

"It's perfect."

Han tried to believe her. "I know . . ." He paused, trying to find the right words. "I know we're going to have to trade out this ship," he said, gesturing to the wealth on display in the suite, "for the *Falcon*. And it's not what you're used to, but—"

"The *Falcon*'s been more my home than anyplace since—" She stopped, redirecting her thoughts. "For more than a year," she finished. "I love it."

"Good. But I'm adding some things for you, at least, to make it more, I don't know . . . homey?" He was doing this all wrong.

"Homey?" Leia asked.

"Chewie's making some modifications. For you. Us. You."

"Like what?" She looked befuddled.

"Well . . . Cleaning up some."

"That will be nice."

"It wasn't that bad!"

Leia didn't bother answering.

"And," Han continued, "adding a kitchen area."

Leia barked with laughter. "A *kitchen*?"

"What? I thought you'd like—"

"Do you think I can *cook*?" She was practically wheezing at the idea.

"Well—I don't know!" Han said. "I just thought—"

"A kitchen!" Leia had tears in her eyes again, this time from laughter.

"I thought it was a *nice* thing to do!"

"Oh, it's very nice." Leia snorted. "I'll be sure to burn you a nice piece of toast, maybe."

"But—well, I—" Han growled, throwing his hands in the air. Try to turn his ship into a home and all he gets in return is mockery.

"It was a very nice thing to do," Leia said in a patronizing tone, choking back giggles. "If you promise never to make me cook for you, I promise to never accidentally poison you with whatever I could manufacture in any kitchen I come across."

"Deal," Han grumbled. Thankfully, Chewie was a good cook.

"Oh, come on, don't be mad."

"I was *trying* to be—"

"Nice, I know." Leia shot him a sardonic, teasing look. "I suppose, despite some evidence to the contrary, that you really are a nice man."

Han's voice dropped an octave. "Why don't you admit you like me just as well when I'm being a scoundrel?"

But Leia didn't rise to the bait. Instead, she trapped him in those big eyes again and said, "Maybe I do."

Well, this was a game he could play. "You sure about that?" he asked. "I noticed there was a magic act going on in the dining room. A nice man would take you out on a proper date, buy you a drink . . ."

Leia rose up on her toes, her lips close to his. "I have all the magic I need right here," she whispered.

"I'm starting to think you're the rogue, not me," Han muttered.

Leia ran her fingers through his hair. "You're right. Let's stay in tonight. It is, after all, our honeymoon."

"Wait, wait," Han said.

"I thought the point was not to wait anymore."

"I just want to savor the moment."

Leia raised an eyebrow. "What moment?"

"The moment where you say I'm right."

Leia groaned. "Don't get used to it, hotshot."

Han gave her his best roguish grin. "Never, sweetheart. But you know," he said, gently running a finger down her cheek in a way that made her sigh. "I could get used to this."

Leia looked as if she was about to snap off a witty retort, but instead, she simply said, "Me too," and pulled him down for a kiss.

ACKNOWLEDGMENTS

I've known ever since I read my first *Star Wars* novel on the back of the school bus—*The Rise of the Shadow Academy* by Kevin J. Anderson and Rebecca Moesta—that I one day hoped to write for *Star Wars*. What I didn't know then was that it wasn't just writing the characters that was a dream, it was working with the people who loved the characters as much as I did. Every single person I've had the privilege to work with throughout the *Star Wars* literary universe has been brilliant.

Special thanks to Elizabeth Schaefer for sharing about a million exclamation marks with me over the course of this project, and Jen Heddle, who read each draft with an eye on where to add more kissing and banter. Matt Martin knows the *Halcyon* inside and out, Tom Hoeler helped me balance Han's bravado, and Kelsey Sharpe and Pablo Hidalgo helped me keep everything in order. Michael Siglain reached out to me in a dark time and embodied what it means to bring light and hope. I am consistently blown away by how awesome everyone on the team at Lucasfilm and Del Rey truly are; these are the types of people authors dream of working with.

Additional thanks go to Jennifer Randolph, who swapped *Star Wars* books with me on that school bus; Merrilee Heifetz, who's been with me from the beginning of my writing journey; and my mother, who had no idea what was going to happen when she taped those old movies off television when I was a kid and let me use a PVC pipe as a lightsaber. Thanks also to Wordsmith Workshops and the friends who did online writing sessions with me and who had no idea I was working on this novel at the time.

At its heart, this is a love story. It's my kind of romance, with a moon crumbling, a space battle, and kissing in between snarky comebacks, but it's very much a love story. I don't know if I could write love without having experienced it, and to that, I owe my heart to Corwin Revis, and an additional thanks to the organ donor who literally gave him a heart so we could continue our story together.

My six-year-old son was less helpful in the creation of this novel, but he was always quick with the advice to add more explosions. I know I don't have enough in this book to suit his taste, and he thinks the kissing is gross. Sorry, kid.

My greatest thanks go to you, dear reader. Thank you for letting me visit your galaxy.

PHOTO: @ CORWIN REVIS

BETH REVIS is a *New York Times* bestselling author with books available in more than twenty languages. She writes science fiction, fantasy, and contemporary novels, including *Across the Universe, Star Wars: Rebel Rising, Give the Dark My Love,* and *A World Without You.* A native of North Carolina, Beth lives in a rural corner of the state with her son and husband.

bethrevis.com
Twitter: @bethrevis

Read on for an excerpt from

SHADOW OF THE SITH

BY ADAM CHRISTOPHER

CHAPTER 1

Wild Space, Coordinates Unknown

NOW

AT FIRST, THERE WAS NOTHING but empty space. And then the ship appeared, mass and form and structure. Here to there, crossing boundless gulfs of space, as easy as pulling a lever. It was almost magical in its simplicity.

Right then, however, the ship's overheating navicomputer begged to differ.

For a moment, the battered old freighter just floated, hanging in space, like a garu-bear coming out of a long hibernation, taking stock of its surroundings.

And then the ship shuddered and began listing to port, carving a long, slow spiral that was suddenly accelerated as an aft impulse stabilizer failed in a shower of white sparks. The ship's nose dipped even further, the starboard engine now sputtering, a loose cover plate revealing a dangerous red glow from beneath.

For the pilot and her two passengers, the situation had just gone from bad to worse.

Two days. That was all they'd managed. Two days out from Jakku, limping along in a ship that shouldn't be flying at all, but was the only hulk they'd managed to jack from Unkar Plutt's scrapyard outside of

Niima Outpost. And it didn't look like they were going to make it much farther.

Just a few hours earlier, they dared to think that maybe . . . they'd made it? They'd gotten out of their homestead, their all-purpose house droid, handcrafted from more scrap and salvage, sacrificing itself as it led the hunters astray. Then they found the ship (truth be told, they had long ago earmarked it for such a day—a day they hoped would never come). Launched it, just themselves, a bag with toys and books and a blanket, a handful of credits, the clothes on their backs. Pointed the navicomputer along a vector that would take them *way* out of range (so they hoped). And buckled in for the ride.

But now? The ship had barely survived the initial trip. Escaping to Wild Space had been a desperate move, but was far from the endgame. It was supposed to be where they could hide, just for a while, take the time to *make a plan* and *plot a course.*

Those options now seemed decidedly more limited as they floated adrift. They'd escaped Jakku, only to . . . what? Die in the cold reaches of space, the old freighter now nothing but a tomb for the three of them, lost forever on the outskirts of the galaxy, their passing unmourned, their names unremembered.

Dathan, Miramir.

Rey.

The freighter's interior was as old and battered as the exterior—the flight deck was cramped and functional, the old-fashioned design requiring not just pilot and copilot but navigator, the third seat at the back of the cabin, facing away from the forward viewports. For this trip, they'd had to make do with a crew of just two.

The pilot's seat was occupied by a young woman, her long blond hair corralled loosely with a blue tie that matched the color of her cloak, the sleeves of her cream tunic rolled up as she leaned over the control console in front of her, one hand gripping the uncooperative yoke, the other flying over buttons and switches as she fought to control the shuddering ship. The forward view, as seen through the angled, heavily scratched transparisteel viewport, showed the starscape ahead sliding diagonally as the freighter's spin accelerated.

Behind her, a young man, his dark hair short, the beginnings of a beard over his jaw, knelt on the decking behind the navigator's seat. His arms were wrapped around it and its small occupant, the child cradled in a padded nest formed out of a bright, multicolored blanket, a stark contrast with the drab, greasy gunmetal of the flight deck.

The man craned his neck around as he watched his wife wrestle with the controls, then he stood and leaned down to kiss the head of the six-year-old girl strapped securely in the seat, a large pair of navigator's sound-deadening headphones over her ears. In front of the girl, the ancient navigation panel—a square matrix of hundreds of individual tiny square lights—flashed in multicolored patterns of moving shapes, a simple game the girl's mother had loaded into the auxiliary computer to keep her daughter occupied on the long journey.

The man looked up at the game board, but the girl had stopped playing. He moved around to the front of the chair and saw she had her eyes screwed tightly shut. He leaned in, embracing his daughter.

"I've got you," Dathan whispered to Rey. "We're all right. I've got you."

There was a bang; Dathan felt it as much as he heard it as another part of the strained engines gave up, the small explosion reverberating through the ship. A tear ran down from Rey's closed eyes. Dathan wiped it away, and closed his own eyes, wishing that, for once, a little good luck would come their way.

"Okay, there we go!" Miramir yelled, following her statement with a *whoop* of triumph. The ship jolted once, and then the steady shaking stopped. Through the forward viewports, the stars were now completely still.

Despite himself, despite their situation, Dathan found himself smiling. He couldn't help it. His wife was a genius and he loved her. He didn't know *where* she got it from, but she was a natural, like it was genetic. She could fly anything, had been—and still was—a self-taught engineer and inventor. Tinkering, Miramir called it, as though it were nothing, as though she didn't realize just how special her talents were.

In the years that he had known her, Dathan had often asked where this gift had come from, but Miramir would just shrug and say her grandmother was a wonderful woman. Dathan knew that to be true—he had met her, several times, before Miramir gave up her life in the twilight forest of Hyperkarn to travel with Dathan. But then . . . where had her *grandmother* learned it all?

Dathan wanted to know, but over time he'd learned not to ask any further. Miramir missed her grandmother. She missed her home.

That was something else Dathan had tried to understand. To be *homesick,* to miss something that you could never return to—that was something unknown to him. Oh sure, he could *understand* it. And yes, he felt something for his days on Hyperkarn, even the years on Jakku, but he wasn't sure it was the same. Neither of those places had been truly *home.*

He did have a home, a place he could legitimately say he came from. It was a place he revisited a lot, in dreams.

Dreams . . . and nightmares.

"That will hold for a while," said Miramir, releasing the yoke and reaching up to flick a series of heavy switches in the angled panel above the pilot's position. "I've rerouted reserve power into the starboard impulse stabilizer, and then pushed the angle of the field *way* beyond point-seven, but that's fine because—"

She stopped as Dathan dropped into the copilot's seat and looked at her, one eyebrow raised.

"I don't know what any of that means," he said, "except that we're safe, right?"

Miramir sat back, her slight form dwarfed by the pilot's seat. She grinned and nodded.

Dathan felt his own grin growing. Miramir's happiness—her relief—was infectious. Maybe they *would* get out of this after all.

"The stabilizers will hold until the hyperdrive resets," said Miramir. "The motivator overheats every time we make a jump, but it's still working for the moment. We should be good for another couple of jumps." She paused, then wrinkled her nose. "But we do need to find another ship. Which means . . ." She gestured at the viewports, to the infinite emptiness that was Wild Space.

Dathan nodded. "Which means heading back to the Outer Rim."

At that, Miramir unclipped her seat restraints and headed over to Rey. Kneeling by the navigator's seat, she gently lifted the headphones off her daughter's head, then unclipped the seat restraints. As soon as she was freed, Rey sprang out of the seat and tackled her mother, arms and legs wrapped around Miramir, her head buried in her chest. Rey was perhaps small for a six-year old, but Miramir didn't mind her daughter's desire for closeness, knowing the girl would soon grow out of it. Miramir turned and sank gently into the navigator's seat, still cradling Rey, and kicked the seat around so she was facing Dathan.

"I know it's dangerous," said Miramir, "but this ship was in Plutt's scrap heap for a reason. We've managed one long jump, and look what happened. It'll be worse each time."

Dathan sighed and gave his wife a nod. "We don't have a choice," he said. "I know."

Miramir lowered her face to Rey's hair, burying her nose in the brunette plait, her eyes focused somewhere on the floor.

Dathan knew that look. He'd seen it plenty of times over the last two days. It pained him to see Miramir like this. His wife, his love, the smartest and most beautiful and best person he had ever met. Certainly the most capable, far better at most things than he was, no matter how hard he tried.

And he knew something else, too.

This was *all* his fault.

But there would be time for that later. Right now, they were out of options, and only one path was open to them.

"Hey," said Dathan. He forced the smile back onto his face.

Miramir looked up but didn't speak.

"Hey, come on, now," said Dathan.

Miramir looked at him, her big eyes beginning to water.

"Mum, I'm hungry."

Miramir looked down at Rey, and—

She laughed. Dathan grinned, then found himself unable to stop himself from joining in.

Rey unraveled herself from her mother's arms and turned to look at her dad.

"You guys are silly," she said. And then she pointed at the front viewport. "Who's that?"

No sooner had the child spoken than an alarm sounded. Dathan toggled a switch to clear it, then turned around to look at what Rey had spotted. The alarm began to sound again.

"What is that?" asked Miramir.

"We've got company," said Dathan, watching as in the distance three stars moved and began growing in size.

Three ships, flying in formation.

Coming right for them.

CHAPTER 2

WILD SPACE, COORDINATES UNKNOWN

NOW

"THEY'VE FOUND US," DATHAN WHISPERED. "How did they find us?" He looked down at the controls in front of them, nearly every one a complete mystery. "Miramir, we have to get out of here."

"Take Rey," said his wife, "let me handle this." As they swapped positions, there was a flash and a roar, the pair ducking instinctively as the trio of pursuing ships split right on the freighter's nose, two disappearing port and starboard, the third flying directly over the top. Lights flashed on the consoles around them as the freighter's antique computer systems kicked into life, tracking the other ships.

"They're turning," said Dathan, looking at a readout on the navigator's console. The display was poor—the freighter should have been in a museum, not lost in Wild Space—but against the burnt-orange grid, three fuzzy markers indicating the other craft crawled over the screen as they looped around and headed back toward them.

"Are we sure it's them?" asked Miramir, her focus on the flight systems. "How did they track us?"

Dathan shrugged. "How did they track us the first time? They're not going to give up, Miramir. They're *never* going to give up. How long until we can make the jump?"

Miramir toggled another readout and blew out her cheeks. "A few minutes. The hyperdrive motivator is still too hot, and if I touch the impulse stabilizers it'll be too hard to get an escape vector anyway."

There was a screeching sound from somewhere far away. Dathan looked up at the flight deck ceiling, alive with dancing indicators. Then there was a bang and the freighter rocked from side to side. Ahead, the blackness of space flashed green as the attacking ships, now back in a new formation, screamed overhead, firing warning shots over their bow. Dathan watched as the ships receded from view, then split and turned back around, careening toward them, another salvo of what had to have been deliberately wide shots lighting up the flight deck.

Heart racing, Dathan turned his attention to Rey. She was back in the navigator's seat, eyes closed, her small hands clutching the edges of the blanket beneath her, the one piece of the only home the girl had ever known that they had been able to bring with them. Dathan felt a tightening in his chest, his love for the child so profound, so real, that it was all he could do to keep breathing as he grabbed the navigator's headphones and slipped them over Rey's ears, buckling her into the seat.

The ship rocked again as another shot streaked almost too close to their hull. Dathan made his way back to the copilot's seat and strapped himself in.

Miramir frowned, reading something on a panel above her. "Maybe I can kick the hyperdrive in manually, bypassing the motivator . . ." She trailed off, then glanced at Dathan. "Might be a rough ride."

Dathan nodded. "How long do you need?"

"Three minutes."

Dathan nodded. "Then three minutes you shall have. Hold tight."

He grabbed the copilot's control yoke, the twin of the one at Miramir's station, and disengaged the autos, about the only control he recognized. Immediately the freighter bucked, then dipped into a steep dive as the overloaded starboard impulse stabilizer blew, unable to compensate now for its already inactive counterpart on the opposite side of the ship. In front of them, the attacking fighters vanished from sight as the freighter's course abruptly changed. Space flashed green, but in silence, the warning shots now distant.

Dathan gritted his teeth. Beneath his grip, the yoke shuddered and shook, the whole ship fighting him as he tried to steer it away from their attackers. He didn't know what he was doing—he couldn't fly *anything* and had never wanted to try—but even the most basic, instinctive maneuvering would give them time while Miramir worked on her new plan.

The attackers were small, were agile, and, as Dathan had suspected, were making fast tracks toward them. As they swung into view, he pulled back and to the left, lifting the nose as the freighter spun on its axis, corkscrewing the much larger ship straight through the center of the attackers' formation, forcing them to take evasive action of their own.

"One minute," said Miramir.

Dathan nodded in acknowledgment, not taking his eyes from the forward viewports, now trying to keep the freighter level. The attackers had regrouped and sped in for yet another frontal approach, but they were still careful with their shots—they wanted the freighter crippled, not destroyed, and were slowly closing the warning blasts in, banking, perhaps, on the shock waves disabling the already damaged craft. Dathan used their caution to his advantage, accelerating again toward the group. As the fighters split once more, he jerked the yoke to port, swinging the freighter directly into the path of one of the other ships.

The freighter rocked as more blasterfire streaked past. Dathan knew he couldn't keep this up forever. He just hoped the ship would hold together for a little while longer.

"Okay, nearly done, nearly done," said Miramir, now standing at the pilot's position, her blue cloak falling behind her as she focused her attention on the multitude of control panels above her. "We just need to set the navicomputer to null coordinates and we can make a jump. Not a long one, but it should be enough to lose them."

That was when there was another blinding flash from the forward viewports, another dull thud of an explosion from somewhere at the rear, the ship rocking hard enough to throw Miramir to the floor. Behind them, Rey cried out in surprise and fear.

Miramir pulled herself back into the pilot's seat. "We're okay, Rey, we're right here," she said, perhaps more for her own benefit than her daughter's, given Rey couldn't hear her with the headphones on. "Not long now. Just hold tight." But as she strapped herself in, she looked back over her shoulder with a terrible, anguished expression on her face that Dathan hated to see. He craned his neck around and followed her gaze, to where their daughter sat, her head buried in her blanket.

"Okay, here we go," said Miramir. She grabbed the pilot's master control yoke, and Dathan felt his own yoke pull away from his grip. He let go.

Far ahead, the three attack ships regrouped again, their ion engines leaving glowing trails across the stars as they flew in a tight arc back toward them.

This was it. They were done playing. They were coming in for a final run, ready to knock the ship out of commission permanently and make their collection.

The ships approached, fast.

"We're not going to make it," said Dathan.

"Yes, we are."

"Not enough time or space, Miramir. They'll box us in. We can't jump with them right in front of us."

"I can do it."

"You know what?"

Miramir didn't pause, didn't look up from the controls, as she kept her eyes fixed on the hyperdrive readout. From his position, Dathan could see data scrolling, almost too fast to read. "What?"

"I love you," said Dathan.

Miramir glanced at her husband, and for Dathan, time seemed to stop, again. She looked like she was going to say something, but instead, she just . . . smiled that smile, a smile he knew so well, a smile he loved, a smile he'd cross the galaxy for, a smile that could light up even this nameless reach of empty space, the smile of his wife, the mother of his child, the smile of Miramir—

There was another flash; this time it was blue. The ship rocked again, but the movement was gentle, the battered freighter not knocked by a shock wave but riding the crest of an energy pulse. Dathan and Miramir turned to watch as the central fighter in the trio flying toward them evaporated in a flash of ionized particles, sending its two companion craft into desperate escape headings.

They were fast, but not fast enough. A second fighter exploded into an expanding cloud of glowing gas, that cloud pierced by the sleek lines of a new ship that spun through the debris.

This new arrival was long, sleek, a finely sculpted nose cone leading a narrow, arrowlike fuselage, engines at the rear, and from the side, four wings with long, spearlike cannons mounted at the ends, the flight surfaces locked into a distinct shape known across the whole galaxy.

"An X-wing," said Miramir, blinking, as though she could scarcely believe their luck. "We're nowhere near New Republic space. What are they doing here?" She turned to Dathan, her eyes wide, now alert to the possibility that maybe, just maybe, they were somewhere safe.

But Dathan shook his head. "Don't know, don't care." He looked down at the copilot's console, wishing he knew more about the ship's systems. "We ready to jump again or what?"

Miramir's eyes were wide. "What are you talking about?" She gestured to the forward viewports. "We don't need to jump again. The New Republic will help us."

Even as she said that, there was another blue flash from outside. The last remaining attacker had peeled away, trying to find room to make a jump to lightspeed. But the pursuing X-wing was faster and more heavily armed, the pilot sending their ship into a tight spiral as all four cannons opened up, sending a blazing corkscrew of blasterfire after its quarry.

No, not one X-wing. Two—*three*. The other two fighters came into view from underneath the freighter, racing away from them to join the first. While Dathan and Miramir watched, their S-foils opened out into attack position and their quad engines flared as they accelerated away.

The attacker didn't stand a chance. The craft spun on its axis, then dived up and then sharply down, the pilot making a vain attempt to break target locks before it could punch the hyperdrive.

Dathan watched as the three X-wings fell into a tight formation and closed the distance behind their target, but he took no satisfaction in seeing the last hunter destroyed. They'd been saved this time, out of sheer luck—what *was* the New Republic doing out here?—but as he knew all too well, there were more hunters where those had come from, their prize far too valuable to give up on.

"Make the jump," he said quietly. Miramir looked at him again, and the two locked eyes. Dathan hoped she would understand, they'd talked about it often enough—hell, she knew *exactly* what he was thinking.

And then, to his relief, she nodded.

They could trust nobody. Not even the New Republic.

They were on their own. Always had been, always would be.

As Miramir refocused on the controls, Dathan looked around again at the navigator's seat, but Rey was simply a huddled mass under the blanket, only the fingers of one hand visible as she clutched at the seat beneath her.

That was when the ship-wide comms crackled into life.

"Attention, unknown craft. Clear your navicomputer and stand by for inspection."

Dathan once again looked at the ceiling. Inspection, by . . . three X-wings? That didn't make any sense.

And then a fourth ship appeared, pulling in close over the top of the freighter, a huge slab of ash-gray metal, the surface studded with antennas, hatchways, sensor blocks, and gun emplacements.

A New Republic gunship. Dathan didn't know what kind, but it didn't matter. Even as he watched the gunship's hull blot out the entire starscape, he felt the slight shudder as tractor beams were locked on and they were pulled slowly to the glowing blue opening of the hangar that now appeared in view.

Dathan sat back, his face behind his hands. He shook his head, and then he felt Miramir's hands on his. He opened his eyes, letting his hands, still held by Miramir's, drop into his lap.

He looked at the viewport as the hangar grew larger and larger. Beside them, two of the escorting X-wings pulled in ahead of them and made soft touchdowns. Then the blue shimmer vanished as the freighter passed through the magnetic shield.

"This is it," Dathan said, with a sigh. "The end of the road."

"We don't know that," said Miramir.

Perhaps she was right. Perhaps he was being too cautious—too *cynical*.

The comms barked again.

"Attention, unknown craft. Proceed to your exit ramp. Please follow our directions."

Miramir unclipped her restraint and stood.

"Well," she said, giving a weak shrug. "At least they said 'please.'"

Dathan stood stock-still, his heart pounding. He felt Rey wriggling her hand in his, trying to break free. He glanced down at her.

"You're holding too tight, Daddy."

Dathan almost laughed, but he did relax his grip, then looked up and watched as Miramir talked to one of the X-wing pilots, the officer still in his blue flight suit, his helmet under one arm. Next to him stood one of the other pilots, her helmet hanging from one hand.

They were standing in the hangar, by their freighter's exit ramp. So far, all the New Republic officers had done was motion them to stay where they were, and when they started asking questions, it was Miramir who volunteered herself to answer them.

She was good with people, Dathan knew that, but it didn't make him feel much better. The fact was they had no identification, no licenses or permits, no official documentation of any kind, and their ship had no ID tags or transponder or . . . anything. Dathan could only hope that Miramir was working her charm on the officers, because he—and Miramir—knew that while the New Republic claimed control of a large section of the galaxy, there were regions that lived happily outside their borders, peaceably, but unwilling, or unconvinced, to join the glorious cause. It had been seventeen years since the second Death Star had been destroyed over Endor, seventeen long years since Dathan's father—even now, he felt the chill, felt the hollow, almost light-headed sensation as he thought of Palpatine—had fallen, the Empire over which he ruled shattered. A long time, to be sure, but the galaxy was big and the fledgling new authority had a lot of ground, both literally and figuratively, to reclaim. To Dathan, watching, *willing* the old order to be replaced with the new, it sometimes seemed that the New Republic had done nothing at all.

But right now, it was all academic, anyway. They were in Wild Space, a literal no-being's-land. Even the New Republic couldn't claim authority here.

Could they?

Miramir glanced back at Dathan, her mouth twisted in an *I have no idea what's going on* expression. She walked back to join him and Rey, followed by the two X-wing pilots. The male pilot stood tall, his back ramrod-straight—the senior officer, Dathan guessed. The pilot looked at Dathan and then at Rey with an expression that wasn't one of distaste, but it wasn't far off. The female pilot looked far friendlier and, crucially, far more relaxed.

The senior officer sniffed, glanced at Miramir, then looked at Dathan again.

"I understand you have no identification of any kind?"

Dathan gave the man a smile that was not returned. "You understand correctly."

The officer's mouth twitched. The other pilot moved to his shoulder, the smile on her face apparently quite genuine.

"We're sorry to have to do this," she said, "but we do need to ask what you're doing out here."

"I could ask you the same question," said Dathan. Beside him, Miramir frowned and gave a slight shake of her head. The male officer didn't react, except to cast his cold gaze at Dathan.

"I am Lieutenant Zaycker Asheron. This is my flight sergeant, Dina Dipurl. You are aboard the *Starheart*, the command ship of Halo Squadron." He lifted his chin, as though it could go any higher. "You are in a very dangerous part of the galaxy, young man."

Dathan nodded. "As we discovered. And also," he added, "a part of the galaxy a long way from the Galactic Core." He spread his hands. "Thank you for the rescue, but we're just travelers. We're not part of your republic, nor do we wish to be."

Asheron bristled but said nothing.

"Then consider this a routine check," said Flight Sergeant Dipurl. "Being attacked by pirates is no small thing." She smiled and dropped into a crouch so she was the same height as Rey. She smiled at the child, then looked up at her parents. "Is everyone all right? Your ship doesn't look in the best shape."

"Our hyperdrive is temperamental," said Miramir. "We were waiting for the motivator to cool before we attempted another jump. That's when we were attacked."

"And do you have any reason to have been attacked?" asked Asheron, sharply. At this, Dipurl stood and shook her head.

"Sir, with all due respect, do pirates and marauders ever need a reason to attack? That's why we're out here, after all."

Asheron raised an eyebrow. "Our objectives are classified, Sergeant." Then, satisfied at his subordinate's downcast glance, he turned back to the others.

"So where are you going?"

"Just passing through," muttered Dathan.

Asheron's expression soured. He was clearly a man who needed things right and proper, to be done according to the rule book. "But to *where*, exactly?"

Dathan and Miramir exchanged a look, then Miramir said, "We don't know."

"Are you some kind of space vagrants?" Asheron sniffed again. "Where did you come from?"

Dathan was about to give an answer, but Miramir got in first.

"Jakku," she said.

"Never heard of it."

He was lying. Dathan knew it—the way Asheron had answered so quickly, showing again the superiority of his position, the power he had over them at this moment. The Battle of Jakku had been sixteen years ago, but everybody over a certain age would remember the name, and Asheron certainly fit the bill.

"We're in danger," said Miramir. "We need help."

"Really?" Asheron's tone indicated he had little to no interest in their immediate plight, only answers to his own pointless questions. He turned to the other pilot. "Sergeant, I'll leave you to wrap this up. This little diversion has cost us too much time already."

Miramir and Dathan looked at each other. Asheron adjusted his helmet under his arm and turned to leave, but Miramir stepped forward and pulled on his arm. He stopped and just looked down at her hand.

"Don't you understand?" she asked. "We need help. Isn't the New Republic supposed to help people?" Exasperated, Miramir reached down the front of her tunic and pulled out a thin silver chain. She held it up, showing the amulet that hung on it—it was stylized, daggerlike, the symbol somehow . . . sinister. "We are being hunted by the Sith."

Dathan felt his stomach drop. The amulet—the hex charm—was his. He'd carried it all his life, even when he fled home . . . he had kept it with him, a symbol of everything he hated and everything he was determined never to be. Kept it with him—but had been unable to stomach wearing it. Years ago, Miramir had taken the hex charm from him and promised to keep it close to her own heart, a symbol now of the way their love could overcome any evil.

Asheron looked at her and smiled, a thin, tight line completely devoid of warmth, or interest.

"Is that so?"

Dathan blinked. Was Asheron really *that* ignorant? He hadn't expected to get any help from the New Republic, but did this senior officer really not even know what the Sith were?

Then again . . . perhaps he didn't. Perhaps he thought they were long dead, as most other people in the galaxy did.

If only that were the truth. Dathan glanced at Miramir, but she was now just shaking her head as she looked down at the amulet in her hands. He wanted to punch the New Republic officer, very, very hard, but he knew exactly where that would land the three of them. He let his fist unclench at his side.

"The New Republic helps its *citizens,* yes," Asheron continued, glancing sideways at Dathan before returning his gaze to Miramir. "But as you have said, you live outside its bounds." His expression softened, and he sighed. "Might I suggest," he continued, quietly, "that you clear this region, find your way to somewhere a little closer to the Core. You might find your travels a little safer." Then he turned on his heel. "Flight Sergeant Dipurl, we will debrief in ten minutes." He marched away, heading toward the main doors on the other side of the hangar.

Miramir and Dathan looked at each other. Dathan felt Rey's hand squeeze his, and he dropped down, bringing her in for a hug. He glanced up at the underside of their ship. It looked exactly like what it was— a pile of junk.

"You have to help us," he said, turning back to the sergeant. Miramir moved to join him, reaching down to take Rey's other hand. "You said it yourself," Dathan continued. "This ship isn't going to get far at all."

Dipurl looked at them with a sigh. "Okay, let me take a look," she said, placing her flight helmet down on the deck next to the freighter's ramp, and gesturing for them all to go aboard. "But this has to be fast. I'll see if there's anything I can patch quickly." She paused. "I think I have somewhere you can reach from here. I have a contact who owes me one—someone who worked with my father, back in the days of the Rebel Alliance. They might be able to take you in, at least until you can get any major repairs taken care of." She waved the family aboard ahead of her. "And I'm sorry, I really am," she said, following them up into the ship. "All I can do is file a report. You can tell me about this Sith and that amulet, and I'll log it all. It might make a difference to someone."

CHAPTER 3

THE SEPULCHRE, COORDINATES UNKNOWN

NOW

SOMETHING MOVES IN THE DARKNESS—A shadow, cast long, crawling through the abyssal night. The shadow is a thing apart: neither alive nor dead.

It is a relic. It is an . . . echo. A presence from an older time, a malignancy that somehow survived, somehow found a way.

Found a *path*.

She can see it now. Black and blacker still, moving, always moving. An intelligence, yes. A mind, but one without form or substance.

But here—*present*—nonetheless.

She closes her eyes. It makes no difference. There is nothing to see but a gulf, a nothing, where the shadow lives.

Where the shadow thrives.

In the darkness, in the forever night inside her head.

And the void is not silent. It is anything but. It is a cacophony, a sound so loud it lights up every nerve fiber of her entire being, even though she knows there is nothing to hear, physically.

It is the sound of pain. The sound of death. The sound of a thousand thousand thousand souls crying out in sorrow and agony before they are snuffed out in an instant. Brothers and sisters. Sons and daughters.

Mothers and fathers. Podlings, branchlings, kithkin. Sporechilds and denmothers; space fathers and their brethren, and their gene-clusters and their shoots. Spawn, and offspring. Children.

Entire generations of the living, consumed, their dying cries absorbed and left to reflect forever, trapped inside a dark vessel crafted centuries ago by a power uncommon, inhuman.

By a darkness.

By a shadow, cast long.

And there is another sound. A voice, from the ancient past. It is far distant, a call echoing across a huge valley of space and time.

The voice is terrible.

The voice is as familiar as her own.

SOON.

She opens her golden eyes. The room is bright and, mercifully, silent. Her ears ring like a bell, the sudden absence of screams almost as painful, the echo of the voice still reverberating in her mind.

Slowly, slowly, she remembers where she is. As she lies on the floor and blinks the world into existence around her, she pulls up a hand and touches her face. It is warm, and wet, the blood on her fingertips the bright blue of the Pantoran sky.

The place is lit by flickering flame, and the flickering flame lights the plinth of meteoric iron, and beside the plinth lies the mask made of the same starstuff. The mask faces away from her. It rocks, gently, like it has just been thrown.

She stares at the back of it, the curve of nothing, of darkness, of deep shadow.

And she hears the voice again.

SOON.

SOON.

She closes her eyes, and she sleeps, exchanging one nightmare for another, in the dead of night, in the dead of space.

She wakes to another sound, one technological, modern. She lifts herself from her nest, ignoring the throbbing in her head, the ache of her limbs.

Because she can't keep them waiting. They are patient, yes. Infuriatingly so.

But they are also quick to anger, and if there is one thing she dares not do, it is make them angry.

She agreed to help them. They agreed to show her the way.

This is how it was.

And she would do nothing to jeopardize that.

Standing, she activates the communicator, and her nest is lit in the sudden electric blue of a hologram. The image shimmers and pulses, tinged with the same static and interference that protects the caller's point of origin.

She kneels before the figure, cloaked in darkness, the hood barely concealing a face that is wrapped tightly in heavy black bandages, in the manner all cultists of the Sith Eternal hide their features.

She doesn't know why. She doesn't care.

But she does obey.

"What is thy bidding, my Master," she intones, repeating the litany that echoed through time like the screams inside the mask she knew she would have to put on again, soon.

The looming figure speaks, and she listens, and she wonders whether this will be the last time or whether they will ever honor their promise.

Perhaps one day, they will ask too much.

CHAPTER 4

THE JEDI TEMPLE OF MASTER LUKE SKYWALKER, OSSUS

NOW

"LUKE? UNCLE?"

Luke Skywalker opened his eyes and looked up from where he was sitting cross-legged in the middle of the stone-flagged floor. The teenager who had called him was standing half in, half out of Luke's hut, the look on his face both expectant and clearly embarrassed that he had accidentally interrupted Luke's meditation.

Luke sighed but didn't move from his position. The fact was, he was glad of the disturbance. His meditation had been . . . difficult.

Again.

"Ben, I've told you before."

Ben Solo ran a hand through his mop of black hair. "I . . . ah, yes, I'm sorry . . . *Master* Skywalker."

"The ways of the Jedi are many," said Luke, "and they include discipline and control."

"Of course, Master."

"And that includes knocking before entering," added Luke, with a smile that was soft and friendly.

Ben smiled back, but the expression was fleeting. He shuffled a little and looked around the stone hut. The small building was no different from any other in the temple grounds, but Luke knew the look on Ben's face.

Luke told himself to go easy, but not just because his Padawan was his nephew. Far from it—family ties had little to do with the teachings of the Jedi Order that Luke had worked hard to reestablish. Detachment and distance were required for the pure focus the Jedi constantly strove to achieve, and for Luke, there was a simple satisfaction in adhering to those tenets.

But Ben was trying his best, and Luke knew it wasn't easy for him, being out here in the forests of Ossus. The land was picturesque, the temple calm and ordered, the life of the Padawans one of training, with little time for leisure and, even when their schedules allowed, few facilities for it.

Ossus was *exactly* the kind of place a sixteen-year-old like Ben Solo would find crushingly dull, the studious life perhaps nice in theory but boring in practice.

But Ben was trying. More than that, he was good—even now, as Ben just stood in the doorway, leaning one shoulder casually against the frame as he ran his hand through his hair yet again, Luke could feel the power in him. It was a beautiful flower, growing inside his Padawan, waiting to blossom into something wonderful. Sometimes Luke thought Ben would one day be as powerful as he was.

The Skywalker legacy ran deep.

Luke raised an eyebrow, then laughed, the growing silence in the hut clearly making Ben even more uncomfortable. That wasn't something Luke had expected in his nephew—he was a fine boy, but there was an edge to him, a slow anxiety that simmered just below the surface. Luke put it down to an eagerness to please him, as the temple's Jedi Master. But it was also reflective of an internal struggle, Jedi versus family, nephew versus uncle, Padawan versus Master. Luke knew it couldn't be easy for Ben, no matter how hard he tried to hide it.

And sometimes he tried to hide it too well.

"So what is it, Ben? You want me for something?"

At this, Ben snapped into focus, even composing himself enough to give his Master a small bow.

"Sorry, Master. You have a visitor."

"A visitor? I wasn't expecting anyone."

"I didn't think I had to ask your permission to see an old friend."

Ben turned at the new voice as another man entered the hut.

Luke pushed himself to his feet to greet the new arrival.

"Of course not," said Luke. The Jedi and the visitor clasped their hands around each other's forearms. "It's good to see you, Lor."

Lor San Tekka released Luke's arm and stepped back to give the Jedi Master a more formal bow. Then he stood and clapped a hand on Luke's shoulder.

"I never take an audience with a Jedi Master for granted," said Lor. He turned to Ben. "Young Ben Solo, you look well. How goes the training?"

Ben gave the older man a stiff bow. "Greetings, sir," he said. "And . . . uh . . ."

Luke laughed. "He's doing fine. In fact, I couldn't hope for a better student."

"I am very glad to hear that," said Lor, before turning back to Luke. "I have some information you might be interested in, Luke, if—"

Now it was Luke's turn to lay a hand on his friend's shoulder. "I'm always interested." He glanced at his Padawan. "And you should be studying, Ben. Lor and I have a lot to discuss."

Ben looked at the pair of them and bowed again, but Luke noticed the frown on his face. "At once, Master." Then he stood tall and, giving a look to Lor, left the hut.

Luke wandered to the doorway and watched his nephew stalk away down the grassy slope. Over by the other cluster of temple buildings, an orange-skinned Twi'lek woman, Enyo, was leading a class of younglings through a series of exercises with training blades.

Luke turned and headed back inside, guiding his friend by the arm. "Actually, I'm glad you're here," he said, stopping in the center of the stone hut.

"They're still happening, aren't they?" asked Lor, facing Luke's back.

Luke nodded, then turned around. "And they're getting worse."

"Worse? Or stronger?" Lor cocked his head. "There's a difference, Luke. You just need to listen to the Force, it will guide you."

Luke's lips twitched in amusement—but the expression was mirrored by Lor San Tekka. He raised a hand.

"I know, I know, an adherent of the Church of the Force dares to instruct a Jedi Master." Lor gave a quiet chuckle. "Maybe I'll learn one day, but I'm an old man with old habits." He folded his arms. "Do you know where your vision takes you?"

Luke fixed his gaze on the old man. "That's where I want your help."

Lor frowned. "I am always happy to guide, Master Skywalker, but only for one willing to follow." He spread his hands. "The Force itself remains a mystery to me. I'm not sure what you think I can do."

Luke stroked his beard. "I want to try something." Luke folded himself down into a cross-legged position again in the middle of the room.

Lor stayed right where he was. "Luke, are you sure this is a good idea?"

Luke glanced up. "I need to find out what these visions mean. If I meditate, try to describe what I'm seeing as I see it—"

"Luke, I'm serious." Lor lowered himself to his knees in front of his friend. "I'm not a Jedi. You know that. There must be someone else in the temple who can assist. Ben, perhaps?"

But Luke shook his head. "You're the only person who knows about the visions, and I want to keep it that way."

Lor lifted his hands, his jaw working as he tried to work up some kind of protest, but in the end he just sighed.

"Very well," he said. "I will stand vigil. Tell me what you see and perhaps the Force will guide me as it guides you."

Luke nodded. "Thank you." He lifted his chin, and closed his eyes, and—

In another world, he opened them, and looked around, and saw—

Nothing. Darkness. A . . . void, empty of anything, a space without limits or dimensions, a place that didn't even exist outside of the confines of his own mind.

And yet a *place* nonetheless.

Luke took a step forward, not really feeling anything beneath his feet, because there was nothing there. His footfalls made no sound, and took him no distance. He looked around, straining to see, even while knowing there was nothing to see, no light, no energy, no anything.

The suddenness of this vision startled him. He had been visiting this place in his meditations for weeks now, but the strange dark world usually took a while to appear, Luke's consciousness drifting away from reality as he focused his mind and body on the meditation. And then, as though falling from a great height, he succumbed to a dark gravity he couldn't escape, and he was there.

Over the years, his meditations had gotten deeper and deeper, as he delved into the recesses of his mind, not just to unlock the potential he knew was there, just out of reach, but to try to commune with the galaxy around him. The Force, he knew, was a living thing, in the crudest terms an energy field that bound the universe together. The Force was not a power, not something to be wielded, or used, or manipulated. Rather, it was something that allowed others to share in it—a thing vast and alive and yet not sentient.

In that respect, his friend Lor San Tekka was right. Adherents to the Church of the Force were not Force-sensitive, but that didn't mean they didn't understand it, or those who could tap into the field that underlined the very fabric of being.

But this time, it was different. He had closed his eyes and suddenly he was *here*. Luke knew that without his own iron grip on his emotions, he would be afraid now, and rightly so. But instead he turned that feeling that even now grew inside him into something else, using it as fuel for his senses, heightening his awareness of his surroundings.

And the void, he realized, was somehow . . . *aware* of him, of this visitor, this intruder from elsewhere.

Luke concentrated.

Yes, he felt it now. It had come and gone before, in previous visions, but whether the presence of Lor San Tekka really was doing something or not, it didn't matter, because it was stronger now.

A presence.

The void was not empty.

He concentrated.

It was dark, but it was different from the black awfulness he had felt in the Emperor's presence, even in the presence of his own father, so many years ago. That was something he could understand. He knew where it came from, knew how the light could be corrupted and twisted, turned to darkness, that darkness wrenched and abused into a tool of power that had no place in the light of the Force.

This void was not a part of that, but it was still alive, and Luke was not alone.

Then the void changed, becoming a reality, not an abstract.

Luke was somewhere ancient, somewhere distant.

Somewhere . . . hidden.

Black ground. Black sky. Both flat, cold, like metal. Lightning flashes, electrical discharges that snapped from sky to ground in great pillars of energy, illuminating gray dust that formed low, suffocating clouds, like the sky itself was pressing down on the ground, the world between it squeezed until it cracked.

Desolation. That was the word for it. The landscape, the place, was blasted, by eons of time, the air dry and charged with a dangerous electricity that danced over a ground of black basalt that was already immeasurably ancient.

And then, he—

"Well?"

Luke opened his eyes. He was sitting on the floor. Lor San Tekka was kneeling in front of him, hands pressed down on his knees. It didn't look comfortable.

Luke pursed his lips, surprised that his vision had gone just as fast as it had arrived.

"Tell me what you saw, Luke," said Lor. "Describe it to me."

Luke stared into the middle distance as he brought the memories back to the front of his mind. He described the void, and the blackened landscape—and the dark presence he sensed.

Lor listened carefully, then he stood and began a slow pace of the hut, stretching out his legs, his knees clicking loudly, each accompanied by a wince.

Luke watched him. "Does any of that mean anything to you?"

Lor stopped pacing and pursed his lips. "We've been to a lot of places, Luke. We've seen a lot of things."

Luke nodded. That was quite true—the two had spent a lot of time in each other's company since the death of the Emperor and the fall of the Empire. Luke was driven by a desire to reestablish the Jedi Order from, essentially, absolutely nothing. It was to Lor that he had come, eager for the old explorer's help in hunting down relics and artifacts that had a connection with the Force. Together they followed the star compass Luke had uncovered from Pilio, mapping out the network of Jedi temples that were scattered across the galaxy—perhaps half of them not even remembered after the Empire's purge of the Order four decades before.

Their voyages had been largely fruitful, too. Luke had amassed quite a collection of antiquities at his own fledgling Jedi temple—books, tomes, papers, and data cards; ritual items, sigils and symbols of power; technology, including lightsabers, the star compass, and more. All of which Luke and Lor had studied, the older man's deep knowledge of the Jedi Order a boon to Luke, who was eager not only to learn but also to *understand* as he tried to rebuild the Jedi.

"I sense a *but* coming," said Luke.

Lor began to pace again. "It could be a real place, or it may just be what it is—a vision, a representation of the darkness that must always exist where there is light."

"But why now? I've never had visions like this before."

"The influence of some artifact, perhaps? We have collected and studied many products of the dark arts, Luke."

The suggestion was plausible, but it didn't feel right to Luke. Truth was, his focus had drifted over the last few weeks, his daily rituals and training with the younglings—a strict, unwavering routine—suddenly became disrupted. Luke had handed basic responsibilities to his senior pupils—Ben included—while he holed himself up in his quarters, trying to understand the visions. But he hadn't handled any Sith relics in a long time. He knew full well the danger such artifacts could pose.

"I'm sorry," said Luke, unfolding himself from his position and standing up. He brushed down his cream-colored robes and ran his cybernetic hand through his mop of ash-brown hair. "I don't know what

I thought this would achieve." He paused, shaking his head. "But this . . . place, whatever it is. I'm seeing it for a reason, Lor. I can feel it."

"Oh," said Lor, clapping a hand on his friend's shoulder. "Of that, Luke, I have no doubt. No doubt at all. I just wish I could help you in some way. Research, fieldwork—the search!—there, I feel like I can be of use. But standing vigil over a Jedi who is looking into his own mind?" He clicked his tongue. "I'm a little out of my depth."

Luke laughed softly, relaxing again in the company of his old friend. "Perhaps you're right," he said. "But why did you come to Ossus, anyway? You said you'd found some information?"

"Well," began Lor, "it's going to sound a little . . . anticlimactic, shall we say, after all that."

"Go on," said Luke. "I'm interested."

Lor nodded. "You ever heard of a planet called Yoturba?"

Luke frowned. "I don't think so."

"Mid Rim, nothing remarkable," said Lor, "but the Lerct Historical Institute is running an archaeological dig out there."

Luke felt his eyebrows going up as his interest was piqued. "Have they found something?"

"No," said Lor. "Not yet, anyway. But they have uncovered a large settlement. I couldn't find any record of the Jedi having a temple on Yoturba, but the period is correct. I thought we should take a look. If, of course, you can spare the time from your own temple."

Luke stroked his beard in thought, then he nodded.

"Of course," he said. "We should go. I could use some time to think, anyway."

He stepped past Lor and walked out of the hut. Standing at the top of the small hill on which it stood, he looked out and saw Ben had taken the place of Enyo in leading the training session.

Luke lifted his hand, catching Ben's attention. The young man nodded in acknowledgment and began to bring the training session to an end.

"He's going to make a fine Jedi one day, Luke," said Lor, joining his friend at the door. "And learning the responsibilities of the temple while his Master is away will do him a world of good."

Luke nodded, then, patting his friend on the shoulder, turned, and headed back inside to prepare himself for the expedition ahead.

ABOUT THE TYPE

This book was set in Minion, a 1990 Adobe Originals typeface by Robert Slimbach (b. 1956). Minion is inspired by classical, old-style typefaces of the late Renaissance, a period of elegant, beautiful, and highly readable type designs. Created primarily for text setting, Minion combines the aesthetic and functional qualities that make text type highly readable with the versatility of digital technology.

A long time ago in a galaxy far, far away. . . .

STAR WARS™

Join up! Subscribe to our newsletter at ReadStarWars.com or find us on social.

 @DelReyStarWars

 @DelReyStarWars

 StarWarsBooks